longer home, and a fiercely political book about what oppressive regimes do to societies. There are few writers that do either as well as Gessen does both."

—*Minneapolis Star Tribune*

"A fresh and often very funny perspective on contemporary Russia."

—*San Francisco Chronicle*

"A very funny, perceptive, exasperated, loving, and timely portrait of a country that its author clearly knows well. . . . If the last two bizarre years have taught us anything, it's that Russia is never irrelevant. I wonder how many more drugged spies, bent elections, and political murders it will take for the rest of the world to realize that, for existential reasons, it would be smart for us to pay it a little more consistent and nuanced attention. *A Terrible Country* would be an excellent and entertaining place to begin."   —*The Guardian*

"*A Terrible Country* . . . has a spare emotional force, as beautiful as it is painful; [the novel] serves as a keen document of history past and present; builds in an unlikely way to the suspenseful climax of a taut (and very human) political thriller; and is the funniest work of fiction I've read this year."

—Christian Lorentzen, *Vulture*

"Taking such an intimate trip through the recent past of Putin's Russia is fascinating, made more so by the presence of Andrei's lively, sorrowful, unpredictable grandmother."   —*Vanity Fair*

"What is everyday life like under Putin's rule? Russian-born Gessen, founding editor of *n+1* magazine, draws on his first-hand experiences to paint a vivid picture of Moscow circa 2008."   —*Esquire*'s "Best Books of 2018"

"*A Terrible Country* positions complacency against resistance, and questions what 'home' really means."   —*Entertainment Weekly*

"Like Gessen himself, Andrei ends up spending time back in Russia, a nation perhaps even more totalitarian than it was when his parents fled almost three decades earlier. He falls in with a group of anti-Putin socialists—a turnabout that, eventually, indicts the values of his adopted homeland."

—Boris Kachka, *Vulture*

D0111866

"[A] funny and very perceptive portrait of a grandson, a grandmother and a complicated country."
—*Jewish Weekly*

"A complex portrait of a misunderstood nation . . . Most of the book's pleasures are traditional ones, welcome reminders of how much an old-fashioned novel can do. It expands the sympathies of its readers, delicately explores the connection between historical experience and the everyday, and offers a picture of a whole social system and what it does to the people who inhabit it. . . . Gessen weaves together many people's stories, so that along the way we glean much about Soviet and post-Soviet life. . . . Gessen is as funny as ever."
—Lidija Haas, *Bookforum*

"An essential addition to the 'Before You Go to Russia, Read . . .' list."
—*The Millions*

"For those of us fond of Moscow's street scenes, the fine descriptions of Andrei's walks along the Garden Ring and his shopping trips and errands will draw out pangs of recognition. . . . The novel's best, sturdiest theme is that life is, if not attractive, then at least possible in that 'Terrible Country' of Russia."
—*Christian Science Monitor*

"A novel where Russia—a character so compelling that it could have sucked the air out of the room—is merely the landscape on which an even more compelling story plays out—about a human being, and his grandmother."
—*Tablet*

"[Keith Gessen] understands how unequally the profits of speaking on behalf of Russians are distributed, and how rarely Russians themselves end up the beneficiaries. . . . *A Terrible Country* refuses . . . easy and individualized solutions: If Andrei alone is saved, that is no salvation at all."
—Gregory Afinogenov, *The Nation*

"Perhaps the most surprising aspect of *A Terrible Country* is how funny it is. Gessen displays tremendous compassion for his characters . . . and that includes the compassion to find comedy in their lives. . . . It's the propulsive energy that keeps the pages turning at a steady clip. . . . Gessen slyly conceals

"With wit and humor, Gessen delivers a heartwarming novel about the multitudinous winding roads that lead us home."

—Library Journal (starred review)

"Gessen's first novel in a decade is both a piercing look at contemporary Russian society and a touching story of the struggle to find your place in the world." *—amNY*

"Timely and engaging . . . Moscow-born Gessen displays an affecting sympathy for the smaller players on history's stage." *—Kirkus Reviews*

"A cause for celebration: big-hearted, witty, warm, compulsively readable, earnest, funny, full of that kind of joyful sadness I associate with Russia and its writers. Gessen's particular gift is his ability to effortlessly and charmingly engage with big ideas—power, responsibility, despotism of various stripes, the question of what a country is supposed to do for the people who live in it—while still managing to tell a moving and entertaining human story. At a time when people are wondering whether art can rise to the current confusing political moment, this novel is a reassurance, from a wonderful and important writer." —George Saunders, Man Booker Prize–winning author of *Lincoln in the Bardo*

"Keith Gessen is one of my favorite writers and *A Terrible Country* is even better than I hoped. By turns sad, funny, bewildering, revelatory, and then sad again, it recreates the historical-psychological experience of returning, for twenty-first-century reasons, to a country one's parents left in the twentieth century. It's at once an old-fashioned novel about the interplay between generational roles, family fates, and political ideology, and a kind of global detective mystery about neoliberalism (plus a secret map of Moscow in terms of pickup hockey). Gessen is a master journalist and essayist, as well as a storyteller with a scary grasp on the human heartstrings, and *A Terrible Country* unites the personal and political as only the best novels do."

—Elif Batuman, author of *The Idiot* and *The Possessed*

"*A Terrible Country* is an engaging and entertaining novel, full of humor and humility, and always after one thing—the truth of contemporary life. Gessen gives us the people of Moscow—businessmen, anarchists, grandmothers, in *A Terrible Country* a serious economic discussion of Russia's past and future. . . . The greatest joke in *A Terrible Country* is that the Russia that Gessen portrays isn't all that far from the America of today."

—Paul Constant, *The Seattle Review of Books*

"Keith Gessen's dark, brilliant, dryly hilarious new novel *A Terrible Country* is about the experience of a modern American—an ex-pat, to be sure, but is there anything more modern and American that that? . . . It is up to Andrei to navigate this country's specific terribleness; or, rather, it is up to Gessen to guide Andrei through the mundane tumult of his life, and Gessen does so with a clarity and grace (and no small amount of humor) that makes for the kind of book that lodges inside your consciousness long after you've finished it, so compelling and provocative are its ideas, so unforgettable its characters."

—*Nylon*

"A novel about life under neoliberalism . . . *A Terrible Country* is not exactly a hopeful book about political protest, but neither is it a fatalistic one. Instead, it suggests what resistance might mean, not as a slogan, but as a life."

—Maggie Doherty, *Harvard Magazine*

"Sad, funny, and altogether winning . . . A compassionate, soulful read that avoids dourness by being surprisingly funny. *A Terrible Country* shows us that while you certainly can go home again, it often turns out to be a lousy idea."

—*BookPage*

"In Gessen's exceptional and trenchant novel, floundering thirty-something professor Andrei Kaplan flees from New York to Russia, the country of his birth, to reassess his future and take care of his ailing grandmother. . . . Andrei's early attempts to reorient himself to post-Soviet Russian society bring about considerable insight and humor—getting rebuffed by a men's adult hockey league, getting pistol-whipped outside a nightclub—leading him back to watching old Russian films with his grandmother. . . . While poised to critique Putin's Russia, this sharp, stellar novel becomes, by virtue of Andrei's ultimate self-interest, a subtle and incisive indictment of the American character."

—*Publishers Weekly* (starred and boxed review)

Praise for *A Terrible Country*

A *New York Times* Editors' Choice
Named a Best Book of 2018 by *Bookforum*, *Nylon*,
Esquire*, and *Vulture

"This earnest and wistful but serious book gets good, and then it gets very good. . . . [Gessen] writes incisively about many things here but especially about, as the old saw has it, how it is easier to fight for your principles than live up to them. . . . This artful and autumnal novel, published in high summer, is a gift for those who wish to receive it."

—Dwight Garner, *The New York Times*

"Excellent . . . In its breadth and depth, its sweep, its ability to move us and philosophize . . . *A Terrible Country* is a smart, enjoyable, modern take on what we think of, admiringly, as 'the Russian novel'—in this case, a Russian novel that only an American could have written."

—Francine Prose, *The New York Review of Books*

"[A] lighthearted yet morally serious novel."

—Vadim Nikitin, *The London Review of Books*

"Hilarious, heartbreaking . . . *A Terrible Country* may be one of the best books you'll read this year. . . . One of the pleasures of the novel is listening to Andrei's hyper-intelligent, wry, and ironic voice. . . . The other unforgettable character is Andrei's grandmother, an indomitable force of nature. Gessen's portrait of her is tender, and readers will be hard-pressed to find a more nuanced and poignant depiction of what it means to lose your memory. . . . Gessen's genius is in showing us how and why Russia is and isn't a terrible country. And how, in its ruthless devotion to market capitalism, the former socialist state bears a striking resemblance to our own."

—Ann Levin, Associated Press

"Hilarious . . . To understand Russia, read *A Terrible Country*."   —*Time*

"[Andrei's] wry observations about Moscow's day-to-day—his tour through his own family history, his grandmother's stuck-in-time apartment, his struggle to join hockey games and party in nightclubs—are completely engrossing. It's portraiture, showing us a place we may think we know but don't.... *A Terrible Country* is a splendid guidebook."

—*Entertainment Weekly*

"My own feelings towards this complexly ambivalent novel aren't complex or ambivalent in the least. I loved it and expect others will too."

—*The Boston Globe*

"*A Terrible Country* is filled with moments of levity.... Gessen has shown how literature, academia, and anti-capitalism—topics often pushed to the periphery of political debate—have in fact much to say about the dehumanizing effects of neoliberalism. Tolstoy, who by the end of his life opposed private property, renounced the copyright to his literary works, and started a school for peasants, would probably like it."   —Jennifer Wilson, *The New Republic*

"Laser-true and very funny . . . Gessen evokes not only convincingly, but indispensably, something exceedingly rare in modern American fiction; genuine male vulnerability. There's enough heart here to redeem every recent male novel that's aimed for it and found solipsism instead.... You won't read a more observant book about the country that has now been America's bedeviling foil for almost a century."   —*The New York Times Book Review*

"*A Terrible Country* tells the reader a lot about contemporary Russia and, importantly, lifts the lid on domestic political resistance to Putin. But what makes this a moving and thought-provoking novel is Andrei's personal struggle to find his way in the world, his sense of obligation to his family, and his realization that his parents' emigration—the very thing that has afforded him opportunities—was 'the great tragedy of my grandmother's life.'"

—Max Liu, *Financial Times*

"Wily, seductive, and deeply affecting . . . Gessen brilliantly captures the daily rhythms, allures, and challenges of Moscow life in 2008–2009. It's as personable a book as it is political.... A great book with a great heart."

—Michael Upchurch, *The Seattle Times*

"Funny and incisive . . . Marvelous . . . *A Terrible Country* is a contemplative and compassionate novel about what it means to return to a place that is no dissidents, baristas, hockey goalies, prostitutes, and FSB agents—not as fanciful characters but with the full force of the real. His affectionate, clear-eyed portrait of one terrible country has plenty to teach us about our own."

—Chad Harbach, author of *The Art of Fielding*

"I loved *A Terrible Country*, and I loved Andrei, the smart, likable narrator, a struggling American academic with a deliciously wry observational intelligence. I'd follow Andrei's voice anywhere, but I was especially glad, at this moment, to go with him to post-Soviet Moscow. A fun, funny but sincere novel that explores with real integrity what it means to be an American ex-pat who can always leave, *A Terrible Country* is one of the most addictive and affecting books I've read in a while."

—Adelle Waldman, author of *The Love Affairs of Nathaniel P.*

"Like *If Not Now, When?*, Primo Levi's masterpiece, *A Terrible Country* makes the emotional case for an unfamiliar politics. Its critique of the Russian mafia state is balanced by a deeply humanistic attention to common decency. I would not hesitate to recommend this novel to a busy person who otherwise refuses to touch fiction. The only up-to-the-minute, topical, relevant, and necessary novel of 2018 that never has to mention Trump."

—Nell Zink, author of *The Wallcreeper* and *Mislaid*

"Keith Gessen has written a poignant yet laugh-out-loud portrait of the new Russia of nightclubs, black Audis, and wi-fi cafés, still haunted by an old Russia of kasha, hockey, and Soviet movies. *A Terrible Country* is a serious book that's a pleasure to read, full of love and sorrow."

—Caleb Crain, author of *Necessary Errors*

"For those of us who have grown up reading Russian literature, from Chekhov to Babel to Svetlana Alexievich, following this Americanized narrator through his return to contemporary Moscow offers an education and pure delight."   —Mona Simpson, author of *Casebook* and *Anywhere but Here*

ABOUT THE AUTHOR

Keith Gessen is the author of *All the Sad Young Literary Men* and a founding editor of *n+1*. He is the editor of three nonfiction books and the translator or cotranslator, from Russian, of a collection of short stories, a book of poems, and a work of oral history, Nobel Prize–winner Svetlana Alexievich's *Voices from Chernobyl*. A contributor to *The New Yorker* and *The London Review of Books*, Gessen teaches journalism at Columbia University and lives in New York with his wife and sons.

A TERRIBLE COUNTRY

A NOVEL

KEITH GESSEN

PENGUIN BOOKS

PENGUIN BOOKS
An imprint of Penguin Random House LLC
penguinrandomhouse.com

First published in the United States of America by Viking,
an imprint of Penguin Random House LLC, 2018
Published in Penguin Books 2019

Translation of Anna Akhmatova's "Requiem" by Stanley Kunitz and
Max Hayward from *Poems of Akhmatova* (Little, Brown, 1973).

ISBN 9780735221338 (paperback)

THE LIBRARY OF CONGRESS HAS CATALOGED THE
HARDCOVER EDITION AS FOLLOWS:
Names: Gessen, Keith, author.
Title: A terrible country : a novel / Keith Gessen.
Description: New York, New York : Viking, [2018] |
Identifiers: LCCN 2018025065 (print) | LCCN 2018026670 (ebook) |
ISBN 9780735221321 (ebook) | ISBN 9780735221314 (hardcover) |
ISBN 9780525560913 (international edition)
Subjects: | BISAC: FICTION / Literary. | FICTION / Family Life. | FICTION / Satire.
Classification: LCC PS3607.E87 (ebook) | LCC PS3607.E87 T47 2018 (print) |
DDC 813/.6—dc23
LC record available at https://lccn.loc.gov/2018025065

Printed in the United States of America
1   3   5   7   9   10   8   6   4   2

Set in Arno Pro
Designed by Francesca Belanger

PART I

For Rosalia Moiseevna Solodovnik, 1920–2015

1.

I MOVE TO MOSCOW

IN THE LATE SUMMER of 2008, I moved to Moscow to take care of my grandmother. She was about to turn ninety and I hadn't seen her for nearly a decade. My brother Dima and I were her only family; her lone daughter, our mother, had died years earlier. Baba Seva lived alone now in her old Moscow apartment. When I called to tell her I was coming, she sounded very happy to hear it, and also a little confused.

My parents and my brother and I left the Soviet Union in 1981. I was six and Dima was sixteen, and that made all the difference. I became an American, whereas Dima remained essentially Russian. As soon as the Soviet Union collapsed, he returned to Moscow to make his fortune. Since then he had made and lost several fortunes; where things stood now I wasn't sure. But one day he Gchatted me to ask if I could come to Moscow and stay with Baba Seva while he went to London for an unspecified period of time.

"Why do you need to go to London?"

"I'll explain when I see you."

"You want me to drop everything and travel halfway across the world and you can't even tell me why?"

There was something petulant that came out of me when dealing with my older brother. I hated it, and couldn't help myself.

Dima said, "If you don't want to come, say so. But I'm not discussing this on Gchat."

"You know," I said, "there's a way to take it off the record. No one will be able to see it."

"Don't be an idiot."

He meant to say that he was involved with some *very serious people,*

3

who would not so easily be deterred from reading his Gchats. Maybe that was true, maybe it wasn't. With Dima the line between those concepts was always shifting.

As for me, I wasn't really an idiot. But neither was I not an idiot. I had spent four long years of college and then eight much longer years of grad school studying Russian literature and history, drinking beer, and winning the Grad Student Cup hockey tournament (five times!); then I had gone out onto the job market for three straight years, with zero results. By the time Dima wrote me I had exhausted all the available post-graduate fellowships and had signed up to teach online sections in the university's new PMOOC initiative, short for "paid massive online open course," although the "paid" part mostly referred to the students, who really did need to pay, and less to the instructors, who were paid very little. It was definitely not enough to continue living, even very frugally, in New York. In short, on the question of whether I was an idiot, there was evidence on both sides.

Dima writing me when he did was, on the one hand, providential. On the other hand, Dima had a way of getting people involved in undertakings that were not in their best interests. He had once convinced his now former best friend Tom to move to Moscow to open a bakery. Unfortunately, Tom opened his bakery too close to another bakery, and was lucky to leave Moscow with just a dislocated shoulder. Anyway, I proceeded cautiously. I said, "Can I stay at your place?" Back in 1999, after the Russian economic collapse, Dima bought the apartment directly across the landing from my grandmother's, so helping her out from there would be easy.

"I'm subletting it," said Dima. "But you can stay in our bedroom in Grandma's place. It's pretty clean."

"I'm thirty-three years old," I said, meaning too old to live with my grandmother.

"You want to rent your own place, be my guest. But it'll have to be pretty close to Grandma's."

Our grandmother lived in the center of Moscow. The rents there were almost as high as Manhattan's. On my PMOOC salary I would be able to rent approximately an armchair.

"Can I use your car?"

"I sold it."

"Dude. How long are you leaving for?"

"I don't know," said Dima. "And I already left."

"Oh," I said. He was already in London. He must have left in a hurry.

But I in turn was desperate to leave New York. The last of my old classmates from the Slavic department had recently left for a new job, in California, and my girlfriend of six months, Sarah, had recently dumped me at a Starbucks. "I just don't see where this is going," she had said, meaning I suppose our relationship, but suggesting in fact my entire life. And she was right: even the thing that I had once most enjoyed doing—reading and writing about and teaching Russian literature and history—was no longer any fun. I was heading into a future of half-heartedly grading the half-written papers of half-interested students, with no end in sight.

Whereas Moscow was a special place for me. It was the city where my parents had grown up, where they had met; it was the city where I was born. It was a big, ugly, dangerous city, but also the cradle of Russian civilization. Even when Peter the Great abandoned it for St. Petersburg in 1713, even when Napoleon sacked it in 1812, Moscow remained, as Alexander Herzen put it, the capital of the Russian people. "They recognized their ties of blood to Moscow by the pain they felt at losing it." Yes. And I hadn't been there in years. Over the course of a few grad-school summers I'd grown tired of its poverty and hopelessness. The aggressive drunks on the subway; the thugs in tracksuits and leather jackets walking around eyeing everyone; the guy eating from the dumpster next to my grandmother's place every night during the summer I spent there in 2000, periodically yelling "Fuckers! Bloodsuckers!" then going back to eating. I hadn't been back since.

Still, I kept my hands off the keyboard. I needed some kind of concession from Dima, if only for my pride.

I said, "Is there someplace for me to play hockey?" As my academic career had declined, my hockey playing had ramped up. Even during the summer, I was on the ice three days a week.

"Are you kidding?" said Dima. "Moscow is a hockey mecca. They're building new rinks all the time. I'll get you into a game as soon as you get here."

I took that in.

"Oh, and the wireless signal from my place reaches across the landing," Dima said. "Free wi-fi."

"OK!" I wrote.

"OK?"

"Yeah," I said. "Why not."

A few days later I went to the Russian consulate on the Upper East Side, stood in line for an hour with my application, and got a one-year visa. Then I wrapped things up in New York: I sublet my room to a rock drummer from Minnesota, returned my books to the library, and fetched my hockey stuff from a locker at the rink. It was all a big hassle, and not cheap, but I spent the whole time imagining the different life I would soon be living and the different person I'd become. I pictured myself carrying groceries for my grandmother; taking her on excursions around the city, including to the movies (she'd always loved the movies); walking with her arm in arm around the old neighborhood and listening to her tales of life under socialism. There was so much about her life that I didn't know, about which I'd never asked. I had been incurious and oblivious; I had believed more in books than I had in people. I pictured myself protesting the Putin regime in the morning, playing hockey in the afternoon, and keeping my grandmother company in the evening. Perhaps there was even some way I might use my grandmother's life as the basis for a journal article. I pictured myself sitting monastically in my room and with my grandmother's stories in hand adding a whole new dimension to my work. Maybe I could put her testimony in italics and intersperse it throughout my article, like in *In Our Time*.

On my last night in town my roommates threw me a small party. "To Moscow," they said, raising their cans of beer.

"To Moscow!" I repeated.

"And don't get killed," one of them added.

"I won't get killed," I promised. I was excited. And drunk. It occurred to me that there was a certain glamor that might attend spending time in an increasingly violent and dictatorial Russia, whose armed forces had just pummeled the small country of Georgia into a humiliating defeat. At three in the morning I sent a text message to Sarah. "I'm leaving tomorrow," it said, as if I were heading for a very dangerous place. Sarah did not respond. Three hours later I woke up, still drunk, threw the last of my stuff into my huge red suitcase, grabbed my hockey stick, and headed for JFK. I got on my flight and promptly fell asleep.

Next thing I knew I was standing in the passport control line in the grim basement of Sheremetevo-2 International Airport. It never seemed to change. As long as I'd been flying in here, they made you come down to this basement and wait in line before you got your bags. It was like a purgatory from which you suspected you might be entering someplace other than heaven.

But the Russians looked different than I remembered them. They were well dressed, with good haircuts, and talking on sleek new cell phones. Even the guards in their light-blue short-sleeve uniforms looked cheerful. Though the line was long, several stood off together to the side, laughing. Oil was selling at $114 a barrel, and they had clobbered the Georgians—is that what they were laughing about?

Modernization theory said the following: Wealth and technology are more powerful than culture. Give people nice cars, color televisions, and the ability to travel to Europe, and they'll stop being so aggressive. No two countries with McDonald's franchises will ever go to war with each other. People with cell phones are nicer than people without cell phones.

I wasn't so sure. The Georgians had McDonald's, and the Russians bombed them anyway. As I neared the passport booth, a tall, bespectacled, nicely dressed European, Dutch or German, asked in English if he could cut the line: he had to catch a connecting flight. I nodded yes—we'd have to wait for our luggage anyway—but the man behind me,

7

about the same height as the Dutch guy but much sturdier, in a boxy but not to my eyes inexpensive suit, piped up in Russian-accented English.

"Go back to end of line."

"I'm about to miss my flight," said the Dutchman.

"Go back to end of line."

I said to him in Russian, "What's the difference?"

"There's a big difference," he answered.

"Please?" the Dutchman asked again, in English.

"I said go back. Now." The Russian turned slightly so that he was square with the Dutchman. The latter man kicked his bag in frustration. Then he picked it up and walked to the back of the line.

"He made the correct decision," said the Russian guy to me, in Russian, indicating that as a man of principle he was ready to pummel the Dutch guy for cutting the line.

I didn't answer. A few minutes later, I approached the passport control booth. The young, blond, unsmiling border guard sat in his uniform bathed in light, like a god. I had no rights here, I suddenly remembered; there was no such thing here as rights. I wondered as I handed over my passport whether I had finally pressed my luck, returning to the country my parents had fled, too many times. Would they finally take me into custody for all the unkind things I had thought about Russia over the years?

But the guard merely took my battered blue American passport— the passport of a person who lived in a country where you didn't have to carry your passport everywhere you went, where in fact you might not even know where your passport was for months and years at a time—with mild disgust. If he had a passport like mine he'd take better care of it. He checked my name against the terrorist database and buzzed me through the gate to the other side.

That was it. I was in Russia again.

My grandmother Seva lived in the very center of the city, in an apartment she'd been awarded, in the late 1940s, by Joseph Stalin. My brother, Dima, brought this up sometimes, when he was trying to make a point, and so did my grandmother, when she was in a self-deprecating mood. "My Stalin apartment," she called it, as if to remind everyone, and herself, of the moral compromise she had made. Still, in general in our family it was understood that if someone was offering you an apartment, and you lived at the time in a drafty room in a communal apartment with your small daughter, your two brothers, and your mom, then you should take the apartment, no matter who it was from. And it's not like Stalin himself was handing her the keys or asking for anything in return. She was at the time a young professor of history at Moscow State University, and had consulted on a film about Ivan the Great, the fifteenth-century "gatherer of the lands of Rus" and grandfather to Ivan the Terrible, which Stalin so enjoyed that he declared everyone involved should get an apartment. So in addition to "my Stalin apartment," my grandmother also called it "my Ivan the Great apartment," and then, if she was speaking honestly, "my Yolka apartment," after her daughter, my mother, for whom she had been willing to do anything at all.

To get to this apartment I exchanged some dollars at the booth outside baggage claim—it was about twenty-four rubles per dollar at the time—and took the brand-new express train to Savelovsky Railway Station, passing miles of crumbling Soviet apartment blocks, and the old (also crumbling) turn-of-the-century industrial belt just outside the center. Along the way the massive guy sitting next to me—about my age, in jeans and a short-sleeve button-down—struck up a conversation.

"What model is that?" he asked, about my phone. I had bought a SIM card at the airport and was now putting it in the phone and seeing if it worked.

Here we go, I thought. My phone was a regular T-Mobile flip phone. But I figured this was just a prelude to the guy trying to rob me. I grew tense. My hockey stick was in the luggage rack above us, and anyway it would have been hard to swing it at this guy on this train.

"Just a regular phone," I said. "Samsung." I grew up speaking Russian and still speak it with my father and my brother but I have a slight, difficult-to-place accent. I occasionally make small grammatical mistakes or put the stress on the wrong syllable. And I was rusty.

The guy picked up on this, as well as the fact that my olive skin set me apart from most of the Slavs on this fancy train. "Where you from?" he said. He used the familiar *ty* rather than *vy*—which could mean he was being friendly, because we were the same age and on the same train, or it could mean he was asserting his right to call me anything he wanted. I couldn't tell. He began to guess where I might be from. "Spain?" he said. "Or Turkey?"

And what should I answer? If I said "New York" it would mean I had money, even though I was wearing an old pair of jeans, and sneakers that had seen better days, and in fact had no money. A person from New York could get robbed, either on the train or once he got off, in the commotion of the platform. But if I said "Here," Moscow, it would technically be true but also obviously a lie, which could escalate the situation. And I was on the train from the airport, after all.

"New York," I said.

The guy nodded sagely. "They have the new iPhone there?"

"Sure," I said. I wasn't sure what he was getting at.

"How much does it cost?"

Ah. Western goods in Moscow were always way more expensive than in the West, and Russians always wanted to know just how much more expensive so they could be bitter about it.

I tried to remember. Sarah had had an iPhone. "Two hundred dollars," I said.

The guy's eyes widened. He knew it! That was a third of the Russian price.

"But," I hastened to add, "you have to get a contract. It's about a hundred dollars a month. For two years. So, not cheap."

"A contract?" This guy had never heard of a contract. Did I even know what I was talking about? In Russia you just bought a SIM card and paid by the minute.

"Yeah, in America you need a contract."

The guy was offended. In fact he was beginning to wonder if I wasn't just making this up. "There must be some way around that," he said.

"I don't think so."

10

"No," he said again. "There must be some way to get the phone and dump the contract."

"I don't know," I said. "They're pretty strict about that stuff."

The guy shrugged, took out a paper—*Kommersant,* one of the business dailies—and didn't say another word to me the rest of the way. A person who couldn't figure out how to dump an iPhone contract was not worth knowing. But there was no gang of robbers waiting for me at the train station, and from there without further incident I took the metro a couple of stops to Tsvetnoi Boulevard.

The center of Moscow was its own world. Gone were the tall, crumbling apartment blocks of the periphery and the old, crumbling factories. Instead, as I stepped off the long escalator and through the big, heavy, swinging wood doors, I saw a wide street, imposing Stalin-era apartment buildings, some restaurants, and a dozen construction sites in every direction. Tsvetnoi Boulevard was right off the huge Garden Ring road, which ran in a ten-lane loop around the center, at a radius of about a mile and a half from the Kremlin. But as soon as I started up toward Sretenka Street, where my grandmother lived, I found myself on side streets that were quiet and dilapidated, with many of the two- and three-story nineteenth-century buildings unpainted and even, in August, partly abandoned. A group of stray dogs sunning themselves in an abandoned lot on Pechatnikov Lane barked at me and my hockey stick. And then in a few minutes I was home.

My grandmother's apartment was on the second floor of a five-story white building in a courtyard between two older, shorter buildings, one of them facing Pechatnikov, the other Rozhdestvenskiy Boulevard. The courtyard's fourth boundary was a big redbrick wall on whose other side was an old church. When I was a kid the courtyard had been filled with trees and dirt for me to play with, and even, during the winter, a tiny hockey rink, but after the USSR fell apart the trees were chopped down and the rink dismantled by neighbors who wanted to park their cars there. The courtyard was also, for a time, a popular destination for local prostitutes; cars would drive into it, run their lights over the merch, and make a selection without even getting out.

I entered that old courtyard now. The prostitutes were long gone, and though it was still basically a parking lot, the cars parked here were much nicer, and there were even a few more trees than last time I visited. I entered the code on the front door—it hadn't changed in a decade—and lugged my suitcase up the stairs. My grandmother came to the door. She was tiny—she had always been small, but now she was even smaller, and the gray hair on her head was even thinner—and for a moment I was worried she wasn't expecting me. But then she said, "Andryushik. You're here." She seemed to have mixed feelings about it.

I went in.

2.

MY GRANDMOTHER

BABA SEVA—Seva Efraimovna Gekhtman, my maternal grandmother—was born in a small town in Ukraine in 1919. Her father was an accountant at a textile factory and her mother was a nurse. She had two brothers, and the entire family moved to Moscow not long after the Revolution.

I knew she had excelled in school and been admitted to Moscow State, the best and oldest Russian university, where she studied history. I knew that at Moscow State, not long after the German invasion, she had met a young law student, my grandfather Boris (really Baruch) Lipkin, and that they had fallen in love and been married. Then he was killed near Vyazma in the second year of the war, just a month after my mother was born. I knew that after the war my grandmother had started lecturing at Moscow State and consulted on the Ivan the Great film and received the apartment and lived there with my mother as well as an elderly relative, Aunt Klava; that the apartment had caused some turmoil in the family, not because of who it came from but because my grandmother refused to let her brother and his wife move in with her, because his wife drank and also because she did not want to displace Aunt Klava; that not long after receiving the apartment she had been forced out at Moscow State at the height of the "anti-cosmopolitan," i.e., anti-Jewish, campaign, and that she had gotten by as a tutor and translator of other Slavic languages; and that she had remarried in late middle age, to a sweet, forgetful geophysicist whom we called Uncle Lev, and moved with him to the nuclear research town of Dubna, vacating the apartment for my parents, and then eventually my brother, before moving back here again, just a few years before I showed up, because Uncle Lev had died in his sleep.

But there was a lot I didn't know. I didn't know what had happened to Aunt Klava; nor what her life had been like after the war; nor whether, before the war, during the purges, she had had any knowledge or sense of what was happening in the country. If not, why not? If so, how did she live with that knowledge? And how did she live in this apartment with that knowledge once that knowledge came?

For the moment, as my grandmother busied herself in the kitchen, I put down my bags in our old bedroom—which, contrary to Dima's promises, was still filled with his crap—and then took a quick look around. The apartment hadn't changed: it was a museum of Soviet furniture, arranged in layers from newest to oldest, like an archaeological site. There was my grandmother's grand old oak wood desk, in the back room, from the forties or fifties, as well as her locked standing shelf, also from that era; and then from my parents' time in the apartment was most of the furniture: the green foldout couch, the glassed-in hanging shelves, and the tall lacquered standing closet. And of course, in our bedroom, our bunk beds, which my father had built not long before our emigration, and which Dima had not replaced; when he'd lived here he'd taken the back room for himself and used our room for guests. There were even a few childhood toys, mostly little cars, now tucked up among the books, that Dima and I had played with. After that came the modern age: Dima had installed a flat-screen in the back room, as well as an exercise bike in our bedroom that was taking up a lot of space. Most of the books on the shelves were Russian classics in their full Soviet editions—fourteen volumes of Dostoevsky, eleven of Tolstoy, sixteen (!) of Chekhov—though there were also some shelves filled with English-language books on business and deal making that Dima had apparently imported. And there was a linoleum-topped table in the kitchen, circa the year of my birth, at which my grandmother now sat, waiting for me.

For no good reason, I was her favorite. During summers when I was little I often stayed with her and Uncle Lev at their dacha in Sheremetevo (not far from the airport), and I had visited them as much as I could when I lived in Moscow during my college year abroad. In the late nineties, when she was still able to travel, she and Dima and I had taken an annual trip to Europe together. All this added up to just a few months together, total, and yet I was the younger and the favorite child of her only daughter, and this was enough. For her I was still that little boy.

She wanted to feed me. Slowly and deliberately she heated potato soup, *kotlety* (Russian meatballs), and sliced fried potatoes. She moved around the kitchen at a glacial pace and was unsteady on her feet, but there were many things to hold on to in that old kitchen, and she knew exactly where they were. She couldn't talk and cook at the same time, and her hearing had deteriorated, so I waited while she finished, and then helped her plate the food. Finally, we sat. She asked me about my life in America. "Where do you live?" "New York." "What?" "New York." "Oh. Do you live in a house or an apartment?" "An apartment." "What?" "An apartment." "Do you own it?" "I rent it. With some roommates." "What?" "I share it. It's like a communal apartment." "Are you married?" "No." "No?" "No." "Do you have kids?" "No." "No kids?" "No. In America," I half lied, "people don't have kids until later." Satisfied, or partly satisfied, she then asked me how long I intended to stay. "Until Dima comes back," I said. "What?" she said. "Until Dima comes back," I said again.

"Andryusha," she said now. "Do you know my friend Musya?"

"Yes," I said. Emma Abramovna, or Musya, was her oldest and closest friend.

"She's a very close friend of mine," my grandmother explained. "And right now, she's at her dacha." Emma Abramovna, a literature professor who had managed to hang on at Moscow State despite the anti-Jewish campaign, had a dacha at Peredelkino, the old writers' colony. My grandmother had lost her own dacha in the nineties, under circumstances I was never quite clear about.

"I think," she said now, "that next summer she's going to invite me to stay with her."

"Yes? She said that?"

15

"No," said my grandmother. "But I hope she does."

"That sounds good," I said. In August, Muscovites all leave for their dachas; clearly my grandmother's inability to leave for her dacha was weighing on her mind.

We had now finished our food and our tea, and my grandmother casually reached into her mouth and took out her teeth. She put them in a little teacup on the table. "I need to rest my gums," she said toothlessly.

"Of course," I said. Without her teeth to hold them up my grandmother's lips collapsed a little, and without her teeth to strike her tongue against she spoke with a slight lisp.

"Tell me," she said now, in the same exploratory tone as earlier. "Do you know Dima?"

"Of course," I said. "He's my brother."

"Oh." My grandmother sighed, as if she couldn't entirely trust someone who knew Dima. "Do you know where he is?"

"He's in London," I said.

"He never comes to see me," said my grandmother.

"That's not true."

"No, it is. Once he got me to sign over the apartment, he hasn't been interested in me at all."

"Grandma!" I said. "That's definitely not true." It was true that a few years earlier Dima had put the apartment in his name—under post-Soviet-style gentrification, little old ladies who owned prime Moscow real estate tended to have all sorts of misfortunes befall them. From a safety perspective it was the right move. But I could see now that from my grandmother's perspective it looked suspicious.

"What's not true?" she said.

"It's not true that he doesn't have any interest in you. He talks to me about you all the time."

"Hmm," said my grandmother, unconvinced. Then she sighed again. She started to get up to try to put away the plates, but I implored her to sit, less in that moment because I wanted to help than because she did everything so slowly. I quickly cleared the table and started doing the dishes. As I was finishing, my grandmother came over and made to ask a question that I could tell she thought might be a little delicate.

"Andryusha," she said. "You are such a dear person to me. To our whole family. But I can't remember right now. How did we come to know you?"

I was momentarily speechless.

"I'm your grandson," I said. There was an element of pleading in my voice.

"What?"

"I'm your grandson."

"My grandson," she repeated.

"You had a daughter, do you remember?"

"Yes," she said uncertainly, and then remembered. "Yes. My little daughter." She thought a moment longer. "She went to America," said my grandmother. "She went to America and died."

"That's right," I said. My mother had died of breast cancer in 1992; the first time my grandmother saw her after our emigration was at her funeral.

"And you—" she said now.

"I'm her son."

My grandmother took this in. "Then why did you come here?" she said.

I didn't understand.

"This is a terrible country. My Yolka took you to America. Why did you come back?" She seemed angry.

I was again at a loss for words. Why had I come? Because Dima had asked me to. And because I wanted to help my grandmother. And because I thought it would help me find a topic for an article, which would then help me get a job. These reasons swirled through my mind like an argument and I decided to go with the one that seemed most practical. "For work," I said. "I need to do some research."

"Oh," she said. "All right." She too had had to work in this terrible country, and she could understand.

Momentarily satisfied, my grandmother excused herself and went to her room to lie down.

I remained in the kitchen, drinking another cup of tea. Throughout the apartment were photos of our family, and especially my mother—on walls, on dressers, on bookshelves. In America our family had become scattered; in Moscow it was exactly where it had always been.

Holy shit, I thought. This was not the state in which I had expected to find my grandmother. Dima said she was on medication for her dementia, but I hadn't really understood.

My first thought was: I am not qualified. I am not qualified to care for an eighty-nine-year-old woman who can't remember who I am. I was a person who had indulged in an unthinkable amount of schooling and then failed to convert that schooling into an actual job. "I just don't see where this is going," Sarah had said at the Starbucks.

"Why does it have to go somewhere?" I said, lamely.

She just shook her head. "I may regret this," she said. "But I doubt it." And she was right. I was an idiot, like Dima said. And I was in over my head. That first day, in the kitchen, was the first time, the first of many, that I would decide to leave.

In my mind I began composing an email. "Dima," it went, "I feel that you misled me about the condition our grandmother is in. Or maybe I misunderstood you. I can't handle this. I'm sorry. Let's hire someone who knows what they're doing. I'll help pay for it." And then I'd go back to New York. There's no shame in knowing your limitations. Though how exactly I'd help pay for it was a mystery. After buying my visa and my ticket, I had less than one thousand dollars to my name.

My grandmother came out of her room and crossed the foyer to the toilet. She had gone to bed, clearly, and then gotten up again: her hair was mussed and she was still without her teeth. Seeing me, she gave a toothless smile and a wave. I felt like she knew who I was in that moment. I calmed down.

So I was to keep her company. Maybe even an idiot could do that. Who cared if she couldn't remember certain things? Her life had been so wonderful, such a parade of joys, that she should sit around remembering everything about it? She wouldn't be able to tell me the story of her life for my would-be article, but I'd find something else to write about. And maybe she wouldn't know who I was all the time. I knew who I was, and I could remind her. I was the youngest son of her daughter, her lone child, my mother, who had gone to America and died. I got up and washed my teacup and headed for my bedroom.

There were banker's boxes in the corner and the large exercise bike jammed against the lower bunk. I had to climb past it to lie down. Now I was really looking forward to getting online so as to yell at my brother, but when I got out my laptop and tried to catch the signal from next door, it didn't work. This may not have been Dima's fault—my computer was old, so old that it didn't work unless it was plugged into a socket, and there were many wireless protocols that it couldn't recognize—and yet it was still something else he had misled me about. I considered going next door and seeing if I could adjust the router, but it seemed unbecoming of the rent collector (this was to be one of my tasks) to be stealing the tenants' wi-fi. They were paying good money for that wi-fi.

I closed my computer and lay back on the bed, the exercise bike looming over me. My grandmother had put out an old towel and some scratchy sheets, and without getting out of bed I managed to put the sheets on. Then I lay there and thought: Fuck fuck fuck fuck fuck fuck fuck. And then: OK. OK. Everything was fine. My grandmother was in bad shape, but I could handle it. My sheets were scratchy, but I could buy new ones. And the bedroom was a mess, but that just meant I had something on Dima. Which was good. Trust me. If you didn't have something on Dima, it meant Dima had something on you.

It was 8:00 P.M. in Moscow, and still light out, but I felt tired, incredibly tired, and quickly, with my clothes still on, fell asleep.

3.

A TOUR OF THE NEIGHBORHOOD

I WOKE AT FIVE in the morning. My window looked onto an alleyway between our building and the Pechatnikov-side building. Since we were on the second floor and it was late August and I had the window open, and since the two stone buildings created a mini echo chamber, I found that I heard distinctly every cough, Russian swearword, door slamming, ignition turning, and radio blaring shitty Russian pop music that took place anywhere in or near the alleyway. All these noises disturbed my sleep, and not just because they were noises. Dima wouldn't have left town in such a hurry unless he was in danger, I thought, and if Dima was in danger, then it was possible that Dima's plenipotentiary, his brother and his rent collector, was also in danger. Though probably not. I lay in bed for a while wondering, and then sat up with a realization.

What if my grandmother wasn't taking her medicine? Dima had been gone for over a month. What if the forgetfulness I witnessed was just a matter of her missing some pills? I went into the kitchen. Moscow is a northern city and during the summer the days start early; the sun was already up. I had seen her take some pills after our supper and put them on the shelf behind her. I retrieved them now and read the labels. One of the bottles was in fact empty. The name of the drug was unfamiliar to me, of course; there was no indication that it was for dementia, nor any indication that it wasn't.

Dima had sent me a list of Baba Seva's medicines, along with what they did, but thinking I'd have wi-fi in the apartment I hadn't printed it out. Again I tried and failed to catch a wireless signal. I would need to find a place with wi-fi, and fast. I went back to my room and retrieved my threadbare towel and headed for the shower.

My grandmother's bathroom—separate from the toilet, which had its own, much smaller room, just off the front hall—was large for a Soviet bathroom. It's possible that it had once been part of the kitchen. Along the wall was a ledge that was used for toiletries. I put mine there now.

The first time I'd returned to Russia after we left, I was a college student. I had received a small grant to travel around and study the "post-Soviet condition." That trip was a shock. I had never encountered such poverty. In Astrakhan, Rostov, Yalta, Odessa, Lviv, but also Moscow itself, and St. Petersburg, what you saw were ruins—ruined buildings, ruined streets, ruined people—as if the country had lost a war.

I was traveling by myself, and every night at the various cheap hostels and dormitories in which I stayed I would take out my toiletries, and every night it was such a relief. The colors were brighter and more attractive than anything I saw around me: my cool slate-gray Gillette Sensor razor (a mere three blades at the time, but a better shave than mankind had yet known); my tall blue Gillette shaving gel; my brilliant red-and-white Old Spice anti-perspirant (that stuff really worked, and no one else in Russia had it, you could tell the minute you walked onto a crowded bus); my bright yellow Gold Bond powder; my little orange Advil caplets. I was walking many miles every day, interviewing people and looking around, and in the summer heat this led to rashes in my crotch and pain in my feet, but the Gold Bond powder made them go away. And Advil! Russians were still using aspirin. The only way they knew to get rid of a bad morning hangover was to start drinking again. Whereas I popped a few smooth pills into my mouth and was as good as new. I felt like James Bond practically, with my little kit of ingenious devices. Now these wonders had arrived in Russia too, though my grandmother didn't use them.

It was that summer trip to Russia that set me on the course I'd been on ever since. I had just finished my freshman year of college. College had come as a surprise to me, a bad one. I had thought it would basically be like high school, just cooler. Instead it was something completely different: vast, unfriendly, and highly competitive. I had dreamed of playing hockey there, but within minutes of stepping on the ice for the varsity tryout I saw that it was never going to happen—the level of play was way beyond mine. And neither did I excel in my classes. I wanted to master the Western canon, but every time I opened *The Faerie Queen*, I fell asleep.

Whenever I saw a Russian class in the course listings I read the description and moved on; why study at college something that I could passively imbibe at home? But halfway through my first year, after I finally quit the hockey team (I had made the JV squad, but wasn't dressing for any games), unsure of what to do with myself and wondering if taking some classes in Russian might not be a bad way to honor my mother, I walked over to the Slavic department. It was on the fourth floor of the gray foreign languages building, and unlike every other place on that campus it was somehow homey. They had managed to Russify it. There was a big samovar in the corner, tea mugs everywhere, old Russian books in their Soviet editions like the ones we had at our house, and an ironic poster of Lenin. My parents would never have hung an ironic poster of Lenin in our house, but Dima had had one in his place in New York. I felt like I had found, for the first time at that large and forbidding institution, a place where I could be at home.

Six months later I got my grant and went to Russia for the summer. It was the first time I'd been there since we'd left. So these were the streets my parents had walked down; these were the people they had lived among. This was our old apartment (I barely remembered it), where Dima was now living. So much made sense that had not made sense until then. I visited my grandmother and Uncle Lev in Dubna; my grandmother was in her midseventies then, but she was amazingly active, translating, reading, watching movies, and taking multi-mile hikes through the woods (which contained a massive particle accelerator). I left Moscow and traveled around; people outside Moscow were more honest about their dreams, more direct about what they didn't know, and more obviously and desperately poor. I remember sitting with a guy in Astrakhan, a large industrial fishing city on the Caspian Sea, now crumbling under the weight of global competition. This man and I met on the train down from Moscow. He was a computer programmer, like my father, but there was no work for computer programmers just then, so to make ends meet he traveled to Moscow to buy cheap clothes from Turkey to bring back and sell at an open-air market in Astrakhan. Now we were drinking beers on the rickety balcony of the tiny apartment he shared with his young wife and baby boy, and at some point he said, "Listen, Andrei, tell me. What's it like over there?" Meaning, in America. "Is it the same as here, in the end?"

I didn't know how to answer. It was the same, yes, in a sense—there were humans in America, they lived their lives, fell in love, had children, tried to provide for them. But it was also not the same. The abundance; the sheer ease of life, at least for people like me; the number and choice and quality of the toiletries: it was not the same. My college dorm room, which I shared with one roommate, was bigger and nicer and better built than this computer programmer's apartment, which he shared with a wife and child. I tried gently but honestly to explain this. "Well," said my friend, whom I would never see again though we exchanged addresses and promised to keep in touch, "maybe I'll get over there someday, see for myself." And in that moment I thought that I, for my part, would like to stay. In Russia, that is. At least mentally, at least intellectually—it was like no place I had ever been before, though in another sense it was exactly like a place that I had been before, that is to say my childhood, my home.

More than a decade later, a decade of Russian books, Russian classes, Russian academic conferences, a meandering dissertation on Russian literature and "modernity" that no publisher ever responded to, I emerged from the shower—it had a detachable showerhead and no place to attach it, so you had to hold it the entire time—and found my grandmother in her pink bathrobe, leaning over and sipping a coffee with great concentration. I scanned the kitchen, hoping to locate a French press or at least a drip coffee machine, but found only a teakettle and a tin can of instant Nescafé. This was disappointing; over the last few years, as the coffee revolution reached Brooklyn, I had become used to drinking some strong fucking coffee. I resolved—my list of such resolutions was growing—to buy a French press and some normal coffee beans at the first coffee store I found.

My grandmother had her radio tuned to Echo of Moscow, the station of the liberal opposition, and was trying to make sense of the news. The Russian army was reluctantly pulling out of Georgia; the Kremlin was claiming that the Georgians had created a refugee crisis; anti-Kremlin critics blamed Moscow for the war. My grandmother's radio was small, handheld, and battery-powered, and though she had it playing at full volume and was holding it to her ear, she still seemed uncertain as to what it was saying. She perked up when she saw me. "Ah, you're up!" she said. "Will you have breakfast?"

I said yes, and as I dressed she fried up some eggs on top of a panful of kasha. When I returned to the kitchen someone on Echo was very sarcastically dismissing Russian claims that Georgia had fired first. "It's like saying, 'The mosquito bit me. I had to kill him and all his relatives.' Of course the mosquito bit you! He's a mosquito." I had forgotten that tone the Russian oppositionists always took—"aggrieved" wasn't the right word for it. It was sarcastic, self-righteous, full of disbelief that these idiots were running the country and that even bigger idiots out there supported them. There was one island of decency, said these voices, and you had found it on your radio dial. I mean, I say that now. In fact it could be intoxicating. Echo, the lone voice of opposition to the regime (by this point all the television channels were firmly under state control): they woke up daily to engage in the battle of good versus evil. But of course you couldn't outright say on the radio that the regime was evil. That would be too much. So they did it with mockery, sarcasm, subversion. It seemed like a pretty good approximation of what Soviet dissidents must have sounded like back in the 1970s—as if the regime wasn't the only one that found itself a little nostalgic for that time.

So Russia had invaded Georgia. Or Georgia had invaded a part of Georgia called South Ossetia, and the Russians overreacted. And of course any decent person would agree . . . I turned it off. I wanted to talk to my grandmother about her medications. Though first I wanted to eat my grandmother's kasha. It was perfect kasha. I had gone through a period not so long ago of trying to make it, but it always came out mushy.

"Andryush, tell me," said my grandmother now as she watched me eat. "Where do you live?"

"New York."

"Where?"

"New York!"

"Oh, New York. Do you live in a house, or an apartment?"

"An apartment."

"What?"

"An apartment!"

Yesterday she had been wearing a hearing aid, but her hearing now was no worse and no better.

"Do you own the apartment, or do you rent?"

"Rent!" I said very loudly.

"You don't have to yell," she said.

"OK."

"Are you married?"

"No."

"No?"

"No."

"Do you have kids?"

"No."

"No kids?"

"No."

"Why not?"

"I don't know," I said. "I don't have anyone to have them with."

"Yes," my grandmother agreed, "that's true. You need to get married."

"Grandmother," I said. "Can I ask you something? I want to help you keep track of your medications. Do you know which of those medications does what for you?"

My grandmother did not look surprised. "I don't really know," she said. "But here, I wrote it down in a book."

And she proceeded to produce a small notebook. There were about a dozen pages, a running list, on which she'd written the names of medications and, occasionally, what they addressed ("heart," "cough"). Her handwriting had always been large and loopy, but now it was larger and loopier. There was nothing in there about dementia.

I looked up from the notebook to find that my grandmother had gone to the fridge and brought out a bottle of red wine. It was half empty and had the remnants of a cork in its throat. She was wrestling with the cork. "Should we have some wine to celebrate that you're here?" she said. "I can't seem to open it."

It was seven in the morning.

"Maybe later," I said. "Right now I need to step out for a little bit to check on something. I'll be back in an hour."

She looked disappointed. "Do you have to?"

I did. Reluctantly, my grandmother put the wine back in the fridge.

I went into my room and retrieved my laptop and my book bag. As I was about to leave, the phone rang. My grandmother was using the toilet, so I answered. An elderly woman asked for my grandmother; I said she couldn't come to the phone but that I'd take a message. The woman identified herself as Alla Aaronovna. My grandmother remained in the toilet. I wrote her a note that Alla Aaronovna had called and left it on the kitchen table. Then I headed out.

My grandmother could hardly have been more centrally located—a fifteen-minute walk to the Kremlin—but it took me forty minutes to find a place to check my email.

I hadn't seen any cafés or internet spots on my way up from the subway the day before, so the first place I headed was the other subway hub, at Clean Ponds, just up the boulevard from our place. It had always been the busiest and most active spot in the neighborhood, and behind the post office there had once been an internet café, filled with sweaty Russian video game addicts. The area was still very busy: next to the subway entrance was the big post office, a McDonald's, a bedlam of small kiosks selling cell phones, DVDs, and shish kebabs, and a statue of the poet Griboedov. Beyond Griboedev lay the eponymous clean pond. Catercorner from this agglomeration was the giant RussOil building, headquarters of the country's largest oil company, built in a black marble that seemed to swallow all the light around it. But the old internet café had been replaced by a German bank. There was no wi-fi.

I retreated to Sretenka and then walked north, along the commercial strip that Sretenka had become. It was a cute, European sort of street, narrower than most, with travel agencies and restaurants and bars, an experimental theater, a Hugo Boss store, and a shitty bookstore with the latest blockbusters in the window that also appeared to have a strip club on the second floor—there was an unlit neon sign hanging before it in the shape of a naked woman. At half past seven in the morning the street was waking up: gleaming black foreign cars sped by on their way out of the center, and once in a while a nicely dressed man or woman stepped out of one while speaking on a sleek mobile phone. This was not the Russia I remembered. I found several European-style cafés, with small tables and little signs in the window that said WI-FI. But they were incredibly expensive. The cheapest item on the menu, a tea, was two hundred rubles—almost nine dollars. On the one hand I needed to figure out if my grandmother had run out of medication for her dementia; on the other hand, nine dollars for a cup of tea. The cafés were filled with nicely dressed Russians, sipping outrageously priced cappuccinos. What the fuck.

I retreated again to our intersection: my grandmother lived just off the corner of Sretenka and the boulevard, although on the other side of the boulevard Sretenka turned into Bolshaya Lubyanka, which headed down to Lubyanka Square, the headquarters of the old KGB, now the FSB. I walked that way now. Compared with Sretenka, just a minute away, it was a desolate walk, as if the organization—thousands of people had been shot in its basement during the terror of the 1930s—had frightened off small businesses. That my grandmother lived so close to the KGB had always been a weird fact of her Moscow existence—on the one hand, central Moscow was where the good property was, so she was very lucky, and on the other hand, it was also where they'd had their execution chambers. It was like living down the street from Auschwitz.

But I needed to check my email.

I walked along the wide, quiet street until I arrived at the KGB. It was a massive building made of dark, heavy granite and it loomed over a large, open rotary, which had once been anchored by a giant statue of the KGB's founder, Felix Dzerzhinsky. But Dzerzhinsky had been taken down in 1991, and the only thing that remained at the center of the rotary was his pedestal, which had been converted into a giant flowerpot.

To my delight and surprise, however, just off this massive and still terrifying square there was a small comfortable café, the Coffee Grind, with cute little tables, wi-fi, and a chalkboard menu on which I spied at least one drink—their signature cappuccino—for a reasonable seventy-five rubles, three dollars. Maybe it was subsidized by the KGB. Well, good. They owed us. I approached the counter. "Hello!" the pretty barista said, as if she was happy to see me. I ordered the cappuccino and sat down.

I now had only fifteen minutes to check my email if I wanted to be back within the hour. I found Dima's message with the medical instructions and quickly copied it into a notebook; I then wrote him a short note to ask why there was an exercise bike in my room and also whether he knew if the wireless in his apartment was working. Then I Googled "dementia." It was a catchall term that included Alzheimer's. Did my grandmother have Alzheimer's? I was out of time. I gave myself exactly sixty seconds to look at the Slavic jobs listings website. This was an anonymous site where people posted leads on new jobs and also complaints about their job search. ("I can tell you right now this job is slated for the inside candidate." "One of the older professors on the search committee is a real creep. He spent the entire interview staring at my boobs.") This wasn't the only way to find out about new jobs, but it was the most fun. Today there was nothing. I gave myself thirty seconds to look at Facebook. My old classmates were arriving at their new posts as college professors. There were photos of new offices, requests for syllabus tips (as a way of reminding everyone: I'm a college professor!), and other stuff I thought I would no longer find upsetting once I was halfway across the world. But I still found it upsetting. Alex Fishman, my nemesis from the Slavic department, had posted a beautiful photo of Princeton, where he was starting a post-doc. What a dickhead. I shut the computer, stuck it in my bag, and went back into the street.

It was eight o'clock in the morning now and even sleepy, scary Bolshaya Lubyanka was stirring to life. Expensive German cars bounced out of the rotary and sped toward Sretenka; others pulled into a large open-air parking lot that must have been for the FSB. Some of the cars made their way onto the sidewalk and parked there; elegantly dressed men and women, on their way to work, maneuvered around them, as if it was perfectly ordinary that someone would park on a sidewalk.

The women, I couldn't help but notice, were exceptionally attractive. In the four blocks between the Coffee Grind and our house I must have seen a dozen very good-looking women. And there was something about them, about their uniformity. They were all thin, blonde, thirtyish, in black pencil skirts, white blouses, and high heels. I don't know why I liked the fact that they all looked alike, but I did.

The men too fit a pattern. Big, kasha fed, six feet tall, stuffed into expensive suits, balancing themselves on shiny, pointy-toed shoes, never smiling. Ten years ago you walked down a Moscow street and ran into a lot of thugs in cheap leather jackets. Those guys were gone now, replaced by these guys. Or maybe they were the same guys? They hogged the sidewalk; they barreled ahead without looking to see what was in the way; they kept their hands by their sides and their fists clenched, like they were ready to use them. I had just come from the land of dudes who grew beards, wore shorts, smiled always at some secret melody playing in their heads, and sipped their coffees as they slowly rode their bikes up Bedford Avenue. This was the opposite of that.

One other thing I noticed: Everyone was white. Some were blond and blue-eyed, others had brown hair and hazel eyes, and some were a little darker, Armenian or Jewish, but still white. The construction sites, meanwhile, were manned by Central Asians, short and thin, while Central Asian women, in orange vests, tidied up the various courtyards.

Before returning home I ducked into a tiny grocery at the corner of Bolshaya Lubyanka and the boulevard. It smelled bad and the two women behind the counter seemed annoyed to have a customer. Beer took up most of the small space, but they also had cold cuts—that must have been the source of the smell—and, more important, what I was looking for: *sushki*. These were round, crunchy, slightly sweet bread rings. Because they were a little sweet you could have them with tea, but because they weren't too sweet you could also have them with beer. I bought two packets, one with poppy seeds, one without. Unlike everything else in the new Russia, sushki were still cheap.

When I got home, my grandmother was sitting at the kitchen table, with four little phone books spread out before her. She didn't hear me come in and I saw her slowly reading through one of them, repeating "Alla Aaronovna" to herself, searching for the name.

"Andryush," she said when she finally saw me, "were you the one who left me this note?"

I nodded.

"I can't find an Alla Aaronovna anywhere. Are you sure that's who it was?"

I was sure. I should have asked for her number! But she sounded certain that my grandmother would know exactly who she was.

My grandmother looked down helplessly at her many phone books. "Andryushenka," she said, holding one out to me like an offering. "Can you find it in here?"

I sat down at the table with her and started going through the books. They were written in her large, round hand. Many names and numbers were crossed out. I asked after a few of them. "She died." "They emigrated." "I don't know." I stopped asking. We had only Alla Aaronovna's name and patronymic, not her last name, so I had to flip through the entirety of each book. There were two crossed-out Allas, but both had died (there were dates), and neither was an Aaronovna.

"Are you sure that was her name?"

I was becoming less sure, but still I was sure. I had written it down right away.

My grandmother continued to look through the books. Finally she said, "There's an Ella Petrovna. Maybe it was her."

"It wasn't her."

"I'm going to call her. Maybe it was."

She dialed the number. The person who answered knew neither an Ella Petrovna nor an Alla Aaronovna. My grandmother apologized. Then, very carefully, as someone does when dealing with the dead, she crossed out the name and number in her book.

"You see," said my grandmother, "all my friends have died. Everyone close to me has died. I have no one left."

"I'm sure she'll call again," I said hopefully.

She never did.

When all this was done I took my notebook out of my book bag and cross-checked the list of medicines Dima had sent me with the ones on the shelf. The empty bottle, it turned out, was a vitamin D supplement. Her dementia pill bottle was half full. So it was not the medicine. This was her.

I opened the bag of poppy-seed sushki and, sitting there in the kitchen, ate the entire thing.

For the next week, I didn't let my grandmother out of my sight. I went with her on her grocery rounds and kept her company while she cooked. I sneaked down to the KGB to work while she took her morning nap, but then I'd be back again. I was having trouble overcoming my jet lag, and found myself very sleepy in the late afternoons, but did my best to accompany her on walks. In the early evenings we ate supper, which was heavy on tea and sweets, and watched the evening news.

Physically, for an eighty-nine-year-old woman, my grandmother was in good shape. She and Uncle Lev had spent years going on interminable walks around the particle accelerator in Dubna and hiking through the mountains of the USSR. This was fashionable among the scientific set, and also he had to travel the vast empire for work, to learn if there was oil under the ground. Even now my grandmother took walks through the apartment, back and forth from one end to the other, like a prisoner. But her mind was failing. After some emails with Dima and a few hours on WebMD I concluded that she had regular old dementia. (A few weeks later Dima got us an appointment with a neurologist; the neurologist confirmed this.) The grooves of her memory were shot. Her personality was slowly disappearing. All the while her heart beat like a perfect little engine. Her body was outliving her mind.

Her days were strictly regimented. She awoke each morning at seven, grated an apple (for her digestion), took her medicines, made her bed, and dressed. Like all Soviet people she had spent her life with limited space, and now each morning she removed her bedding and placed it in the drawers underneath her bed, thereby converting her bed into something more like a sofa. She still took care of her appearance, with a rotation of two pairs of pleated, light-green khaki-style pants and several pastel-colored collared shirts. She had a blue cotton hat that she wore to keep off the sun. These feminine touches were the ones that had, once upon a time, kept her from being lonely even in the postwar years, when most of the men didn't return from the war and the ones who did could choose just about any girl they liked. It was a tough dating scene for a woman, and yet my grandmother had done OK.

She still did her own grocery shopping, going on a tour of the stores (and a "market," as she called it, which consisted of six plastic kiosks on an empty lot) within a two-block radius. Most of the neighborhood had undergone radical gentrification, with restaurants and clothing boutiques and banks muscling out the depressing Soviet-era groceries, but a few remained, and she went from one to the next to the next. Eggs were cheaper in one place, cheese in another, a beet salad with too much mayonnaise that she liked in a third. For special items we ranged a little farther. "Do you want chicken for lunch?" my grandmother said one morning. I said sure. So we walked ten minutes down Sretenka to the Sukharevskaya metro stop, where there was a rotisserie chicken stand run by some Azeri dudes. My grandmother ordered a half chicken. They handed it to her in a little paper bag.

The grocery run wasn't always smooth—I caught, or thought I caught, one of the saleswomen shortchanging my grandmother by eighty rubles—and because most of the groceries were Soviet style, that is, you had to ask for everything from behind the counter and then pay at the register and then come back with your receipt and get your items, and because my grandmother went from place to place to place to get the best prices, and because she did everything slowly, it took much, much longer than it needed to. At the end of it, she needed help getting up the stairs to the second floor. Still, that she was able to do so much by herself was a triumph.

Aside from Emma Abramovna, still ensconced at her enviable dacha, my grandmother had, as she told me over and over again, no friends: she had lost touch with them, they had moved with their children to Israel, they had died. One courtyard over from ours, there usually sat a little knot of old ladies—a few years younger than my grandmother, and much sturdier, thicker, cruder, dressed in cheap leisurewear, while my grand-mother still dressed in cheap business attire—but when I asked my grandmother about them, as a way of introducing the concept of their potential friendship, she pulled me a little closer (we were walking by them) and said, "I used to sit with them. But then I stopped. They're anti-Semites." So it was down to me.

The evenings were simple enough: we'd watch the nightly news and play anagrams, where you pick some large word out of a book, write it on a sheet of paper, and then try to form out of its letters the maximum number of different words. You got one point for a word with four let-ters, two points for a word with five, and so on. My grandmother loved this game, was ruthless at it, and typically beat me about 60 to 8. So that was good. But before we got to anagrams and the evening news, we had to survive the late afternoon—the witching hour. This was the time my grandmother had the most trouble filling. She could no longer read for long stretches, as she once had done: sitting in a chair and looking down was hard on her back and neck, whereas lying in bed and holding up a book was too exhausting. She had taken to tearing out chapters of books, making it easier to hold them above her face as she lay in bed, but her memory was so bad that she had trouble enjoying anything of any length. Over the course of those first few weeks I saw her read the same

Chekhov story—torn out of a paperback edition of his stories—over and over again. Aside from reading, there wasn't much my grandmother knew how to do inside the house to entertain herself. She had lived a difficult life and had never really learned how to take her leisure. There'd always been too much to do. Now there wasn't, and on these long afternoons she would become bored and even desperate if there was nowhere to go. But going somewhere wasn't easy.

Moscow was enormous. It had always been enormous. Stalin had widened the avenues to the point where you needed underground passageways to get from one side to the other. My little grandmother had to go down a flight of stairs, walk through a passageway, then up some stairs again, just to cross the street. If she wanted to cross back she'd have to do it all over again.

Moscow's subway, also built by Stalin, was justly famous. In the center of the city the stations were glorious, laid out in marble, decorated in colorful mosaics depicting the heroic achievements of the working class. Some still featured giant statues of Lenin or Marx or Red Army soldiers fighting off the Nazis. The stations were spotless, and even in the stuffy final days of August they were always cool. Trains came quickly and efficiently, and a digital clock at the entrance to the tunnel in each station indicated to the second the time that had passed since the last train departed. By the time the clock reached two minutes and thirty seconds, another train had usually arrived.

But riding this famous metro with my grandmother, I quickly came to see its limitations. It was incredibly crowded: because all the lines but one were radial, that is, running from the center of the circle that was Moscow to its outskirts, there was no way to transfer from one line to another without going through the center, meaning that basically all travelers were routed through a few stations near the Kremlin, which is where we lived. Every time we got on a train, it was packed. And packed here meant something different from what it did in New York. In New York during rush hour the trains could be so crowded that people couldn't get on, and had to wait for the next train. In Moscow when this happened, people got on anyway.

The trains themselves were OK, but, unlike the station platforms, hot and stuffy, filled with the body odor of a hundred Russian men. And finally and worst of all, there were simply not enough stops. No matter where you arrived, you still had some walking to do.

We tried to head out to Sokolniki Park, just a few metro stops away, while the weather was still nice. But the subway ride and the walk to the park tired my grandmother out. The sway of the fast trains made her nauseous. The jostling and bumping upset her. "Let's go home," she said, just about as soon as we emerged from the metro.

"We just got here," I said. "Let's at least make it to the park."

"I'm telling you I want to go home!"

I stopped. She was holding on to my arm and stopped as well. We were just outside the Sokolniki metro, with people going in and out of the heavy swinging doors. My grandmother was so small. She had put on her little light-blue sun hat for our trip, and her light-green summer pants. "Whatever you want," I said, though I was upset.

"Fine," my poor tired grandmother said at last. "Let's just go to the park and then go back."

We walked to the park and sat for a while on a bench just inside it. Then we headed home again. Neither of us had found the trip much fun. I knew that I was to blame for not coming up with something better. But I didn't know what that could be.

My grandmother had once been devoted to cinema, taking the train in from Dubna on weekends to see whatever was playing at the House of Cinema near Mayakovskaya—she received hard-to-find passes from a man she'd once dated, before she met Uncle Lev. She liked to complain to whoever would listen that the movies at the Dubna House of Culture were always six months out of date. Now she told me she could no longer stand the movies. "It's just *bakh-bakh-bakh*," she said, miming a gun with her hand. "I can't watch." She had a paper with entertainment listings that she still bought, out of habit, every single week from a newsstand next to the Azeri chicken guys, and one morning she handed it to me. "Andryush," she said, "can you find something for us to see?" She had marked up the film section with checks and circles and crosses, but I got the sense that she was doing this at random. The trouble was, I didn't know any better than she did. I took the paper to the Coffee Grind so I could use the internet to puzzle out which movies it was referring to, since most of them were American or British, and I didn't recognize the titles in translation. Once I'd puzzled them out, I saw the problem: almost all the foreign movies playing in Moscow (and since the collapse of the Russian film industry in the early 1990s, almost all the movies playing in Moscow were foreign) were shit. It was *Kung Fu Panda*, *The Mummy: Tomb of the Dragon Emperor*, and *Madagascar: Escape 2 Africa*. No offense intended, but many of these movies were cartoons; the rest were *bakh-bakh-bakh*, just as my grandmother said. In the end, to avoid the *bakh-bakh-bakh*, I found us an artsy Danish film that was showing at what seemed from its website to be a quasi-underground film place not far from our house. The address for the cinema was Red Army Avenue, 24, which I naïvely thought would mean it was on Red Army Avenue; it turned out the cinema was in an inner courtyard *off* Red Army Avenue. While we were searching for it, it started to rain; my grandmother pleaded for us to give up, but I insisted I could find it, left her under an awning, and ran around for five minutes until I did. I came back to fetch my tired and slightly wet grandmother and dragged her to the theater. Inside were several dozen young Moscow hipsters, wearing Converse. My people! They would think I was pretty cool for bringing my grandmother. Except that they did not. She got hushed twice for asking me what was happening in the film. The hipsters looked annoyed when we went past them halfway through so my grandmother could use the bathroom. At the end of the film, she asked me what I thought, and I sort of shrugged, not wanting to get into it. She then declared very loudly, "It was so boring!" A few of the hipsters shot us dirty looks. But she was right. The movie was boring. After that I put our film viewing on hold.

My grandmother's problem was not that she couldn't handle the tasks life still put before her. She could handle them. Her problem was loneliness. "The thing is," she would say to me during our walks, or over lunch, or over breakfast, "all my friends have died. Everyone close to me has died. Borya Kraisenstern died. Lyubima Gershkovich died. Rosa Pipkin died. Look," she said, picking up her phone books, "these are just lists of the dead now. Just dead, dead, dead." Occasionally I would try to argue (What about Dima? What about me?), but in its broad outlines it was true. Her lone remaining friend was Emma Abramovna, with whom she talked on the phone quite frequently, but since Emma Abramovna's dacha lacked a landline, their conversations consisted primarily of my grandmother saying, "What? I didn't hear that!" They would have this conversation multiple times a day. Once in a while I would hear my grandmother bringing up the dacha. "How is Peredelkino?" she would say. "Is it nice there?" Hearing an answer in the affirmative, she would say sadly, "Here in the city it's so stuffy. I can hardly breathe."

Unable to travel to the park, worried about seeing another bad movie, we contented ourselves with walking along the little green pedestrian mall in between the traffic lanes of the boulevard. Our stretch of it went from the statue of Lenin's widow, Nadezhda Krupskaya, to the giant scary RussOil building across from Clean Ponds. We walked back and forth between these, arguing. My grandmother argued that she was neglected and abandoned, that Dima didn't love her, and that I wasn't going to stay very long. I argued that Dima was busy, that she was not abandoned, and that I would stay as long as necessary. I thought it was important to correct the things she was mistaken about, or even to challenge the things she was right about, just to keep the grooves of her memory working. This was often frustrating, as she didn't seem to believe me, and only sometimes because I was lying.

Once in a while I tried to jog her memory about Soviet history—Stalinism, the purges, the war, the "thaw"—but I never got anywhere. She didn't remember, and she didn't seem to want to try. Someone more committed to getting at the truth might have forced her to remember whether she wanted to or not. I don't know. But I couldn't do it.

The one thing I did manage to do on our walks was remind her of who I was. This I enjoyed.

"Do you remember who I am?" I said.

"You're Andryusha."

"But do you remember how I know you?"

"How you know me . . ."

"Do you remember your daughter?"

"My daughter?" There was almost always a pause. "My little daughter? My Yelochka?"

"Yes."

"She died."

"Yes."

"And you?"

"I am her son."

"You are her son." I could practically see as her mind went back to the dacha at Sheremetevo, me as a little boy running around the yard, my father coming one weekend and teaching me how to ride a bike. Then she'd look up at grown-up me. "Andryusha?"

"Yes."

And we would continue walking, and I would try not to cry.

4.

I TRY TO FIND A HOCKEY GAME

YOU HAD TO BE fundamentally *stupid*, I sometimes thought, to become the sort of academic specialist that hiring committees liked. You had to be thick somehow. You had to block out all the other things in the world to focus on one narrow, particular thing. And how, without knowing all the other things out there, could you possibly choose? I was enjoying this thought one day while walking to the Coffee Grind. It wasn't the only time in the day that I had to think, but it was the most concentrated. I always walked past the little grocery where I got my sushki and then I was on creepy, deserted Bolshaya Lubyanka. I had no choice but to think.

If I looked at my classmates, the ones who started at the same time as I did, what was the difference between them and me? It wasn't that they were actually stupid. Most of them were smart, and some were quite a bit smarter than I was. That wasn't the difference, though. The difference was their willingness to stick with something. The successful ones were like pit bulls who had sunk their teeth into a topic and wouldn't let go until someone shot them or they had tenure.

To the ongoing frustration of my adviser, I was not doing that.

"Pretend I'm a hiring committee," he said once. "What is your pitch to me?"

"My pitch is that I love this stuff. I love Russian history and literature and I love talking about it to people."

"OK, but a university is also a place for research. What's your specialty?"

I had been through this with him before. "Modernity," I said,

39

knowing already that he wasn't going to like it. "I am a specialist in modernity."

My adviser, a six-foot-four former basketball player from Iowa, did a very girly imitation of my voice. "'I'm a specialist in modernity,'" he said. "'I study the ways in which modernity affects the Russian mind.'"

I waited for him to finish.

"I'm a specialist in my own butt!" yelled my adviser. "That's not what got me this job!"

"What's wrong with modernity?"

"It covers three centuries! It's not a specialization. Three *years* is a specialization. Or better yet, three months. Three days. If you were a specialist in, like, Tuesday through Thursday of the first week of February 1904, but *also* in total command of Russian modernism, I could get you a job anywhere you wanted."

I didn't say anything.

"I mean, look at the writers you've studied." We were in my adviser's tiny office, the two printed-out sheets of my CV lying on his desk between us. Despite his unorthodox advising methods, he was a good guy. He said he'd gotten serious about studying Russia after he realized he wasn't going to the NBA. ("It took me a long time to realize that," he said, "because I am dumb.") He was a great teacher, a truly inspired teacher, but his own academic career had not gone smoothly. He wanted me to avoid his mistakes. "Who is Patrushkin?" he asked now, looking at the description of my dissertation. Grigory Patrushkin was an early-nineteenth-century poet. He hadn't actually written very many poems, nor were the poems he wrote very good, but I wanted someone from that era who wasn't Pushkin. Although Patrushkin knew Pushkin.

"Patrushkin was a friend of Pushkin's," I now said.

"A friend?"

"He sort of knew Pushkin."

"And does this mean you can teach Pushkin?"

"I don't know."

"Because there's no course on Patrushkin!"

"I just didn't want to write about the usual suspects. I thought . . ." I sort of trailed off.

"Look," he said. "Do you think I want to be studying the architecture of early Russian huts?" In his one smart academic move, my adviser had developed a theory that medieval Russian huts lacked chimneys— they discovered chimneys some two hundred years after Western European peasants—and this gave early Russian peasants brain damage, which explains why they didn't develop some of the farming strategies that radically increased crop yields in early modern Europe and helped bring about the Renaissance. "Do you think I wanted to become another of these people who come up with a monocause for Russian backwardness? No, dude. I wanted to be Isaiah Berlin!"

"I know I'm not Isaiah Berlin."

"I know, OK. I'm just saying. I know you love teaching. That's a good thing. But in order to teach, you need a teaching job, yes? And right now, at this point in time, that means finding a topic that's going to appeal to a hiring committee."

Back in July he was very excited when I told him I was going to Russia.

"This is great!" he said. "You'll be on the ground. You can find something new and original. Or something old." It was my adviser who suggested I interview my grandmother. "She'll tell you stories about the USSR. You can weave them in and out of a tale of modernity. That shit is gold, my friend. People *love* that shit."

"Hiring committees love it?"

"Yes. Who did you think I meant when I said 'people'?"

Now that was out. If I couldn't use my grandmother's stories, which she didn't remember, I would have to think of something else. But what? I really had no idea. People like Alex Fishman made their careers repackaging Russian dictatorship. "Gulag," said Fishman, then "internet," and granting institutions swooned. (He was now doing an online history of the Gulag.) People loved reading about the Soviet Gulag—it made them feel better about the U.S. of A.

Of course it wasn't like Russia was now a flourishing democracy. But it was complicated. Back in Brooklyn on the internet, and now in my grandmother's kitchen on Echo of Moscow, all I heard about was what a dangerous place Russia was, what a bloody tyrant Putin had become. And it was, and he was. But I had half expected to be arrested at the airport! I thought I'd be robbed on the train. In fact the only thing I was in danger of being arrested for was accidentally buying too many cappuccinos at the Coffee Grind and not having enough cash on me to pay. (They did not take credit cards.) The only robbery going on was the price of croissants on Sretenka.

The country had become rich. Not everyone was rich—my grandmother wasn't rich, and in fact, speaking of robbery, she *had* been robbed of certain things—but overall, generally speaking, a lot of people, especially in Moscow, were pretty well off. Looking out the window, it was hard to square all the talk of bloody dictatorship with all the people in expensive suits, getting into Audis, talking on their cell phones. Was this naïve? Didn't people in Saudi Arabia drive fancy cars and talk on cell phones in between chopping off the heads of dissidents? Yes. Maybe. I don't know. I'd never been to Saudi Arabia. For me—and not just for me, I think—Soviet oppression and Soviet poverty had always been inextricably intertwined.

Not everyone was happy about the new conditions. The liberals on Echo complained about press censorship and the marginalization of opposition politicians. Sometimes they held small protests to express their anger at the regime. And there were also occasional local issue-oriented protests, for example against the building of a mall in Pushkin Square. Most of these were tolerated, but some were violently dispersed, and my grandmother had apparently seen such a dispersal because every time we walked past a larger than usual group of people—whether waiting in line or watching a juggler perform, and especially if there were police nearby—she would say, "Let's get out of here, it's a protest, the police are very harsh toward protesters," and pull us in the opposite direction. Nonetheless she remained very curious about the news, and every time she found me in the kitchen with the radio on or *Kom-*

mersant or the *Moscow Times* in front of me, she started asking questions. "What are they saying?" she'd say.

"About what?"

"You know, about the situation. What's the situation?"

What was the situation? I couldn't tell! It was some kind of modern authoritarianism. Or authoritarian modernization. Or something. I tried to keep her up on the latest, and she gamely nodded her head.

In the meantime, the fall PMOOC sections had begun. I was in charge of four online sections of Jeff Wilson's class on the classics of Russian literature. It was an OK class. Jeff was in his midforties and taught a kind of hepped-up version of the classics. He would say things like "Vronski is a bro in a hipster outfit" and "Tolstoy was sort of the Kanye of Russian literature—he was always making embarrassing public statements and then being forced to apologize." The idea was to make the books relatable to a younger audience. I didn't mind, even though, having TA'ed for Jeff quite a bit in grad school, I had noticed that he also compared Pushkin, Gogol, and Dostoevsky to Kanye, to the point where I wondered if he knew any other figures from popular culture. ("Pushkin is really the Tupac of Russian literature, though, don't you think?" my adviser quipped once, when I complained about it to him.)

The class began in early September, and so in the Coffee Grind across from the FSB I would watch Jeff's lecture, skim the assigned book to refresh my memory, and then log on to the different class blogs, where the students wrote responses to the text and then commented on those responses and then commented on the comments—forever.

In my many years of grad school I had taught all sorts of people. I had taught arriving freshmen in their first semester, when they still resembled children, their upper lips irritated from their first shaves; they thought that Tolstoy or, better still, Dostoevsky was trying to communicate directly to them and responded accordingly (often without doing the reading). I had taught cynical seniors who had learned to manipulate the limited belief system of contemporary literary studies and receive good grades. They knew that Tolstoy was just a name that we gave to a machine that had once written symbols on a piece of paper. It was ridiculous to try to assign some kind of intention or consistency to this machine. The seniors floated in and out of class, making fun of me. At the end of the year, I watched them all get jobs at hedge funds. I experienced it as a personal failure when they left literature; the only thing worse was when they remained. But the PMOOC students were something else altogether—a volatile mixture of the young and old, the over-educated and the autodidactic. They wrote me a tremendous number of emails.

The first book we read that fall semester was Tolstoy's *The Cossacks*. It was one of Tolstoy's early novels, about a spoiled young officer from Moscow who is sent to do his army service in a Cossack town on the southern Russian frontier. Back home, the young officer has gambling debts and a bad reputation, but in the Cossack village he starts over again, falling in love with the simple, straightforward, earthbound ways of the natives. He falls in love too with a handsome, strong-boned Cossack girl named Dunya, and though she is engaged to be married to her childhood sweetheart, the spoiled young officer eventually convinces her to break it off. Though skeptical, she knows she'd be a fool to turn down a wealthy Muscovite. And then, just as they're about to make it official, there is a raid on the village and Dunya's former fiancé is killed. Somewhat unfairly, Dunya blames the young officer for her friend's death. Unable to muster a defense of his actions, he packs his things and goes back to Moscow. The end.

The students did not like the book, primarily because they didn't like the young officer. "Why read a book about a jerk?" they said. After reading seven or eight responses along these lines, I wrote an impassioned defense of *The Cossacks*. Books weren't just for likeable characters overcoming hardships, I said. Some of the world's greatest books are about jerks! I wrote the post and uploaded it and waited. The blogging software we used allowed people to "like" posts, as on Facebook; after my heartfelt essay received just one like, I spent an hour in the Coffee Grind figuring out how to disable that function, and did.

At the end of my work sessions at the Grind, I would check the Slavic jobs listings page—in early September it was, predictably, pretty fallow—and then give myself the dubious treat of scrolling through Facebook. Sarah hadn't bothered to unfriend me after our break-up and it would have been churlish on my part to unfriend her, and now I saw her posting solo photos of herself, looking cuter and cuter with each one, here on some beach over Labor Day, there on some college campus that was definitely not our college campus . . . Her status was still "single," and she was alone in all the photos, and it was possible that it was just a friend of hers who was taking them—maybe her friend Ellen?—but they didn't *feel* like photos that Ellen would take. Sarah was going into her third year in the English department, and she had said that all the boys in English were ridiculous, but maybe she had found one who wasn't. Or maybe she was dating a guy from anthro. I tried not to think too much about it. I went back to studying the Facebook posts of my stupid former classmates: A syllabus completed! A manuscript accepted! An issue of the *Slavic Review* with their peer-reviewed article in it! Oh, how I hated all of them. Through gritted teeth I pressed "like" on all their posts, pretty much without exception.

I tried to be helpful around the house, but like much else this was more difficult than I had expected. The place was so old and had been adjusted over the years in so many ingenious but ad hoc ways that a person without deep knowledge of it was lost. I had lived in an old building in Brooklyn, at least as old as my grandmother's, but it had been built to last, and when something broke down we called the super, Elvis, who took his time but eventually came up and more or less fixed what was broken. If you gave Elvis twenty dollars at Christmas, he would start coming up faster. In Moscow it would never occur to a group of residents to employ and house a permanent handyman. Every man of the house was his own handyman. Except, as it turned out, me.

One morning I got up to find my grandmother at the kitchen table, looking worried. "Ah, Andryush, you're up," she said. "We have a problem. There's no hot water."

"Oh?" I said.

I half expected to turn on the tap and find hot water coming out and explain to my grandmother that she had been mistakenly turning the cold water knob, but this was not the case. I turned the hot water knob, let it run, and nothing but cold water emerged. She was right.

The hot water, I knew, was regulated by a mini-boiler that was mounted in the corner of the bathroom. It was like a stove in that it had a little blue pilot light always working; when you turned on the hot water, the pilot light lit a big blue flame that warmed the water as, I guess, it went through the boiler. I went into the bathroom and, sure enough, the pilot light was extinguished. So I had identified the cause of the problem. But that was only half the battle.

Dima had left me the number of his handyman, Stepan, to call in case anything broke. But surely I could fix this myself? I tried fiddling with the knobs on the boiler, none of which were labeled, to no effect; then I tried fiddling with them while holding a lit match next to where the pilot light used to be, to equally little effect. Then I tried to do all this with the hot water on. Then I tried it with the cold water on. Some of these attempts required the participation of my grandmother, who kept mumbling, "We're ruined, we're ruined," over and over as she turned on the hot water, the cold water, and both of them at once. These attempts in their various combinations took about an hour and didn't get us anywhere. Finally, I broke down and called Stepan.

"Did you try turning the knob at the back to the left with the hot water on?" he asked right away.

"Yes."

"All right, I'll come by. The traffic's bad so it's going to take a while, and I'll need to charge you for that."

"How much?"

"All told, fifteen hundred."

That was sixty dollars at the time. It seemed like a lot. But we needed hot water. "OK," I said.

Stepan was there two hours later, a gruff giant with a bushy mustache. He said hello to my grandmother, whom he knew by name, and headed for the bathroom. It took him exactly two seconds to get the pilot light back on. "You have to hold the knob in position for a bit," he said. "Otherwise the gas doesn't get there."

I handed him the rubles, which I'd prepared, and he took them with an air of profound regret, as if this was really something that should not have happened. I tried to cheer him up.

"Next time I'll be able to do it myself!" I said.

"You should have done it yourself this time," Stepan said gloomily, bid farewell to my grandmother, and left.

Otherwise, around the house, things were OK. I grew used to my scratchy sheets and instant coffee (when I finally found a place that sold French presses, I discovered I could not afford one), and even the lack of wi-fi started to seem like a blessing, keeping me away from student blog posts and fruitless rage-filled Facebook sessions. The one real problem was that I couldn't sleep. I kept waking at five in the morning and then lying in bed hoping to get to sleep again before I gave up and got out of bed. Then in the late afternoon I would become unbearably sleepy; as this was the time my grandmother most needed company, I would try to stay awake, but I didn't always manage.

The time difference was mostly to blame, but so too, I thought, was my sudden lack of exercise. Back in New York I either played hockey or went jogging or used the university gym just about every day of the week. Now, suddenly, I did not. I tried to go jogging a few times but jogging along the street was miserable, because of the cars sitting in traffic and spewing exhaust, and jogging along the pedestrian strip on the boulevard was too annoying, since you had to either wait at a large intersection every tenth of a mile or turn back and run the same section again. As for gyms, I had looked up a few that were within walking distance and not one of them cost less than three hundred dollars a month. The solution was hockey. I had lugged all my stuff to this so-called hockey mecca, but Dima had so far failed to provide me the game he had promised, and I could learn nothing on my own online—there was no information about recreational hockey, or even the location of hockey rinks. It was like the rinks were nuclear research towns, to be kept top secret.

The worst part of the sleep situation was that it was making me irritable. I didn't realize just how irritable until one day I heard my grandmother shuffling past my bedroom door while I was working. I tried whenever possible to work at the Coffee Grind, but it was sometimes such a production to get out of the house (Where was I going? To a café? But we had plenty of food in the house! No, I'm going to the café to work. To work? Did I have a *job* at the café?) that I was trying, as an experiment, to work at home. I would certainly save on cappuccinos. But it wasn't going well. When I tried to work in the kitchen, the room in the house with the most light, my grandmother came in and sat with me and started offering me food. I went into my room and shut the door. But she pursued me there as well. She'd knock, ask some question—What time did I want to have lunch? Did I want chicken? Did I remember her husband Lev?—and then, having received an answer, would promptly forget it and return in five minutes to ask again.

On this afternoon that I'm remembering, about two weeks after I'd arrived, I was sitting in my room, making my way through a digital pile of student blog responses I'd pasted into a Word document at the Grind, when I heard my grandmother shuffling toward my door. I braced for her knock, but she shuffled past instead. About forty-five seconds later, she was by my door again, and again she failed to knock. This was impossible. I waited for her to come back, and when she did I rushed to the door and opened it. I found her there, in her robe, with her hand up in a small fist, preparing to knock at last.

"WHAT IS IT?" I shouted.

My grandmother looked at me with such pathetic fear and surprise that I immediately regretted it. "I—I don't know," she said. "I can't remember. I'm so sorry."

"It's OK," I said, trying to soothe her. "I'm sorry."

But she walked away.

At that moment I concluded that I needed to solve this sleep situation before it got any worse. I needed to find some exercise. If I couldn't jog or afford a gym, then I would need to find a hockey game.

The next day I wrote Dima to ask if he'd found out anything at all, and he apologized and said it was trickier than he'd anticipated and that the only thing he'd learned was that there was a game at Sokolniki, at the Spartak arena. He didn't know when or who, but maybe I could just show up there and figure it out? It's certainly what you'd do in America. So one day I finally packed all my gear into a large blue Ikea bag I found in the closet—I had, somewhat rashly and also to save on baggage fees, thrown out my ragged old hockey bag before leaving Brooklyn and simply stuffed my gear into my big red suitcase—and in the evening took the metro to Sokolniki.

I reached the rink without any trouble: it was an actual stadium, the home rink of Spartak, and unlike most buildings in Moscow it was neither surrounded by a tall metal fence nor insanely and unreasonably guarded. There was a guard at the entrance, but he saw my hockey stuff and nodded me along. I made my way down to the ice. It was a nice, modern, professional rink, with about five thousand seats; I had never played on a professional rink before; presumably Spartak was out of town or simply wasn't using the ice that evening, and whoever ran the rink rented it out to earn some extra money. Very cool. Only in Russia, I thought. For about five minutes, the country struck me as a vast informal arrangement, outside the reach of modernity and regimentation, an ever-evolving experiment. I liked the place. Like I say, this feeling lasted about five minutes.

A pickup game was in progress. The level was mixed, with a few excellent players weaving through mostly mediocre ones. It was a little incongruous to see these middle-aged nonprofessionals on a professional ice surface and on the professional benches, in this beautiful arena, but it was definitely a game I could play in. And there weren't too many guys—three on each bench, in fact, which is a couple too few.

On one of the benches stood a guy in street clothes, like he was a coach. He probably wasn't a coach—I had noticed that there were always guys like this hanging around in Russia, without any apparent purpose, just because—but I figured he'd know what was up.

As I walked toward him I realized that since I'd arrived I had hardly interacted with anyone who wasn't my grandmother, and I wasn't sure in this situation whether to use the familiar *ty* or the polite *vy*. Back in Boston my parents had said *vy* to just about everyone except their close friends, but the culture had moved on, and my sense was more people now said *ty*. But I wasn't sure. *Vy* was safer, and I went with *vy*. "Excuse me," I said, using the polite form. "Can I play with you guys?"

The pseudocoach thus politely addressed looked at me in a neutral fashion and said, "You'll have to ask Zhora," then turned back to the game.

"Excuse me," I was forced to say again, again very politely. "Where is Zhora?"

Zhora was on the other bench. I went over. The guy closest to me on the bench was older than I was, past forty, but in good shape and with a scar on his cheek. I asked him (*vy*) if he could point out Zhora. He could. Zhora was on the ice, a big right-handed forward who could barely keep himself on his skates. Unlike most guys who can't skate, however, he was fed a constant diet of passes from his teammates and given plenty of room by his opponents. I intuited from this that Zhora paid for the ice.

When he came to the bench at the end of his shift I saw that he was about my age, with smooth, almost babylike skin and a tan. All his equipment was brand-new and he held somewhat awkwardly a very expensive stick.

"Zhora, hello, my name is Andrei," I said quickly. Increasingly uncertain of my *vy*, I added, "I just moved to Moscow and am looking for a hockey game. Do you have room?"

Zhora looked at me. I was saying *vy* to everyone, like a foreigner. Instead of a proper CCM hockey bag, I had a big Ikea bag with my stuff falling out. And I was wearing my favorite short-sleeve, collared shirt, from some thrift store in Massachusetts, that had a picture of a gas station and the name "Hugo" on the chest. I either looked like a very committed hockey player or a total idiot.

Zhora decided it was the latter.

"We're full up," he said.

This was patently untrue.

"Every single time?" I said. "Maybe you're full today, but not next time?"

"Where'd you play?" said Zhora. He used the familiar *ty*, like he was my boss. I could now continue saying *vy* to him, in a sign of deference, or I could also switch to *ty*, which could be seen as aggressive. Or I could avoid expressions that required a choice.

"Where did I play?" I asked, not quite understanding.

"Yeah," said Zhora. "For example, that guy played at Spartak." He pointed to the rough-looking guy who'd helped me locate Zhora; he had jumped over the boards when Zhora came back to the bench and was now skating with the puck. Spartak was effortlessly dodging guys half his age; he was a tremendous hockey player.

And, to be fair, the question of where one played was not unreasonable. In hockey you don't want to play with people who suck. They disrupt the flow of the game, for one thing, and for another, skating on a slippery surface and holding on to sticks, they can be dangerous. Zhora himself, for example, was such a player. So I didn't exactly resent his question; it's just that there was no way for me to answer it sensibly.

"In Boston," I said.

Zhora chuckled. "Where in Boston?"

"In school," I said. In Russian there is no word for high school—all school, from first grade to tenth, is referred to as "school"; more important, as I did not quite understand at the time, there is no such thing as high school sports in Russia. Youth sports take place in so-called "sports schools." They can be affiliated with one of the major professional teams (Red Army or Dynamo or Spartak), or they can be independent. They train kids from a young age, sometimes for free, encouraging those with talent and discouraging those without it. Whereas my answer to Zhora made it sound like I'd played shinny on the pond behind my elementary school.

"School, huh?" Zhora laughed again. "No, it's all right, we're full up." Then, in English: "*Sorry.*"

"All right," I said, though I was pissed. At least I hadn't had to call him *vy* again. As I walked away, I watched the game a little longer. There really were three or four terrific players out there, but the rest of the guys were at my level or worse. They had not played at Spartak.

My stuff felt heavy as I lugged it back to the metro, and to add further humiliation to the previous humiliation, I got stopped by two cops and asked for my "documents." This had happened to me all the time when I was younger—the police usually stop non-Slavic-looking men, in case they're illegal migrants or Chechen terrorists—but it hadn't happened to me since I'd been in town, presumably because I had aged out of the illegal immigrant/Chechen terrorist cohort. But my bag must have looked suspicious. I showed them my passport, they started practicing their English but I answered them in Russian, and then they lost interest and rudely (*ty*) sent me on my way.

What the fuck was wrong with these people? In America, at least in 2008, you didn't have to show your documents all the time. And you could play hockey! You showed up at a rink, found out the schedule, put down ten dollars—maybe twenty if you were in New York—and played hockey. That was all. "Open hockey," it was called, or "stick time." Beautiful words! As long as you had a full face mask, you could play. And here? I had come to Moscow to take care of my grandmother and I couldn't even get into a hockey game. When I went to the store to buy groceries, the cashiers were rude. The people on the subway were pushy. The baristas at the Coffee Grind were always smiling, but that was clearly because someone had instructed them in Western-style customer service, and they would lose their jobs if they cut it out.

A few days after my failed attempt at Spartak, my grandmother and I were at her pharmacy, waiting to refill some prescriptions. Most Russian pharmacies don't make a distinction between over-the-counter and prescription medicines and just keep everything behind the counter. This leads to lines. We were waiting in the line, then, when two huge guys in black jeans and black sweaters walked in, took a look at the line, and cut it, elbowing aside the woman who was waiting at the window. These guys were thugs, just like the old 1990s thugs, though with a difference. They were less fat and dressed a little better; I had begun noticing guys like this around the neighborhood, mostly sitting in black SUVs and coming in and out of the Grind, and I had concluded, rightly or wrongly, that they were from the FSB. So that was what had become of the post-Soviet criminal class—they weren't all dead or in fancy suits; they were working for the state! I looked at the line: it was five women, aged forty to sixty, plus my grandmother and me.

"Excuse me," I called out. "What's going on?" The men ignored me. One of them was giving directions to the pharmacist, who was taking notes, and pointing to something in the back.

I said it louder. One of the men turned around and walked toward me.

He said, "What's the problem?"

"We have a line here."

"Yeah?" said the giant. He was ugly, very ugly, with enormous jowls and a shaved head and small beady eyes.

My grandmother didn't pick up on the threat and seemed to think this was a new friend of mine. Very politely, she said, "Hello!"

The giant gave her a look. "Hello," he said neutrally.

Then he looked back at me. "It's a good line," he said. "You should stay in it." The ugly giant used the *ty* on me, and then turned around and went back to his buddy. They got whatever it was they came for and left. On the way out the giant gave me a long look, to make sure I understood him, and after a moment I looked away.

"Andryush, who was that man?" asked my grandmother, as if she'd been waiting for an introduction.

"I don't know," I said.

"Oh." She sounded confused.

It was humiliating. Minor, but humiliating. We walked home with her medicines.

"That man was very fat," said my grandmother finally. "I don't like fat men. I was married two times, and there were many men in between. None of them was fat."

"Grandma!" I said.

"What?"

"It's not nice to be mean to fat people."

"What can I do? I don't like fat people."

I looked at my grandmother, who held on to my arm as we walked, just to steady herself a little. I wasn't able to get her to open up about Stalinism, but I knew from my mother that she had despised the Soviet regime. It had poisoned her life, thwarted her career, and caused her daughter to emigrate to a foreign land, where, far from her loving mother, she became sick and died. When the regime collapsed, my grandmother cheered. And now? The neighborhood in which she'd lived on and off for sixty years had changed. It had become terrifyingly expensive. My brother was subletting his apartment next door for several thousand dollars a month. There were expensive coffee shops, expensive supermarkets, expensive clothing boutiques all around us. Most of the residents were new residents; the old residents had been bought off or died off or were pushed off to make room. All around us buildings were being refurbished, renewed, knocked down, and sometimes all three—several buildings on Pechatnikov were in the process of being totally rebuilt, with the exception of their nineteenth-century brick facades. You'd be walking along this quiet side street and see a facade still standing and some kind of work happening behind it. Then you looked, and it was an entire construction site back there, even the foundation was being replaced, but they'd kept the facade for some reason. And then among all these gleaming new objects and massive open-hole construction sites walked my grandmother, in her pink shirt and green pants, like a ghost haunting her own life. She was looking for some inexpensive cheese.

She must have sensed something in my mood because now she said, "Did I ever tell you how we lost our dacha?"

I was surprised. No, she hadn't. I knew it was the result of some kind of financial machinations in the early nineties, but not anything besides that.

"It was Lyova's friends," she said. "And, you know, RussOil. When Lyova was still a student he came up with a theory that there were oil deposits on Yamal." This was the Yamal Peninsula, in the Arctic. "But there was never any time to explore that. Then, when the institute"—his research institute, in Dubna—"started falling apart, some of his friends asked him to start a business to see if they could find the oil."

Uncle Lev was a geophysicist tasked by the mighty empire with helping it find its oil. Alongside the great Jewish-Italian physicist Bruno Pontecorvo, who defected to the USSR in 1950, Uncle Lev had pioneered the use of neutron physics in well logging. This discovery radically increased the efficiency of Soviet oil exploration, helping the workers' state become the largest oil producer in the world. It was oil that bankrolled the Soviet military buildup of the 1970s and the invasion of Afghanistan, and it was the collapse of oil prices in 1986 that caused the Soviet Union to start unraveling. Through it all, Uncle Lev worked on figuring out the physical structure of matter, the better to discover whether it had oil in it.

As my grandmother now told the story, and as Dima later pieced it together for me where she had gaps in her memory, Uncle Lev and his friends started their company with a small investment from the institute in the hopes of finding oil on Yamal. They made a plan, hired equipment, and started exploring, using the best and latest methods. But of course there were delays and cost overruns. As the exploration of the site started eating through the new company's small capital account, all the founders, Uncle Lev very much included, started raising money so they could finish the exploration. My grandmother and Uncle Lev had already lost all their savings in the various currency "reforms" that had been undertaken by the government, but they still had all their old stuff, plus an apartment in Moscow, a dacha in Sheremetevo, and an apartment in Dubna. First they sold their old clothes, books, and skis. When this was not enough, my grandmother and Uncle Lev took a loan out with their dacha as collateral. When even this was not enough, my grandmother came to Moscow intent on mortgaging the apartment. This was only prevented by Dima, who was living in the apartment at the time, with his first wife. He succeeded in convincing my grandmother that it was a bad idea. This was good, because what happened next was that the group ran out of money and was forced to seek funding from its partners, one of which was a subsidiary of RussOil. Apparently this subsidiary resented the additional request because a month after the funding came through, oil was struck, in very impressive quantities for a field of that size and in that place, and on the very next day the geologists came to their office to find the locks changed and guards with RussOil insignia on their uniforms posted at the doors. They weren't even allowed in to retrieve their stuff. There were court battles and attempts to reach out to the press, and at the end of it, one of the geologists had been beaten up in front of his apartment building, one was run over by a car—perhaps accidentally—and Uncle Lev had had a mini-stroke, after which he could no longer use his left arm. And of course he and my grandmother lost the dacha.

"He was very philosophical about it," my grandmother said now, as we reached our building. "He kept saying, 'That's capitalism. We didn't know the rules, and we lost. It's our own fault.' But I always thought his friends betrayed him.

"So that's the story," she concluded. "Should we have some lunch?"

Lunch! Lunch. Of course we should have some lunch. But Jesus, I thought. What a fucking shithole. What a fucked-up, good-for-nothing, awful country. Just like my grandmother always said.

"Grandma," I said, "let's move to America. You and me. We'll live in New York. There are lots of nice parks there."

"I don't like New York," said my grandmother matter-of-factly. "I prefer Boston."

My grandmother had never been to New York. But she had been to Boston for my mother's funeral.

"All right," I said. "We can live in Boston."

"Andryush," my grandmother said, "I'm not going anywhere. I'd be dead before we got off the plane. I'm staying right here. Next summer I'm going to Musya's dacha, and then I can die."

In this shithole? I thought, but didn't say. In this particular shithole of a country? Dying is all it's good for. Why give them the satisfaction?

But I did not bring up America again.

As for my sleeping problem, I started drinking a big Russian beer before going to bed. I bought it at the smelly little grocery at the corner of Lubyanka and the boulevard, or at another smelly little grocery on Pechatnikov, closer to our house, accessible through a little gap between the building next to ours and the church wall. This little alleyway off Pechatnikov was also where our dumpster was, and sometimes at night there was a guy eating food out of it. Was he the same guy who used to eat from that dumpster years before? If so, it spoke well of his longevity. Anyway, the beer put me to sleep faster, and kept me asleep longer, though in the morning I'd always have a bad feeling of some kind. The water used in Russian beers was not known for its purity. But imported beer cost twice as much and a minor tummyache was, in the final analysis, a small price to pay for some sleep.

5.

I TRY TO MAKE SOME FRIENDS

In the second week of September, my grandmother's best friend, Emma Abramovna, came back to town from her dacha. We went to visit her right away.

Emma Abramovna was originally from Poland but had moved to Moscow in advance of Hitler in the late 1930s; she had met my grandmother in the forties at Moscow State, where both of them were young professors. Jewish women in an official environment that was becoming increasingly hostile to Jews, they became friends. Unlike my grandmother, though, Emma Abramovna had somehow managed to remain at the university throughout all the changes that took place in the USSR. She was a tremendously charismatic, outspoken person, with absolutely no fear of authority, and she was often, according to my grandmother, in conflict with the university administration; perhaps her very outspokenness had protected her. In any case, even after her daughter emigrated to Israel in the late eighties, she remained in Moscow. Her two sons had remained in the city, and this was a tremendous help.

Emma Abramovna lived in an old building off the huge Tverskaya thoroughfare, up the street from Patriarch Ponds, about a mile and a half from us. Though it was nearby as the crow flies or the young person walks, on the subway there was no direct route; we had to go south on the red line and then transfer and head northwest on the green one. My grandmother was a little wobbly by the time we arrived, but at least we didn't need to climb any stairs; some years earlier, when Emma Abramovna started having trouble with her hips, her sons traded her apartment on the fourth floor for a similar apartment, in the same

58

building, on the first. We came in, walked down a corridor, and were at her door.

We were greeted by Emma Abramovna's caretaker, a large, round, friendly woman from Moldova named Valya. While I took a quick tour of the apartment, she helped my grandmother orient herself and get ready in the mirror. "What an old lady," my grandmother kept saying, "what a scary old lady"—visiting Emma Abramovna brought out my grandmother's fear that she was not attractive. And I was having simultaneously my own insecurities. The apartment was incredible. The floors were new, the walls and ceilings had fresh coats of paint, and Emma Abramovna's sons (or someone) had installed a special stand-up shower booth, with handles all along its perimeter, to make it easier for Emma Abramovna to get in and out. It made me feel powerfully ashamed of the job Dima and I were doing on Sretenka.

"Musya," my grandmother was saying when I joined them in the living room, also Emma Abramovna's bedroom. Emma Abramovna half sat, half lay on the couch, a blanket across her lap, while my grandmother perched on a small chair that Valya had pulled up for her at the foot of the couch. "Musya, look at you, you are so beautiful."

It was true. Emma Abramovna was Baba Seva's age almost exactly, and she was not in the best of health: her hips barely functioned; she used a walker and needed a great deal of help getting in and out of chairs. And yet unlike my grandmother she glowed. She had thick curly hair, now gray, that came up from her head in a small Afro, and her olive skin color and brown eyes suited her still. It was strange to see someone from my grandmother's generation so animated and even cheerful; my grandmother apparently found it strange as well.

"Look at your hair," she went on describing her friend's beauty. "It's so thick!"

"Sevochka, cut it out," Emma Abramovna said.

"What?"

"I said stop it!"

"It's not my fault you're beautiful!" my grandmother insisted.

59

"Andrei." Emma Abramovna turned to me. "How are you? How long are you here?"

I told her I didn't know, but a few months at the least.

"That's wonderful," said Emma Abramovna. "Seva is very happy you're here."

"But he'll leave eventually," my grandmother said sadly.

"Yes, but he's here now!"

"That's true," my grandmother said, still very sadly. "That's true."

And on it went, over a variety of subjects as disparate as the state of contemporary film to the outcome of the Second World War. My grandmother would say something pessimistic, to be corrected by Emma Abramovna, or alternately Emma Abramovna would say something optimistic, to be contradicted by my grandmother. And then of course there was the dacha.

"Did you have a good time at Peredelkino?" asked my grandmother.

"Yes, it was lovely. Borya"—her youngest son—"made a lot of improvements over the winter. And I had visitors throughout August. I don't know what I'd do without Peredelkino."

Emma Abramovna always said exactly what she thought. This was an admirable trait, and yet it also meant that she didn't pick up signals from people who were more subtle or indirect about things, like my grandmother.

"I had a dacha once," my grandmother said now. "We always went there during the summer."

"I know, Sevochka." Emma Abramovna softened momentarily.

"Now I have nowhere to go," my grandmother said.

This was clearly an opening for Emma Abramovna to suggest that my grandmother come visit her next summer, but she didn't seem to think so and let it pass.

"You're so lucky that you had three kids," my grandmother continued. "They take such good care of you."

"You could have had more kids!" Emma Abramovna lost her temper a little. "No one was stopping you!"

"Yes," my grandmother said, in the way one does when actually deep down disagreeing. "Maybe."

Still and all, the whole thing was about as animated and happy as I'd seen my grandmother since I'd come to Moscow. This was her one remaining friend and contemporary. And surely Emma Abramovna would eventually catch the hint about the dacha.

As soon as we were out the door, my grandmother turned to me, as if she'd been waiting to do so the entire time, and said, "Poor Musya. She can't walk anymore. Imagine that? I don't know what I'd do if I couldn't walk."

For our trip home we caught a car. One of the undeniably non-terrible things about Moscow was that you could hail a random car on the street and it would give you a ride for a reasonable price. It had been one of the ways Russians adapted to the shortages of Communism—there weren't nearly enough cabs to go around, so people just started offering each other rides. When I was little my father used to go out a few nights a week and look for fares; it was an ordinary activity for people with cars, including people with cars and advanced engineering degrees. This practice lasted well into the post-Soviet era, though one thing I had noticed since I arrived was that fewer and fewer Muscovites felt like earning three dollars for driving someone a mile down the boulevard. You had to look for beat-up old Russian-made cars; their drivers were poor enough to take you. On this occasion we got lucky, and one of the first cars my grandmother hailed was old and Russian, and stopped. On the ride home she was in a garrulous mood and quizzed the driver about his dacha. He was from Armenia, it turned out, and had a dacha outside Yerevan. It had a beautiful garden, he said, though he hadn't been there in three years, as he was here in Moscow trying to earn some money.

"Yes," said my grandmother. "A dacha is a very good thing."

As we entered our apartment, she turned to me. "It's terrible about Musya's legs, but in another sense she is very lucky. Her kids take such good care of her. That was my mistake. I only had one kid. Don't only have one kid. Have three kids. Then they'll take care of you."

I went to bed that night and thought: Didn't my grandmother have a daughter, and didn't that daughter have two sons, and weren't we taking care of her now? My grandmother's suggestion was that no, we were not. And compared to what Emma Abramovna's sons were doing for her, it was hard to argue. I was there, yes, but also I was not there. My PMOOC classes were more arduous than I had expected: I had sixty students across the four sections, which meant hundreds of blog posts and, as the semester progressed, hundreds of emails, which meant hundreds of emails that I had to answer in a timely fashion because the PMOOC administrators swore by the student evaluations—they really had nothing else to go on—and there was nothing students took to less kindly than someone not answering their emails. Whether I wanted to or not I had to spend hours at the Coffee Grind. And, in truth, I did want to. My grandmother did not make it easy to keep her company. She was depressed; she complained. She complained about everything. Had I been doing great myself I might have been more sympathetic, but I too was a little bummed out. After my initial hope of interviewing her was disappointed, I hadn't thought of another way forward. All the topics seemed taken; the field was crowded. I would never find something unique and my own. Perversely, this made me spend more time at the Coffee Grind looking at people's Facebook pages. My failure as an academic was not making me a success as a grandson.

Meanwhile, back home, the American financial system collapsed. From my perch at the Coffee Grind, I watched events unfold on Facebook and the website of the *New York Times*.

Some of my old classmates joked about the news—"Good thing I work in an industry where no one makes any money," Sarah wrote on Facebook—but on the Slavic jobs website things were grim. One search got canceled when the funding for the job fell through. And there were rumors of further cuts.

"We're fucked," my adviser told me over Gchat. "Nelson"—Phil Nelson, the outspoken president of our university—"has been treating the endowment like his own personal poker game. I bet we're about to lose some unthinkable chunk of it. And if oil prices collapse, the campus in Qatar is in trouble." The satellite campus in Qatar had been one of President Nelson's signature gambles, and it had been turning a nice profit during the era of $100 barrels of oil.

"Won't more people go back to school if the economy is bad?" I said. I'd read that somewhere.

"Sure," said my adviser, "but they'll go to an affordable school. They'll go to a good school."

"I swear to God," he went on, "I could get fired any minute. I'm afraid to check my email!"

"Aren't you on email right now?"

"Yes. But I'm afraid."

This conversation freaked me out. I felt momentarily like a person who had escaped a great cataclysm, but of course I had not escaped it. My adviser did not get fired, though neither would the Slavic department survive the crisis intact; as for me I eventually received an email from the university administration that in anticipation of declining PMOOC enrollment for the next semester, the maximum number of classes per instructor per semester was now three. This was effectively a 25 percent cut in my pay.

Back in Moscow, my grandmother and I watched the evening news in the back room three or four nights a week. All the channels were controlled by the state, but they weren't gray or boring. The newscasters were attractive and spoke clearly, with conviction; the production values were top-notch. With terrifying music and fast cuts, the news presented a world in crisis: there was trouble in Georgia, there was trouble in Iraq, there was trouble in Africa. Luckily, we in Russia had Putin. Wherever trouble reared its head, Putin was there to tame it. Putin was no longer even president—his hand-picked successor, Dmitry Medvedev, was president, and Putin was prime minister—but when push came to shove, Putin was still in charge. Everything was OK. Russians could sleep at night.

And now there was trouble in America too. The Russians really enjoyed the financial crisis, at least at first. The news showed footage of American bankers carrying boxes out of their ruined companies. Soviet propaganda had always stressed the problem of homelessness in the United States, and those images of the bankers with their boxes made you wonder—were they going to sleep in them? Meanwhile the Russian finance minister came on to explain that we had nothing to worry about: Russia was an island of stability in a sea of troubles. He did hope, however, that this experience would teach the Americans a valuable lesson.

One evening around this time my grandmother and I were out for a walk along the boulevard; we had ventured farther than usual and arrived at the small park on the other side of the Clean Ponds metro station. On this evening there was a group of people gathered at the Griboedov statue; they were surrounded by an even larger group of police. "It's a protest," said my grandmother. "Let's get out of here."

This time she was right. It was a protest. I maneuvered us across the street, at a safe distance but so that I could see what was going on. The protesters were mostly middle-aged and educated looking—glasses, shaggy hair, short-sleeve dress shirts, and some argyle sweaters. They looked like my parents. They held signs that said FRIENDSHIP WITH THE WEST and AMERICA'S CRISIS IS OUR CRISIS TOO! There were even some signs in English. These were the liberals, the Echo of Moscow listeners, the people whom Putin's political adviser Vladislav Surkov had recently compared to a fifth column inside the country. Surrounded and significantly outnumbered by burly, stone-faced police, they seemed harmless and pathetic.

And then I noticed a group of what looked like teenagers, all in black, scrambling to the roof of the metro station. Once they got there they shot a flare into the sky. For a second I wondered if this was the direct action wing of the protest, the reinforcements. Then they unfurled a banner that read DON'T ROCK THE BOAT and started chanting it: "Don't rock the boat! Don't rock the boat!" These were counterprotesters, regime supporters, sent to intimidate this small protest as if the massive police presence weren't enough. The police didn't even pretend to try to stop them. Neither did the protesters. It was depressing.

We went home to watch the news. Our protest wasn't on it. But Putin was. In truth you had to admire his mastery. The world saw in him a cold-blooded killer, a ruthless dictator, the gravedigger of Russian democracy. But from the Russian perspective, well, he was *our* cold-blooded killer, *our* ruthless dictator, *our* gravedigger. And he was good at what he did. He could be charming when he needed to be, or menacing, or full of pathos. He loved playing against type. If you expected tough Putin you'd get sensitive Putin, but if you started expecting sensitive Putin—kablamo! Tough Putin would sock you in the jaw. During one interview my grandmother and I watched, he was asked about the criticisms the opposition was making of his administration. Instead of dismissing them outright, he said sadly, "Some of these criticisms are fair. I think we need to listen to them and take them into account and work harder. But some of the criticisms are too much. They are directed not just at my administration, but at our country. And the truth is, our country is troubled. It has still not recovered from the turbulence that took place under my predecessor. I think we all know: Mother Russia is sick. But when your mother is sick, there is only one thing you can do: you have to help her." It was a devastating response. And all the opposition's yelling and screaming about Putin's crimes, his corruption, his recklessness—all true, by the way, as far as I could tell—could not penetrate it.

My grandmother usually went to bed after the news ended; I stayed up to watch some more. You can learn a lot about a place by watching TV. Many shows were imports: American action movies, South American soap operas, even *The Simpsons*. But there was also some native programming. I enjoyed the reality shows. They were mostly rip-offs of American or European concepts, but with more sex and violence. The sex in particular was impressive. Even in Russia, a place where you'd think people would be worried about surviving, staying out of jail, and not getting run over by a car—even here people wanted to fuck one another.

One of my responsibilities as Dima's replacement was to collect the rent once a month from the guys next door. They were a group of ex-pats, but my grandmother called them "the soldiers," for reasons that were not entirely clear—it's possible she had misheard my brother or me when we'd mentioned "subletters" (but why in English, unless it was one of the soldiers introducing himself as a "subletter"?) or it's possible she couldn't understand why three unmarried men would be living together, rather than with their mothers (or grandmothers), unless they were in fact soldiers. In any case, they weren't soldiers: they were a beautiful Italian guy named Roberto, who worked in real estate; a soft-spoken American blond from Seattle named Michael; and a chubby British journalist named Howard, who worked at the English-language expat newspaper, the *Moscow Times*. They were all in their midtwenties, and the first time I'd gone over there to collect the rent I found them arguing about whether to go to a particular nightclub. Actually, Roberto was arguing with Michael that it was Michael's moral duty to go to the club, because girls liked him. Michael was arguing back that he didn't want to go, he had a girlfriend back home, and anyway he had to be up early the next day. Meanwhile the third roommate, Howard, was watching a Premier League soccer game on Dima's big flat-screen TV. It was a shock to go over there; the apartment was the same size as my grandmother's and had once had the same layout, but Dima, under the direction of his second wife, Alina, had knocked down several walls to create an open space and then three small bedrooms off of it. If my grandmother's place was a museum of Soviet furniture, Dima's was a testament to refined Russian taste circa the turn of the millennium. It felt like I had crossed the landing and traveled forward in time fifty years.

"I just got back together with Susan," Michael was saying. "I don't want to go hit on Russian girls."

"But they *like* you," Roberto said.

"No, they don't. They just do it to make the rich Russian guys jealous."

"Michael, who cares *why* they do it? It is not for us to understand."

"Why does everyone in this town just want to sleep with hot chicks?" Michael asked. He seemed almost pained by this. "It's like, there are other things."

Roberto shook his head sadly. "You do not understand life," he said. "Life is for *living*. Look at Putin. Or Berlusconi. He is an old man. He has unlimited power over his country. And still he is chasing after the girls."

"I don't want to be like Berlusconi!"

"OK, OK, no Berlusconi. But Russian girls are the most beautiful in the world. Most generous. You are being unreasonable!"

"Come on, you wanker!" cried Howard. He was looking at the television as he said this. We all turned to the game. The sequence ended with the player addressed by Howard kicking the ball over the goal. Howard deflated and turned momentarily to Roberto and Michael. "I'll go," he said.

Apparently this did not meet with Roberto's approval. "You ask too many questions," he said to Howard. "Girls don't want to feel like they are being interrogated." Now to me: "He says: Where are you from? What do you do? How many siblings you have? Do you want to do a photo with me? They think he's from FSB."

"I'm curious," said Howard.

"I'm going to Rasputin," Roberto said menacingly. "If you cannot get in, I will still go."

"I'll take that chance," said Howard.

"This is life." Roberto sighed. "Those who can, don't want to. Those who cannot . . ."

"Are full of passionate intensity!" Howard supplied. "You'll see," he said. "Tonight is my night." And he hopped off the couch and headed into his bedroom to put on some nicer clothes.

Those were the guys across the landing. They paid their rent in rubles on the first of the month. Having received it, I then had to take it, with my grandmother, to Dima's bank, which was several subway stops and one transfer away. I had to bring my grandmother because, due to some Russian law meant to prevent either capital flight or capital infusion, it was illegal for a foreign citizen (me) to deposit funds into the account of a Russian or dual citizen (Dima). So I had to drag her to the bank. When we did this the first time she was so tired from the subway ride that she practically collapsed in a chair the minute we walked into HSBC. I went up to the window and explained that I was depositing money into my brother's account and that our grandmother would sign for it. I received a form and walked it over to Baba Seva. As she signed it, she asked what it was. Very loudly I said, "We are depositing the rent from Dima's subletters into his account!" I said this loudly because it was plain for everyone to see that actually I had found some elderly lady on the street and asked her to help me deposit stolen money into an offshore account. When I mentioned the subletters, she said, "Who?"

"The subletters! Dima's subletters! The soldiers!"

"Oh, the soldiers."

I brought the form back to the window. No one said a word. I withheld two hundred rubles from the rent so we could take a car home, but by the time we got out of the bank, the traffic was so bad that we had to take the subway again anyway. I kept the two hundred rubles.

I wasn't sure if, as the rent collector, it was appropriate for me to hang out with the soldiers; nor whether, as a thirty-three-year-old academic who had never been to a real nightclub, much less one with face control, it would be pathetic of me to want to do so; nor was I sure I even wanted to. It was a relief to speak English, to not have to worry about whom to address as *ty* and whom as *vy*, and to be welcomed back into the long luxurious adolescence of the contemporary Western male. This wasn't of course what I had come for. It felt like a cop-out. But I didn't have a lot of other options.

I had a brief social outing in mid-September with Dima's friends, whom I thought I could perhaps borrow as friends while I was there as I had once hoped to borrow Dima's car. A guy named Maxim had been, apparently, the one to blame for the exercise bike clogging up my room. That is to say, Dima, when leaving, had asked him if he wanted it, and Maxim said yes and then failed all summer to pick it up. When he eventually did stop by for the bike, he said he was having a birthday party just around the corner that weekend, and I should come.

I met him and a few others at a small French restaurant called Jean-Jacques down near the Tsvetnoi Boulevard subway station. It wasn't terribly expensive, for Moscow, but it was definitely out of my price range. Before I could think up some excuse to leave, Maxim bought me a French beer and introduced me around; the small group of friends—Alla, Borya, Kristina, Denis, Elena, Fyodor—were all also Dima's friends, closer to my age than to his. They seemed nice enough. Dima was a business mogul but he had always chosen his friends from the circle of art students, bohemians, and journalists. As they talked, I gathered that these Moscow friends worked in advertising and magazines and public relations. They were interested in politics—Maxim and Elena had been at the protest at Clean Ponds that my grandmother and I had run into the other day—and dispensed their opinions with that mixture of bluster, sarcasm, and despair that I'd grown used to already from Echo of Moscow. "These goblins think they're going to weather the world financial crisis while everyone else goes under," Maxim said. "It's a joke."

"Whereas I think the Americans," said Fyodor, turning to me, "they're going to right the ship pretty quickly, don't you think?"

He said *ty*. But I had no idea. I knew that back home people were withdrawing their life savings from banks and discussing which root vegetables they should buy in case supermarkets closed down for the winter. And it was the people closest to the world of finance who seemed most frightened. To Fyodor I said, "I don't know. My friends in America are pretty freaked out."

"They'll be fine," Maxim said with authority. "America will be fine. But Russia is fucked. This country is run by idiots."

Soon the conversation turned to culture. There was a long and intricate discussion of the first season of *Breaking Bad;* asked to weigh in as an expert on all things American, I had to admit I'd never seen the show, nor been to New Mexico, nor tried crystal meth. And in general I think I was a disappointment to them. When they learned that I lived in New York they started asking me about the art galleries and restaurants they knew there, which I had never been to or even heard of.

Every minute I spent with them made it clearer how much more money they had than I did.

The one bit of common ground we found was in our anger at Russia. When I told them about my experience trying to play hockey at Sokolniki, they were properly indignant. "That's typical Russian lack of culture," said Alla, a marketing director. "Disgraceful."

"Don't worry," said Borya, who worked in advertising, "there are still some normal people left in this country."

"Do you know any hockey games?" I asked.

"No. I prefer tennis."

"For hockey you really need *blat*," said Kristina—an in, a connection.

This made me angry all over again. "That's ridiculous!" I said. "Hockey should be for everyone."

"To be fair," Maxim said, "if you let just anyone play, they'd probably ruin it."

So these were the Russian liberals who opposed the Putin regime. It turned out they hated Russia. They sort of lived there, but they also sort of lived somewhere else. None of them watched Russian TV. I tried, as part of the general pop culture conversation, to mention my affection for the Russian reality programs, only to be told by Elena that the one I liked best—a hyperviolent version of *Cheaters,* about cheating husbands and (mostly) wives—was fake.

"What do you mean fake?"

"It's fake. All the so-called reality shows are fake."

"How do you know?"

"I'm a journalist," she said. "I know these things." Elena was blond, my height, stocky, with a haircut that framed her face and pretty blue eyes. She was a kind of Slavic version of Sarah, actually, and I found myself gravitating toward her. I must have looked stricken at the information about my show, because she added, "Sorry."

But of course it made sense. The structure of the plot was always the same, and the idea that they actually captured as much illicit footage as they claimed was risible. It was obvious to me now.

"It's still an interesting cultural product?" I said.

"It's trash. Everything on Russian TV is trash."

"I'll tell you what I watch," Maxim interrupted. He was a former magazine editor who now managed an upscale wine store. "My weekly schedule is *Mad Men* on Monday, *House* on Tuesday, *Breaking Bad* on Wednesday . . ." These were all a day later than the shows aired in the States. That's how long it took before they appeared on one of the online TV sites.

"And what about Russian TV?" I asked.

"Never in a million years," said Maxim. "I couldn't watch it if I tried, to be honest. I don't have an antenna. My TV is a screen for my computer, nothing more."

I wanted to leave. I wasn't sure I liked these people; I didn't know whether to say *ty* or *vy* to them; and, more to the point, if I stayed I'd have to buy Maxim an expensive French beer. On the other hand, Elena. She had insulted my favorite show, but I liked the way she'd done it. I checked her right hand for a wedding band (Russians wear their wedding rings on their right hands), and there was none; just in case (who knew with these people), I checked her left hand also. There too she was unmarried. We were all standing, though not at the bar, and I decided to get Maxim a beer, and one for myself so I could relax a little, and I also asked Elena if she wanted anything. "Why not?" she said, which seemed like a good sign, and asked for a glass of grenache. It cost twenty dollars, which with two nine-dollar beers put me out thirty-eight dollars, plus tip. I had to ask the bartender to repeat himself, because it sounded like a mistake. It wasn't a mistake.

Nonetheless, when Elena finished her drink and announced it was time to go, I asked if I could walk her (*vy*, I said) wherever she was going.

"If you want," she said, using *ty*. This meant that I should also switch to *ty*. Or not?

Elena was parked on Pechatnikov, on the way to my grandmother's place, and as we walked—it was a nice night, in the brief autumnal interim between summer and the bitter cold—I asked her where she worked as a journalist. "Echo of Moscow," she said.

71

"I listen to that all the time!" I said. "It's my grandmother's favorite station."

"I'm glad to hear that," said Elena. "For me it's just where I work."

"OK," I said. Now I said lamely, "I will listen for your show, then." (*Vy* again! I couldn't help it.)

"OK," she said.

Elena was clearly not into me. On the other hand, Russians are very reserved. Maybe this taciturnity bordering on outright hostility was actually her way of being into me?

"That was a fun party," I said.

"It was OK."

"Where do you live?"

"Zamoskvorechie," she said. "Do you know it?"

I didn't. And we had arrived at her car.

"Well, good night," said Elena, and started to open her car door.

"Wait," I said. I could tell she didn't like me, but somehow her physical resemblance to Sarah convinced me that just maybe she did.

Elena turned toward me reluctantly, and as she did so, I leaned in to kiss her. She deftly turned her head so that I gave her cheek a kiss instead.

"Andrei," she said, pushing me away with her hand, not unkindly, "you seem like a nice young man. But I don't think you're cut out for this."

"For what?" I said. Did she mean kissing?

"For this," she said, gesturing up the street and around it. From where we stood on Pechatnikov, you could see some of the church steeples and oil and gas headquarters of downtown. "For Russia."

"Oh," I said. But I didn't understand. "In what sense?"

"I don't know," she said. "Just a feeling I have."

And with that, Elena got into her car. Her driver's seat was on the right-hand side—this usually meant the car had been bought used by an enterprising young man in Japan, taken by ferry to Vladivostok, and then driven straight across Russia to be sold in Moscow—and she spent a few moments studying the rearview mirror and trying to figure out if there were cars coming up Pechatnikov.

Then she thought of something and rolled down her window.

"You don't have to say *vy* to everyone," she said. "It makes you sound retarded."

"OK," I said. I tried to think of a sentence in which I would address her with the familiar *ty*, but I couldn't. "OK," I said again, stupidly. "It's a deal."

Elena nodded and drove off.

What did she mean, I wasn't cut out for Russia? It felt insulting, though I couldn't quite locate the insult. Was I too much of a wimp? I hadn't been in a fight since college (it was more like wrestling, and a draw), and though I was in pretty good physical condition for an academic, it's true there was an air of violence on the streets here that I didn't know how to handle. Or did she mean something else? Was I too boring for Russia? Like in a spiritual sense? Was I too callow?

As I tried to figure it out, I noticed that the evening had another effect as well. My attempt to kiss Elena, though a failure, had reminded me of the existence of women. I hadn't realized until then how bummed I still was about Sarah; if her breaking up with me was mostly just embarrassing, the creeping realization since I'd gotten to Moscow that she was sleeping with someone else had made me sexually depressed. I wasn't even interested anymore. And living with one's grandmother, I had to admit, was something of an anti-erotic experience.

But now, as I walked the streets around our house on various errands, or sat at the Coffee Grind, or occasionally turned on the TV, I realized: I wanted to fuck every woman I saw. I couldn't tell if it was me or it was them: me because I was sexually deprived, or them because they dressed so well, took such good care of themselves. Either way, once I started thinking about it, I couldn't stop. In the Coffee Grind, frequented not just by FSB goons but by young office workers from the adjoining neighborhood, I watched the women's thin blouses ride up their bare backs as they leaned forward to sip their espressos. I watched them cross their legs. On the street, where they walked in high heels, I watched their ankles, their hips. Why should flesh in one place or another matter so much? It was just skin and muscle and fat. But still.

Was it me or was it them? I could swear it was them. Russian men had been drinking and yelling and shooting at one another for so long that there weren't that many left. *There were not enough men to go around.* This produced intense competition for the ones who remained. Women worked out; they dressed up; they spent hours at beauty salons getting their skin smoothed, their brows plucked, their butts massaged. What I was seeing as I looked around me with a boner stirring in my pants was a calculated response to a tragic situation of scarcity. I was wrong to enjoy it. I kept telling myself that.

Still, I had no idea how to talk to these women, and they didn't seem interested in helping me figure it out. Embedded in the university for most of my life, I didn't know how to strike out on my own, with no context, no institution through which to meet other people. I tried, a few times, to start conversations in line at the Coffee Grind, to no avail.

It was while feeling these feelings at the Grind one day that a thought occurred to me: Russian online dating. I entered the words into Google, and after some missteps I found myself on a Russian dating site. It was filled with beautiful girls. Or at least photos of them. Huh. I dug up an old photo of myself from my computer, slapped together a profile, and wrote some notes to girls who seemed like they were educated. Before the week was out I had a date with a cute blond twenty-five-year-old named Sonya. "I'm going to be in your neighborhood tomorrow night," she wrote me. "Let's meet up."

Wow, I thought. The modern world! And I continued thinking it as I met Sonya at an incredibly expensive bar called Sad (pronounced Saad) around the corner from the Tsvetnoi Boulevard metro station. Sonya was pretty, just about exactly as she had appeared in her profile photo, and smart. She was studying fashion at Moscow State and wanted to become a hat designer. She had come to Moscow from the southern city of Rostov, which was totally crime-ridden and danger- ous, she said. Her best friend from high school had been raped and killed a week after their graduation. Moscow was no picnic either—she had to scrimp and save each month to make the rent—but compared to Rostov she found it a great relief. For my part I told her a few select things about my life in New York and how I'd come to Moscow to take care of my grandmother and find an interesting topic for my next academic article. She seemed sort of impressed, or at least not entirely bored.

We had two drinks each, for a ruinous total of fifty dollars, but it didn't matter, because Sonya seemed to like me. To my great relief she did not order food, and after about an hour, she asked if I wanted to go. I wasn't quite sure what this meant but I said yes. We walked out into a beautiful night and toward the subway, me wondering once again whether I should make some kind of move. But before I could think about it too much, just as we rounded the corner onto the boulevard, she curled into my arms and kissed me.

I was made a little dizzy by it. My first Russian kiss! It was like an American kiss but better, more intense, and it was in Russia. It turned out that all I had to do was go online and fill out a form.

Then Sonya broke off our kiss and put her hand on my chest. "Andrei," she said, "listen, I'd love to take you home with me. But there's a cleaning fee."

"A cleaning fee?"

"Well, yes, if we go to my place we'll definitely make a mess." She sort of cuddled into my arms again.

It finally dawned on me what this was. At some level I didn't care. I said, "How much?"

"Three thousand," she said.

"Dollars?"

"No, of course not," she laughed. "We're in Russia, after all. Rubles."

A little over a hundred dollars. I had brought exactly that amount with me, as a kind of upper limit on the night's spending, and had already spent half of it on drinks.

"Can we make it fifteen hundred?"

"Sorry," she said, "those are the rules. Maybe we can go to a cash machine?"

I was horny, but this was too much. I shook my head no.

"All right," she said sweetly and stepped away from me. "Call me if you change your mind." Then she turned around and walked into the subway.

I walked home to my grandmother's out fifty dollars. The construction sites all around me, as well as the buildings that had already gone up, had never seemed so ugly. Noisy teenagers were drinking beer and yelling on the pedestrian strip along the boulevard. As I turned onto Pechatnikov and started walking up, I passed another fancy restaurant. Wealthy men and their pretty young—I now assumed—escorts sat inside having dinner. This place sucked. And it sucked in a completely different way from the one I'd been led to expect. What happened to the scary dictatorship? What happened to the bloodthirsty regime? I had thought I was going to be arrested, but no one was going to arrest me. No one gave a shit about me. I was too poor for that. I was now getting $493.53 direct-deposited into my account by the university every two weeks for my PMOOC classes, a not totally risible salary by Russian standards, but I still had exactly as much in the bank as when I arrived— a little under a thousand dollars. And my paycheck was going to become more like $375 every two weeks come January. Anything besides rent and food and a daily cappuccino at the Coffee Grind would remain beyond my reach. This wasn't like getting taken to the Lubyanka in the middle of the night, but as a form of social control, money worked. If people couldn't afford to do anything but barely survive, they probably wouldn't form a political organization and seize power. You didn't actually need to pack them off to the Gulag. What a fucking scam. The world, I mean. The world was a fucking scam.

6.

I GO CLUBBING

SO THIS WAS my life—a series of errands for Dima punctuated by a series of rejections by Russians and a slate of activities with a roommate—my grandmother—who only remembered the ones she didn't like. My trip to Russia was not going as planned. On top of everything else I had had this notion that coming here would raise my stock back home. I wasn't just some bookworm who sat in New York and contemplated Russia; I was in Russia itself! But that didn't seem to have been the effect; in fact an opposite effect could be observed. One day while sitting in the Grind and considering my situation I received an email. "Dear Andrew Kaplan," it began:

> My name is Richard Sutherland. As you probably know I teach cultural studies at Princeton. I'm coming to Moscow soon to talk with some culture-makers about their concepts of "modernity." Our mutual friend Sasha Fishman said you're there now and would be willing to help. I don't of course speak any Russian but I've got some research funds for the trip (Princeton is really being quite good about it) and can pay you for your time—how does $8/hour sound? I arrive October 3 on the Delta flight from New York; if you're able to pick me up some seltzer water, I am always very thirsty after a long flight!
>
> Thanks in advance,
>
> Richard

I stared at this email amid the bustle of the Coffee Grind, across the way from the KGB. My first impulse was to delete it, but then I chickened out and undeleted it. I was flabbergasted—I should not have been, but I was. Would someone write to anyone they had the slightest shred of respect for and suggest they pick them up at the airport with some seltzer water? I didn't know. But I suspected not. Worse still, this person had funding from Princeton to research a topic that was *basically my topic,* even though *he did not know the first thing about it.*

But if this was an insult—and it was—the insult really emanated from Fishman. Sasha fucking Fishman! I was so mad that without thinking too long about it, I pressed "forward" on the undeleted email and put in his address.

Dear Sasha,

I realize I'm not a great academic star like you, but this is a bit much. Next time you know someone who needs a servant in Moscow, please do it yourself.

Andrei

I sent it off immediately and immediately regretted it. Not because I was wrong but because it would allow Fishman to say something condescending. I had to wait a day for it, but sure enough it came. He wrote using my American name:

Andrew,

I'm sorry you feel that way. I'm sure you have far more important things to do than take around one of my colleagues.

All best,

Alex Fishman
Visiting Professor of Slavic Literature, etc.

All right, Alex, I thought. We'll see.

But what would we see? I didn't know. If there was some way to shame and humiliate Alex Fishman, I had yet to find it. He seemed in certain ways beyond shame and beyond humiliation. He had once written an exuberant five-thousand-word blog post about the wonderful academic achievements of the chair of the Princeton Slavic department—*at the same time as he was applying for a job there*. How do you shame a person like that?

So had I made a mistake? Not just in coming to Russia, though that too. Had I totally mislived my life? My parents had taken a great risk and undergone a great trial to bring me to a country where I could do, basically, anything I wanted. And what had I done? My friends from college and high school were now doctors, lawyers, bankers. Some of them were in Hollywood; their visions were being beamed daily to millions of people, and on top of that they were rich. They lived in nice houses in Los Angeles and gave birth to multiple children. Whereas I had chosen to read books. What a joke! I liked reading books, and I had thought that reading them would help me understand the world. But I did not understand the world. I knew nothing of the world. And to be a grown man—as I was now, no denying it—and still to be reading books? It was pathetic. And within this pathetic world, Sasha Fishman at least had a job. He didn't have to teach four online classes just to keep the lights on. No one would ever think to hire him at minimum wage to drive them around Moscow.

The worst part of the whole Richard Sutherland business was, I could have used the money. I would have had to neglect my grandmother but, after a few days of fetching Sutherland some seltzers, I could have called Sonya back and paid her cleaning fee. After the exchange with Fishman, though, I couldn't go back. I wrote to Sutherland and politely begged off.

My grandmother was disappointed in me. She had an insatiable appetite for company, but all her friends, as she repeatedly said, were dead or gone, and there were only so many times in a day she could call Emma Abramovna and drop hints about her dacha. Then there was me. I could be talked to. But I had my own issues. Once my class had made it through *The Cossacks*, we moved on to *Fathers and Sons* and then straight into *War and Peace*. The students became infected by Tolstoy's amateur historicizing. They started coming up with all sorts of theories. Some had studied Hegel in college, and quite recently; others hadn't been in an educational setting for forty years. One of my older students had a historical theory about Muslims that may or may not have been in violation of the university policy on hate speech; I had to delete his comments and then talk to him about them, after which I re-posted them with a short introduction saying why I was doing so. And this was just one section. I hadn't made any rules about when the students could or couldn't post, so they posted whenever they felt like it and I had to read it all to make sure it wasn't too unhinged or too racist or blatantly false. In short, this was taking up more and more of my time, and meanwhile I wasn't getting any closer to finding myself a job for next year. And because of this, I had less patience for my discussions with my half-deaf grandmother than, in retrospect, I wish I'd had.

The saving grace was that I thought she wouldn't notice. She heard so little and forgot so much. We'd go to the park or to Emma Abramovna's and the next day she'd give no indication that she remembered. She couldn't remember what we were discussing five minutes ago. Why would she remember if I ran off to the Grind after lunch without sticking around to chat?

Occasionally Howard from next door would come by to eat sushki and talk about his reporting—once he learned I had a PhD in Russian literature, he started asking me for literary references with which to sprinkle his *Moscow Times* articles. But pretty quickly the conversations would devolve into tales of Howard's sex adventures. The first time I saw him after his trip to Rasputin, he told me he had been roofied by someone at the club and bundled into a cab by Roberto (who thought he was just very drunk); next thing he knew he was waking up on the ground on the outskirts of the city without his wallet. His cabdriver had robbed him. He tried calling his roommates, but was still so messed up that he was unable to make them understand what he was saying. "I thought I was going to die out there," he said. Finally he managed to hail a car and somehow explain where we lived, but the driver did not trust him to go upstairs and get money, and Howard ended up paying for the ride by giving the driver his phone. "That was very resourceful of you," I said.

"Thanks," said Howard. "But it was a three-hundred-dollar phone."
Nonetheless, he was uncowed. He had gone to Rasputin again, in fact; he
had also started using a website that allowed you to order prostitutes after
viewing their profiles and reading *customer reviews* of their performance.

"Are you serious?" I cried. I was shocked and amazed.

"Yeah," said Howard. "Want to see?"

"No!" I said. "Or, I don't know. Maybe later."

When he left I saw that my grandmother was standing in the doorway to her room, watching us. For a second I feared she had overheard
Howard's description of the hooker website. But we had been speaking
in English, and anyway my grandmother could hardly have heard us
from over there. She was upset, it turned out, about something else.

"You never talk to me like that," she said.

"Like what?"

"With so much animation. So much interest."

"Sure I do," I said.

"No," she said. "You don't."

I was at a loss. I mean, this was a very interesting website Howard
was describing. But of course my grandmother was right. And instead
of apologizing I denied it. "We talk all the time!" I said. "We're always
talking! Even right now we're talking! We can talk some more. What do
you want to talk about?"

My grandmother pursed her lips. She knew I was being unfair but
she was willing to give me a chance. "OK," she said. "Tell me about the
situation. What's the situation in the country?"

For some reason this question set me off. "How should I know?" I
said. "I sit here all day trying to answer your questions. I have no idea
what the situation is!"

I was looming over her as I said this.

"You don't need to yell," said my little grandmother as she stepped
back into her room and with trembling hands closed the door behind her. I felt awful.

Later I apologized, and she forgave me, but this sort of thing kept
happening in different variations: her criticizing my shitty caretaking,

me becoming defensive and unhappy and an even shittier caretaker than I had been.

What was the situation in the country? It was true I didn't know. But it wasn't true that I had no idea.

Everyone in Moscow seemed to drive a black Audi and there were websites where you could order a prostitute after reading all her customer reviews. Outside of a few stinky Soviet-era groceries, food was expensive, rent was outrageous, and hockey games were closed to outsiders. Every time I walked into the Coffee Grind and bought the cheapest item on the menu, I was amazed at all the other customers. Where did they come from, in this traumatized and wounded country? Some of them were walking over from the KGB building across the street, but not all of them, and anyway this was the cheapest café in my grandmother's neighborhood. These people were buying a couple of double espressos and pastries and sandwiches and being charged thirty dollars. The worst part was, they didn't even argue! You'd have thought some of them at least would have said, "What?" None of them said it. They handed over the money. They didn't even blink.

So this was the Putinist bargain: you give up your freedoms, I make you rich. Not everyone was rich, but enough people were making do that the system held. And who was I to tell them they were wrong? If they liked their Putin, they could have him.

Of course complacency was a sin. At the beginning of the Stalinist terror, Mandelshtam said contemptuously that people thought everything was fine as long as the trams still ran on their tracks. But how else are you supposed to know that things *aren't* fine? In Moscow they had long ago torn up most of the tram tracks to make room for the cars. If the remaining trams stopped running, it would be a while before anyone noticed.

I still sometimes had trouble sleeping. Though I had lost my favorite show about cheaters, I kept staying up late and watching TV. Thanks to nineties-era Dima we had a cable channel that showed American sports, including football. I had always loved watching football, college football in particular, with its pageantry and crowds. In college I looked forward to being woken on Saturday mornings by the sound of our marching band on its way to the stadium. And then in Moscow, there it was again. The only catch was that the sound was off—of the crowd and the announcers both—and instead you had to listen to the Russian announcer, who was still learning the game. "Now of course they're going to punt," he'd say on a fourth down, except sometimes they didn't. "Actually, they've decided not to punt. They're not punting." One of the first games I watched had a safety in it, and the announcer knew what a safety was, but he was confused by an ineligible receiver downfield (understandably) and also, less forgivably, by the ground not causing a fumble. "For some reason they are not giving them the ball," he said of the defensive team that had caused (or, rather, not caused) the fumble. For an American of course "The ground cannot cause a fumble" was as self-evident as "All men are created equal." But the announcer wasn't American. I wasn't in America. That's the lesson I kept being taught, though I didn't seem willing to learn it.

One weekend toward late September I was sitting in the back room, trying to experience LSU–Auburn despite the artificial hush in which it was being played, when my phone buzzed with a text message. I remember being startled to realize it was the first text message I had received since arriving in Moscow. "It's Howard," said the text. "We're going to Teatr in an hour. Want to come?" Teatr was a dance club not too far from our house. I'd passed it a few times while running errands in the neighborhood. It occupied an old theater building and had a big garish fluorescent sign out front.

I held my phone and wondered what to say. On the one hand, I hated clubs and dreaded especially the prospect of spending fifty or more dollars at this one. On the other hand, it was the weekend, and my grandmother was asleep and wouldn't for once miss me. Also, I was curious. And lonely. Without internet at home I'd taken to downloading videos of naked people at the Coffee Grind for later private viewing, but they must recently have installed some kind of megabyte counter, because the last few times I'd tried to download porn while I was in there, it hadn't worked.

I looked at the television. The young men of LSU were running the option in silence. The announcer sounded tired. This was no way to live. I put on a dress shirt and a jacket and presented myself across the hall. "He'll be OK, don't you think?" Howard said when I came in.

"I think so," Roberto said, evaluating me. "Teatr's face control is pretty relaxed."

So we had a few shots of vodka and some beers and headed to the club in a cab. Crammed in the back with an excited Howard and a reluctant Michael, all of us in sport coats, I felt drunk and a little excited. I was finally getting out of the house.

Teatr was pulsating with dance music; we heard it as soon as we pulled up. As Roberto predicted, the two goons at the door merely patted me down for weapons and then let me in. Once inside, we were greeted by a throng of young people writhing on a dance floor that ran down at a slight angle to a stage; it was an old theater, and they had simply torn out all the seats. They'd kept the stage, though, and the DJ with his tool kit was up there playing music very loud.

Immediately I regretted coming. This was hell. The other guys melted away, leaving me alone. I did not know how to dance, nor did it seem like anyone would have been willing to dance with me if I did. Everyone in the club was twenty years old; there were some men in there a little closer to my age, fat and bald and sweating in their suits, but they were surrounded by young women—you could almost see the dollars flying out of these guys' pockets. I tried to dance for a while, but after joining a few dancing groups and watching those groups sort of gradually turn away from me in a coordinated movement, I slunk off in the direction of the bar, where I bought an expensive beer, which I tried to drink very slowly and purposefully, as if I had something to do.

This is where Howard found me. He was with a tall, thin, blue-eyed girl with high cheekbones and perfect hair. I was shocked. "There you are," said Howard, as if he'd been looking for me. "Natasha," he said, "this is my landlord, Andrew."

"Landlord?" said Natasha, in English.

"More like a representative of the landlord," I said, in Russian.

"You're Russian?" she said.

"Yes, basically."

"Well, and a landlord. That's very impressive."

Things seemed to have turned around for me. I had seen girls like this on the street and occasionally at the Coffee Grind, but I had never actually spoken to one. It was just like speaking to a regular person, but one who was more beautiful.

"Natasha wants to get out of here and go party somewhere else," Howard said to me. "Want to come?" Did I! But I hesitated, not knowing whether Howard would rather be alone, and whether he was a paying customer of Natasha's. But he seemed to want me to come along, and Natasha said, "Landlord. Come with us."

I don't think she knew what was going to happen—at least, I hope she didn't. I think she really thought we were going to continue the party somewhere else. But Howard's bad luck was about to rub off on me. We made our way through the dancing throng and back out into the crisp autumn air. It was great to be outside, and with a beautiful girl. I was beginning to think that finally I'd made a correct decision.

As we stood outside and Howard smoked a cigarette, Natasha was busy with her phone, occasionally muttering something in annoyance. "What is it?" Howard asked.

"My boyfriend is an asshole," she said.

This was the first I'd heard of a boyfriend, but Howard took it in stride. Who didn't have a boyfriend, after all? And a girl like Natasha probably had lots of beautiful friends. "He says he's picking me up and we're going home," Natasha continued. "But I bet I can talk him into coming out with us."

The club was on the pedestrian strip of the boulevard, about a mile from our place; to meet Natasha's boyfriend we had stepped over the short fence and into the street. We stood there awhile; it was around two o'clock on a Saturday night, now Sunday morning, and the street was alive with activity. This city was fun. We could feel the club pulsating from where we stood; occasionally people came out for a cigarette, or to get in a cab; there was an informal line of unofficial taxis waiting out front. The old pastel-colored nineteenth-century buildings along Clean Ponds Boulevard, converted to luxury clothing shops, gleamed yellow and pink in the moonlight. There was a Benetton, and a restaurant called Avocado that looked like it was still open. Natasha kept tapping at her phone, in an increasingly foul mood. I remember thinking, though, how ordinary this scene was—some people out partying, waiting for our ride, hoping to keep the night going—and, really, how much fun.

Everything after that happened pretty fast. A black Mercedes SUV—the ubiquitous black Gelenvagen, which resembles a hearse, rare in the U.S. but very popular in Moscow—pulled up, and a tall, blond young man emerged from the front passenger seat. This would be the boyfriend. We all turned and looked at him, Howard and I putting on friendly, nonthreatening faces. I figured that as the native Russian speaker I should be the one to introduce us, so I stepped forward and started to say something along the lines of "I'm Andrei and this is my friend Howard" when I noticed that the boyfriend had raised his hand, as if telling me to stop speaking, that in his hand he had something black that I could swear was a gun, and that the hand with this possible gun was flying at my face.

The gun hit my face before I had a chance to process the sequence of events; my knees buckled and I fell to the ground. "Hey!" Howard yelled. Then came the pain. It was a throbbing in my left cheekbone and a kind of spinning in my head. I was preparing to get hit again and I even put my arm up to block it, but when I looked up the Gelenvagen and Natasha were gone. The boyfriend who'd hit me hadn't even said a word. I remained sitting awkwardly on the ground. I felt like I was very close to crying; the whole thing was so humiliating, this whole country was so awful, why was I even here?

"Jesus, fuck, I'm sorry," said Howard. He was crouching down next to me, looking very upset. It hurt to speak so I didn't say anything, but it wasn't Howard's fault. "That car had government plates," he said. "That cunt was probably the son of a Duma deputy. Jesus!" He hailed a car to take us home.

It was a five-minute ride but it felt like forever. Howard sat up front with the driver. I held my cheek with my hand, hoping thereby to keep it from falling off my face. I wondered if it was broken.

"They fucked your friend up, huh?" the cabdriver said to Howard.

Howard nodded. *"Pistolet,"* he said, meaning "gun."

"He hit him with a gun?" said the driver. He seemed genuinely concerned. "You foreigners," he said, "you need to be careful. *Nash chelovek inogda voz'met i po yebal'niku dast, prosto tak."* "Our person"—that is, a Russian—"is liable to just up and hit you in the fucker"—that is, the face—"for no reason." He shook his head.

We stopped at the traffic light at the Clean Ponds metro, next to the big post office, not far from the statue of Griboedov where my grandmother and I had seen that protest. I kept taking my hand off my cheek to see if it was bleeding. It was, but only a tiny bit. Was that bad? I wondered. Would it have been better if it was bleeding profusely?

The driver seemed to feel bad about the whole thing, on behalf of all Russians, and reached his hand into his jacket pocket. I thought for a second that it was going to be another gun, but it was a flask. He handed it back to me.

"Russian medicine!" the driver said to me in English and laughed.

"Thank you," I said in Russian. I took a drink from the flask—it was vodka.

"What, you're Russian?" said the driver.

"Sort of, yes," I said.

The driver now shook his head in disgust, as if, as a Russian, I should have known better. "But I'm not Russian," I wanted to say to him. "I'm American. I'm from a place where shit like this doesn't happen. I am going to leave here and you will never see me again." I found even thinking this a humiliating experience. But I meant it. I had made up my mind to leave. I was a shitty caretaker of my grandmother and neither was I having the time of my life. I would write to Dima finally to ask when he was coming back, because as soon as he came back, I was gone. This was a terrible country, and I was not cut out for it.

The next morning I woke up with a very badly swollen but by all appearances not broken cheekbone. The pain was bad but worse than that was my grandmother's shock at seeing me. I hadn't thought to think of an excuse, but I did so now. The other day I had seen some Central Asian construction workers playing soccer in a dirt lot off Pechatnikov, and I now told my grandmother I'd been hit with a soccer ball. "It looks terrible," she commented.

It really did look terrible, and continued to look terrible for two weeks. But the worst part might have taken place that afternoon. I decided to stay home from the Coffee Grind and ice my face as much as possible; in the middle of the afternoon my grandmother and I had some tea and listened to Echo of Moscow, when who should we hear being interviewed by Elena but my brother.

The week before, some protesters from a group called September had infiltrated a construction site on the new Moscow–Petersburg highway. I knew about this highway because Dima had bid to build gas stations on it and lost. The protesters draped signs over the bulldozers declaring that forests were for the people, not the oligarchs—the highway was going to be built through a large forest north of Moscow, destroying a sizable portion of it in the process—and tried to prevent construction crews from operating their machinery, including by pouring sugar into the gas tank of one of the bulldozers, apparently destroying its engine. In response they were roughed up by soccer hooligans hired by the construction company, and in the next day's papers appeared photos of these nice young protesters, both men and women, getting attacked by thugs wearing MMA gloves. The construction company turned out to be part owned by a RussOil executive who was also a Duma deputy from the United Russia Party. There was enough outrage about it that the Duma deputy had to make a public statement. His statement was that this regrettable incident was the fault of "certain businessmen living abroad" who had been disappointed by the "operations of the free market" and were now trying to destabilize the situation. "We are a country of laws and respect for property," he said. "When property is ruined at the behest of some foreign businessman, that's something law enforcement needs to look into." It seemed, I thought, like a potential reference to my brother, but at the time this struck me as so far-fetched that I put the thought away.

Now here was Dima on the radio, discussing this very thing with Elena. She was asking him about the deputy's remarks, and whether he took them to be addressed to him.

"It's Dima!" I cried.

"Oh?" said my grandmother, not immediately understanding. And then, "It's Dima!"

"Do I think he was referring to me?" Dima was saying. "I have no idea. I can't read the sick minds of the representatives of this sick regime. But I also think deflecting blame is a perfect sign of this sickness. So is lying. I can't tell if they're lying or they believe it, and I don't care."

"That's true," said my grandmother, but I was taken aback. First, by the thought that the official's accusations might be true, and that Dima had organized some kind of rebel army. And second, by the way he spoke: this did not sound like a person who was planning to come back to Moscow anytime soon.

That evening Howard texted me to see how I was doing, and I asked if I could come over and check my email on his computer. From there I wrote Dima, said I'd heard him on the radio, and demanded to know what his plans were about coming back. I did not mention that I'd been pistol-whipped in front of Teatr, since he'd probably just call me an idiot for going there in the first place. In any case he wrote back right away to say he'd be coming to town at the end of October—we could talk about it then. This was an entire month away but I figured I could handle it. The swelling in my face would go down and then when Dima came I could tell him that I wanted to leave.

I wrote to the rock drummer who was subletting my room that I would probably be taking it back in a month or two, and that he should start thinking about his next move.

7.

WE GO TO THE BANK

THEN I WAITED: I waited for the swelling in my face to go down and for the days to pass until Dima came back and I was released. I was too embarrassed to show up at the Coffee Grind looking like I did, so I did my classwork at the post office on Clean Ponds; it turned out they had a bunch of old computers upstairs in a stuffy windowless room and you could pay by the minute for online access. I didn't spend a minute longer in there than was absolutely necessary, and as a result I was around the apartment more often. My grandmother kept remarking how nice it was to have me there. Sometimes I was pleased that she was pleased with me; other times I felt resentful that it required a violent and unintentional grounding for this to happen.

In late September, the tsunami of the financial crisis finally reached our little island of stability. There wasn't a lot of warning. It was all "island of stability, island of stability," and then one day the ruble plunged 10 percent against the dollar and the euro. Within a week, just about every item in the groceries in our neighborhood went up 10 percent in price.

Soon everyone was talking about the *krizis:* the liberals on Echo of Moscow, the propagandists on the television news, and then, all of a sudden, my grandmother. I was still staying home and waiting for my face to heal when she walked into my room and said, "Andrei, I have a question."

She handed me a little booklet, just barely wider and taller than a credit card. It was from her bank, the state savings bank, and listed all her transactions from the last few years. At the beginning of the book they were recorded by hand, then at a certain point they started to be recorded by a little dot matrix printer—the bank clerks must have shoved the little book into the printer somehow.

My grandmother handed it to me now and said, "Andryush, how much money do I have?"

I studied the little document and determined that she had twelve thousand somethings—if it was dollars, it was a lot, but if it was rubles, it was not. Eventually I found the small print: it was rubles.

"You have twelve thousand," I said.

"Dollars?"

"No. Rubles."

She looked crestfallen.

Then, "How much is that?" She meant in dollars.

"Five hundred," I said.

"Five hundred dollars?" Now she sounded impressed.

"Yes."

"OK."

She took her bankbook and left. The financial consultation was over. Then she returned.

"Andryush. Is my money in rubles or dollars?"

"Rubles."

"Should I change it to dollars?"

Ah. The radio had frightened her with talk of the ruble's collapse. But in fact it was too late. The ruble had already lost a tenth of its value. When I said she had five hundred dollars, I was rounding up. It used to be five hundred dollars. Now it was four-fifty. But the ruble could bounce back, for one thing, and also, this just wasn't very much money. The hassle of going to the bank and getting this done far outweighed the potential losses from a further devaluation. So it seemed to me. For a day or two my grandmother relented, then we had the same scene all over again, and then after she concluded it was no use asking me, she started sitting in the kitchen doing little calculations on a sheet of paper. I looked at them once, but as far as I could tell they were just numbers being multiplied at random.

A few days later, on a Friday morning, with my face more or less back to normal, I made my triumphant return to the Coffee Grind. I was voraciously catching up on American views of the election, now just a few weeks away—the Russians hated McCain for his hawkishness and seemed optimistic that Obama would be a more reasonable American—when I got a Gchat from Dima.

"Hey, have you deposited the rent yet? It hasn't shown up in my account."

"No. Sorry. It's been busy."

"Can you do it today, please? The ruble is going to collapse over the weekend."

Dima had wisely set the rent in dollars to isolate it from fluctuations in the exchange rate, but there was a hitch: Howard and the guys paid in rubles at the going rate on the first of the month, and in between their payment and my deposit lay danger. If the ruble were to collapse before I could get to the bank, Dima would lose money. Nine days had passed already since the first of the month. And Dima didn't like losing money.

I said, "How do you know about the ruble?"

"Because I know!"

"I read that the Central Bank was defending the currency with all its might."

"Listen, could you please just deposit the rent? By Monday morning the ruble is fucked."

"OK, OK."

"Thanks!"

But I was annoyed. If it was so important for Dima that his rent get deposited in a timely fashion, he should have set it up so that I didn't have to drag our grandmother halfway across town to the HSBC. Furthermore, as I did not feel like explaining to Dima, over the past week with my swollen face it hadn't seemed like a good time to go to the bank to perform a potentially illegal transaction.

After the Gchat, though, I figured I might as well do it. I finished up some student emails and headed home.

When I got there my grandmother was drinking tea in the kitchen.

She always sat with her back to the door, facing the window, and sometimes she didn't hear me come in.

"Hello!" I called out, so as not to frighten her.

She turned around in her chair and smiled. "Coo-coo!" she said happily. Her teeth were out, which gave her a look of childlike joy when she smiled. "You're home early. Should I heat up lunch?"

And then I remembered—my grandmother's life savings! She hadn't mentioned it in a few days, but if the ruble collapsed she would never forgive me. I would never forgive myself.

"Listen," I said now. "Do you want to convert your account into dollars?"

"What?"

"Your bank account. Do you want it to be in dollars?"

"Of course!"

She might have forgotten the devaluation but she knew that she had faith in the dollar.

"OK," I said. "Let's go to the bank."

My grandmother put in her teeth, got dressed in her best slacks, a sweater, her pink coat and hat, and off we went. Her bank, Sberbank, the state bank, was just around the corner, and I figured we could go there first and then deposit Dima's rent, which I brought with me.

But the Sberbank was packed. The branch was just too small—a row of cashiers' windows and a narrow waiting space before them, maybe five feet deep. It was impossible to form any kind of line in that space, so people stood haphazardly wherever they could. "Who's last in line?" I asked.

A bespectacled man in his fifties said he was.

"And all these people are in front of you?" I asked.

"That's how a line works," he confirmed.

"Then we're after you," I said, to complete the transaction. There was no telling how long this would take. I could have the guy hold my place in line and walk my grandmother home, but if the line was quicker than it looked I'd have to run after her soon and drag her back here again. Probably better to just wait it out. As I contemplated the possibilities, I heard my grandmother thanking someone; a woman had offered her the lone chair.

Now a woman came through the door, looked stoically at the long line, and asked who was last.

"I am," I said.

"I'm after you," she said. I nodded.

"Why are there so many people?" I asked the man who had been last before me, wondering if he'd also heard about the coming devaluation.

"It's always like this on Fridays," he said. He thought a moment. "And other days too."

In the end, we would wait for more than two hours. When it was finally our turn, an exhausted and irritated clerk converted my grandmother's life savings to dollars and handed us a brand-new bankbook.

"Is that it?" my grandmother asked me as we walked away from the window.

"Yes," I said. "You now have dollars."

My grandmother, who was holding on to my arm, patted it. She was exhausted but pleased. It was not too late to go to Dima's bank, but I couldn't do it to her. She was much too tired. We went home and I spent the weekend at the Grind checking the news sites for word of the collapsing ruble. Instead, the news was still dominated by the American presidential race. Just in case, I turned off my Gchat so that my brother couldn't yell at me. In the event, the ruble opened Monday even a little stronger than it had closed on Friday. We made the trip to HSBC first thing that morning and deposited Dima's money. My delay had actually earned him some money, though I wasn't going to harp on that, especially as, two weeks later, the ruble did have another bad day—Bad Tuesday—and slipped another 10 percent. But my grandmother's life savings had ridden out the storm mostly intact.

In those first few weeks after getting hit in the face, every time I went out of the house I was skittish. I kept thinking I saw the guy who hit me, and my heart jumped: Should I run and confront him? If I did, would he hit me again? Once you realize that other people can physically harm you, with no warning or provocation, you start seeing things differently. I hated going out of the house those first weeks, though I had to get groceries and a couple of times I went for a jog so I wouldn't get too depressed. This lasted, as I say, for a few weeks, but eventually it wore off. My heart stopped racing every time I saw a tall, blond guy on Sretenka or in the Coffee Grind. Anyway, I figured I'd be leaving soon.

Obama, I sensed, would win the election. I looked forward to returning to an enlightened, post-racial America just as soon as my brother came back.

In the meantime, in the aftermath of the ruble's devaluation, I'd grown richer. My cappuccinos were now 20 percent off. Once or twice in the weeks after the devaluation, I even bought myself a sandwich. Live it up, Kaplan, I thought. Live it up.

8.

MY GRANDMOTHER DEMANDS
SOME SLIPPERS (FROM BELARUS)

ONE OTHER THING turned my way before Dima came to visit. My grandmother announced that she needed new slippers from Belarus. That she needed new slippers was true. Like all Russian people, my grandmother took her shoes off when entering her apartment and replaced them with slippers. Since she did perpetual laps around the apartment, the slippers were getting serious mileage, and it showed. The rub was that she liked her current slippers, and believed that they were from Belarus. So it had to be Belarusian slippers again.

This was not easy. There was a shoe store on Sretenka where I had bought my own slippers—they had a black insole and an argyle pattern; they were pretty cool slippers—but the store did not have anything from Belarus. I tried a few more stores in the neighborhood and came up empty. I wrote to Dima to ask if he knew where the supposedly Belarusian slippers came from and he said he didn't, and couldn't I just get our grandmother regular slippers? No, I could not, though I was beginning to wonder why. Her slippers were not so extraordinary; there were many Chinese and Russian and Ukrainian slippers just like them. But she insisted. A famous historian had once defined the Soviet people—*Homo Sovieticus*—as a "species whose most highly developed skills involved the hunting and gathering of scarce goods in an urban environment." I had never developed these skills. It seemed unfair to demand of me that I develop them now.

Finally I confessed to my grandmother that I was having trouble finding Belarusian slippers. "Have you tried the market outside

Olympic Stadium?" she asked. I had not. "Let's go there," said my grandmother, so we did.

Olympic Stadium was just one stop from us on the subway. It had been built for the 1980 Summer Olympics, the ones that had been boycotted by the West over the Soviet invasion of Afghanistan, and had hosted the boxing tournament (the Cubans won). In the 1990s, it had been taken over by small clothing stores, and though it was now active again as a stadium—Metallica was playing next month—the large open space in front of it had become a clothes market. We approached it from the Prospekt Mira (Peace Avenue) subway stop, across a large chaotic square that included a small church, a McDonald's, and, cutting across the square, an active tramline. Periodically a tram would rumble through and people would clear out of the way for it. Moscow was crazy.

Eventually we reached a sea of little stalls. We toured them as quickly as we could, though my grandmother was in no hurry. She seemed, for once, to be having a good time. There were a fair number of dedicated shoe stalls, and my grandmother would go over and ask if they had any slippers from Belarus; after enough of them said no, she agreed to try on some slippers that were not from Belarus. Each of the little stalls had a stool she could sit on as she pulled off her loafers and experimented with some slippers. The salesladies were understanding. You spent half your life in slippers, after all. Choosing a pair was serious business.

My grandmother rejected all the slippers. This felt discouraging to me, but she didn't mind. I guess we were shopping. After about an hour of this, we finally headed back to the metro. But I would not be relating this exciting tale were it not for what happened next. As we made our way through the square with the McDonald's and tram tracks and church on it, I noticed two teenage girls ahead of us carrying gym bags and figure skates; they looked flushed, as if they'd just been skating. Ordinarily I'd have been too shy to say anything, but an hour of watching my grandmother try on slippers had apparently lowered my inhibitions. I hailed the girls and asked if there was an ice rink nearby. They said yes and pointed back toward the stadium. "If you bend around the stadium and under, it's right there, across from the swimming pool."

"Do they play hockey there?"

"I think late in the evenings, yes."

If that was true, and if I could get into a skate there, it would signal a remarkable change in my fortunes—this place was really close to our house.

I went the next evening after my grandmother had gone to bed. I didn't bring my Ikea bag full of stuff this time. The entrance was across from the pool, just as the figure skaters said, and it had the usual Moscow security guards in cheap black suits stationed at it. When I asked where the hockey rink was, they pointed me down the corridor, and when I asked if it was all right for me to go there, they shrugged. This meant yes. I walked down the hall, descended some stairs, noticed some locker rooms to my left, and then opened a metal door to find— a hockey rink. It was not a professional rink like at Sokolniki, there were no stands for thousands of fans, and since it was under the stadium it was something like a secret rink—but it was a hockey rink nonetheless, it had that smell of mildew mixed with sweat mixed with trapped cold air, and guys were playing hockey on it.

I decided this time that I'd check the locker rooms. One was locked, another was empty, but in the third I found two guys about my age, one big, blue-eyed, and bald—I later learned his name was Grisha—the other smaller, a little older, with dark blond hair and a mean look on his face—Fedya. They were both sitting down next to unopened hockey bags and taping their sticks. Hockey players.

And then the same thing happened all over again. They didn't want to let me play. I insisted. They said no. They couldn't understand who I was. By this point the swelling in my cheek was gone, and I'd been speaking Russian continually for almost two months, meaning my small accent was also gone, and so I seemed to them like, basically, a regular guy. Why didn't I have a network of people to whom I could appeal for an introduction to their hockey game? Grisha actually got up at one point and yelled, in his frustration at my refusal to leave, "Who are you and what do you want?!"

"I just want to play hockey," I finally said. Grisha turned away in disgust, but Fedya, who had seemed like the mean one, said, "Come on Wednesday. Bring five hundred rubles." I thanked him and got out of there before Grisha could rescind the invitation. Five hundred rubles would have been twenty dollars before the devaluation; now it was seventeen. I could live with that.

That was on a Friday. I spent the next five days imagining what playing hockey in Russia would be like, and then I found out. When I came in smiling to Fedya and Grisha's locker room, Fedya barely looked up and without a hello simply said, "You're on the other team," and sent me to the neighboring locker room. The guys in there moved aside for me but otherwise paid me no attention. Out on the ice, Fedya and Grisha's team subjected me to an extraordinary level of physical violence. I got hooked, hit from behind, and slashed, not least by big, bald Grisha. At one point one of their guys—not Grisha—slashed me so badly in the leg that I couldn't take it anymore and slashed him back. He took real exception to this and made as if he were going to slash me in the head. At that point I didn't care—I was not enjoying myself. One of the guys on my team pulled him back, marking pretty much the first acknowledgment from one of our guys that I was even there.

Fedya and Grisha's team was good; they wore matching white jerseys and played together seamlessly. Our team was less good. We all wore different nonwhite jerseys (our goalie even wore a bright red one in the style of the old Soviet Olympic jerseys, with CCCP across the front) and did not play well together. On top of that, we had a bad attitude. On my first shift I got the puck in the offensive zone, chased it into the corner, and got plastered from behind by Grisha. The puck squirted away; my right wing, Anton, picked it up and tried to hit my left wing, Oleg, in the slot. But the pass was a little out of Oleg's reach and got picked up instead by Grisha, who made a nice outlet pass to the right wing, who gave it to Fedya, who gave it back to the wing, who scampered down the boards and scored.

Our line came off; as soon as we reached the bench, Anton and Oleg started yelling at each other. They were big guys, over six feet tall, and a few years older than me; Anton wore a blue Ovechkin jersey from when he (Ovechkin) played for Dynamo; Oleg wore a red Karlovy Vary jersey and had a chubby, friendly face.

"What the fuck, Oleg!" Anton said. "Where were you looking?"

"*Blyad'*!" said Oleg. "What do you want from me? Put the pass a little closer to my stick and I'll fucking get it. Fuck."

This went on for the entire game. None of the guys yelled at me; they barely seemed to see me. But they kept yelling at each other.

In Boston, where I grew up playing, hockey players never yelled. In New York things were a little different; there was a Long Island school of hockey that was more exuberant, where guys talked more trash—but only to the other team. In Boston, entire skates could go by in total silence. If someone from the other team happened to say something to you, you were to give him a disdainful look and say, "Fuck you." If he continued talking you could skate away or drop your gloves and fight. But more often than not, no one said anything. They just played.

I was, frankly, disgusted. We must have lost by six or seven goals and in the locker room afterward the mood was grim. No one invited me back for the next skate and I didn't go. I would rather not play hockey, I thought, than play hockey with these dicks.

But by the next Wednesday, I was ready to try again. When I came into the locker room half an hour early, as a way of trying to establish a presence in the space, our goalie was already there. He was a small, thin guy, about my age, but a good goaltender—it wasn't his fault the other team was much better than we were. "Ah," he said now, "y-y-you're here!" He had a slight stutter, and he was using the *ty* in a way that was clearly friendly. "We were wondering if you'd come. You may not have noticed, but we need some speed up front." I was immensely grateful for this and laughed. "By the way, my name is Sergei," he said. "Hello, Sergei," I said, using the *ty* myself. We shook hands. Then we went out and lost again. Nonetheless, despite plenty of slashing and hooking against me, I felt better out on the ice. The guys were violent, but they were slow; I could take an extra half second and make sure my passes were accurate and then brace for a hit. I didn't do anything extraordinary, but I began to have a sense of where I was. In the locker room afterward, one of the guys turned to me and said, "You coming on Friday?"

Another *ty*.

"Do you think I should?" I asked, using *ty* as well.

"I think you have to."

"All right," I said. I was on the team. It wasn't a good team, and it was badly overmatched and indeed frequently humiliated by the white team, but nonetheless I was on it. One of the guys even asked me about my Ikea bag. "Is that comfortable?" he said.

"It's OK," I lied. "It lets my stuff breathe."

The guy nodded—a little skeptically, but still.

As for my grandmother's slippers, a few weeks after our failed trip to Olympic Stadium I was walking through an underground crossing on my way to a hockey store to get my skates sharpened when I saw a lady selling slippers. They looked sort of like my grandmother's. "Excuse me," I said, "where are these from?"

"Gomel," said the woman.

"In Belarus?"

"Yeah, so? They're just as good as Russian ones."

"No, that's great!" I cried, much to her surprise. Belarusians were sensitive about their products, post-Chernobyl. I bought two pairs and stuck them in my Ikea bag. My grandmother was very pleased and bragged continually on the phone about it to Emma Abramovna. I'm sure Emma Abramovna was thrilled.

And in the meantime, Dima had come to visit.

9.

DIMA COMES TO MOSCOW

ALL HAPPY FAMILIES are alike; ours, obviously, was not a happy family.

What had we done wrong? By most measures, you would have thought we'd done everything right. For a few years in the late 1970s, the Soviets allowed the emigration of their Jews. First they sent the criminals and critics ("Let them rob and criticize the Americans!"), but there were only so many criminals and critics, and they eventually started letting out computer programmers like my father and literary scholars like my mother. My parents weren't stupid. When you are given a chance to emigrate from a poor, decrepit, crumbling country to a wealthy, powerful, dynamic one, you take it. They took it. They filed their application, bribed someone who said they'd help, sold all their stuff—and off we went.

It wasn't easy. I was six years old when we came over, and even I could tell. We stayed with another family at first, then in a weird apartment in Brighton, at the very edge of respectable Boston. Someone stole our security deposit. With my father's first substantial paycheck we bought a giant, ugly car. As my parents drove around Brighton visiting their Russian friends—all their friends were Russian—I sprawled on the backseat and slept.

Eventually they figured it out, my father went from good job to better, and my mother became one of the few literary Russians to actually find a literary job. We moved from Brighton to Brookline to aristocratic Newton. But through it all Dima flung himself at the frustrations and limitations of our new life. He denounced the Russians my parents hung out with as losers; he dismissed his new classmates as idiots. He had hated the Soviet Union, he said, but at least in the Soviet Union there were people you could talk to.

The only person he seemed to like was me. As he started making money in his first jobs in America—he got a job as a gas station attendant, which included, he told me proudly, both a wage and some tips—he always bought me little gifts and let me in on his theories about capitalism. He sought to enlist me in his ongoing battle with our parents, and let me in on all the (limited) family dirt.

As Dima moved out into the world—he left home the minute he turned eighteen, declared to my flabbergasted parents that he wasn't going to college, and incorporated his first company before the year was out (they made some kind of video game)—I watched him with profound fascination. What was this new world and what could a Kaplan hope to do in it? How could you live? I had no idea. My parents were good people but they lived in a Russian ghetto. It wasn't just their friends who were Russian, it was everyone: our doctor was Russian, our dentist was Russian, our car mechanic was Russian, the clown who came to our house for birthday parties was Russian, the guy who fixed the roof was Russian. How the fuck did they know so many Russian people? The thing is, I knew this world, this close-knit community, would not be available to me. It was as if, yes, my parents had emigrated, but only to the Russia that existed inside America; Dima and I would have to emigrate all over again into America itself. Dima was the one who went out into the world and figured it out. He was the advance party for the two of us. I did not have to do what he did—in fact in most ways I would do the exact opposite—but from him at least I could learn the possibilities. Until I was about sixteen there was no one I admired more.

Then our mother died. She got sick when I was a sophomore, endured the terrible treatments, and still died, two years later, in terrible pain. My brother was in New York by then, working on Wall Street, and he spent a week with us in Newton after the funeral. All of us were in shock, more, I think, than we even realized at the time.

With my mother gone, it was like our entire history, our emigration, our lives no longer made sense. She had been at the center of it, she and Dima. Now we scattered: I left for college; my father sold the house and moved to Cape Cod, eventually marrying an American woman and starting a new family; and Dima quit his job and moved to Moscow. I don't know if he thought of his return as a rebuke to my parents or an homage to them. Maybe it was both.

I don't know all the things that he got into while he was making his way in the new Russian capitalism. He would periodically report on this or that exciting foolproof scheme on his increasingly rare visits to the States—he was investing in a demolition company in anticipation of the destruction of Soviet housing stock; he was buying a warehouse for auto parts; he was chopping down forests outside Moscow and selling them to the Norwegians—and then the next time he came it was on to something else. It was the same with his wives and girlfriends. He got married and divorced before I was done with college, once more while I was in grad school, and was now married a third time.

It wouldn't be right to say that I noticed some kind of change in him over time; I didn't. He was the same person. But certainly as he became more successful and accrued more stuff, he became more himself. The Dima I had known growing up had been impatient, aggressive, and aggrieved—qualities that had made his teenage years a living hell for him and for our parents. But in Russia he found a suitable arena for these qualities. It was a place where being impatient and aggressive could pay off. I remember visiting him once, not long after I'd started grad school. He had just bought the apartment across the landing from our grandmother and was getting his floor replanked. The workers had done a less than perfect job—there was a slight gap between the last of the floorboards and the wall. By slight I mean a quarter of an inch— I would not have noticed it had Dima not pointed it out to me. Nonetheless when the contractor, a burly Russian guy in work overalls, came by to get paid, Dima laid into him. The work was shit, he yelled, and he wasn't paying for it. "You and your incompetents are going to come back tomorrow and do the whole thing over again," said Dima. The contractor, whose large belly was about at Dima's chest, looked like he was considering taking a swipe at Dima. But he tried to make peace instead. "Why don't we take up the two or three adjoining ones and fix those?" he said. "It'll look the same."

Dima smelled weakness. "You will take up every single board, do you understand me, you fucking bear?"

The contractor puffed up his chest for a moment and then deflated. He must have made a calculation: If he took a swipe at Dima, he wouldn't get paid, he might get arrested, and maybe even worse—if someone this small was yelling this loudly, it must mean he had all sorts of protection behind him. "All right," said the contractor dolefully, and the next day his workers came back and redid the entire job. The contractor even seemed to take something of a liking to Dima, who by this point was all sweetness and light.

"No hard feelings, OK?" said the contractor, offering his hand.

"Of course not," said Dima, and meant it. The contractor was Stepan, who now fixed stuff for Dima, and sometimes (grudgingly) for me.

Eventually Dima's fierceness won out over whatever flaws were inherent in the Russian free market, and he returned with some success to the moneymaking platform of his youth—gas stations. He built a small network of them, about ten, throughout Moscow and the Moscow region, and started making money. But then the Moscow–Petersburg highway project was announced, and with it a tender for the gas station contract. It was a large contract, twenty stations, plus the opportunity to sublease store space in the future rest stops—tens of millions of dollars, a whole new level for Dima. And here his problems began, because he wasn't the only one who was interested. In the end, he lost the bid to our old friend RussOil, in what he claimed was a rigged process, and started raising a terrible fuss. That was about as much as I knew about it, and as far as I could tell that was why he'd had to leave the country.

My hope was that he'd straightened it out, one way or another—maybe his appearance on the radio was part of a tough negotiation—and would now be coming back.

When I told my grandmother that Dima was coming to visit, she freaked out.

"Where will he stay?" she said.

"In our room," I said.

"Your room?"

I took my grandmother to my room to show her the bunk beds that we had once slept in as boys. I had played hockey for the first time the night before and left my stuff to dry, a little haphazardly, on the floor. And the rest of the room wasn't exactly a model of cleanliness.

"Dima can't stay here!" said my horrified grandmother.

"Half this junk is his!" I said, which was true. But it didn't matter. "I'll clean it up before he gets here," I said.

"All right," said my grandmother.

The next day—six days before Dima's arrival—she came into my room. I had cleaned up some of it, but she was unsatisfied. "Andryush," she said. "I've been thinking. Maybe you can move out of this room while Dima is here?"

"And where will I stay?" I said. Theoretically I could have stayed in the back room, but this would have meant walking through my grandmother's little room to go to the bathroom or get a drink of water. And anyway I didn't feel like getting kicked out of my room for a week.

"This room will be fine for Dima," I said. "He'll like it."

"Are you sure?"

And on and on it went. One afternoon I came home from the Coffee Grind to find that my grandmother had set the table for three. She'd brought out her nicest plates and even the half-empty bottle of red wine that was still in the fridge for special occasions. I had no idea how long it had been there and we had not yet made any progress in finishing it. "What's this?" I asked.

"Dima is coming today," said my grandmother proudly. "Do you know my grandson, Dima?"

"I do know him," I said, "because he's my brother, and he's coming on Thursday."

"Well, what's today?"

"Monday."

"Are you sure?"

That day I put a note on the fridge that said "Dima arrives Thursday," but my grandmother took it down. "I know when Dima arrives," she said. So we continued having these conversations until he was finally there.

Dima was my brother. We had emigrated together, acclimated to America together, we had attended our mother's funeral together, and then we had helped my dad move out of our house together. We had had many arguments, but he was my brother; he had always been my brother. What else does one build a life out of if not people, and time? People multiplied by time. But people can change. Circumstances can change. Money can change—money can change everything.

He came in the late afternoon, off the British Airways flight from London. My grandmother had spent the entire previous day cooking. She made borscht and kotlety and kasha. Dima in general ate very little, he seemed to exist on an inexhaustible fund of nervous energy, but when he came in, with his rolling suitcase, in a beautiful gray coat and expensive leather boots, he immediately agreed to eat. This pleased my grandmother immensely. "Dima!" she said. "I am so proud of you!"

"Thank you, Grandma," said Dima.

"You are a really impressive person!" my grandmother insisted. She was beaming. Here was Dima! "We heard you on the radio!" she said.

"Thank you, Grandma," Dima said again.

"If only you'd get a haircut," said my grandmother. Dima's hair was a little on the long side. "And come see me more often!"

"I'm in London right now."

"What?" My grandmother hadn't heard him.

"London!" Dima said more loudly. "In England!"

"Ah!" said my grandmother. "England," she said. "Yes, that is a nice place." She had already forgotten why this was relevant. She said, sadly: "If only you would come see me once in a while. No one ever comes to see me."

"I'm here right now," said Dima.

"Yes," said my grandmother, in the same sad tone.

Dima finished his borscht and saw that my grandmother had put water on to boil. He regarded the teakettle for a moment and then said to me accusingly, "Where's the electric teakettle?"

"What?" I said.

"Grandma," Dima said. "What'd you do with the electric teakettle I got you?"

My grandmother looked at him uncomprehendingly.

Dima got up. He started rifling through the kitchen cabinets. Finally, from behind some pots in one of them, he pulled out a brand-new electric teakettle.

"I got her this because she burned the last three of those," he said, indicating the one in which water had just started boiling on the stove. Dima turned it off. "Grandma," he said. "I got you this because it's easier to use."

"I don't like it," said my grandmother, waving it away. "It's noisy."

"It's *noisy*?!" Dima almost yelled. He shook his head. "It's safer, Grandma. You should use it."

He left it on the counter. I could see he was investigating the kitchen further. "Where's the trash can?" he asked me.

"What?" I said again. "It's under the sink."

Dima looked under the sink, where my grandmother kept a tiny little trash can; it was so small that it usually filled up in a day, sometimes twice a day, but that was OK because the dumpster was nearby and I was glad to throw our bag out whenever it got full.

"Grandma," Dima now said, "what did you do with the trash can I got you?"

"I don't remember," said my grandmother a little stubbornly.

Now Dima set off to look for his trash can. My grandmother and I sat in the kitchen like guilty children. Eventually Dima emerged from the back room with a large, modern, stainless steel trash can. "This was in the closet in the back room," he told me.

"Grandma," he said, "this is a nice trash can. Bugs can't get in." (We had had some flies in the kitchen in August.) "And it looks good."

"I don't like it," said my grandmother. "It takes up too much space."

"It fits right here," said Dima. He put it next to the refrigerator. It almost fit there.

"Won't you have some tea?" my grandmother said.

"I don't have time," Dima said to her. Then, to me: "I need to write some emails. After that maybe we can get a drink?"

I said sure. Dima got out his laptop and right on the kitchen table started banging away at it—apparently his computer communicated with the soldiers' network just fine. I cleaned up from dinner and my grandmother, after trying and failing to get Dima's attention a couple of times, went to her room. When Dima announced himself done with his emails and asked if I was ready, I felt like I was betraying my grandmother by saying yes, choosing him over her. But in truth I was also eager to get outside. I stuck my head into her room and said we'd be back in an hour. She was lying in bed, reading Chekhov. Without turning around, she gamely waved good-bye.

It was evening now, and Dima suggested we go to the strip club on the second floor above the bookstore. "Have you been already?" he asked.

I shook my head.

"Wellll," he said, drawing it out in disappointment. "*Nuuuu.* You must change your life."

We headed out. It was so strange walking down the street with Dima. He was thin and small and elegant and dark-haired, with a thin, very Semitic nose, the exact opposite of the big, ungainly, flat-faced Slavic men who walked down the street toward us. He was the opposite of a typical Russian, he was an anti-Russian, and yet he fit in here. He knew no one liked him, and it put him at ease.

The strip club was called Gentlemen of Fortune, after a famous

Russian film of that name, and it consisted of two large rooms. The first was set up pretty much like a café, with tables and chairs and topless girls going around serving drinks, and the second room was an open space with benches along the walls, where the men sat and the girls danced for them. The girls looked like they ranged in age from about nineteen to twenty-four, and though some were blond and blue-eyed and others were dark-haired and brown-eyed, and in fact were of multiple nationalities, they were almost all uniformly slim, petite, and very attractive. I found it disturbing, in fact, how attractive and fresh-faced they all seemed. Dima and I sat down in the café part; Dima ordered an expensive drink and I ordered a beer, and then as I tried to ignore the topless girls he told me what was happening with his business. As he told me more I forgot all about the girls.

"Basically," Dima was saying, "they've shut me down. I filed a lawsuit to demand an audit of the highway tender, and they didn't like it. My stations started getting raided by the tax police. I tried to get in touch with the people I know in the Kremlin and they stopped answering my calls. The tax people closed my stations. There's fucking police tape around them, like a murder took place there. I had to leave to avoid criminal prosecution, and they still have a case at the ready should they ever need it."

He paused to see what effect this was having.

I said, "That's not good."

"No, it's not. Now that they have me by the nuts they're going to take my stations; if I don't give them up, they're going to continue with a criminal prosecution. So I'm getting out."

"What?" I didn't quite understand.

"I'm not coming back. This is it. I'm done with this place."

I had not expected this. "You're just going to leave?"

"Yes. What do you want me to do?"

"I don't know!" I said. I didn't know, of course. "Stay? Fight?"

"And get put in prison like Khodor?" Khodor was Mikhail Khodorkovsky, the oligarch who stayed and fought and had been in prison, by that point, for five years. "No, thanks."

"OK," I said. I wasn't going to argue with him about it.

"So here's the thing," said Dima. Apparently what he'd said until then was just a prelude. "How long are you planning on staying?"

"Here? I was planning on staying until you came back. I thought it was going to be soon." A pathetic note of reproach entered my voice, though I tried to suppress it. "I already told my subletter I need my room back."

"OK, great," said Dima. "Do you still want to do that?"

"Well, I don't know. I—why?"

"Because my legal bills are insane, and I need to start liquidating assets. And I want to start with the ones that are the least devalued right now."

"OK." I didn't see what this had to do with me.

Dima said, "The least devalued assets are real estate."

"What?" It was more the way he said it than what he said that made me realize what he was talking about. "Do you mean the apartment?"

Dima nodded.

I said, "Isn't it also down?"

"Not like my other stuff. Have you seen the MICEX?"

"What's that?"

"The stock exchange, professor. It's down eighty percent. Eighty! The apartments are down ten, fifteen at most. I'm not moving on those shares until they're back."

"But you can't sell Grandma's apartment. It's not yours!"

"It is, actually. It's in my name and I have power of attorney. And it's the best thing for her. She can't get up those stairs much longer, and this will give us some cash on hand to hire someone to take care of her."

"She's been in that apartment practically her entire life."

"What does that matter? She can't remember what she had for breakfast."

"But she knows where stuff is. She can orient herself."

"We'll set up the new place with her stuff, we'll put it in the same places. Like at Emma Abramovna's."

I thought a second. "Why don't you sell your own apartment?"

"Oh, I will," said Dima. "But the buyer I have wants both apartments so he can combine them. He's willing to pay a premium for that."

"No," I said. "You can't do that to her."

"*I* can't?" Dima looked at me like he was studying something on my nose. "I'm sorry. I must have missed all your contributions to Grandma's health and well-being these past fifteen years. Did you do them in secret?" Dima paused as if waiting for an answer. "No? You didn't? So you haven't actually been here all this time, and you haven't actually set foot in this country in however many years, and you don't actually know anything about what's going on? I thought so."

He sat back momentarily with his expensive drink. It had an orange peel in it. He was so much older than me that we had never wrestled or fought the way brothers do, and anyway he wasn't the wrestling type. He was all brain, and the brain was devoted to maximizing profit and proving he was right. And in this instance he was right. I'd been in America all this time. My grandmother had descended into senility without me. That I had finally showed up didn't change that.

I asked, "When are you planning on doing this?"

"As soon as possible. If you leave around Thanksgiving, that would be great, we could probably get three hundred for the place. I might need to borrow a hundred out of it for my legal fees. The rest, two hundred thousand, we put in a Grandma fund—for renting her a place, hiring a live-in nurse, and any medical expenses that she incurs in the coming years. If her burn rate is about three thousand a month, that's, what, sixty-six months, five and a half years. That's a long time for her."

"Yeah," I said. Our grandmother was not going to live another five and a half years.

"Half that money is yours and I should be able to get it back to you within two to three years. We can draw up a contract."

"I don't need any money."

"OK, Mr. Moneybucks. We'll cross that bridge when we get to it."

I sat in silence. I had been looking forward to going back but this was different; if I left, it would mean my grandmother having to move to some random place.

"So what do you think?" said Dima.

"I don't know," I said. "I need to think about it."

"OK," said Dima. "Think about it."

He then made some gesture that I didn't catch, and one of the girls came over and sat in Dima's lap. She was topless, and she clearly knew Dima; he whispered something in her ear and she laughed. He turned to me. "Vera says she has a friend who'd like to meet you. Should we invite her over?" Then he added, in English, "It's on me."

Part of me wanted to take him up on it but another part did not. In any case I was too confused by Dima's news. I thanked Vera and Dima and said I was going to head home. Dima shrugged. "See you there," he said, and that was the end of our conversation.

I took a roundabout way home so I could clear my head. The evenings were growing colder. I was in a sweater and a fall coat but it was not enough. Until now I had been so eager to leave. I walked past the expensive cafés that I didn't like, the Hugo Boss, the experimental theater.... I was just getting used to this place. And I had maybe found a hockey game. But maybe too it was for the best. I was not exactly the world's greatest caretaker of my grandmother.

Did I think Dima should stay? I mean, between going to prison and leaving, of course he should leave. But it didn't sit well with me somehow. There had always been a kind of moral argument that Dima made alongside his moneymaking. He wasn't just coming to Russia to make a killing; he was coming to build capitalism, democracy, a modern nation. He was continuing the work begun by the great Soviet dissidents whom my parents so admired. That's why he could get so high and mighty on Facebook or when Elena interviewed him on Echo. It's why he could sleep with strippers and still think of himself as a righteous dude—he was building the new Russia! Of course he had to blow off some steam! Now he was leaving. And that was OK. But if the idea had been to build something, and it was still unbuilt ... did that mean the idea had never been to build anything at all?

Maybe I was being unfair. But one saw the same thing in academia. People came to Russia, interviewed Russians, wrote their articles and books—and then they got a job, or tenure, or the Nobel Prize, and what did the Russians get from it exactly? All this money that the Russians now had, it wasn't from Dima coming over and building gas stations, and it sure as hell wasn't from some academic writing articles. It was from Uncle Lev and the great Jewish-Italian defector Pontecorvo figuring out the goddamn molecular nature of oil. It was from Uncle Lev building instruments to detect neutron emissions. No Americans ever came over and showed the Russians how to find their oil; the Russians did it all on their own.

When I got home, my grandmother was in the kitchen in her nightgown, drinking a cup of tea. She had her teeth out and gave me a toothless smile when I sat down across from her. She always looked very cute without her teeth, like a very old, wise, gray-haired baby.

"Andryush," she said, "you're home. I was worried. Where did you go?"

"I was out with Dima."

"Dima? Is he here?"

"Yes."

"He's my grandson, you know," said my grandmother sadly. "He lives in London now."

"I know," I said.

"Are you hungry?" she asked. "There's some pancakes with jam. Do you want some?"

She started to pull herself up by the table and I stopped her. "I'll get them," I said.

The pancakes were on the windowsill—it was really more like a window alcove, it was two feet deep—in an aluminum dish, covered by another dish; my grandmother owned no Tupperware. I put two on a plate and came back to the table. My grandmother was slowly, methodically sipping her tea.

Dima and I had just spent I didn't know how much money on those drinks. Thirty dollars? And Dima was no doubt going to spend quite a bit more. How much was Vera's cleaning fee? Two hundred dollars? Five hundred? I had no idea, but five hundred struck me as plausible. That was the entirety of my grandmother's life savings.

"My mother used to make these pancakes," my grandmother said suddenly. "She wasn't a good cook. She was a dancer. And she was very good at chess. She was one of the best female chess players in Moscow."

I had never heard any of this before.

"Yes," said my grandmother, "she was very talented but she didn't like children. But once in a while we would come home from school and she'd be there and she'd have these pancakes for us to eat."

My poor little grandmother, I thought. She had lived such a long life, but she still remembered her mother's pancakes.

It was wrong that she was alone like this. And it happened because we had emigrated. It didn't seem that way at the time—at the time it was a great adventure—but by leaving we had ruptured the generations. We had abandoned my grandmother. It took a while to unspool all its ramifications, but that emigration, more than anything, was the great tragedy of my grandmother's life.

"Do you want to play anagrams?" I asked her.

Her eyes widened. "Of course!" she said. And we played three games. She slaughtered me. Then we went to sleep. Whenever it was Dima came home, I did not hear him.

The next morning I wrote to the drummer that my plans had changed, and if he hadn't yet made other arrangements, he could stay. He wrote back right away to say that he hadn't, and would be happy to stay.

Telling Dima was more difficult, but—uncharacteristically for me, it must be said—I decided not to put it off. I told him I wanted to stay a few more months, that I was just getting started here, and that I didn't think we should move my grandmother while I was still around to help. He took it better than I expected. "All right," he said. "If you're here to help her up the stairs, we save on a caretaker, so fine. But if the place loses value, I'm taking it out of your end."

"OK," I said.

Dima was in Moscow an entire week. We ran a couple of household errands together and watched the election returns come in, and Obama's speech, on his computer, but other than that I hardly saw him. He slipped in and out of the apartment like a ghost, either very early in the morning or very late at night. He was avoiding my grandmother, I think, and she could tell. Every time she saw him, she said, "Dima! I'm so proud of you! You've made such a great career for yourself! We heard you on the radio! If only you would come see me once in a while! I'm right here!"

"Grandma, I have to go," Dima would say, looking at his phone and putting on his coat and boots and hat. "We'll talk about this later, OK?"

"Can't you stay a little bit?" my grandmother would say. "We'll play anagrams."

"I can't right now."

"Just one game?"

"I can't."

"You never can."

"I'm very busy!"

The more she pressed, the more he pulled away. I recognized the dynamic. *He* thought she was criticizing him, minimizing or even ignoring all the time he had spent with her over the years, all the attention he had given her, whereas *she* was merely stating a wish and also, I now saw, helplessly trying to think of something to say. There was Dima. What to say to him? And the first thing that came out was always some kind of rebuke. She was just trying to make conversation, to get him to stick around a moment longer, to engage.

I watched it and became so sad. Perhaps I could do things differently. Dima was going to leave. But I was going to stay.

PART II

1.

IT GETS COLD OUT

AFTER DIMA LEFT it grew cold. First it was a little cold, but one could manage, and after that it was a little colder—and then it became very, very cold.

It wasn't a wet cold, and there wasn't a lot of wind. It was just really fucking cold. Ten degrees Fahrenheit was ordinary. If it got down to zero, that was tough. If it got up to twenty, people loosened their collars and took off their hats.

On an average day, before leaving the house, you had to wonder: Will I freeze to death? Anywhere you wanted to go, you were going to end up walking. The city was very big. The streets were very wide. As you walked there wouldn't be any pockets of warmth to hide in. What if you fell? What if you got lost or discouraged? In blockaded Leningrad during the war people would just collapse on the street from hunger and cold and that was it. Others would step over them. Eventually someone would come to collect the frozen body.

After a week of this cold I made the determination that the winter coat with which I'd been making do in New York wouldn't cut it, and with my grandmother's permission I raided the standing closet in the back room. There to my amazement I found a green *telogreyka*, literally "body warmer." I had seen them in old photos of Soviet workers, including in the Gulag—they were work jackets with a green outer lining stuffed with cotton wool batting. Most important, they were warm. Uncle Lev must have gotten one while working at an oil field. And it must have been when he was a younger, more robust man, because when I tried it on it fit me perfectly. I now had a winter jacket, albeit one in a somewhat hipsterish vein. There was also a red hiking backpack with the word СПОРТ on the back into which I could, with some creative arranging, fit all my hockey stuff. I discarded my Ikea bag and from there on out made my way to hockey with a nice red Soviet backpack.

Soon I was going to hockey a lot. Our team was getting badly beaten by the white team each Wednesday and Friday, and yet I couldn't get enough. I was dazzled by the white team. They were not, individually, superskilled players, but they had played together a long time and they knew how to use the large ice surface. Their breakout (from the defensive zone) was different from anything I had ever seen. Growing up, our breakouts had been simple: as the defenseman got the puck down low, the wings waited near the blue line, and if they were open, they received the first pass, which they redirected either to the center or up the boards; if the wings were covered, the center looped back toward the goal and received a short pass from the defenseman and tried to go from there. The white team played a longer game: they sent their wings to the opposite blue line and then had them curl back toward the puck; the defenseman rifled the puck to the wing coming back, and the wing redirected it to the center coming out of the zone. It was in certain ways the same play—the defenseman passed to the wing, who passed to the center—and in this variation the center received the puck just a few feet farther along than in the breakout I was accustomed to. But both the players and the puck traveled a greater distance, and this in itself was valuable, as it stretched the defense and made the ensuing attack more difficult to defend. And it required a skill in passing—both in making passes and in receiving them—that was remarkable. With one exception—a pudgy young forward named Alyosha—the white players were not fast, but every single one of them was a good passer. Alyosha played with Fedya, whom I had met on my very first day and who I'd since learned was the owner of a small chain of restaurants in the city center, and consequently a man who had to deal with all sorts of criminal and semi-criminal organizations. Fedya had a preternatural sense of where everyone was. Perhaps he had developed it while looking out for the mob. Now he used it to deliver the puck to Alyosha quietly, swiftly, and with deadly accuracy. Then Alyosha scored. We were powerless to stop them.

But maybe I could stop them, I thought, if I could just get better. Every time someone mentioned a different skate, provided that it was in the evening, I would go. "There's a game on Saturday nights near the Kyrgyzia movie theater," one of our defensemen, Ilya, said one day. "Three hundred rubles. Want to come?" I did. It was way out on the edge of the city, at the last stop on the yellow line, just past the movie theater, and the locker room was a little shed in the parking lot. There weren't any showers. But the ice was good, the price was half what we paid at Olympic Stadium, and the guys were friendly—they were simpler, poorer, and some of them had gold teeth. They laughed a lot, looked forward to heading for their dachas (even in the dead of winter) and to drinking some beer. After I found this game, I also found a third, on Mondays: it was at the Institute of Physical Culture, which I later learned was the birthplace of Soviet hockey; the rink was decrepit, with poor heating in the locker rooms, and on the ice a gulley several inches wide along the boards, where if the puck fell in you had to stand there and fish it out. I didn't care. I wanted more hockey. Soon I was playing six nights a week. The puck began to stick to my blade. The ice came to seem a more natural place to be than the ground.

Traveling all over to play hockey, I saw the strangest things. Once you left the center of the city—which, to be sure, had its own strangenesses—but once you escaped the immediate vicinity of the Kremlin, it was as if civilization fell away. Or rather it was as if some other civilization—the Soviet one—had come here, like the glaciers of the Ice Age, and erected its massive apartment towers, twelve and sixteen stories high, some of them the length of an entire block, some of them so long that the builders had slightly curved them, as if taking into account the curvature of the Earth. And then, like the glaciers, this Soviet civilization retreated. Now a new civilization had taken over these decrepit apartment blocks and erected its own monuments: car garages, giant ugly shopping malls, horrible mazelike markets the size of airports. But also, to make up for all that: hockey rinks. For one skate, on Sundays, I had to take the subway as far as it would go, get on a crowded trolleybus, walk through a semi-apocalyptic landscape along a raised highway and a massive aboveground gas line, before finally arriving at the rink, which was nestled between some apartment blocks as if it were a secret.

There were streets out here, and sidewalks, but most people and cars ignored them. All the spaces between the apartment blocks had been converted into streets. If it was not a house, it was a street; if not a street, then a house. That was all.

Going out into the exurbs like this—riding the metro to its last stops, transferring to a bus, and still having to walk through a barren landscape—was revelatory. This is how most of the people in the city lived. The distances were unbelievable. No wonder they were always in such a lousy mood.

I never felt unsafe when going out to these places, though there were always some drunk people hanging around, and occasionally I'd see gangs of teens looking for trouble. I was still a little skittish from getting hit in the face with a gun. But for one thing, the guy who'd hit me with a gun had jumped out of a black Mercedes SUV, and there weren't a lot of those rolling through the courtyards and onto the sidewalks of outer Moscow; out here you got more of a taste of what Russian auto manufacturing had been up to (mostly it was making cars that looked like Hyundais and cheap compact Fords). And for another thing, I had a hockey stick in my hands and I knew how to use it. So I kept going, and playing, and getting better.

Even so, we couldn't beat the white team. There were just so many of them, and no matter how fast I got, the puck was always faster. It didn't help that my team sucked. I remember one time during this period—I was probably in the best shape of my hockey life postcollege—when I got the puck in the neutral zone and saw that Grisha was on his way. I sent the puck against the boards, sidestepped Grisha, and picked the puck up again on the other side; but now Grisha's partner, Sasha, the most violent person on their team (Grisha was merely the most dirty), was coming at me. There was no escaping this one; just before he made contact, I managed to slip the puck through his legs to my right wing, Anton, who was charging beside me. Sasha clobbered me to the ice but Anton was in alone. Then he blew it. He chugged in, awkwardly hugging the puck, and as the goalie went down, shot it over the net.

"What the fuck d'you do that for?" Oleg, my left wing, asked him when we were back on the bench.

"I was trying to get it over him," said Anton.

"You just have to hit the net, you asshole."

"I was trying! And where were you? Andrei was getting fucked over there and where were you?"

"Fuck you," said Oleg.

And so on. They always yelled at each other, never at me. And of course we lost again.

Walking to hockey in the cold, my breath visible before me, I thought about money. I had never not thought about money, but until now it had been in the nature of a game: Could I make do on $25,000 in New York? What about $22,000? And so on. But it had never seemed like a crime on my part that I didn't have money. Now it did. If I could only buy out my brother's share of the apartment, my grandmother wouldn't have to move. But there was no way I could get my hands on that much money, and it was just a matter of time before he kicked her out.

At hockey—my original hockey, where we kept getting whipped by the white team—the guys talked about money. I tried to follow their conversation in case it yielded useful advice. This was not easy. I had grown up speaking Russian with my parents, I'd been in the country speaking nothing but Russian for three months, and still I had trouble keeping up. The problem was their cursing. They did not merely curse; they *replaced* ordinary words with curses. Verbs were the most common victims. "I've been taking my rubles and cunting them across the border," Tolya said once. "They fuck there for a while, and I cock them back here again." I think Tolya was describing a simple currency maneuver, changing rubles to euros to take advantage of the faltering ruble. But I couldn't be sure.

With the exception of Sergei, our goalie, who drove an old Russian car and hardly spoke in the locker room, the hockey guys all worked in some kind of business. Oleg, my left wing, owned property that he leased out; Anton, my right wing, was a corporate lawyer; Tolya was a banker; Vanya owned a sugar factory; and Ilya was CEO of an agricultural concern. They drove expensive German cars. But they were not like Dima's friends—they were cruder, less educated, and they were not already spiritually half in the West. They were Russian, they had made their money in Russia, and they were going to die Russians, even if they died in a house they'd bought on the southern coast of Spain.

The guys traveled a lot, and not just to fuck rubles. They knew the flight schedule from Moscow to Frankfurt as well as businessmen in Boston know the Delta shuttle schedule to New York. But they were not under the illusion that they belonged anywhere but where they were.

"Frankfurt is a fucking airport," Tolya said. "I like to get there early for my flights and fuck a beer or two."

"Frankfurt is nice, but have you been to Istanbul?" said Vanya. "I fucked through there on my way to Dubai last year and I just cocked out. The fucking Turks! I was ashamed, to be honest. You'd be cunted to find a hotel in Russia with furniture as nice as they had at this fucking airport."

"Yes," said Anton. "That's what happens when half of every dollar doesn't get cunted. You can fuck something nice."

There were so few actual words that sometimes the guys themselves got confused. "Everything in Germany is cunted," Vanya said at one point. My understanding was that "cunted" usually meant "bad," but the way Vanya said it, drawing it out, "cuuunted," like he was impressed, left room for interpretation.

"You mean good cunted or bad cunted?" Anton asked.

"Good cunted!" Vanya said. He thought about it for a second and added: "If I'd said things in Russia were cunted, that would mean bad."

Everybody laughed.

"What do you say, Seryoga?" Ilya addressed our goalie, Sergei. He was putting on his red CCCP goalie shirt. "In the USSR things were different, no?"

Sergei smiled. "W-w-well yeah," he said. "Things were stable. You guys wouldn't have to worry about cunting your rubles. You could sleep well at night and think about hockey."

"You're right," said Tolya, standing up. "It's time to play some hockey."

We went out and played and lost, 8 to 1.

There was no way I'd ever earn enough money to buy Dima out. A hundred and fifty thousand dollars was a hundred and fifty PMOOC classes—it would take me twenty years. Even if I got a real professor job with a real professor salary I'd be making only about sixty or seventy grand a year. If I miraculously saved half my salary it would still take five years. By then it would be too late.

Still, getting an academic job wouldn't hurt. A couple of times a week there was a lecture or reading by a writer or scholar at a bookstore/bar called Bilingua, and I started attending these. I listened to talks on the use of Pushkin in Soviet propaganda; the concept of "Ukraine" in nineteenth-century Russian thought; and the "indigenization" campaign in the Soviet ethnic republics in the 1920s. All of it was interesting, and though nothing was quite up my alley, I felt like there might be some kernel of a project for me to pick up. One evening I came home from a lecture—they were always at six, i.e., when my grandmother became most restless—to find that she was gone. Her slippers were by the door, her coat was not on the rack, there was no note on the kitchen table. She had just up and left.

This was not totally without precedent. My grandmother still did her own grocery shopping, though with the onset of the cold she was more likely to ask me to do it. She would occasionally go for a walk in the neighborhood by herself. A few times I had returned from the Coffee Grind to find her gone, and yet she had returned safely. But it had not been her practice to leave by herself during the evenings. As I was thinking this through I got a call from Emma Abramovna. "Andrei," she said, "is Seva there?" My grandmother had told Emma Abramovna that she was coming over. But she was supposed to have been there an hour ago. It was not like my grandmother to be late.

I hung up in a panic, put my telogreyka back on, and rushed outside. I ran down to Tsvetnoi Boulevard, which was on the way to Emma Abramovna's, in case my grandmother had failed to hail a car and just started walking. Nothing. I ran back to Clean Ponds in case she had started walking in the wrong direction: nothing. I even ran down to the police station on Sretenka, where I was greeted by a fresh-faced young cop who was obviously perplexed by my Gulag coat—the only other person I'd seen wearing one like it was the guy who ate from our dumpster—but nonetheless took my number and said they'd call me if they found a confused elderly lady in the neighborhood. Eventually I decided that the best place for me to be was at home, in case she called, and about twenty minutes after I returned I heard her key scratching at the door. I ran out and found my grandmother half frozen to death and frightened. She had hailed a cab, she told me, as I covered her with a blanket and gave her hot tea, but there had been a lot of traffic, and the driver had left the usual route to Emma Abramovna's. My grandmother found that she did not remember the address. They got hopelessly lost and drove around central Moscow for a while. Finally she gave up, and the driver started heading back in this direction. She had caught an actual taxi, a rarity in Moscow and significantly more expensive than an ordinary private car, and she saw that the meter was approaching a thousand rubles. "But we never reached our destination," she said to the driver.

"That's not my fault," he said. The ride to Emma Abramovna's usually cost one hundred rubles, and my grandmother had only five hundred with her. She told this to the driver, who told her to get out. She knew how to get home from there, but it was almost a mile, and it was cold. As she told this story Emma Abramovna called and my little grandmother picked up the phone and started telling her what happened. Then she became exhausted and said she'd call her back. When she got off the phone, she began to cry. She sat in her chair at the kitchen table, cradling the phone receiver, and cried.

After that I stopped attending the lectures at Bilingua. I could see them some other time. If my grandmother wanted to go to Emma Abramovna's, I went along. I even cut down a little bit on my hockey playing, though the games at Olympic Stadium were late enough at night that they never interfered with something my grandmother and I might be doing.

Of course we kept losing to the white team, and I felt increasingly frustrated. During one game not long after my grandmother's terrible adventure, I got the puck from Oleg at the top of the slot. I should have taken a wrist shot but I was feeling angry. I wound up for a slap shot instead. When my stick hit the ice it broke in half. The top half stayed in my hands, the bottom half went flying into the corner, and the puck dribbled feebly toward the goal. Anton loaned me his stick for the remainder of the game. In the locker room afterward he asked if I wanted to cut the stick down so it was my size and keep it. I did not like the lie on his blade but a new stick would cost $150. "Yes," I said. "Thank you." And from then on I played with Anton's shitty stick.

2.

I EXPAND MY SOCIAL CIRCLE

I WENT ACROSS the hall once in a while to have a beer with the soldiers, but I never went out with them again after the incident at Teatr, and in general my social life was pretty barren. Periodically, Dima's friend Maxim invited me to a party or art opening. I never went. I knew that if I went out with that crowd there would always come a moment when I would be called upon to chip in fifty dollars for a bar or restaurant tab, and that it would mean I wouldn't be able to go to the Coffee Grind for a week. Also, I was embarrassed about trying to kiss Elena. So I stayed home.

I was perplexed by the hockey guys. That they rarely exchanged pleasantries or smiled was now something I was accustomed to—Vanya once tried to smile at me, as a way of making me feel at home, and instead resembled a wolf flashing his teeth. But it was odd that they never wanted to have a beer. In America it was traditional to have some beers in the locker room after a skate, even if you didn't know the people you were skating with; if you played with guys for a while, you'd eventually go and drink at a bar and learn things about them. In Russia, where you could sometimes end up drinking with people you just met on the street, I figured we'd be having beers in no time. But it never happened. One evening I decided to force the issue and brought some beers with me, to see if anyone wanted one. All the guys politely declined, and I carried the beers home with me like an idiot.

Still, I noticed that my linemates, Anton and Oleg, had begun staying in the locker room later and later, taking their time and chatting after getting dressed. They were funny guys. Anton was probably the worst player on our team—a poor skater, he also had a shoulder injury that caused him to keep only one hand on his stick most of the time—but he was a garrulous presence in the locker room and had been on the team a long time. He drove a large black Mercedes to the arena. Oleg was a different story: he was a talented player, tall and rangy, with a terrific slap shot. But he was lazy. If the puck wasn't right there for him, he declined to skate for it; then he would come to the bench to complain. This was not my brand of hockey. And it was possible that I had been put on a line with Anton and Oleg because no one else wanted to play with them. In any case, my line it was.

I gradually learned their stories. Anton was just under forty. He had a math degree from one of the top Moscow universities; if he'd graduated a few years earlier, he'd have gone into one of the research institutes, like Uncle Lev, and then spent years trying to figure out how to escape. Instead he went straight into business. He and some programmer friends created a piece of workflow software they thought might be useful for human resources departments, but this went nowhere; then they made a video game, which went better. The legal environment for Russian business in the 1990s was so complex that Anton started taking law classes at night, in part to keep himself and his partners out of trouble. Eventually he had enough credits for a law degree, and with his help the company pivoted out of the volatile (and dangerous, even in video games) retail environment and into legal services. For over a decade now he'd been making a good living providing legal advice to new Russian businesses; one of their most popular services was setting up offshore shell companies to avoid onerous (or any) Russian taxes.

Oleg had a more exciting history. He was a few years younger than Anton and was from a humbler background, so had not had the wherewithal to avoid the army; as a fairly bright young man, though, he'd done his service in the Far East as a radar operator, monitoring American signals traffic. This was considered prestigious and intellectual, and when he got out he was offered work at the KGB and a spot at a top university for diplomats (with ties to the KGB). That wasn't Oleg's bag, and he decided instead to go into business. His first scheme was to arbitrage the limited hours that liquor stores were open during

Gorbachev's anti-alcohol campaign. Young Oleg bought up cheap wine at the liquor store in the evening and then headed to the same store early in the morning the next day to sell it at a markup to winos who were already in line, waiting for the store to open. Having thus accumulated some capital, he invested it, after the USSR collapsed, in an old car that he drove to Ukraine to buy cheap cigarettes, which he brought back to Moscow to sell. He'd fill the entire trunk, then sell them on the street or to middlemen, all the while hoping he didn't get pulled over by the police, who would need to be bribed. This was hard work, but it paid well and eventually Oleg had enough money and contacts to buy, very cheaply, ninety-nine-year leases on two commercial properties in central Moscow. Now he rented them out to foreign banks—a European bank on Tverskaya and, incredibly, the HSBC where my grandmother and I deposited the soldiers' rent. He had revenue of about $25,000 a month and very few expenses and basically just hung out all day and took people to lunch.

Oleg and his wife and young son lived on the Rublevka highway, an elite section on the outskirts of the city where a lot of government officials, including Putin, also lived, mostly in large houses. Anton lived with his father and a teenage son in the old family apartment near Moscow University. He had another son, who lived with the son's mother in Spain; he visited them frequently. Oleg had a summer house in Spain. They often talked about how they would figure out a way to see each other over the summer, when they both planned on being in Spain.

Oleg was very nervous about the financial crisis, and occasionally asked me if I had any insight into how his bank tenants were viewed in the West. "Are people saying they'll pull through this thing?" he would ask, to which I would say, "I have no idea," and he would nod ruefully, as if, yes, I was right, no one really had any idea.

One night after hockey, Oleg suggested the three of us go out. I immediately agreed. I thought we'd go somewhere and have some beers finally, but instead we went to one of the expensive cafés along Sretenka and Anton and Oleg both ordered fruit juices. It turned out the reason no one ever had any beers was that there was a de facto zero tolerance policy for drunk driving. If you had even the bare minimum of a whiff of beer on your breath, you'd get shaken down for a serious fine. But also, these guys, when they drank, they drank a lot. "When I drink," said Oleg, "I tend to drink for several days. So I try not to drink."

But mostly, of course, we talked about money. "So listen," said Oleg. "How much is a house in America?"

I told him it depended on the location.

"Could I get something nice for a lemon?" A "lemon" was a million dollars.

"Yes," I said. "Definitely."

This pleased Oleg.

"You know what I'd do?" said Anton. "I'd get a small house in a small town and use it as a base and just go everywhere on my motorcycle." Anton, it turned out, loved traveling by motorcycle. He'd traversed all of Europe and parts of South America on one. "I'd come back to the house, get some sleep, and then go out again," he said.

"So how much is a little house?" Oleg asked me.

"It depends."

"Could Anton get one for fifty things?" A "thing" was a thousand dollars.

"No," I said. "But he could get something for one hundred fifty."

"How about New York?" said Oleg. "What's commercial property like?"

"Expensive," I said, guessing.

"What if I wanted to buy a ground floor to rent it out?" asked Oleg.

"Like your banks?"

"Yes."

"I don't know." I had no idea. "We could look it up. But in Manhattan, my guess would be five million."

"For just the ground floor?"

"I don't know if you could buy only the ground floor. But if you could, then yes, something like that."

"Even now?" He meant with the financial crisis.

"Even now," I said. To the best of my knowledge, Manhattan was still expensive.

Oleg took this in. Five million was clearly more money than he had. And it turned out there was a deeper reason he was asking these questions. "Motherfucker," he said now. "My Europeans said they're leaving." HSBC was staying but the European bank on Tverskaya was pulling up stakes. Oleg was in the process of searching for a new tenant. "If I don't find another tenant soon," he said, "I'll be cunted."

"Don't worry," said Anton. "Something will turn up."

"Yeah, probably," said Oleg, though he looked worried.

The guys had another round of fruit juices, and then we headed home.

We were getting into December and the semester was winding down. Jeff, the professor, liked to add a book at the end of the syllabus that was from the twentieth century or later, to try to bring things into the modern era. For this semester he assigned Shalamov's *Kolyma Tales*.

I had not read them. I had taken an entire seminar on Solzhenitsyn in grad school and by the end of it I had had my fill of the camps. It was as much a reaction to my fellow students, who became so melodramatic when discussing the Gulag, as it was to Solzhenitsyn, who seemed to be yelling all the time. I couldn't take either of them.

At least I understood why Solzhenitsyn was yelling. But why were my fellow grad students so sad? *We* weren't in the Gulag. You'd think this realization would have made them happy.

"Why such a long face?" I finally said one time as Fishman was going on and on about how terrible the camps were. "We're in New York. Look outside!"

"It's important to bear witness to this suffering," said Fishman. "It's the least we can do."

So I was, I thought, done with the Gulag and hesitant to start in on Shalamov. But almost the first thing I learned about him—from an edition of his memoirs I found at the bookstore under the strip club—was that he hated Solzhenitsyn. This was encouraging. He had, it turned out, a different vision of the camps. He wasn't bitter about them. He did not seek vengeance in this life for the misfortunes that had befallen him, in part because he knew that many of the men who had harmed him in the camps had themselves been harmed much worse by others—they had been shot, or tortured, or beaten to death, just as they had beaten others to death. He had no interest in preaching about the meaning of his time in the camps. But he did want to record it. From this, people could draw their own conclusions. You might say that Shalamov had a touching belief in the power of art.

I had Shalamov on the table, then, when my grandmother came into the kitchen and asked me what I was reading. I showed her the book.

"Shalamov," she said sadly. "Yes."

She sat down across from me.

"Klavdia Giorgievna knew him," she said.

I had never heard of a Klavdia Giorgievna but somehow I figured it out. "Aunt Klava?" I said.

"Yes. She was in Kazakhstan."

"I didn't know that," I said. I had not known that.

"She wasn't anyone's aunt, of course," said my grandmother.

"What?"

"I told people she was my aunt. From Pereyaslavl'. I even told Yolka that."

This was correct. Aunt Klava, who had lived in the apartment when my mother was growing up, had died before my parents were married, so I'd heard very little about her. My understanding was that she'd survived the war in Ukraine and then come to Moscow alone.

"Her husband was a big Hungarian communist," my grandmother said now. "He came to build Communism. They gave him this apartment. Then they arrested him. And Klavdia Giorgievna too. He died, but she survived. And then she came back.

"We were already living here. With Yolka. She came back and I didn't know what to do. It had been her apartment."

Somehow I had never thought about the fact that for my grandmother to receive a Stalin apartment, someone else had to lose it.

"So we agreed that I'd keep the apartment but she could live here in the meantime. She lived in your room and helped me with Yolka. She was a wonderful woman, a doctor."

"I didn't know," I said.

"No one knew. I didn't even tell Yelochka. I didn't want her to have to lie to people. And then when it no longer mattered it was too late."

My grandmother played with the little iron saltcellar on the table.

"I sometimes think I should have moved out then and there," she said. "The minute she showed up, I should have left. Andryush, what do you think?"

What did *I* think? Who cares what I thought? And yet I had noticed this happening more and more—my grandmother treating me like someone who could be appealed to for moral guidance.

"I don't know," I said. I was still taking in the news about Aunt Klava. "You also needed somewhere to live."

"That's true."

"And . . ." I began, thinking of what to say. A whole ethics had grown up around Stalinism that was, at times, hard to parse. Solzhenitsyn, who had suffered so mildly in the camps, had declared the principle "Do not live a lie," meaning, "Do not participate in the deceptions of the regime." This would certainly include taking an apartment from Stalin for your work on a propaganda film and staying in it after the repressed former owner returned. My grandmother had lived a lie. But what did Solzhenitsyn do? He proclaimed his principle; he won the Nobel Prize; then in his later years he cozied up to Putin, surrendering in one widely televised smile (Putin came to visit him) the moral authority it had taken him fifty years to build.

I had been reading Shalamov. What would Shalamov say? Shalamov saw things differently from Solzhenitsyn. He saw them doubly, ambivalently. He thought Solzhenitsyn was a windbag. Physical pain, hunger, and bitter cold: these could not be "overcome" by the spirit. Nor did the world divide neatly, as it did for Solzhenitsyn, between friends and enemies of the regime. For Shalamov, in the camps there were people who helped him and there were people who brought him harm (who beat him, stole his food, ratted him out), but the majority of the people he encountered did neither. They were just, like him, trying to survive. There was great brutality in the camps, and very little heroism. In his memoirs he told a remarkable story about learning, at one of the darkest moments of his camp life, that his sister-in-law, Asya, with whom he was close, was in a nearby camp. Shalamov was in the hospital with dysentery, and one of the doctors wanted to know if he wished to send Asya a message. Only half alive, Shalamov scribbled her a short and unsentimental note. "Asya," it said, "I'm very sick. Send some tobacco." That was all. Shalamov clearly remembered this with shame, but also with understanding: he was weak, on the edge of death, and had been reduced to a bare animal existence. There was no great lesson in this, except that in certain conditions a man quickly ceases to be a man.

It was nothing personal, as the saying goes. Just the twentieth century. I now wondered if, having learned this fact, I was under an obligation to contact Aunt Klava's relatives and try to return the apartment to them. But I put it out of my mind. My grandmother had discharged the debt when she housed Aunt Klava. At least, as far as such debts could be discharged.

So I did not know what to say to my grandmother. She had lived a lie but she had done so alone and in silence, in order that no one else should have to live it as well. To me this was courageous. But that her conscience still worried her, that it was, maybe, part of what animated her and kept her alive—that was not something I should try to eliminate. Though at the same time it was OK for me to try.

"You earned this apartment," I said. "You earned it by working on that movie. And when Aunt Klava came back, you opened your door to her."

"Yes," my grandmother reluctantly agreed.

"Not a lot of people would have done that," I ventured. People released from the camps often did not have permission to return to Moscow, and certainly not to move back into their old apartments. Aunt Klava was probably breaking the law by coming back, and my grandmother protected her.

"That's true," said my grandmother. "Unfortunately," she said with certainty, "that's true."

135

Now she looked sad again, but only in her usual way.

"You see, Andryushik," she said, "all my friends have died. All my relatives have died. I am all alone."

"You're not entirely alone," I said.

"No," she insisted. "I am."

It was weird. After conversations like this, and at other times—while we were watching the nightly news together, or playing anagrams, or just sipping tea after lunch—I felt that she had accepted my presence there, however finite, as a real and solid thing. It was rarely something in particular that I did for her that she appreciated; it was just my showing up. When I would get dressed to go to the Coffee Grind, or out for some groceries, she never failed to express admiration. "Andryush, I'm so impressed with you," she'd say. "You are so tall."

I was and am barely five foot seven. But my grandmother was now so tiny, I must have looked tall to her. Or so she said.

One day I went out to the so-called market and bought a bunch of groceries; since you had to pay for a plastic bag I always brought my Labyrinth bookstore tote bag with me, and on this occasion I had filled it to the brim with clementines, potatoes, sushki, and my grandmother's favorite poppy-seed pie. While doing the shopping I had developed an overwhelming need to pee, so I set the tote bag down when I came home, shuffled off my sneakers, and ran to the toilet. When I eventually emerged I saw my grandmother pulling on the handle of the tote with all her might and slowly, slowly dragging it along the floor toward the kitchen. It was an incredible sight. She was an indomitable person. I intercepted her and picked up the bag.

"Are you able to carry all that?" she asked, in awe.

But just as often she could reveal a profound distrust of me. Two incidents stand out. The first took place during a rare visit from Emma Abramovna. She apparently felt bad about my grandmother's aborted attempt to visit her, and also her son Arkady was staying with her for a few days while his wife and daughter were out of town, so she had access to a car, and she decided to come visit us. My grandmother was thrilled and made elaborate preparations, including sitting down with me and asking very seriously whether I thought the old bottle of wine in the fridge was still good enough to drink, and if not, what I thought we should replace it with. I suggested a bottle of Abkhazian white and went out and got it. The day of the visit, my grandmother put out the plates and silverware and her best napkins early in the morning and we ate breakfast at the table in the back room, so as not to disturb them.

Finally lunchtime arrived and with it Emma Abramovna and Arkady. Arkady was in his early fifties, a quiet computer programmer; he spent much of the visit looking at his phone. In any case, the visit was about my grandmother and Emma Abramovna. It went, as the visits between them usually went, with a discussion of Emma Abramovna's children (wonderful!) and my grandmother's grandchildren (neglectful, except for me), their mutual acquaintances (mostly in Israel), and the lousy cold weather. Arkady and I occasionally tried to introduce fresh topics of conversation, with limited success. And then my grandmother—I could practically see this happening—fell into her usual post-lunch funk. "Yes," she said, "yes," and then, before I could stop her, "you see, the thing is, everyone has died. Everyone I know has died. All my relatives, all my friends. They died and left me all alone."

"Come on, Seva," said Emma Abramovna.

"But it's true!" my grandmother insisted.

"I'm still alive," Emma Abramovna said, taking the bait.

"Yes, you, it's true. But who else?"

"How should I know?!" Emma Abramovna cried. "I'm sure there are other people alive besides me!"

"Yes," said my grandmother sadly. "Maybe." And with that, her melancholy filled the room.

After Arkady took Emma Abramovna home, I couldn't help myself.

"Grandma," I said. "You so value Emma Abramovna's friendship. You were so worried whether she'd have a good time. And then she's here and all you talk about is how lonely you are and how depressed you are."

"So?" said my grandmother, looking up at me (I was turning around from doing the dishes, and she was relaxing at the kitchen table—social activity always took the wind out of her). "It's true, isn't it?"

"That's not the point! People don't want to hear how depressed you are!"

"You don't need to yell," she said. Then she stood up, placed her mug of tea in the sink, and left the kitchen. I hadn't been yelling, I didn't think. But I hadn't not been yelling either. I watched her walk to her bedroom and close the door behind her. Why I thought I could change my grandmother's behavior by criticizing it I don't know. What a jerk I was. I went back to doing the dishes.

The other incident occurred about a week later, when my grandmother announced that she was going to attend her annual physical. How annual it was I had no idea, but I was eager to come along. My grandmother complained of many ailments, but none of them ever seemed to stop her from doing anything, and at the same time she kept going to the pharmacy and bringing home medicines to treat them. So I was looking forward to running her list of medicines past a doctor to see if they seemed about right.

I was not disappointed. The doctor was a nice woman in her fifties with her brown hair tied in a bun; she spoke seriously with my grandmother, listened to her breathing and her heart, and generally gave her a clean bill of health. Then she looked at my grandmother's list and said to me, "Are you out of your mind?"

"What?"

"Who made this list? Did you make it?"

"She goes to the pharmacy and comes back with these."

"But half of them are counteractive. Look here, this is a medicine for low blood pressure, and this one is for high blood pressure. She shouldn't be taking both at once!"

My grandmother had apparently been self-medicating, with the help of the local pharmacist.

"What should she take then?"

The doctor went through the fifteen medicines and crossed out ten.

"These are fine," she said. "And no more additions unless they're prescribed by an actual doctor."

I agreed with this approach, and when we got home I threw out all the medicines the doctor had crossed out. My grandmother's faith in the doctor was total—she had brought a box of chocolates with her as a gift, and had laughed at all the doctor's jokes and been immensely grateful for the fifteen minutes of attention she received—so I did not anticipate any problems, nor did I even really think she'd notice. But she noticed right away. "What happened to my medicines?" she said after supper.

"The doctor told us to cut down on the medicines you take," I said. "Here's the new list."

"But what happened to the other ones?" she said.

"I threw them out."

"Why?!"

"So you wouldn't take them by accident! They weren't good for you!"

My grandmother put her head in her hands. "How could you do this to me?" she said. "I needed those medicines." Then: "You don't want me to get better, do you?"

"What?"

"You want me to be sick."

"That's not true!"

"Fine," she said. "I'll be sick." She pursed her lips and, once again, left the kitchen.

I was upset, though this time, at least, I was in the right. And by the next day this whole conversation was forgotten; my grandmother occasionally asked who had crossed out all the medicines on her list, and I told her it was the doctor, and she accepted this. From there on out I tried to make sure she didn't introduce any new medicines on her own. But this incident stuck with me—that she could turn on me so suddenly, with such conviction, was not good. And in the months ahead it would get worse.

3.

I ATTEND A DINNER PARTY

IN A FLURRY of final blog posts on Russian literature—some of them pretty good—my first full PMOOC semester came to an end. I read them over and made individual comments, and by the time the second week of December rolled around I was done.

I had imagined that I'd be back home by now, but as it was I couldn't afford to fly back and there wasn't much reason to. My father and his family were going skiing, I no longer had a place to stay in New York, and no one had invited me to any of the holiday Slavic conferences. So I stuck around. I went back to some of the skates I'd been skipping, and played anagrams with my grandmother.

As I was finishing up the semester, I was rewarded, in a way, by a dinner invitation from a postdoc I knew named Simon. He was in Moscow for the year working on his long-standing project about Czech–Russian cultural relations, and he was having a party, he wrote, in honor of the visit to town of the delightful Alex Fishman. He actually said that—"delightful." Fishman was coming to town over break and Simon was throwing him a dinner party.

Since I'd arrived I had avoided Simon and the rest of the expat academics. They were all in Russia for a reason, with specific goals and projects, whereas I was doing who knows what and living with my grandmother. It wasn't really a conversation I felt like having. This dinner party, however, was a different matter. Whatever else it was, Moscow was my town. I was born here. Fishman didn't get to show up for a visit without having to deal with me. Also, I had to admit, I was lonely.

The evening did not go as planned. My first mistake was arriving an hour late. This was my grandmother's fault. I had spent the day writing the last "narrative" evaluations of my many students. This was one of the perks of the PMOOC, as opposed to a regular old MOOC that you didn't have to pay for; in addition to a grade, you got a narrative evaluation! When I finally got up to go, my grandmother blocked the way and asked if I would play anagrams with her. "We already played today," I said. This was true. We'd played after lunch.

"We did?" said my grandmother. She looked, standing in the hallway in her pink robe, a pen and piece of scrap paper already in her hand, terribly disappointed. I couldn't do it to her.

"OK," I said. "One quick game."

We ended up playing four games—as usual, a total slaughter—and then I was able to leave.

By the time I arrived, people were already eating, and Fishman, I could tell, had already monopolized the conversation. I could hear him from the front hallway as I came in and took off my shoes and shook Simon's hand. Simon's apartment was in a compound owned by the Czech embassy, and it was recently refurbished and was on the twelfth floor, with a great view of Triumphal Square and the Mayakovsky monument. He escorted me to the kitchen so I could put the bagful of beers I'd brought—there was no such thing as a six-pack in Russia—into the fridge and take one for myself. (I noticed that someone else had brought a superior brand of beer, but it would be gauche at least at first not to drink the inferior Russian beer that I'd brought, so I took that.) "Listen," said Simon quietly as I opened my beer, "are you and Alex cool?"

I was surprised. I thought I had managed to keep my hatred of Fishman pretty much to myself. I resolved to continue doing so. "Sure," I said. "Why?"

Now I saw that it was Simon's turn to be surprised. He apparently thought I knew something that I did not know. And he had inadvertently half revealed it to me.

"Why?" I said again.

Very reluctantly Simon said, "Because of Sarah?"

"Sarah," I repeated, nodding as if I knew what he meant. And then I did know. Of course. That's who she was seeing; that's who was taking all those photos. If I hadn't mentally muted Fishman's Facebook posts after his obnoxious photo of Princeton, I'd have figured it out sooner. "Well," I said now. "That's nice. For them." I had no right to be angry— they were grown-ups, I was living in Moscow, and anyway Sarah had dumped me—and I did not want to ruin Simon's party. He was a good guy, when you came down to it. But I followed him out into the dining room in a bit of a daze.

There were about ten people sitting around a large rectangular glass table and drinking wine. The lights were dimmed and the furniture was modern (though, I suspect, Czech), and if you couldn't see the Maya-kovsky statue out the window you'd have thought you were in a condo in midtown Manhattan. I recognized half the people at the table from various conferences and lectures, as well as Fishman, of course, who had grown a hipster beard since last I saw him and now gave me a some-what wary nod, before continuing to hold forth on his favorite topic, that is to say, Fishman himself. The one notable thing about Fishman on this occasion, aside from the fact that he was wearing a very expen-sive shirt, was the pretty girl sitting next to him. I didn't catch every-one's name as I was hurriedly introduced, but I caught hers—Yulia. By the way she dressed and said hello, I could tell she was Russian. How did she know Fishman?

Simon had made a big vat of spaghetti and I was able to hide behind a mound of it as I tried to adjust, first, to the thought that Fishman was sleeping with Sarah, and next to being around people who were neither profanity-spewing Russian hockey players nor my grandmother. I had thought it would be annoying but—whenever Fishman stopped talking for a minute—I found to my surprise that it was not annoying. It was nice. The group was a mix of Russians and Americans, all of them grad students or post-docs. Some of the stuff they were working on was very interesting—one of the Russians was writing a biography of the contro-versial formalist critic Viktor Shklovsky. Another was studying the Ma-rina Tsvetaeva archive at the NKVD. These were sweet, earnest people who had gone into academia because they cared about knowledge. The Americans among them brought news of the financial crisis: there was talk at some of the universities of doing away with Slavic departments altogether, merging them into the history or literature departments, and cutting staff—enrollment was already down, no one wanted to learn Russian anymore, and now money was tight. I felt a surge of warmth toward my fellow Slavicists. I spent so much time on Facebook being envious of their successes, their plum posts or brilliant futures, but they were good people! That they were now all stuck in a demeaning pursuit of professional advancement, and in a shrinking field to boot, was not their fault. They had gone into this with the purest motives. Even Fishman, maybe. Though maybe not.

Why did this happen to people? All of us could have pursued more lucrative careers. There were people in our field who had left academia and prospered. Aaron Bloom had dropped out of our program after two years and gone to law school and was now an intellectual property attorney in Washington, D.C.; he was making hundreds of thousands of dollars a year. Or Eugene Priglashovkin, an émigré like me and Fishman, who had thought one of his research topics—the post-Soviet existence of a former Gulag town in Siberia—was so interesting that he made a documentary about it. Now he was in Hollywood directing actual films. Reports of Priglashovkin's new life in Los Angeles filled conversations in the Slavic department like rumors of another world. Priglashovkin was dating an actress. Priglashovkin went to a party at Leonardo DiCaprio's! Fishman himself, actually, when I ran into him in the library the year before, had pulled me over to a computer and showed me Priglashovkin's house on Zillow.com. It had been bought for $2.2 million. By Priglashovkin.

And yet the people in this room had stuck it out! And I too had stuck it out! We might have been frustrated, thwarted, bitter, poor, but at least we still had the dream. The dream of scholarship, of teaching, of learning, of the advancement of human knowledge. Anyone who stayed in academia for this long was my brother, I thought to myself as I put another serving of spaghetti on my plate. Hell, even Fishman.

But Fishman was resolved not to allow me these generous thoughts— not about him, not about anyone. He wouldn't stop talking, and the more he talked, the more I felt like I was being pulled back into all the pettiness of academia, like Fishman was magically conjuring it by sheer force of will.

"I mean," he was saying now, "the thing to do is get an appointment in Slavic and then start your own 'research center.' Those things are the biggest scams going. But it makes the university feel like it's engaging in contemporary debates." My mother had worked at a research center. It was a precarious existence, but hardly a scam.

Fishman! Sarah wasn't my girlfriend anymore, obviously. But it was also the case that Fishman had a thing for other people's girlfriends. It was something he talked about, back when we'd still been friends, during our first year in the department. During our second year this predilection caused everyone a lot of trouble: Fishman, at a party, made out with the drunk visiting girlfriend of a first-year student named Jake, who was from Wisconsin. This was one of the nice things about Slavic grad school—people came from all over the place, it wasn't just the children of Russian immigrants. And I don't know how someone not from Wisconsin would have handled it, but Jake, who was a head taller than Fishman, grabbed him by the collar without saying a word and flung him down on the floor and left the party, with his remorseful and now slightly less drunk girlfriend trailing behind. All this would have been unfortunate and upsetting, but still within the bounds of the sort of stuff that happens at grad school, had Fishman not then complained to the department about the "physical assault," saying that he now felt "unsafe" at school with poor Jake. My adviser was then head of the department, and he tried his best to talk Fishman into dropping the whole thing. "As long as you stay out of people's relationships," my adviser said to him, "you'll be perfectly safe." But Fishman was adamant—it was a matter of principle, he said—and took his case to the university disciplinary board. As a result, Jake was kicked out of school for a year, and my adviser was officially rebuked by the university for not responding more promptly to a student's concerns about his physical safety. My adviser took the whole thing philosophically—"I'll tell you what creates an unsafe environment—that rat Fishman!"—and at the end of the year resigned from his position as department head, which in a way he was all too happy to have the excuse to do. But Jake did not return after his enforced sabbatical. I was still friends with him on Facebook, but he didn't post there very often.

So that was Fishman. Ever since the Jake incident I kept waiting for him to be punished, to get his comeuppance from the just and vengeful God of Slavic Studies, but it just never seemed to happen. There were a few jobs that he didn't get, to be sure, because at the end of the day you could only snow so many people with your fashionable work on digitizing the Gulag, but he always seemed to land on his feet. He had finished his dissertation a year before I did and gone on a Fulbright to Moscow; then he'd started his post-doc at Princeton. He was luxuriating in it now. "It's such a supportive atmosphere," he was saying. "Whether you're new faculty or old faculty, it's all the same—a very collegial place."

I listened to Fishman but stole as many glances as were not obviously inappropriate at the girl next to him. Was it possible that in addition to Sarah, Fishman was also seeing her? For the first few minutes of dinner I tried to convince myself that she wasn't as cute as she seemed. Was she a little too thin, maybe? And her teeth were crooked! But it didn't work. She was cute. She had short black hair and big green eyes and thin shoulders and she held herself very erect, like a Soviet icon. And she was self-conscious about her teeth, so when she laughed at a joke, for example by Fishman, she ducked her head a little so that her teeth weren't showing. It was an endearing gesture. She was clearly connected to Fishman somehow, but how? If Fishman was sleeping with this girl, was I obligated to tell Sarah? No, I would not tell Sarah. But Jesus! Fishman turned to her several times during dinner to say something too quietly for others to hear, and once he even put his hand on her arm. Fishman was always putting his hands on people in a conspiratorial manner. What an asshole.

"Princeton, Princeton, Princeton," said Fishman, to a group of people who would have been willing to gnaw off their left arms if, by reducing themselves in mass, it would enable them to squeeze through that university's heavy oak doors. I kept waiting for one of them to rebel, to throw off the shackles of Fishman: who did he think he was, talking to them like this? Instead, these sweet Russian and American grad students and post-docs lapped it up. One of them asked, of a famous Bakhtin scholar, "What's Caryl Emerson like?"

"Oh," said Fishman, "very collegial. I was just the other day telling her about my new project—she was very supportive. You know, she's really very down to earth."

He said it as if the rest of us thought that Caryl Emerson got around everywhere in a helicopter. Which, in fact, we sort of did.

His latest project, Fishman went on, was a scheme to put something or other from the Lenin Library on the internet. In fact Fishman was in town this week to negotiate with the library for digital rights, though they were being stubborn. "They said, 'Why look at the internet when you can visit the library?'" Most people around the table laughed; Yulia, sitting next to Fishman, did not. Did she hate the internet, love libraries? I loved libraries too! "They're still using a card catalog," continued Fishman. "At a certain point you have to interpret this as being an act of hostility toward knowledge." People nodded. I finished gulping down my beer and retreated to the kitchen for another.

Goddamn Fishman. This was a guy who'd once asked me what the big deal about Lotman was. "He's just a second-rate Barthes, don't you think?" No, I didn't think. Fishman was an idiot.

I decided to start drinking the better beer—a Czech Budweiser, which I had never seen in a can before—and took one out of the fridge and popped it open. Yum—thick and a little sweet, just as I remembered it. I considered bringing a whole bunch with me to the table, but Simon had set up everything so nicely that I didn't want to spoil the view with a mountain of beer cans. At the same time I didn't want to keep sneaking off into the kitchen to fetch beers. I was wearing a blue cardigan with side pockets, pretty deep pockets actually, and I stuck one of the Budweisers into my left pocket. It protruded a little bit, but that was OK; no one was really paying attention to me anyway.

Fishman wasn't just an idiot; he was a dangerous idiot. His parents had come from the Soviet Union, as mine had, and at around the same time. Like many of us, he'd grown up speaking Russian, and like many of us he'd inherited his parents' ambivalence toward the country they'd escaped. Our parents had been so skeptical of Russia, so fearful of the Russians, that they had uprooted their lives, put everything in boxes, and gone to the post office dozens of times to ship their books to America, just so they could get away. But they had also remained bound to Russia by a million ties of memory and habit and affection. They watched Russian movies, shopped at Russian stores, and preferred Russian candy. My father, back in Massachusetts with his American wife and non-Russian-speaking children, now downloaded new Russian TV shows from the internet and watched them for hours as he rode his stationary bike. Whereas we, the children of these émigrés . . . if we were involved in Russia, we were critical of Russia and Russians, somewhat as our parents had been, but also, somehow, not. We did not maintain the same bonds; we did not experience the same attachment. I sometimes remembered Gershom Scholem's accusation against Hannah Arendt during the furor over *Eichmann in Jerusalem,* a book that was deeply critical both of Israel and of the many Jews who had, according to Arendt, been too accommodating to those who wished to exterminate them. Arendt's book was learned and acute, Scholem said. But it lacked *ahavat Israel*—"a love of Israel," a love for her people. The accusation may have been unfair toward Arendt, but I think it was fair to us, to the children of the émigrés. In everything they did, even in the very ferocity of their rejection of Russia, our parents had held on to a love of Russia. Their children had not.

Something about Fishman making fun of the Lenin Library really irked me. Or maybe it was this beautiful girl sitting next to him that irked me. And of course there was the not irrelevant matter of his sleeping with my ex-girlfriend. And maybe too, on top of all that, there was my frustration at this beautiful apartment that Simon lived in all by himself, and at Simon's wonderful career prospects studying Russian-Czech cultural exchange, becoming himself an avatar of cultural exchange—a speaker of both Russian and Czech who lived in a Czech apartment in Moscow, while I lived with my grandmother, in a room still partly filled with Dima's boxes, and no one even responded to the résumés and cover letters I sent anymore, and I no longer expected them to.

Anyway, I returned to the table with my beers. Fishman was now expatiating on his theory of Putin's Russia. "I was just saying to my colleague Richard Sutherland that really the pedagogy around Russia should be focused around totalitarianism. We need to understand totalitarianism. Because the Putin regime is just totalitarianism in a postmodern guise. He's turning the whole country into a Gulag."

Ahh, people said. That's so true.

I couldn't take it anymore.

"Fishman," I said, before I could decide not to, "do you even listen to yourself?"

"What?" said Fishman. He looked at me like he'd forgotten I was there.

"'The people at the Leninka are barbarians. I'm at Princeton. Putin is totalitarian.' Do you listen to yourself?"

"As much as anyone else does," said Fishman, looking directly at me. "I'm my own worst critic, in fact." He was being very cool, whereas I was practically hyperventilating. "But tell me, what is the matter with what I've said?"

"You run down Russia so much! You complain about it and make jokes about it *all the time*. And yet you also profit from it. It's your job to study Russia and yet you seem to have nothing but contempt for it."

"Criticism is not the same as contempt. Criticism is part of a dialogue."

At this point I could still have backed off. I could have let it go. But I had lost my temper. "WHAT HAVE YOU DONE FOR RUSSIA?!" I yelled. I don't know exactly what I meant by this, but what my statement lacked in clarity it made up for in volume. "What have you ever done for Russia, Fishman?"

Fishman looked like he thought I might jump across the table and grab him by the throat. It wouldn't have been the first time Fishman was physically assaulted by someone in our department. I looked down at my hands. They were gripping the edge of the table—including my left hand, which until now had been holding on to the beer in my pocket to make sure it didn't fall out.

"I'm not a social worker, if that's what you mean," Fishman said, regaining his cool. "But I like to think that people aware of my criticism find it tonic. But tell me, what have *you* done for Russia?"

"I don't know," I said. It was a fair question. "Maybe nothing. But I would like to."

"Terrific," said Fishman. "Good luck."

There was a moment of silence. I looked around the table to see where people were at; I half hoped to find everyone staring at Fishman with the disgust that he deserved. They were not. In fact some people were staring at me instead. Yulia was looking at me with what I can only describe as an inscrutable expression, and others were staring at their plates in embarrassment. But their embarrassment, I couldn't help but notice, was not for Fishman. It was for me—a guy who couldn't get a job and came to dinner parties and yelled with little or no provocation at former classmates who had become more successful than he was. And it was hard to disagree with them. I was embarrassed for me too.

I got up to leave. As I did so the Budweiser can finally tipped out of my pocket and onto the floor. We all watched it roll toward the wall and then come to a stop. For a moment I considered pretending that it wasn't mine, but this was impossible. Fishman was laughing. "Why do you have a beer in your pocket, Kaplan?"

I ignored Fishman's question. With what dignity I could muster, I bent over and picked up the can. "Russia is sick," I said, straightening up again. "When someone is sick, they do not need criticism. They need help."

As I said it, I knew that I was quoting someone. But who? Was it Shalamov? Was it Dostoevsky's speech about Pushkin, which we'd read over the Thanksgiving break? I couldn't quite place it.

It was Fishman who figured it out. "'Russia is sick,'" he mimicked me. Then, bursting into a grin: "Wait, Putin says that. You're saying what Putin said!"

"Enough with your Putin!" I yelled. He was right, I realized; the words had sort of bubbled up out of me. But also he was wrong. I said, "Just because Putin said it doesn't mean it's not true."

"Hmm," said Fishman, smiling. Yulia, next to him, continued to look at me with an expression I couldn't quite read.

Anyway, it was time to go. "I'm sorry to disrupt your dinner," I said to Simon, who gave a small cry of acknowledgment. He clearly wished for me to leave.

In the hallway it took me a long time to put on my shoes, and as I did so no one back at the dinner table said a word. I finally hopped out into the hallway with one shoe half on; only in the elevator did I get it on entirely. I had held on to the beer I'd picked up, and in the elevator I opened it. Fizz sprayed out violently and all over the sleeve of my telo-greyka. I must have lost a quarter of the can. But the rest of it I drank as I walked home from Simon's in the cold.

What had I done for Russia? I hadn't done much. I had read many books written in Russian and I had for years taught Russian literature to students—I suppose that was something. But I hadn't really changed anyone's mind about Russia. I had not discovered anything new about Russia. To really do something for Russia, as an academic, would mean coming up with a new interpretation, a new way of seeing, that would change the way people talked about Russia and thought about Russia, and that would change Russia itself. This wasn't impossible. But it wasn't easy and I hadn't yet done anything close.

I spent a miserable night in my room and most of the next day, a Sunday, with my grandmother, trying to forget the whole embarrassing incident. That night I played hockey at the weird rink next to the elevated gas line. On Monday, I received an email from YuSemenova @yandex.ru—Yulia Semenova—Yulia from Saturday night. She had pulled my address from Simon's initial invitation, she said. She was sorry for the imposition, but she was organizing a small discussion of neoliberalism in higher education at the Falanster bookstore in a few weeks, just after the New Year, and if I had time to come she'd be delighted if I could say a few words about the American system. The event was scheduled for 7:00 P.M.; she hoped there'd be a nice crowd.

I was perplexed. What had I said or done to make her think that I would be a good person to address the state of neoliberalism in higher education? Was it that I had caused a ruckus and stolen a beer at Simon's dinner, and she wanted me to cause a ruckus and steal a beer at her discussion? That didn't make any sense. Perhaps she had seen, through the noise of my craziness, a good and loyal heart? It seemed unlikely. But there was only one way to find out. I said I'd be happy to go.

4.

REVELATION

I SPENT New Year's Eve at home, but it was not uneventful.

First, we received in the mail a New Year's greeting from Prime Minister Putin. It was addressed directly to my grandmother. "Dear Seva Efraimovna!" it read. "May you have a wonderful New Year. Our country is grateful for your sacrifices. We will not forget and we will not forgive!"

My grandmother was not taken in. "They can go to hell," she said, and threw out the postcard.

A little while later, as I sat in the kitchen sipping instant coffee and listening to Echo, my grandmother came in and handed me a key.

"Andryush," she said. "I just found this key. Do you know what it's from?"

It was a small, old-style desk or cabinet key, and I figured there couldn't possibly be too many answers to that question. "Let's see," I said. With my grandmother trailing behind me, I went into her room and tried it on the desk drawer, which was already unlocked. Happily, it was not the key. And then I tried it on the standing shelf in her room, which had been locked the entire time I was here, and which now, voilà, opened.

"Hooray!" said my grandmother.

"Did you need something in here?" I asked.

"I don't know!" said my grandmother. "What's in there?"

There were many things. My grandmother's old work papers. Her old photos. Various other documents. And then, above it all, there was an old chocolate box full of letters. They were from my mother to my grandmother, after we emigrated. And then my grandmother's letters to my mother—my father must have sent them back to my grandmother at some point, after my mother died.

I spent all day reading the letters. My mother's were filled with long, lively, not always ecstatic descriptions of our life in America, my childhood, Dima's rebellion, her occasional alienation from my practical father; my grandmother's contained sad evaluations of the home lives of the friends and relatives my mother had left behind. About her own life my grandmother spoke with a kind of hollow bravado. Even in letters designed to assuage her daughter's guilt about leaving her, my grandmother couldn't help but let a note of sadness enter. The winters in Dubna were so drab; the movies that she saw in Moscow disappointed her. And there was an envy or even resentment of Uncle Lev, disguised as wonderment. "He is entirely consumed by his work, he won't even tear himself away from it when we're traveling—when we were in Koktebel last month he started wondering why no one had ever checked for oil there. An amazing person!" This was not sarcastic exactly, but it was a little rueful: my grandmother had chosen a profession that turned out to be implicated in all sorts of political nonsense, and she had had, essentially, to abandon it, whereas Uncle Lev had become a scientist, and, tempted as the Party had been at times to meddle in science, it left its oilmen alone.

Above all, in my grandmother's letters there was a longing to be reunited with her daughter, a feeling that the center of her world had disappeared. The letters were incredibly frequent—as many as one a week for the first few years, and then never less than one a month until the late 1980s, when telephone contact became easier. My mother had a nickname for my grandmother; my grandmother addressed my mother as "my beloved little daughter." And though the letters were sophisticated, ironic, full of conversation about movies they'd seen and books they'd read, they addressed each other with total, unaffected honesty. Though it made perfect sense—my grandmother had raised my mother all alone, through some of the most difficult years of the century—I had had no idea, really, how close they had been. I had no idea how much they had missed each other. There was even talk, as the Soviet Union started falling down around their ears, of my grandmother and Uncle Lev coming to Boston to live. It never happened. Uncle Lev had a security clearance, and even in the final years of the USSR people like that were not allowed to leave. And then my mother died.

"It's my fault, you know, that she left," my grandmother said after reading through a few of the letters herself.

"In what sense?"

We were in my grandmother's room—I on the green armchair next to her bed, she in the bed that turned into a sofa, resting.

"I told her the truth," said my grandmother. "Even when she was a little girl, I told her the truth about this place, about what a terrible country this was. So when she became old enough, she left."

I didn't say anything. My grandmother hadn't told her all the truth—she hadn't revealed the secret of Aunt Klava, for example—but that wasn't the point.

"And it's my fault that she died," my grandmother went on. "When she worked here, they had mandatory mammograms. But not in America. If she had stayed here, they would have caught it in time."

"You don't know that," I said automatically. But now I understood what she had meant all those times she said that my mother had gone to America and died. I had thought it was a statement of two unconnected facts. But my mother had died of breast cancer after a diagnosis that arrived too late. My grandmother had a point.

That evening, I got us a bottle of wine and we drank to the New Year. "It's so nice to have you here with me, Andryushenka," my grandmother said. I was very moved. She called Emma Abramovna to wish her a happy New Year and went to bed early. For my part, I went across the landing to see the soldiers. They were going to a big party later on but for the moment they were having a mini-pre-party at their place.

After we'd had a couple of beers, Howard took me aside.

"Listen," he said, "I need to ask you a favor."

He had met a girl through his customer-reviewed sex worker website and gone over to her place. "I show up, and her mother is there in the kitchen. A very nice lady. We drank tea together and then this girl takes me into her room and fucks me. Can you believe that? I felt like a teenager. It was one of the most erotic experiences I've ever had."

Howard paused. What favor could he possibly have in mind to ask of me?

"I'd like to write her a very good review, but in Russian," said Howard. "If I write it and email it to you, will you check it over so that it doesn't have too many mistakes?"

A few days later, I received some interesting news. My adviser called me on the phone. "*S novym godom!*" he shouted. Happy New Year.

"Thank you," I said.

"I have some sad news," said my adviser. "Frank Miller has died."

Frank Miller was a beloved professor of Russian studies at a place called Watson College. Watson was a small undistinguished liberal arts school located in the far frigid reaches of upstate New York, but it had going for it that an eccentric alumnus, who had made millions manufacturing weapons systems at the height of the Cold War, had endowed a permanent professorship in Russian history and literature. Frank Miller had occupied it with distinction. He was also a close friend of and mentor to my adviser, and when Miller had gone on sabbatical a few years earlier, my adviser had arranged for me to take over his classes. I had done my best, both to teach the classes and stave off depression, and the student evaluations had been good.

"I didn't know he was sick," I said.

"No, he kept it quiet. And it was pretty sudden. Over Thanksgiving he got the news that it was in his liver, and from there it happened really fast."

"That sucks," I said.

"It does suck," said my adviser. "But here's the thing. Get your CV in order. I think they're going to do a search for his replacement and they're going to do it fast. I'm going to tell them they had better look at you."

"OK," I said. "Thank you."

"But also," he went on, "you need to publish something. Everybody's obsessed with publication right now. Has your grandmother told you a lot of cool shit about the USSR?"

"No."

"Well, think of something else, then. You need to get a publication. That'll help you a lot."

It was a strange phone call to get. I had pretty much resigned myself to my new Moscow life, and now here was my adviser pulling me back in the direction of the life I'd had. I wasn't sure how to feel about it. But I updated my CV.

The Falanster bookstore, which was to host the discussion of neoliberalism in higher education, was hard to find. After dropping off my grandmother at Emma Abramovna's, I walked there in the bitter cold and then wandered around the vicinity of the address for about fifteen minutes, going in and out of a courtyard through a big archway and growing increasingly cold and worried that I would miss the event. Why did I still think that just because I knew the address, I'd be able to locate a place, even after all the times this had proved not to be the case?

Finally I asked someone and they pointed me to the archway. Over the generations Russians had taken these old tsarist-era buildings and divided them up in a million different ways, and here was an actual bookstore inside the structure of the archway.

You could tell right away that it was a good bookstore. They had all the academic books from the legendary New Literary Observer, and a terrific journals section. There were no posters of Putin above the cash register, as there were at the bookstore under the strip club on Sretenka, no lurid books on *America's Plan to Steal Our Oil,* no obscure tracts on revealed religion. There were serious books of poetry, philosophy, and political science. And there was a small plaster bust of Karl Marx in the corner, against which was leaning a stack of old journals.

The bookstore was filled with about a dozen people, and I saw Yulia, in a red sweater and brown wool skirt, looking both severe and sexy. She was talking to some dude and didn't appear to see me. Did she forget she'd invited me? I was pretending to study the stacks of books in the middle of the store when I saw a very familiar-looking person enter the space. I had positive associations with him, but where from? He was so decontextualized that for a moment I couldn't figure it out. Then I did. "Sergei!" I said. It was the goalie from my hockey team. He looked up and smiled and came over to me. "What are you doing here?" I asked.

"I'm speaking," he said. "What about you?"

"I'm also speaking." This sounded somehow unconvincing, like I was imitating him, so I added, "Yulia invited me."

"Ah, Yulia," said Sergei. "Well, great." He patted me on the shoulder and moved off to speak to someone who had been trying to get his attention.

"Ah, Yulia," meaning what exactly? I had to put the thought aside as Yulia now came over. "Thank you for coming," she said, putting her hand on my arm momentarily. "Sergei Ivanov"—our goalie!—"is going to give a lecture on his path through contemporary education, but I thought it'd be useful to have a bit of global context, so if you don't mind, I'll introduce you and ask you to say a few words about the American situation, and then I'll introduce Sergei. Does that sound all right?"

"What do you want me to say about the American situation?"

"Just whatever you think. The situation of professors and adjuncts and the job market."

I knew exactly what she meant: the shitty and embarrassing position of adjuncts, the humiliations visited on them and their students by the university, the rise of PMOOCs as the solution that solves nothing. How did she know I'd know all this? Maybe she had talked to Fishman about me. Or maybe she just knew. I wanted to ask but I couldn't think of how to word it, and in any case once she'd explained what she wanted, she left me, moved to the front of the room, and asked everyone to take their seats. Looking around, I saw people in their twenties, many of them with glasses, ratty sweaters, poor posture; they looked a little like the group from dinner the other day but more unkempt—they were grad students who might not actually have been grad students. I liked them all immediately.

"Our first speaker," Yulia said, beautifully, "will be Andrei Kaplan, from New York, where he is an adjunct professor of Russian studies. Andrei?"

I got up and, a little nervously—I would have been nervous in any case, but speaking in front of a group in Russian made it worse—gave a short description of the plight of adjuncts in the United States. My main complaint was inequality: if you won the academic sweepstakes and got a full-time job, you were paid about fifteen thousand dollars a class. If you didn't, you might be paid something more like three thousand. (Or one thousand, for a PMOOC.) This was unfair. There was, in my opinion, no justification for such a huge disparity in payment, especially in institutions that considered themselves models of democracy and liberalism.

I said all this as quickly as I could. People nodded in agreement or understanding and then gave a small round of applause when I finished. Yulia got up, gave me her smile, ducked her head to hide her teeth, and thanked me. I sat down, relieved and happy, and then Yulia introduced Sergei.

"As s-s-some of you know," Sergei began, with a little stutter, "I quit the university three years ago in protest over the increasing privatization of education in Russia. My initial impulse after I quit was to do something else entirely. I thought I might write a novel. But I found this boring and in any case I had no talent. And I started thinking more about what my experience in the university had meant for my experience of life in our country.

"The term 'neoliberalism' has come into vogue of late in foreign academic and political writing, and for a long time I was pretty sure that it had nothing to do with us, with me. It was a foreign word and our realities were different from the realities being described, even in such an apparently analogous situation, as Andrei Kaplan has just outlined, in the United States.

"But the more I thought about it, the more clear it became. It's an ugly word but it describes an ugly phenomenon. It's a description of the privatization of matters that were previously public, of the marketization of human relations and affairs. And in Russia it explains a lot of what we see.

"We're used to thinking of our dictators as Stalin: Is this Stalin or is this not Stalin? Is this 1937 or is it not 1937? And if that's the question, the answer is always going to be: it's not 1937, and this is not Stalin. The supermarkets are overflowing with goods, the people have new televisions, some are driving new cars: everything is fine.

"But not everything is fine! You know it and I know it. Stalin is no longer the benchmark. Because there is a dictator that is as tough as Stalin and as brutal as Stalin but is also more acceptable than Stalin, more popular than Stalin ever was. It's called the market.

"What we've seen in Russia in the last twenty years is the replacement of a stagnant, sometimes violent and oppressive, but basically functioning state with a dictatorship of the market. People have died, of starvation, of depression, of alcoholism and violence, and not only have they done so quietly, they have done so *willingly*. They have praised their conquerors. We all know about the Bolsheviks who confessed to terrible crimes in the 1930s of which they were innocent. This was a lot like that. Except the Old Bolsheviks had been tortured! People like our parents did it of their own free will. They had built a country; they had served it loyally and to the best of their ability. Now they were confessing to sins attributed to them by neoclassical economics. They were willing to renounce everything they had ever thought because they believed that, in the grand sweep of history, they were in the wrong.

"And, you know, for a long time I agreed. I thought Communism was the worst thing that could happen to a country. The lies, the shortages, the violence against dissidents. It was abominable.

"A lot of us knew that things in the nineties were bad. That the new capitalism was in many ways more destructive, more deceptive, and more violent than the Soviet Union had been in the seventies and eighties. When Putin became president, a lot of people thought that he represented the return of the USSR—that we had failed to 'cleanse' the country of the communist menace, and that now we were in for it again. As you recall, others argued that Putin was young and a 'reformer,' that the KGB was the only businesslike structure in the USSR, and that he would continue the 'reforms.'

"What I realized at the university in 2001, 2002, 2003, as I watched the administration adopt more and more of the lingo and practices of big business, was that the reforms were in fact continuing. And that Putin *was* a reformer, just as the optimists had said, but that, as the pessimists had said, he was adopting Soviet methods of political repression, control of the press, and so on. It appeared to be a contradiction. But it wasn't one. As I read more about it, I understood: *This is what capitalism looks like on the margins of the world system.* Turkey, China, Mexico, Egypt . . . all of them had governments that looked like ours, economies that looked like ours. Whether this was a permanent state of things, I didn't know (though I had some guesses). What I did know, what I continue to know, is that this was a state of affairs, and a regime, that needed to be resisted. And it needed to be resisted in the name of anti-capitalism. Not anti-communism, as the liberals thought, and think, and which aside from being a misdiagnosis of the situation also aligns them with the worst forces in international life, but anti-capitalism, which happens to be correct and also aligns us with the best of those forces—with the radical students in Greece, with the striking autoworkers in Spain, with the protesting oil workers in Kazakhstan, with the newly conscious academic workers in the United States." Sergei nodded at me. "So, that's what I finally understood."

Sergei paused for a moment and took a drink of water. As he did so, I tried, as unobtrusively as possible, to turn around in my seat in the front row and see how the audience was taking it. I had felt like something very special was happening here, but now, looking at the others, I saw nothing more nor less than a group of students politely listening. A few of them were even taking advantage of Sergei's short pause to look at their phones. "You could come to them with the Sermon on the Mount," my adviser once said, "and they'd just sit there taking notes."

This wasn't the Sermon on the Mount, I knew that—but to me, in that room, at that time, it might as well have been. I couldn't believe it. Sergei was a good goalie, but not an outstanding one. He seemed like a nice guy, but not a superhuman one. In the vulgar yelling and joking of our locker room, I hardly ever noticed him.

Yet he had figured it out. Suddenly everything I had been looking at—not just over these past months in Moscow, but over the past few years in academia, and over the past fifteen years of studying Russia—became clear to me. Russia had always been late to the achievements and realizations of Western civilization. Its lateness was its charm and its curse—it was as if Russia were a drug addict who received every concoction only after it was perfectly crystallized, maximally potent. Nowhere were Western ideas, Western beliefs, taken more seriously; nowhere were they so passionately implemented. Thus the Bolshevik Revolution, which overthrew the old regime; thus the human rights movement, plus blue jeans, which overthrew the Bolshevik one; and thus finally this new form of capitalism created here, which had enriched and then expelled my brother, and which had impoverished my grandmother and killed Uncle Lev. You didn't have to go and read a thousand books to see it; you just had to stay where you were and look around.

Yulia sat a few chairs from me. If I were her I would be in love with Sergei. But she appeared not to be. She was watching the audience more than she was watching him. She had organized the event and wanted it to go well. I went back to listening to the lecture. In addition to everything else, I noticed that Sergei's stutter disappeared when he was speaking like this.

"It was hard for me to leave the university, despite all the reasons I had to do so. We had a small child, and though my salary was meager, it was something. And I believed in the university as an idea. I believed in education. But then again, what is the point of education? The end point of education is liberation. There can be no total liberation, and so education never ends. What I realized is that you do not have to remain inside an institution of education to continue your education and to continue educating others. The goal of our movement is freedom, and in order to be free, we must first learn how to think. We must learn how to think together; we must practice solidarity; we must organize ourselves and we must organize others. Only that way can we move forward against the darkness; only that way can we build equality and democracy here on earth."

Sergei paused.

"I'll be happy to take some questions."

The question-and-answer session lasted an hour. When it was over, Yulia told me that she and Sergei and some others were going to a nearby bar for a drink. I would have loved to get a drink with Yulia or near Yulia but I needed to pick up my grandmother at Emma Abramovna's. I walked in that direction down Tverskaya, pondering what I'd just heard.

It was the first time I'd walked through Moscow that I didn't see only expensive restaurants and execution chambers. Yes, there were expensive restaurants and execution chambers. But there were also the homes of the people who had been executed in those chambers. There were the books they'd read and the books they'd written. And then, arriving at last at Emma Abramovna's, where she sat with my grandmother playing anagrams, there were the homes of those who had, one way or another, survived.

The next day at the Coffee Grind I looked up Sergei on the internet. His break with the university and the regime that supported it had been public and, it turned out, controversial. He had announced it on his LiveJournal page and then spent weeks arguing with people in the comments. I read all of it. He was accused of abandoning the education of young Russians, of exaggerating the level of corruption within the private university, of being a communist. Sergei calmly and methodically answered every accusation. He was abandoning the education of the rich, he said, but he intended to continue educating those without resources; he was not exaggerating; and, yes, he was a communist.

Where did he think the money for the university—for the physical plant, for the library collection, for the salaries of lazy professors like him—was going to come from? Sergei answered that it should come from the government, that education was something people should pay for through their taxes, as individuals and as corporations. "If the state can reform its military and put billions of dollars into superhighways, why shouldn't it help its universities provide free education to its children?"

"People like you teach children godlessness and all sorts of other idiocy," said one person. "Why should I pay for that?"

"Ah," said Sergei.

But he had not backed down.

We had hockey that night and I came early in case Sergei did too. But he arrived with the others. He said hi to me and complimented my talk from the other night; I spent at least part of the game wondering how I would broach the subject of our talking again. Sergei was the one who suggested it. In the locker room after we lost he asked if I needed a ride home. I'd been getting a ride home from Oleg but I immediately said yes. Oleg didn't mind. He had recently found a tenant for the bank space vacated by the Europeans. When he mentioned this in the locker room, and named the group he was renting to, I saw several of the guys raise their eyebrows. Not understanding, I asked, "Is it a bank?"

"Not exactly," said Oleg. It turned out they were a criminal outfit. When Tolya wondered aloud if this was wise, Oleg laughed. "I'm not going into business with them," he said, "just renting them a space." He seemed giddy with the news, as if he'd once again managed to pull a great trick on the world, and I realized then that Oleg was less careful, less reserved, than the other guys we played with. It was part of his charm, but I could see that the guys were worried about him.

Sergei had a boxy old Lada and we loaded our stuff in the back. If I was worried about striking up a conversation with him, I need not have been. He seemed happy to basically continue his talk from the night before.

"One of the important political events of my life was the Iraq War," he said. "Or, rather, watching the reaction to it inside Russia. I saw people who opposed Putin, which I instinctively agreed with, supporting the Iraq War, which I instinctively disagreed with. So either my instincts were wrong, or there was something the matter here.

"Until then I'd been a fairly standard liberal. I voted for Yeltsin. But I started thinking about my parents and grandparents. They were good people, hardworking people. And they had been totally decimated by the reforms. I started looking into it. I studied literature, like you. I wrote my thesis on late Soviet nonconformist poetry. But I started reading about politics, world politics and Russian politics. And the more I read, the more I understood that it wasn't my parents who were the problem, it was the reforms that were the problem, it was capitalism that was the problem, and Putin was a particular kind of capitalist. Once I saw that, I saw a lot of things."

By now we'd reached Trubnaya Square; Sergei pulled over next to one of the big construction sites.

A few years ago, he said, he and some friends had started a political group called October. It was still small, like twenty people small, but it was growing.

"And Yulia?" I couldn't help but ask.

"Yulia joined the group with her husband, Petya Shipalkin, a year ago. But then they broke up. We kept Yulia, and Shipalkin joined the anarchists." Sergei laughed. "Yulia's a very good organizer," he added.

It was the first I'd heard about a husband, but he was now an ex-husband, and I had a more immediate question, about Fishman.

Sergei was surprised. "Sasha Fishman? You know him?"

"Yeah, he was in my department."

"Well." Sergei laughed again. "Fishman is Fishman. A little sneak. He's a friend of Shipalkin's, but now that they've split up he calls Yulia when he comes to Moscow."

"Ah."

"Yeah," said Sergei. "That's Fishman."

"There's another group," I said, "called September?"

"Oh, that's us. I mean, it used to be us. It was like, the revolution is in October, and we were in the month *before* the revolution."

"And now the revolution is closer?"

164

"Well, no, we just decided it was a stupid name."

"Did you guys do that protest against the Moscow–Petersburg high-way?"

"Yes."

"My brother is Dima Kaplan. People accused him of being involved in that."

"That's your brother?" Sergei was amused. "No, we had nothing to do with him, nor would we ever. He's a capitalist snake. No offense."

None taken. I thanked Sergei for the ride and retrieved my stuff from the trunk.

"I'll see you next week," said Sergei, before driving off.

I had finally found some people I could talk to.

5.

I GET SICK

I DID NOT SEE Sergei the next week because that weekend I got sick. I had somewhat miraculously avoided getting sick before now, but it began with a scratchy throat and before I knew it I had a fever. It was still winter break, so I could stay in bed for a few days.

As I lay there, I thought about my grandmother, who came and checked on me heroically every five minutes. She had been robbed by capitalism, I now saw. Or an accidental conspiracy between capitalism and Communism. Communism had nationalized the country's resources: all the oil that Uncle Lev found was owned by the state. When that state collapsed, it sold control of the oil for a pittance to a few well-connected men. It was in fact the explicit policy of the Russian reformers to create megacapitalists—the oligarchs, as they eventually came to be called—who would modernize the Russian economy and drag the country into the future. "People who grew up under Communism have a slave mentality," Dima told me the first time I visited him in the 1990s. "They don't do anything on their own. You have to make them. And, yes, it's going to be ugly sometimes. You can't build a capitalism omelet without breaking some eggs!" It was people like this, with ideas like this, who formed the conditions under which my poor grandmother lost her dacha and Uncle Lev had a stroke.

I had never been a socialist. In fact I'd been an anti-socialist. It was how I was raised. We had escaped the Soviet Union, where you weren't allowed to keep anything you made or earned, and had come to America and changed our lives. My father had voted Republican in every election since they'd let him start. Under the influence of college and grad school, I had moved to the left and become a liberal, but at the word "socialism" I drew the line. It just struck me as one of those things my otherwise intelligent American friends were stupid or naïve about, like iPods. A person did not need an iPod, in my opinion, when he could get music on the radio for free. And likewise we did not need socialism when democratic capitalism was working just fine.

"These people think Karl Marx is a nice old man with a beard," my adviser once said to me when a group of grad students demanding a union took over one of our campus cafeterias. This annoyed my adviser on a number of levels, not least of which being that this cafeteria made his favorite chicken parm sandwich. "They think he's Santa Claus!" he said, of the grad students. "I'd like to plunk these friends of the working class down in Petrograd in 1917. See how long they'd last."

Over in the Slavic department, we'd all read Mandelshtam, Akhmatova, Mandelshtam's widow, Grossman, Solzhenitsyn, Brodsky. . . . We were steeped in memories of the violent Revolution and its even more violent Stalinist sequel. Whenever some bright-eyed grad student from the English department said "socialism," we reached for our bookshelves. "We live without feeling the ground beneath our feet / from a few steps away you can't hear us speak. / Though if someone does begin talking / we know that the man in the Kremlin is watching." The Stalin epigram by Mandelshtam. Any questions?

But *Russian* socialists? That was different. That was interesting. From listening to Sergei I could tell that he did not need any lessons from me in Soviet history. He knew about the camps, the purges, the lies. But there was more to socialism, he seemed to be saying. It wasn't just camps and insane asylums. And what replaced it—"the reforms"— had not made things any better.

At the height of my fever I had a dream about my mother. She was not dead, it turned out; she had merely gone away for a while, and now she was back. We were in Newton, in our old house. My father still lived there. "I'm living with Baba Seva," I told my mother. "I know," she said. "I'm hoping to get a job teaching soon," I half lied. "I know," she said. "I don't have any children," I said, because my mom loved children. "That's

OK," she said. "It's not too late." I wanted to tell her that we had thought she was dead, but it was a misunderstanding, and I was so happy that she was still alive. But in the dream I wasn't able to tell her these things. I woke up with a profound warmness running through my body, and soon I was feeling better again.

6.

OCTOBER

JUST AS I WAS starting to feel better, Sergei invited me to attend an anti-fascist protest at the Clean Ponds metro stop. It was a bitterly cold day and when I showed up there were only six other people there. But one of them was Sergei, and another was Yulia. She wore a puffy black jacket with a fur-lined hood, the kind gangster teenagers wear in New York, and underneath the hood a fur hat with earflaps. Her nose and cheeks were red from the cold and there were tears, it looked like, also from the cold, in her big green eyes.

"Hi," I said.

She nodded.

I wanted to tell her about how I'd been sick, and my thoughts about socialism, and the dream I'd had about my mother, but it was obviously too early for that, and I tried instead to concentrate on the protest. Someone had made a big banner, which we unfurled, that said END FAS-CISM. We were going to stand in front of the metro station, near the entrance to the park, and hold this banner for thirty minutes, in the cold. "That's it?" I said to Sergei. In anticipation of the protest and un-aware of any fascists in Russia at this time, I went online and looked it up. It turned out there were plenty of fascists; their activities included attacking and sometimes killing Central Asian migrants and posting videos of the attacks on YouTube. They also engaged in fighting and sometimes killing anti-fascist activists, or antifa. I had gone to the event prepared for just about anything. That wasn't the plan. "For the mo-ment," Sergei said, "we just need to show people we're not afraid, and they don't need to be, either. That's enough."

We took turns holding the banner. We chanted anti-fascist slogans—"No to fascism!" "Fascism will not pass!" People came out of the subway and walked past us. Most of them didn't look at us. Nonetheless it felt like we were doing something.

Yulia didn't pay much attention to me. But I enjoyed hearing her say that fascism wouldn't pass.

And then we noticed a commotion at the entrance to the Clean Ponds metro. It was the pro-regime protesters, scrambling up to the roof, where they dutifully unfurled their banner urging us not to rock the boat. Our small protest had not attracted any police, but these guys were vigilant.

Sergei wasted no time. As soon as they were up with their banner, he walked closer to them and yelled, "This is an anti-fascist protest! Are you guys for fascism?"

"What do you mean?" one of them yelled back.

"Our banner says, 'End fascism.' Do you think the regime is fascist and that therefore saying no to fascism is going to destabilize the regime?"

"What?"

"Come down here and we'll talk," said Sergei.

The counterprotesters were clearly confused by this. They talked among themselves and eventually came down and joined our protest. After Sergei worked on them for a while, they even held our banner for a bit. They were just kids—college students. They admitted that they were paid five hundred rubles apiece to do these counterprotests. One of them tried to hit on Yulia. Eventually they grew bored and left, though not before taking some socialist literature Sergei had brought with him.

"You can talk to just about anybody," Sergei said to me. "You won't necessarily talk them into it, but the total absence of any real political discourse in the country means that there's an openness to ideas, since people aren't used to hearing them."

We stayed out another fifteen minutes in the cold and then Sergei announced that it was time to get some tea and warm up. At this point Yulia excused herself. "I have a deadline tomorrow," she said.

She started to head toward the metro entrance. It had been a week since the bookstore event and I hadn't heard a peep from her. She may have been separated from her husband and she may not actually have liked Fishman, but that by no means indicated that she liked me. Nonetheless I stepped over to her and asked, using the polite form of "you," when I would see her again.

She looked at me without surprise. "Soon, I think," she said, and smiled. I saw her beautiful crooked teeth, and then she ducked her head, and she was gone. I found this encouraging. When Sergei asked if I wanted to get some tea with the rest of the protesters, I wondered if I was already becoming part of the group.

The answer, for the moment, was no. In the basement café that they took me to, part bohemian hangout, part place where middle-aged men sat grimly drinking beers though it was still relatively early in the afternoon, I was treated politely, but as a guest. Everyone decided to order cranberry vodkas instead of tea, and then the guys explained their socialism to me. In addition to Sergei there were two grad-student types—blond, skinny, handsome Misha; dark-haired, chubby, cerebral Boris—and a computer programmer named Nikolai, who had a ponytail. It turned out they knew all about Dima—they felt like they'd been arguing with him for years. "Liberals like your brother think that if we just had a functioning free market, if we just had 'good' capitalism, then everything would work itself out," said Boris. "What they don't understand is that this *is* capitalism. We're in it already. And if you took the restraints off, it would get even worse."

"But how can you say there's capitalism when there's no free market?" I said. "When a market is this skewed by corruption, it's not really a market, right?"

"Yes and no," said Boris. "You're right that it's not an efficiently functioning market. But you still have wage labor; you still have profits that are invested; you have companies buying up other companies. Just because a market is distorted doesn't mean it ceases to be a market. But even if you imagined that all the corrupt bureaucrats disappeared—if they were all taken out tomorrow and shot—that money wouldn't go into the pockets of the workers. It would go into the capitalists' pockets. It would be used to buy yachts and foreign sports teams."

"So what's the solution?" I said. "Revolution?"

"Yes," said Boris. "That's correct. Expropriation of the capitalists. Worker councils to elect leaders. Common ownership of property."

"That's been tried in this country."

"Lots of things have been tried. Capitalism has also been tried, including in this country. And it's led to exploitation and misery and death. That doesn't keep people from trying it again."

"Look," said Misha, leaning into the group. We were sitting around an old wooden table and it was cold in that basement and most everyone had kept their coats on. "The point is simply that life cannot go on as before. The oil companies are in league with the state to suppress wages, strip us of our rights, and destroy the planet. And it's important to understand that they do this in league with the rest of the capitalist world system, whether the individual figureheads get along with one another or not. We need to fight them."

I must have looked unconvinced, because here Sergei stepped in.

"You're living with your grandmother, right?" he said. I nodded. "She did what in the Soviet Union?"

"She was a college professor. Her husband was a geophysicist."

"And were they bad people? Did they lie, cheat, steal? Or did they try to build a country, despite various obstacles?"

"They tried to build a country," I said.

"That's how our parents were too. They were doctors and architects and engineers. They were trying to build a good place. They did what they could. And then everything they built was seized by a small cabal of people who had connections to the Yeltsin administration. That's not right."

"It's not just not right," Boris said. "It was entirely and fully predictable. This is what capitalism looks like. And in order to resist it you need to know what it is. That's the difference between us and the liberals. They think it's all one bad man named Putin. We know it's an economic system that's been in place for hundreds of years."

We sat there for three hours—at one point, I ordered a plate of dumplings and Boris criticized me for putting too much sour cream on them, but I told him my father had done the same thing, and he backed off—and at the end received a bill for twelve hundred rubles—forty dollars. This was remarkably cheap, given that the five of us had been drinking for so long, but it seemed to make a deep impression on the Octobrists. "Holy shit," said Misha. "I can't believe we drank so many vodka cranberries!" I made sure to put in more money than the others, because of my dumplings.

Watson College officially announced its search for Frank Miller's replacement. I waited a decent interval and then sent in my application.

On the one hand, it felt like a betrayal of everything I was doing. On the other hand, who knew what things would be like eight months from now, when the fall semester began? My grandmother might not even be alive. Heaven knew—she kept telling me—that she hoped not to be. And it was unlikely I'd get the job—I had, after all, been rejected for all the others. So I decided to apply. And in the meantime that meant following my adviser's advice and seeking some kind of publication.

"Listen," I wrote him one day when I saw him in the Gchat bar. "I met some young socialists here. Is that an interesting subject, do you think?"

"Absolutely," he said. "The return of the repressed. The incorrigible Russians. Whatever. Yes. Do it."

Would Sergei find the idea craven? He wanted to liberate himself and others from academic institutions so they could begin to change the world. Here I was proposing to make him and his comrades the object of academic study. But we had hockey again in two nights, and I decided to ask. He was open to it. "We'll have to discuss it internally," he said, meaning within October, "but I don't see why not. It's possible that talking to someone who isn't us might help us formulate our ideas better. I'll put it to the group." The next time we had hockey he told me that they had agreed, and that I was invited to start attending their weekly Marxist study sessions. "But of course as we don't believe in objective scientific discourse, you have to participate. That was one of the conditions the group put forth."

I didn't have a problem with that. I was in.

The study sessions met on Tuesday evenings at Misha's apartment near the Belarus train station. Misha lived with another graduate student, also named Misha, in a large studio apartment that had once been his grandmother's; it was just a kitchen and one room, though a large room, and the two Mishas slept on sofa beds on opposite ends of it. The other Misha studied Greek and his end of the room was piled high with Greek texts, while our Misha studied history and sociology, and his side of the room was piled high with Weber, Marx, and Wallerstein. On Tuesday evenings, the second Misha had some kind of Greek-related seminar, and we usually had the place to ourselves.

The other regular members of the group were Boris and Nikolai, whom I'd met at the anti-fascist protest; Vera, a precocious high school student with thick glasses; and, most important of all, Yulia. Sergei came to about half the sessions; he was the only one of the group who was married and had a child, and I was beginning to get the impression that his home life was not unclouded, so he sometimes begged off.

The reading group had only existed for a brief time, and they had apparently spent the first several sessions arguing over what to read. Part of the group wanted to read the works of contemporary Marxist writers, while others wanted to go back to the source and read Marx's *Capital*. In the end, the *Capital*-ists had scored a narrow victory, and a few weeks ago the group had embarked on Marx's masterpiece. During my first session there was a half-hour discussion as to whether the vote should be revisited in light of the fact that there was a new member. The initiator of the discussion was Boris, who apparently wanted a recount, but the rest took it up eagerly and debated the fine points of my participation, their voting procedures, and consensus politics, until finally Yulia said that I was an associate and nonvoting member and in any case they had already started reading the book! It was agreed then that we'd take a break and have a snack and start in on the book immediately afterward.

In short, I was not surprised to learn that they were still on the first chapter and that I could catch up.

Since Misha was a bachelor and didn't have anything in his refrigerator except beer and vodka, all of us brought some kind of food to reading group—I stuck with basics like black bread and salami, others brought little pies or salads that they'd made. Yulia sometimes brought wine for her and Vera. In advance of the meeting, everyone would read a portion of the text, but one person was selected in advance to lead the discussion. That person would spend the next week studying the text with particular care and also doing outside reading to better understand it. The first time around I was allowed to skip my turn, but the next time, everyone said, I'd have to go.

In the meantime, I was becoming more and more infatuated with Yulia. She was, it turned out, a grad student in Russian literature; she was writing her thesis on some medieval Slavic texts I'd puzzled out a little bit in grad school. In short talks during our breaks, I quickly gathered that she knew about five times more about Russian literature than I ever would. She wore conservative clothing—button-down shirts and sweaters and long skirts—but these if anything accentuated her figure. She was cute. She was also exceedingly polite. She addressed me as *vy*, which initially I thought had to do with my age—she was twenty-nine, four years younger than I was—but which I eventually concluded had to do with her traditional upbringing. She was not the most vocal member of our study circle—that was either Misha, who liked to drink beer at the sessions and became especially voluble on the subject of capital once he'd had two or three of them, or Boris, who seemed to have read everything and had total, if sometimes slightly robotic, recall of it—but she was always engaged, had always done the reading, and took it all very seriously. I loved watching her talk, the precision she insisted on in discussing this very difficult text, and when someone said something funny, I loved watching her duck her head and laugh. I was starved for female non-grandmother companionship, yes, but I think I would have felt the same about her even if I hadn't been.

I had been a little dismayed initially at the number of dudes in the study circle, but it soon became clear that they didn't care about Yulia. Boris didn't seem to be interested in girls at all, only socialism, whereas Misha was apparently involved, in an on-and-off manner, with one of Yulia's roommates, Masha. As for Nikolai, he may have been interested in girls, but I did not get the impression that girls were interested in him.

That said, it didn't seem like this particular girl was interested in me, either. During the study sessions she was always focused on the discussion, and even afterward, when we all left together and walked in a bunch to the Mayakovsky monument, where we split up, I was never able to get her to talk to me. She kept quizzing Boris on the political situation in one Central Asian country after another, and I was left to fend off Nikolai, who, it turned out, was in the process of building a dacha outside the city and was always trying to get people to help him. Everyone had begged off, however, and now he had his eyes on me. I told him that I tried to stay with my grandmother on weekends, but he kept asking. And Yulia kept asking Boris about Central Asia. And then we'd arrive at the Mayakovsky monument and all go our separate ways.

One night as Sergei was dropping me off after hockey, I finally brought it up with him. "Remember that night at Falanster?" I said. "When I told you that Yulia had invited me, you sort of said, 'Ah, Yulia.' What did you mean by that?"

"What did I mean?" Sergei said.

"Yes. Come on. You meant something."

"OK. Well. Yulia is a very good recruiter. She can really spot people who might be sympathetic to us. You might say she has an intuition."

"OK."

"Well, and sometimes it happens that the person she spots is a man, and he then gets ideas about her."

"I see," I said.

There is a play in hockey called slew-footing. It's when you slide (slew) your foot behind an opponent's skates and kick it forward so that his legs get taken out from beneath him. It's considered a very dirty play, because the victim falls straight back, sometimes smashing his head on the ice. When Sergei told me that guys often fall for Yulia when joining October, I felt like I'd been slew-footed.

Sergei could sense this, maybe. "Listen," he said. "I don't actually know what her situation is. Shipalkin wasn't a very good comrade and he wasn't a very good husband, and my impression is he's still coming around. It's very confusing for her, I imagine. He was the same with us, you know, in terms of his politics—first he was a democratic socialist, then he was an accelerationist, now he's an anarchist.

"So I don't know exactly what's going on. But I think if someone was serious about Yulia, that could break the situation."

I nodded. Sergei had said more than enough. I extracted my hockey stuff from the car and headed up the boulevard toward our place. On the way I bought a big brown can of Zhigulovskoye beer from a kiosk. At some point I'd noticed it had stopped making my tummy hurt.

Who were these people and where had they come from? Why weren't they more like Dima's friends, who had gone to many of the same schools and had read at least some of the same books?

I didn't have a ready answer for this, but it had something to do with their experience of post-Soviet life. In the Maxim group, I knew, the parents were prosperous. They had converted their anti-Soviet credentials into jobs on television or in publishing, or in the murky world of "consulting." My impression of the October group was that the parents were barely hanging on. I don't know if this was the decisive factor, but it was certainly something the Octobrists talked a lot about.

I found myself gradually but unmistakably looking at the world a little differently. I had once thought it so strange that across the street from the KGB was a cute café with wi-fi. But it wasn't strange. It wasn't any more strange than the fact that my university back home, a place where people were supposed to live silent and monklike lives in the pursuit of knowledge, had a beautiful multimillion-dollar gym; or that in my old Brooklyn neighborhood the violent displacement of people from the homes in which they'd lived for decades and the stoops on which they were used to sitting took place to the accompaniment of . . .

cute cafés. Cute cafés were not the problem, but they were also not, as I'd once apparently thought, the opposite of the problem. Money was the problem. It had always been the problem. Private property, possessions, the fact that some people had to suffer so that others could live lives of leisure: that was the problem. And that there were intellectual arguments ardently justifying this—that was a bigger problem still.

In the reading group my presence was taken in stride. I was an observer on the one hand, but also an observer-participant on the other, and finally it was assumed that I was a sympathizer. My total lack of knowledge about Marx and Marxism was chalked up to a general American ignorance of everything, while my slightly ambiguous remarks about my own past were always interpreted in the best possible light. One time Misha, who had once been kicked out of school for protesting, asked me if there was student agitation on my campus. Yes, I said, recalling the grad student unionization drive and cafeteria takeover. Misha didn't ask if I had been part of the drive—he assumed that I had. "What was the result?" he asked. The result was that in exchange for the students leaving the cafeteria and liberating the chicken parm, the university agreed to create a committee to investigate grad student unionization. The committee ended up proposing that in lieu of a union, there would be a new committee (a different committee) to examine grad student grievances. Four years later, there was still no union, and I happened to know that the university was using the financial crisis to strip away some of the protections the grad students had finally managed to win. "*Svolochi*," said Misha.

Svolochi. Bastards. It was true. In fact, as I knew from Gchatting with my adviser, not only were they busting the nascent union, they were breaking up the Slavic department. One or two people whose work was more historically oriented were being pushed into the history department; the others were being sent into the German department, which was being renamed the Germanic and Slavic Languages and Literatures Department. The Germans were in charge. And a few professors with really low enrollments, though not yet my adviser, were being asked to take early retirement. "Yes," I agreed with Misha. "They're bastards."

If the Octobrists were from families that had been victimized by the reforms, what about me? My father, over in the States with his new American family, was no victim, though sometimes I wondered, as I thought of him on his exercise bike watching Russian TV shows, if he was lonely and wished he'd never left. My brother, the would-be business tycoon, painted himself as a victim of the new regime, but he was in fact its accomplice. If anything he was a victim of the regime's corrupting influence, like so many others who'd been corrupted by the riches that flowed into the country along with high oil prices, and the partial reforms.

Whereas my grandmother—my grandmother really had been robbed.

One day around this time we were out walking along the boulevard. A light snow was falling and my grandmother held tightly on to my arm. Moscow didn't tend to get a lot of snow all at once, but it remained so consistently cold that once the first snow fell in early November, it didn't melt until the spring, so the snow accreted gradually, turning brown and hardening, occasionally freshened by new snow. In New York, the sidewalks were the responsibility of the landlords, who got fined if they didn't clear snow and ice in a timely fashion; in Moscow, the city still owned most of the buildings, and in any case most of the houses faced inward, into courtyards, and so it was left to the city to clear the sidewalks. This sometimes took weeks. Walking outside became treacherous.

We were out for our walk, then, when we passed the towering Krupskaya statue, which depicted a young Nadezhda Krupskaya, Lenin's wife, wrapped in a flowing shawl. With a light coat of snow on her she looked even more dramatic than usual, which may be what caused my grandmother to remark, after walking by her almost daily for the past five months: "Look at her! She was a very modest lady. But here she's a—ballerina!"

I looked at my grandmother. She was making her way carefully, but indomitably, forward through the snow. The other day at the reading group, while discussing Marx's account of the extraction of value from the worker through his exploitation, I started talking about the expro-priation of Uncle Lev's oil and sputtering about the unfairness of it. Boris urged me onward. "What does fairness have to do with it?" he said. "We're talking about the laws of capitalism."

"But they're not fair!" I said. Boris shrugged.

"Grandma," I said now. "What do you think of Communism?"

"Communism?" She sighed one of her patented sighs. "What do I think of Communism? I think it was worth a try. In this terrible coun-try, nothing is ever going to work. But it was worth a try."

"Was life better under Communism?"

"For some people it was better. For us it was better. We had a dacha and this apartment and everyone had work. But there were bad things about it too. You couldn't say anything in the papers. There were books you couldn't get. I don't know, Andryush. What do you think?"

"I don't know," I said. "I wasn't there." The other day Vanya had come into hockey in a foul mood. His sugar factory was being asked to keep its prices artificially low so that sugar wouldn't become too expensive for people whose salaries were being affected by the finan-cial crisis. "Fuck your mother, it's the same thing all over again," he said. Back in the Soviet Union he'd worked as the head of a shoe fac-tory. "We were making boots for fifteen rubles apiece and selling them for five. Sergei, no offense"—it was well known in the locker room that Sergei was sympathetic to the Soviet experiment—"but that shit had to stop."

"Now they're just doing the same thing but from the other side," he went on. "We've got a market, we've got prices, I own the factory, but they're still fucking with us." He'd kicked the local officials who'd made the request out of his office and a few days later got a visit from the local prosecutor, who already had a case against him, for tax infractions, all drawn up. "So I'm going to do it. But it means I won't be able to index the salaries of my workers"—to inflation—"but of course no one cares about that."

"I knew Putin in Petersburg," Tolya said. Putin had worked as the deputy mayor there in the 1990s, before his move to Moscow and meteoric rise to the presidency. "He had dirt on everyone. That's how he got people to do things. He had all the dirt."

"That's right!" said Vanya. "Now the whole state is run that way."

"So what's the solution?" Ilya said. He was addressing Sergei.

"Democracy," Sergei immediately said. "Workers' councils. Vanya, do your workers own the factory along with you?"

"Of course not," said Vanya. "We bought all their shares in the nineties."

"There you go," said Sergei. "If the factory was owned by the workers, no prosecutor could show up and threaten them. Is he going to put the entire factory in jail? Then there'll be no sugar at all. That's worse than expensive sugar."

Vanya considered this. "What about me?" he said. "I know how to run that factory."

"No problem," said Sergei. "The factory still needs a good manager. You still have the respect of your coworkers. But maybe your salary is not as great."

"Instead of you flying to Spain every weekend, the whole factory flies there once a year," Tolya said. Everyone laughed. They pictured Vanya's workers—gold-toothed, uneducated, awkwardly dressed— enjoying the warm beaches of Spain. But it was a warm laughter. No one seemed to think it was a bad idea.

My grandmother and I had reached the end of our portion of the boulevard, with the huge RussOil building darkening our way. It reminded me of Dima—the other day he'd sent me an article on the rapidly deteriorating Moscow real estate market. Residential property in central Moscow had declined 4 percent since we'd last talked. "You owe me $6K," he had written. I didn't answer that email.

"If it had worked out," my grandmother now said, of the Soviet experiment, "that would have been nice."

We turned around and headed back toward Krupskaya, bride of the Revolution, Lenin's faithful wife.

7.

SERGEI'S PARTY

YULIA DID NOT comment on my political awakening, if she even noticed it. She was guarded during our reading group; I saw her smiling during my stammering expressions of indignation, but whether this meant she was charmed or just politely embarrassed on my behalf, I could not say. On our walks to Mayakovka she continued to talk pretty much exclusively to Boris about Central Asia. A couple of times Boris and Nikolai took me for a beer at a Czech beer place not far from Mayakovskaya, but Yulia never joined us. And always in the background there was the figure of her Shipalkin. I brought it up once during beers with Boris and Nikolai. It turned out that Boris, in particular, really disliked the anarchist group, Mayhem, that Shipalkin had joined after leaving October. "The thing about them," said Boris, "is they don't have a political position. They think they're going to overthrow the regime by spray-painting police cars!" Mayhem had recently done precisely this in Moscow, posting a YouTube video afterward. "It's just as Lenin said," Boris concluded. "Anarchism is an infantile disorder."

"OK," I said. "But what's the deal with him and Yulia?"

Boris looked at me like he couldn't understand why someone would care about such a triviality when we had the opportunity to denounce anarchism. "You mean personally? I have no idea. I do know she shares my views on anarchism." That was all he'd say.

"Are you guys doing anything this weekend?" Nikolai asked. "Because I could use some help on the dacha." And both Boris and I had to think up excuses for why we couldn't go.

Then after our fifth or sixth session, the whole group of us was met outside by a nervous-looking dandy. Yulia had been laughing at something Boris said and the moment she saw him she stopped. "Petya," she said, "what are you doing here?"

"I wanted to talk to you," said the dandy, who I immediately understood to be Shipalkin. He wore a wool car coat and a scarf thrown over his shoulder and leather gloves and Converse high-top sneakers, the outfit of a Moscow hipster. The other notable thing about his appearance was that he looked like me—he was a short, olive-skinned, Eastern European Jew. We weren't identical twins or anything, but where previously I had wondered if Yulia could even entertain the prospect of going out with a guy who looked like me, I now had my answer.

And something else, as well. Shipalkin shook hands with Boris and Nikolai and said *privet* to Vera. Then he looked inquisitively, and even it seemed with some hostility, at me. "This is Andrei," said Yulia quietly.

"Ah," said Shipalkin. "I thought so."

There could have been a hundred reasons for this reaction, in theory, but the simplest one was this: Yulia had said something to him about me in such a way that he'd deemed me a threat. I mean, there might have been other explanations. But that one was plausible. Men aren't as stupid as we pretend to be. A jilted husband knows.

A week later, Sergei invited a bunch of us over for a party at his place. His wife had gone for the weekend with their four-year-old to visit her mother in St. Petersburg, and Sergei said he felt lonely and wanted some company.

"Is your wife mad that you didn't go with her?" I asked.

"I think so, yes," said Sergei matter-of-factly. We were sitting in his car after hockey.

"And you don't care?"

"I care," he said. "But I didn't want to go. In the end, I've found that it's better not to do things I don't want to do. It's better for everyone."

So a party it was. Sergei lived way out in the endless exurbs of the city; I took the gray line north, caught a bus, and walked past five identical sixteen-story blocks until I reached the sixth, which was his. The neighborhood was a particularly pure example of what the modernist architects, led by Le Corbusier, had once imagined: giant blocks where people lived, between which they would transport themselves in automobiles. Meanwhile the ground between the blocks would be filled with parks and trees and other recreations.

What an asshole, I thought as I walked the six long blocks to Sergei's. Because if people were supposed to get everywhere in their cars, why would they spend a lot of time tending to the gardens in between their buildings? The answer was, they wouldn't. As with the big public housing projects built in the United States, the grounds between the big apartment blocks had not automatically filled themselves with park space and trees and children playing. Maybe in the Soviet era it was different, but now they were filled with trash, cars that people had nowhere else to park, more trash, and construction projects. I must have passed at least half a dozen construction-like holes in the ground on my way to Sergei's, though what exactly was being dug I had no idea, and in any case it was already dark. Dogs were barking. The street I walked along was so desolate that I worried there wouldn't even be a store for me to buy beer at, but finally when I reached Sergei's place I saw one in the basement of his building. I bought a bunch of beers and then rang upstairs. Someone buzzed me in. I pulled on the heavy metal door and entered a cramped, poorly lit foyer; it was the same exact design as my grandmother's old building in Dubna, with a little screened-in booth for the building "superintendent," who usually sat inside watching television—in fact, he was doing so now—and scowled at people who came in. This wasn't exactly a doorman whose visitor book you had to sign, but it wasn't not a doorman, either; I made the mistake of saying hello, to which the man, who looked to be in his late sixties, asked without acknowledging the greeting, "Who're you here to see?"

"Sergei Ivanov," I said.

The man grunted. "You having some kind of party up there or what?"

"Just a little one," I said, smiling.

He didn't answer, and I kept going. I walked past the mailboxes, which were in the same spot as in my grandmother's Dubna building and in the same condition—smashed, half open, covered in graffiti—then up three short steps and to the elevator. It smelled like piss. I held my breath and pressed the number 9.

As soon as I reached his floor, things got better. I heard music coming from his apartment, and it was Yulia who opened the door. "Andrei!" she said, in a way I had never heard her say it. She was wearing a white cotton dress with flowers on it, and beaming, and when I stepped in she gave me a kiss on the cheek. She was drunk. She told me to throw my coat on the bed and then danced off into the living room. Still processing this, I went into the kitchen to drop off my beers and take one for myself. There I found Misha and Nikolai and a few people I didn't know sitting at the kitchen table and drinking. Misha was telling a story about growing up in a neighborhood on the outskirts of Moscow before inheriting his grandmother's apartment. As little Misha navigated the area in the early nineties, gangs of kids would approach him. "Grunge or metal?" they'd say, meaning, which do you prefer? The right answer could be either, and if you gave the wrong answer you'd get beaten up. "Though usually the right answer was metal," said Misha. "They'd say, 'Oh, yeah? Which groups do you like?' But you could bluff, because they didn't have any more access to it than you did. I'd say 'Deep Purple.' And they'd be like, 'OK, Deep Purple, cool,' and let me go."

"In my neighborhood it was 'Rap or metal,'" said Nikolai. "And the answer was always definitely metal, because otherwise it meant you liked black people. That made it easier. Though I'd still sometimes get beaten up."

I liked these guys so much. It was like they'd lived some heightened version of my own life, where Western popular culture filtered in slowly, at first merely in the form of rumors about rap and metal, but gradually nudging out the older Russian literary culture that our parents had passed on to us. For me, in order to fit in, learning American pop culture was merely a matter of catching up. For them it was a kind of decision that they lived with, and had to remake, almost every day. To be Russian was in some way constantly to have to choose, not between rap and metal per se, but between the Russian and the Western—in what you ate, what you listened to, what you thought. And Misha, Yulia,

Sergei, Boris, my friends, had settled on an appealing hybrid: no one I met in Russia had studied Western culture as deeply as they had and extracted so much that was so good in it, while staying true, as best they could, to the place where they were from. In their politics it was the same. Marx was a German philosopher who had fled his native land for Paris and then London. But he had had his greatest success, his most devoted students, in the Russians. And here he had them still.

I stood in the kitchen and looked out the window. We were close to the edge of the city; an apartment like this, as far from the center and then as far from the metro as this was, went for pretty cheap, and yet what a view it had. From Sergei's kitchen you could see a highway, a train track, an elevated subway track, an elevated highway, and another train track. In the dark the cars and trains raced by in both directions; it was, on the one hand, a vision of modernity, the future, but on the other hand it looked shabby and improvised, clearly the result of not doing things right the first time. You had the distinct impression that one of the cars or trains was about to fall off and collide with something. In between these rail lines of the future were tall buildings like the one I was in; they looked like bookshelves left behind on a street corner, tottering.

I took my beer and walked down the corridor to the living room, where dance music was playing and about ten people were somewhat awkwardly dancing. I was still pondering the kiss on the cheek from Yulia; as I stepped into the living room and my eyes adjusted to the relative lack of light, I couldn't find her. Momentarily I feared that she was here with Shipalkin, that this accounted for her happy mood, and that they were somewhere together right now. Then someone grabbed my sleeve and pulled me toward her: Yulia. I even thought I saw a mild look of impatience in her eyes. We danced. I am a terrible dancer, but so was Yulia, so it was OK. At one point during "Stayin' Alive," Yulia did a pretty credible disco dance, and I copied her. Then she pulled me close to her and straightened up and kissed me on the lips. It was only a momentary kiss, but it was on purpose, and after she released me she looked at me in a way that seemed to say that she was not blind to the fact that I'd been following her around with my eyes for the past two months. We kept dancing, and we kissed some more, and more intently, and then it was late, and she, Boris, Misha, and I shared a car back to the center, since by then the metro was closed. Boris and Yulia and I huddled in the backseat, and for the entirety of the ride Yulia had her head on my shoulder and was asleep. We dropped her off first, then the guys, and me last. I had the driver drop me at the corner of Sretenka and the Garden Ring, so that I could buy a pastry from the Azeri chicken guys. I walked the few remaining blocks home in the cold, eating it. I wasn't sure exactly what had happened back there between Yulia and me, and whether she would care to continue it the next day and the day after, but I didn't care. All of Sretenka was lit up on this night, and all of it seemed to smile on me.

The next day, my grandmother fell down the stairs.

8.

MY GRANDMOTHER FALLS
DOWN THE STAIRS

A FEW WEEKS EARLIER I'd finally gotten wi-fi in the apartment. The new semester was in full swing and I was sitting at the kitchen table one evening, answering emails offline from students who thought Tolstoy was making too big a deal out of Anna Karenina's divorce, when my grandmother came in and asked if I wanted to have some tea and pancakes. I continued working as she made them—was it the end of the world to choose love over your children? Yes, my friends. It was the end of the world, or a world—and when she was done, I lazily put my computer on the windowsill alcove instead of taking it back into my room. As I did so a message popped up from the wireless icon that I had a signal. I didn't get too excited—when first trying to get internet in the apartment, I'd seen many promising signals—but when as an experiment I opened my browser and typed in the *New York Times* web address, there was the Gray Lady, telling me the news. I had internet! When I left the windowsill, I lost the signal. But as long as I kept my computer there, pulling up a chair backward and sitting astride it, I was in. I was on the internet.

My life was changed. I didn't need to spend five hours at the Coffee Grind every day if I didn't want to. I didn't need to download everything before I left the Coffee Grind, or compose my various emails in a word processor at home and then cut and paste them into my Gmail once I was online again. Almost without noticing it, over the months I had developed an entire ad hoc system, held together with wire and string and my own nervous irritation, for communicating with the world. I could now discard it.

I still went to the Grind just about every day, but not for as long, and I began to spend hours sitting on a chair in the kitchen and working from the windowsill. This meant that I was around more. "Are you going to go to work?" my grandmother, now used to me doing so, asked one morning.

"I'm going to stay here," I said, "if that's OK?"

"Of course!" my grandmother said. She was very pleased.

But the windowsill internet also made me less attentive to my grandmother. My emails from students never seemed to end. And beyond that was the fact that there was so much I wanted to read. The October group had an email list that people were always sending things to—articles, proposals for protests, arguments. There was an anarchist, an associate of Shipalkin's, who occasionally wrote in and accused the Octobrists of dictatorial tendencies, and a communist who wrote in and accused them of sectarianism. The long and sometimes interesting arguments would stretch out over days. I read them from the windowsill, munching on oatmeal cookies and sushki and drinking mug after mug of instant coffee, converting toward the end of the day to tea.

The night after Sergei's party I was reading such an argument from the windowsill—I couldn't now tell you what it was about—when my grandmother told me she was going for a walk. It was snowing out, a little, and slippery, I could see that, but it wasn't *too* slippery. Despite the cold my grandmother had been out earlier in the day to get some groceries and had done fine. I felt like maybe I should go with her but I also wanted to continue reading. Was I just going to be trapped my whole life walking out with my grandmother whenever the notion struck her? That was no way to live. I went over and kissed her on the forehead and told her to have a good walk.

Not thirty minutes later I heard a sharp cry in the stairwell. At first I thought it was a dog or a child, but then I realized exactly who it was. I ran out onto the landing; my grandmother was lying at the bottom of the stairs. She was on her back, and her eyes were open, and she was holding the back of her head and looking at me, and she was scared. I went down the stairs—they were wet and slippery from people clomping snow onto them—and helped her up; her thick pink coat had cushioned the fall, but when I looked at the spot on the back of her head that she was holding, I saw there was blood. "Oh, Andryushenka," she said as I slowly helped her up the stairs. "I'm so stupid. I'm so stupid. My head is spinning."

I got her upstairs, helped her off with her stuff, lay her down on her bed, and then ran to my computer at the windowsill and looked up the emergency number for an ambulance. It was 03. I dialed it and explained that my grandmother had hit her head. The woman on the other end asked if I thought she was in danger. I had no idea. "Is she conscious?" the woman asked. I said yes. This apparently helped her make a determination as to where to send us. She said an ambulance would be there in twenty minutes, and it was.

In retrospect, I don't know what I should have done. I've asked some doctors I've met, and some have said that a blow to the head such as the one my grandmother received when she fell might have been damaging but not life threatening; others have said that all sorts of dangerous bleeding could take place at her age, and that I was right to take her to the hospital. As I say, I don't know. The ambulance came, two pale young guys in scrubs with a stretcher, and as they gently lay my grandmother on it they suggested I pack her some toiletries and changes of clothing and any books she'd liked to read. My grandmother had no travel bags that I knew of and so I went into my room and dumped the hockey stuff from my спорт backpack and then filled it with some clothes and her toothbrush and glasses. Then we left.

I'll never forget the view of Moscow I got from the back of that ambulance as we stopped and started through the traffic on the Garden Ring. After a while my grandmother fell asleep on the gurney next to me; one of the paramedics was sitting in the back with us, playing with his phone, and when I asked if it was all right for her to fall asleep he said yes. I watched the city out the back window. It was covered with a thin white layer of snow, the same snow that my grandmother had slipped on while I sat at my computer, reading my email. From inside the ambulance you could see how cold it was. People walked, in black coats and black hats and black shoes, trying to keep close to the buildings, for warmth. As we stood in traffic at one intersection I saw two cars get into a small fender bender. Without pause, the drivers jumped out and headed for each other. One of them was bigger but the smaller man was quicker; he delivered a couple of long hooks, the bigger guy grabbed his head in pain, and then it was over. They got back in their warm cars and waited for traffic to start moving again.

When we finally got off the Garden Ring and onto the Kiev highway, I asked the paramedic sitting with me how much longer it would take. "About an hour," he said.

"An hour? There's nothing closer?"

"They told us to route her to the neurological clinic," he said, "because it's a head injury. Don't worry, it's a good clinic."

We kept going through the industrial neighborhoods and forests at the city's southern edge. The hospital the ambulance finally arrived at was in the woods. In the dim lights of its driveway I could see an old, long, four-story yellow-brick building; given its distance from the city it might have been a village hospital from before the Revolution. Or after. Who knew. The paramedics carefully rolled my grandmother, covered with a warm blanket, off the ambulance and into the hospital. She was now awake. She did not seem disturbed by the proceedings; in fact, she seemed to like them. Her health had been troubling her. Now here were some people who were taking it seriously. "Thank you," she kept saying to the paramedics. "Thank you."

From inside, the hospital looked even older. A rickety elevator took us to the top floor and then we walked down a dimly lit corridor. It was getting late now, and most of the doors to the rooms were closed. Cheap old wooden chairs out in the hallway suggested that during the daytime there might have been visitors.

We arrived at an open door, where a young man in green hospital gear with dark circles under his eyes sat smoking a cigarette. This turned out to be the head neurologist. "Hello, Arkady Ivanovich," one of my paramedics said. "Woman fell down, hit her head, there's some minor bleeding. Dispatcher said we should take her to you."

"Take her to examination room four-ten, please," said the neurologist, and then followed us there.

I felt a little as my grandmother felt—it was a relief to have her and her health, finally, in the hands of professionals—but I was also apprehensive. This place was dirty and far from home. I wasn't sure if I could trust these people. For reasons I didn't understand, the paramedics hung around outside the doorway of the examination room even after they'd moved my grandmother to the examination table and repossessed their gurney. Noting this, the doctor looked from them to me.

"You know," he said very quietly, "they don't get paid very much."

"Oh!" I said. I pulled out my wallet and found five hundred rubles and handed them to the paramedic who'd sat in back with me.

"Thank you," he said, and finally left.

In the examination room the young doctor checked the back of my grandmother's head, shone a light in her eyes, and asked her some questions. When it was done he told her and me that she was safe for the moment but that it would be wise to keep an eye on her and run some tests while she was here.

"What do you think, Seva Efraimovna?" he asked her gently.

My grandmother turned to me. "Whatever Andryusha thinks is best," she said.

I straightened up. "Would we be able to go home tomorrow?" I asked.

"No," said the doctor. "This will take a week."

"A *week*?" In America, I would have been concerned about the cost; in Russia, it was something else. The medical care was free. But I was concerned about leaving my grandmother for such a long time. I looked around the room, with its tall ceiling and chipped blue paint. I was concerned about leaving her here.

The doctor followed my gaze. "It doesn't look like much but this is a decent hospital," he said. "But I can't force you to keep her here. Sometimes the cranial bleeding from a fall like this doesn't show up right away. But of course there may not be any bleeding. It's up to you."

I felt the pressure of medical expertise. If she dies, or suffers brain damage, or is otherwise hampered in her functioning, he was saying, because you thought that our peeling paint meant that we didn't know anything about medicine—it'll be on you, not me.

"Grandma," I said, "do you want to stay here a little while so they can run some tests?"

"OK," said my grandmother. "If you think I should, I will."

I didn't know what to think. But I also felt like I had no other choice. "I do," I said.

"Then OK."

"OK," said the doctor. "Visiting hours are noon to eight. I'll have a nurse bring her to her room."

And he left us. A few minutes later a nurse came in with a wheelchair and with my help put my grandmother in it and wheeled her to a bed in a large room down the hall. The lights inside the room were dimmed; there was a curtain, on the other side of which appeared to be another bed and, it seemed, another patient. At the nurse's signal we lifted my grandmother from the wheelchair to the bed. She was incredibly light.

The nurse was a big blond woman in her forties. She was careful with my grandmother and seemed to know what she was doing. After we put my grandmother in bed, she left.

My grandmother had been awake but subdued since we'd arrived. I now took out her toiletries and extra clothes and placed them on her bedside table. I also wrote down my phone number. "I will be back tomorrow," I said.

"OK," she said. "Do you have the key to my apartment?"

"I do."

"Good. There is still some soup left over—make sure you eat it."

"OK," I said. I kissed her on the forehead and left.

The metro was closed by the time I got out of there and I had to get a cab home. It cost twenty-five dollars. When I returned to the empty apartment I cleaned up the mess I'd made when I packed, put on the potato soup to heat up, and opened my computer. In the Gchat bar, Dima's little green light was on. I messaged him.

"Grandma's in the hospital," I said.

He wrote back right away. "What??"

"She fell down the stairs and hit her head. The doctor says it's not dangerous."

"Where were you when this happened?"

"I was in the apartment."

"I told you about those stairs!"

I didn't say anything to that.

"Are you home now?" asked Dima.

"Yes."

"I'll call you."

A minute later the phone rang.

"Which hospital is she in?" said Dima.

"Neurological Clinic Number Eight," I said. I had taken a card with me and studied it. "It's way out at the end of the Kiev highway."

"Fuck!" said Dima. "That's a state hospital. They have private hospitals now where you can get decent care."

I didn't say anything. Of course I'd had no idea. Probably I should have called Dima right away, but everything had happened so quickly.

"Can you move her?" Dima said.

"This place is OK," I said. "It's not bad. And it's devoted to neurology."

"Move her to the American Clinic," said Dima. "It's right near Prospekt Mira. You'll be able to walk there."

"How much does it cost?"

"I'll pay for it," said Dima.

"I'll think about it," I said. I didn't want to put my grandmother back in an ambulance for two hours while she still had a head wound. And I didn't want Dima paying for her.

"If you keep her at this place at least give the doctor some money," he said. "Give him three thousand rubles." A hundred dollars. "And give the nurse five hundred. It'll help."

"OK," I said.

"You had one thing to do," said Dima. "You had one fucking thing you were supposed to do."

I didn't say anything.

"Unbelievable," said Dima, and hung up.

My soup had partly boiled out of the saucepan. I ate what remained and spent an hour online reading about head trauma. Then I went to bed. It was the first time in my life I'd had the family apartment all to myself. I slept badly.

Over the course of the next week the hospital tested my grandmother for every manner of neurological ailment. They took her through machines, hooked her up to monitors, and told her to read letters and numbers from a big board. She did it all obediently; she was relieved that someone finally thought she was sick.

I spent that week on the bus that ran from in front of the hospital to the nearest metro station and back. The bus did not seem to keep a regular schedule, and often in the interest of getting out of the cold I boarded it going in the wrong direction, since there was only one bus on the route and it would be coming back in my direction anyway. It was warmer on the bus than it was outside, though never quite warm enough.

I decided not to move my grandmother. She was comfortable in her room, and the staff was attentive. I was nervous about paying money to the doctor but it worked out. I had been unable to find any unused envelopes in my grandmother's apartment and so folded my three 1,000-ruble bills into a ripped-out page from one of my notebooks; this looked pretty ridiculous and when I caught the doctor in his little office and thrust it at him, he demurred. But I insisted. "Please," I said. Finally he agreed and, opening the top drawer of his desk, stuffed the makeshift envelope inside. "It's unnecessary," he said, looking at me with dignity, "but thank you."

And that was that. No receipt, no exchange of goods, and afterward I went back to my grandmother's room. But the payment worked, at least for me. I felt like I had bought a small part of the hospital. I was no longer a stranger there. And after I paid off the nurses too I noticed that my grandmother had an extra blanket and that they rolled a television into her room.

My grandmother's neighbor turned out to be a garrulous woman named Vladlenna. She was just a few years younger than my grandmother but large where my grandmother was small and loud where my grandmother was quiet. On the morning of my first visit I found my grandmother in bed and Vladlenna regaling her with tales of her health. "Oh, Vladlenna Viktorovna, this is my grandson Andrei," said my grandmother.

"Nice to meet you, Andryusha!" Vladlenna hollered from her bed. She was holding some kind of yellow half-knit object in her lap and working on it as she spoke. She weighed two hundred pounds if she weighed anything. "Seva," she hollered, "is this guy married?"

"I'm afraid not," my grandmother said.

"Well, we'll take right care of that!" said Vladlenna. "I know lots of girls!" And she cackled. I smiled politely. The truth was, if it weren't for the recent advent of Yulia, I'd probably have asked Vladlenna for some phone numbers.

My grandmother had been changed into a green hospital gown, and there was still a bandage on the back of her head. I couldn't tell if it was fresh or not. Other than that, she looked OK. She still had her strength. She smiled when she saw me.

"How is the food here?" I asked.

My grandmother shook her head, as if to indicate that the food was unspeakably bad.

"It's pretty good!" Vladlenna shouted from her side of the room. "This morning they gave us oatmeal with jam and some nice tea!"

"Is that true?" I asked my grandmother.

She looked confused. "You know," she said, "I don't remember."

"Ha!" Vladlenna said. "I'm not saying it was the most memorable thing that's ever happened and we all need to remember it for the rest of our lives. Ha-ha!"

I sat with them for a while and then went and found the cafeteria. I ate a bowl of borscht and a plate of kasha and kotlety, all for about three dollars, and bought some small pies they had by the cash register to take up to my grandmother and Vladlenna. I stayed until eight, alternately hanging out, working on my laptop while my grandmother napped, and exchanging pleasantries with Vladlenna. Then I started on the long, cold ride home.

And so it was every day. I was able to get some work done in the morning, get on the subway to the bus, and then spend the remainder of the time (it took almost two hours to reach the hospital) with my grandmother and her roommate. The CT scan showed no internal bleeding, but they proceeded to do the whole raft of other neurological tests, as they said, "while they had her." All these came back negative. My grandmother was in good health.

"Are you sure?" I asked the doctor when, on the final day, he delivered this report to me. I said, "She's always forgetting things. Basic things."

"How old is she?"

"Eighty-nine."

"Exactly right. She has medium-stage dementia, which for her age, after the life she's led—it's good. It's above average."

"There's nothing she could take? She's pretty depressed."

When questioned by the doctor earlier about these very symptoms, I had underplayed them. But now that he was giving her a perfectly clean bill of health, I wanted to argue.

"You live in America, is that right?" said the doctor.

I nodded.

"I know that in America they prescribe medication for this sort of thing. Maybe they're right to do so. But these are powerful drugs. They have side effects. Here, we're more careful. My advice is to keep your grandmother as mentally engaged as you can. Talk to her. Argue with her. Her memory is going to disappear, but you can slow that down. And she can still enjoy her family. She can still enjoy the outdoors. These drugs can slow some of the processes but they might break

197

something else in her brain or body—I would avoid them." The doctor nodded, as if to say, "Enough." He had never said so many words to me at once, and I was surprised and grateful. "*Vot tak,*" he said. "So that's that." "Good luck." And he reached out his hand for me to shake.

All this for a hundred dollars.

It was time to go home. I called a cab and went to fetch my grandmother, who was now dressed in her ordinary clothes again, and helped her up out of bed.

She nearly collapsed in my arms. The nurse was there and saw it. "She's been lying in bed for a week," she said. "It'll be a little while before she gets her strength back. But she will."

We said good-bye to Vladlenna, who handed us a piece of paper with her phone number on it, and I supported my grandmother down the hall and to the elevator. The young doctor came out to say good-bye to us. "It's been a pleasure having you, Seva Efraimovna," he said.

"Thank you," she said, beaming.

They seemed to have genuinely cared for her and were sorry to see her go.

But a terrible thing had happened. Forcing an elderly woman who was used to walking several miles a day, even if only back and forth through her apartment, to lie in bed for such a long stretch of time was hugely destructive. They had meant her no harm! But my grandmother came in with a mild head injury and left with a limp. On our way out we bought her a cane in the hospital shop.

In the cab, I asked my grandmother when she intended to call her new friend Vladlenna.

"That woman?" said my grandmother. "I'm not going to call her. She's an anti-Semite."

"What? How do you know?"

"I know," said my grandmother. "I could tell by the way she said 'Seva Efraimovna.' Let me see her phone number."

I handed her the little sheet. My grandmother crumpled it up and then, before I could stop her, rolled down her window a little bit and threw it out.

"Hey!" said the driver. "If they pull me over you're paying the ticket."

My grandmother didn't hear him. As for me, I was in shock.

"Did you hear me?" said the driver.

"Yes," I said. "Don't worry about it."

We drove on. My grandmother had outlived all her friends, but that didn't mean she was in the market for new ones.

9.

HOUSEKEEPING

THROUGHOUT THE TIME my grandmother was in the hospital I had not seen Yulia. We had texted a bit—I'd never texted in Russian before, and I enjoyed it; I'd gotten a cheap Russian phone after my Samsung started acting up, and it corrected my spelling—but it wasn't like I was going to drag her to the hospital, and I had no time for anything else. On the bus to and from the hospital I had spun out numerous fantasies about our next date, but as soon as my grandmother returned I was confronted with another problem.

The morning after we got back I woke up to find my grandmother in the kitchen, slowly grating an apple, as usual. I kissed her on the back of her perfectly healed head, which still had a little bandage on it.

"Oh, Andryush," said my grandmother, twisting around. The cane we'd bought at the hospital was leaning up against the wall next to her chair. She said, "What are we going to do?"

"What do you mean?"

"What are we going to eat?"

"I can make breakfast," I said.

"And for lunch?"

"For lunch we'll go to a café." I decided this on the spot. We'd go to the Coffee Grind! It would be a wonderful opportunity for my grandmother to get some exercise, and also to see where I spent so much time, and for lunch she could eat one of their tuna sandwiches. The other time we'd stopped at a café, on one of our walks, she'd declared the food inedible, but maybe the Grind would be different. It was too expensive to be a long-term solution, but it would get us through the day, and then tomorrow I could cook.

"A café?" said my grandmother incredulously. The way she said it I could tell she was thinking of a short counter, a couple of tables, maybe an espresso machine. "They won't have anything to eat at a café."

"It's more like a restaurant. We're going to a restaurant."

"A restaurant?" Now she was thinking of a banquet hall, a meal with multiple courses, lots of vodka, loud music, probably dancing. It was something you went to once a year, for a birthday or wedding. "That's very expensive."

"No, it's not."

"Of course it is! It's a restaurant."

"This isn't a fancy restaurant. It's more like a cafeteria."

"Oh, a *cafeteria.*" She pictured a large spacious room, picking up a tray and getting some kasha and kotlety and soup ladled onto your plate, like in an American prison. "OK."

So later that day we went to the cafeteria. It was a five-minute walk down Bolshaya Lubyanka, maybe six, and as we made our way my grandmother oohed and aahed as we tried not to slip on the ice. I held her tightly by the arm, and she began gingerly to make use of her cane. We walked by an art gallery that had recently appeared, and some girls were outside, with their coats off, smoking. "Look at those girls," said my grandmother loudly, of the scantily clad smokers. "They're not wearing any clothes!" She was weaker and had a limp but she was at least getting her spirit back.

I kept my head down and finally we were there. We navigated the step up into the Coffee Grind, the pretty barista greeted us brightly from across the room, as she greeted everyone, and I guided my grandmother to a seat. It was strange to be here with her—I felt nervous, as though, if she didn't like it, the Grind would fall in my esteem. I had to make sure she didn't see the prices, so I asked her to stay put while I got some food. She agreed. I ordered a pot of tea, two little cabbage pies, and two tuna sandwiches. It cost twenty-five dollars. I paid quickly and shoved the change in my pocket. My grandmother, back at our table, hadn't noticed the prices. Then, to my surprise, she ate her food without any complaint. Perhaps at the hospital her high standards had been slightly adjusted down.

"Andryush," she said, as we drank our tea after the meal. "You are a good person. You're not going to stay here, are you?"

"In what sense?" I wasn't sure what she wanted to hear.

"In this country. Don't stay in this country. It's a terrible country. Good people become bad people, or bad things happen to them."

She bent over slowly and sipped at the tea, which was still hot. Sometimes, when her tea was too hot, she would pour it out into a dish to cool it down, and sip it from the dish. She did so now.

"Did I ever tell you about Leva's company?" she said.

"A little," I said.

"He had a wonderful idea, and he made a company with his friends," she said. "They were people he trusted. And then"—I saw her struggling to remember—"something bad happened." She couldn't remember the story, but she remembered its lessons. "He trusted them and they betrayed him," she said. "That's what happened."

I nodded. It was, basically, what had happened, and in addition to everything else it saddened me that this is what my grandmother spent her final years thinking about.

"So," my grandmother concluded, "don't stay in this country. It's a terrible country."

She finished drinking her tea and leaned back a little in her chair. Yes, I thought, it's a terrible country a lot of the time, but here we were, across the street from the KGB no less, and it wasn't so bad. You could find little oases here, little islands of peace. Then, before I could think of a way to stop her, my grandmother took out her teeth and put them in the dish where the tea had been. I'd never seen her do this in public, though of course we'd hardly ever eaten out together. I glanced around the Coffee Grind; I had put us at a corner table, out of the way of things, and no one seemed to be paying attention. I relaxed.

We sat in contented silence for a while. My grandmother had lost a lot of weight at the hospital, and she was pale. Well, we'd take care of that! Eventually I cleared our plates. As I deposited them at the counter,

I heard a wail behind me. I turned to see a little boy, about age three, with his mother; they had been sitting at an angle to us but now, as the mother was getting the boy dressed to leave, he saw my grandmother and her teeth and was pointing at them. "Mama," he was yelling, terrified, "what happened to her teeth?" I turned to my grandmother. She couldn't understand why he was screaming and was making toothless faces at him to try to cheer him up. She loved little kids. The more she made faces at him, the harder the boy cried. I didn't know what to do; I walked back to my grandmother and then stood helplessly beside her. The mother gave me a reproachful look as she finally finished dressing the boy and picked him up and out of the Coffee Grind. Oblivious, my grandmother put her teeth back into her mouth and announced that it was time to go.

As we made our way slowly out the door, the pretty barista who had greeted us approached and, speaking quietly enough that my grandmother couldn't hear, told me not to bring her back again.

My grandmother nodded politely at her. "Thank you very much," she said.

On a parallel track, I was indignant. "I come in here every day and you're telling me I can't bring my grandmother?"

The barista was unfazed. "We need to keep up certain standards here. And as for you, I'm sorry, you come in every day and buy the cheapest item on the menu and then sit for five hours with your computer."

This was low. "You know what?" I said. "I won't be troubling you anymore."

"So be it," said the barista, and bowed slightly.

"And your cappuccinos are inedible."

She bowed again, though I did see some color come to her face.

I turned my head and walked out with my grandmother.

"Andryusha," she said, once we were in the street. "Thank you for that lunch. For supper we can have some cottage cheese with jam. But what will we do tomorrow?"

I was seething. My grandmother should not have taken her teeth out, it's true. But it's not like she came in every day and took out her teeth. This was an emergency. And as for my sitting there for five hours, that was also true. But it was the purpose of a café that people could sit there for a while! Ahhh!

"Andryush," my grandmother said again. "What will we do tomorrow?"

"I'm going to cook," I said roughly.

"Do you know how?" said my grandmother.

"You're going to teach me."

"OK," said my grandmother, and patted me a little nervously on the arm.

We walked back up Bolshaya Lubyanka. "You know," said my grandmother, "that is the big scary building." She gestured to the KGB headquarters across the street. "But this"—she gestured to a small, cute, green nineteenth-century building to our left—"is where they carried out most of the executions."

"Really?" I said. I'd always assumed it was the big building across the street.

"Yes," said my grandmother matter-of-factly. "Bolshaya Lubyanka Eleven. This is it."

And we kept walking.

I got up the next morning to a worried grandmother. "Andryush," she said, "what are we going to do?" I reminded her that I was going to be cooking and proceeded to make us some eggs and instant coffee. But of course more generally she was right. Even if we did find something to eat, *what were we going to do*? In general. With our lives. I didn't know.

I had never learned to cook. This hadn't felt like a moral failing on my part; now it did. Many factors had conspired to create this failing in me. I had spent much of my life in universities, with their cafeterias and pizza nights and free sandwiches in exchange for attending someone's lecture. I had lived in New York, where you could always buy a hot dog or chicken on a stick, and if you were in a part of town where the guys charged too much, you could bargain with them. I had dated girls who cooked, and when there was no one else to cook and I didn't have enough money to buy a sandwich, I went to the store and bought a can of chickpeas and a can of tuna and a packet of pasta. Chickpeas plus tuna plus some olive oil was a salad; pasta plus butter was an entrée. In this way I would feed myself. But of course I could never feed someone else this way. I had never had to.

My grandmother had grown up in a country where, for all its promises of communal living, there were very few public places to get something to eat. If you were not able to cook, and cook frugally, make the most of the paltry ingredients available, then you would go hungry. You had to cook or you would starve.

So maybe I could finally change. After breakfast I placed pen and paper before my grandmother and demanded a shopping list. I was going to make kotlety and potatoes, plus potato soup. This would provide us two or three days of food, depending on how quickly we ate the kotlety. Then I would cook again.

In her large round hand my grandmother produced a list: a kilogram of meat at the basement butcher's on Sretenka, preferably with not too much fat in it, a loaf of bread, and milk—the bread was cheapest at the bakery on the boulevard, my grandmother said, and milk was cheapest at the so-called market. For potato soup, a quart of milk and two kilograms of potatoes, also cheapest at the market. Onions and flour we had.

I considered disobeying her instructions as to where to buy what but knew that she'd be able to tell, and so I went to the butcher on Sretenka, the bakery on the boulevard, and finally the market. Then I returned and laid the groceries proudly on the counter. Sitting in her chair at the kitchen table, my grandmother instructed me in the grinding of the meat—I cut it up and then trimmed it of as much fat as possible, something that was difficult to do because the fat was thickly intertwined with the meat, so that after picking at it with my knife and ripping off a certain amount with my fingers, I gave up. I began to grind the meat, mixing in bread and a little bit of milk as I went. The meat grinder was manual, meaning I had to turn a handle like in olden times, and I enjoyed this until, about halfway through our cut of meat, the grinder slowed down. Then it stopped. "What happened?" I asked my grandmother.

"The fat has gummed it up," she said. "You need to take it apart." I took it apart and laboriously scraped off the fat. Then I washed it and put it back together again. There were only a few parts to the meat grinder so it wasn't complicated, but getting one of the smaller iron fittings back in place took a while.

Eventually I had ground the kilo of meat, half a loaf of white bread, milk, and an onion into a ground beef mixture. That turned out to be the easy part. Next I covered the countertop in flour, caked my own hands in the flour, like an Olympic weight lifter, and with these floured hands rolled the ground beef into little spheres. "You don't want them too small or too dense," my grandmother instructed. In the end, unfortunately, they were not dense enough, and when I put them in the frying pan, they began to crumble. I watched over them with trepidation and tried with a wooden spatula manually to solder back the pieces that were falling off. But this was not possible.

In between these activities or after them my grandmother taught me how to make kasha. I had not known. Kasha, or *grechka,* buckwheat, was the staple of the Russian diet, eaten in the morning with milk, in the afternoon with kotlety, in the evening in little buckwheat cakes, if you were lucky. Without kasha there was nothing, and until this day I did not know how to make it.

Kasha was easier than kotlety. You take a cup of kasha, pour it into a small pot. Pour cold water over this, to let the dust and kasha bits burned during the roasting process rise to the surface; drain the water; rinse once more; then pour twice as much boiling water on this as you have kasha. (This first time and several times after, I showed it to my grandmother, who eyeballed the level: good.) Place on a burner and bring to a boil (about three minutes); now mix in butter and salt and lower to a simmer; cover. In fifteen to twenty minutes, you have perfect kasha.

To watch this happen—to be the vessel through which kasha is brought into the world, after a lifetime of eating it—how to describe this feeling? Tolstoy had eaten kasha; Chekhov had eaten kasha. With the power of kasha in my hands, I needed to rely on no one ever again. I still make kasha just about every day.

But that was my one success. The kotlety fell apart, as I've said, and my grandmother's simple potato soup recipe—potatoes, some water, some onions, some milk—ended up too watery. (And yet, to be fair: I made soup.) We ate the food quietly. Before we sat down, after I had finished cleaning all traces of flour from the kitchen, I looked up at the clock. It was a few minutes past four. I had started the grocery shopping at nine in the morning. In its entirety the process had taken seven hours; these flaky kotlety and the watery soup would last us three days, more realistically two if I came home hungry after hockey. Then I'd be off to the grocery store again.

My grandmother ate the lunch with some gusto. "I need to get my strength back," she said. "The only way to do that is to eat more." I hadn't seen her so cheerful in a long time. But soon a shade of worry once again crossed her face.

"Andryush," she said. "This will last us two days. Then what will we do?"

That evening I looked up an old email from Dima to find the number of a woman named Seraphima Mikhailovna—she used to come clean and cook for him when he was in between wives. Seraphima Mikhailovna agreed to come by the day after tomorrow. She turned out to be a gregarious former math teacher from Ukraine, whose town had stopped paying salaries to schoolteachers years earlier, and she cooked a terrific batch of kotlety and mashed potatoes and borscht that would last until she came again three days later. Her kotlety were good, and her borscht was even better. She charged five hundred rubles per visit, or sixteen dollars, plus supplies, which she picked up herself. It was a good deal. Initially my grandmother found it a little trying, having this relative stranger in the house doing what she used to do and having, my grandmother felt, to supervise her. "Oy, it's exhausting," she said. "To cook and clean yourself is intolerable. But to have someone else do it is exhausting!" Still, she grew used to it. And as long as Seraphima Mikhailovna came to cook and clean, my grandmother never asked where our next meal was coming from. It was in the fridge. It was taken care of. That was the end of my experiment in good housekeeping. Aside from making kasha, I still haven't learned how to cook.

10.

SHIPALKIN FOILS MY PLANS

BY THIS POINT two weeks had passed since Sergei's party. It's not that I thought Yulia would forget me, exactly. But I did worry that whatever spell had been woven or whatever illusion she was laboring under so that she would kiss me at a party would be broken if any more time passed. And then it *was* broken. On Friday morning, the first day after the advent of Seraphima Mikhailovna, I texted Yulia asking if she wanted to hang out the next day, a Saturday. I suggested, since it was so cold, that we could go to the Tretyakov museum.

Yulia did not text back right away and I opened my laptop on the windowsill to check my email. The first thing I saw was a message to the October list from Misha with the subject line "Urgent." I opened it. "Guys," read the email, "last night our old comrade Petya Shipalkin was arrested during an action against the FSB. I know we've had our differences with him but none of that matters now. He's being held at the precinct on Sretenka—if you're able, let's meet there at noon and show our support. There will no doubt be some Mayhem people there—let's try to stay out of debates for now and just show our solidarity."

The uncharacteristically somber email from Misha went on to describe logistics and share phone numbers. I wrote them down on a notepad but the entire time I was thinking: Shipalkin. Fucking Shipalkin. This was why Yulia hadn't texted me back. If she had—if she had texted me to say this had happened—that would be one thing. But she had not.

I worked distractedly for a couple of hours, saw that my grandmother was resting after a hearty late breakfast, and then put on three sweaters and my Gulag coat and headed out into the cold. "Civil activist Pyotr

Shipalkin," I heard on Echo of Moscow radio as I was putting on my things, "was arrested last night in front of Lubyanka as he staged a protest against political violence." Already, he was being turned into a hero.

I arrived at our police station just after noon. There was a surprisingly large crowd, maybe fifty people, milling about outside. It looked to be broken up into three distinct groups. One was Sergei, Misha, Boris, and the rest (though not Yulia yet), in their cheap, puffy winter coats and old hats. My people. Then there was a small group of more arty-looking types, some of them in leather jackets and even leather pants, all of them stylish and in black. That must have been Mayhem. And then there was an even larger group of better-dressed people, among whom I recognized one of Dima's friends from the night of Maxim's birthday party, and then, holding a microphone and interviewing someone, Elena from Echo of Moscow.

She noticed me and came over. "What are you doing here?" she asked.

"I live near here," I said. "What about you?"

She lifted up her microphone to indicate that she was working. "Do you know this guy?" she asked.

"Not really," I said.

"Hmm," said Elena, losing interest in me and scanning the crowd for likely interview subjects.

"I think that's his crew," I said, nodding to the Mayhem crowd.

"Oh?" said Elena. "Thank you." And she went off toward them.

I didn't mind. Elena's spell had been broken, definitively, by Yulia. And for a moment I allowed myself to wonder if Yulia's absence from this quasi-protest meant that she was having a different reaction to Shipalkin's arrest than I had anticipated. Maybe she still thought Shipalkin was an idiot; maybe she thought it was nobler to visit one's grandmother in the hospital than to pull stunts in front of the KGB. But then Misha told me that she was inside the building, with Shipalkin's lawyer. I knew then that we weren't going to be seeing each other again anytime soon. She had been trying to forget about Shipalkin and now he had made that impossible.

As Misha now told it, a drunk Shipalkin had achieved this coup by showing up the night before on Lubyanka with a canister of tomato sauce. He started flinging the sauce at the big FSB building with his hand, yelling, "Hands in sauce, hands off!" To the surprise of the Mayhem colleagues who had been observing his "action," no one came out of the Lubyanka building to confront him; instead, a few minutes in, a police car pulled up and the officers tackled him. He had spent the night at the station. What happened next would depend on whether they believed he was primarily part of a political movement or primarily drunk. Drunk would be a lot better, in terms of getting out.

The whole thing was so stupid, I thought. Here was a regime that had systematically undermined workers' rights; had prosecuted several nasty wars, most recently with Georgia; and had imprisoned labor activists and dissidents, and encouraged the far right. And Shipalkin was going to defeat it by throwing tomato sauce at the FSB? What a joke. Boris—and Yulia—were right.

Finally Yulia came out, with the lawyer, and went over to where Misha and I and the other October people were standing. She hugged all of us without distinction; she looked like she'd been crying. I didn't know what to do or say.

Now the lawyer asked people to pay attention, and the three groups pulled up together to listen. He said Shipalkin was being charged with political extremism. "We're trying to talk them down but it could be serious," he said. "I would urge you, if possible, to be careful what you say in the next few days and weeks online and to the media. If you want Petya to be free soon, you won't try to turn him into a political martyr."

"What kind of martyr?" I heard myself say. "What if we say that he's a fool with zero political analysis or sense?"

The lawyer studied me for a moment. "Well, actually, from a legal perspective, that would be fine," he said.

But my remark had caused a commotion. "Who's this asshole?" one of the Mayhem guys said from behind me, loudly enough so I could hear.

I began to turn around, to introduce myself, but at this moment a young police officer came out of the building. "I'm sorry," he said politely. "You can't all stand here. We'll have to consider it an unsanctioned public meeting."

"We're leaving now," said the lawyer. "Right, guys?"

The three groups, October and Mayhem and the liberals, which had come together to listen to the lawyer's report, now caucused separately and briefly on this question and decided to depart. "We could go to the Coffee Grind," someone proposed.

"That's expensive," one of the Mayhem people said.

"They don't have waiters," said Misha. "We can order one cappuccino for all of us and that'll be enough." The proposal was accepted. A few people gave me dirty looks before heading in the Grind's direction, but that was it.

Without saying anything to me, Yulia headed after them.

"Hey," I said, catching up with her. "I'm going to go back and check on my grandmother."

"All right," she said. She kept her gaze on the ground as she said this.

"Can I see you soon?" I asked.

She looked up at me now, and I saw she was angry. "Why did you say that about Petya?" she said.

Fairly or unfairly, I got mad again. "Anarchism is an infantile disorder!" I cried. "You used to think so too."

Yulia looked me square in the face. "First of all," she said, "please don't tell me what I did or did not used to think. Second, how dare you? Whatever you and maybe I think of Petya's politics, right now he's in there and we're out here. And what's more, before too long you'll be over there." She pointed over her shoulder, toward America. "It's indecent to criticize someone whose position you'll never have to occupy," she said.

I felt exposed. One month ago I'd had no idea that anarchism was an infantile disorder. Now I was proclaiming it to the world. And though I might claim to myself and to Dima and to my grandmother that I was staying, I also knew that eventually I would leave. I didn't say anything.

"Well?" said Yulia, giving me an opportunity to respond. "Fine," she said. "I'll see you at study group."

And that was that. She headed for the Coffee Grind. I turned around and ran into Elena. She was looking at me like she'd discovered something about me. "That was an interesting statement about the protester," she said. "Do you want to say it on air?"

I had, by this point, lost all interest in Elena. "No," I said, "I don't." And I headed home.

The next week, for some reason, the Marxist study group was moved to Wednesday, meaning that it conflicted with hockey. I called Sergei to see what he thought. "I think we play hockey," said Sergei. "Marx isn't going anywhere." I agreed. As a result I didn't see Yulia again until the week after, almost two weeks after Shipalkin's arrest. Shipalkin was still in jail, now in Lefortovo, the special FSB prison. Part of the discussion that evening was about what could be done for him. Yulia had visited him in prison—she was able to, as they were still legally married. She said he seemed scared and upset. Our walk along Tverskaya with Boris and Nikolai was awkward; Yulia and I behaved as total strangers. How could we not? Lefortovo was serious—it's where they put terrorists and major criminals and fallen oligarchs and other people they planned to send away for a long time. Another activist who'd been arrested for defacing a government building—he'd drawn a picture of Medvedev fellating Putin on a police station in Novosibirsk—had recently received a three-year sentence. Would Yulia be forced to wait that long? It wasn't impossible. She looked unhappy, and there was nothing I could do.

11.

TO CHEER OURSELVES UP,
WE GO SHOPPING

I HAD FINALLY found someone, and not just anyone, but Yulia, and then I had lost her. Russia had taken her. My grandmother was right.

I redoubled my efforts to advance myself for the Watson position. I wrote to my recommenders, updating them on my Russian activities so they could incorporate that into any follow-ups they felt like sending to the search committee, and I read up on old Marxist groupuscules, the better to compare October to them. If I submitted my article to one of the Russia journals soon, there might be time for it to get accepted before Watson made their decision. They had a late start, and probably wouldn't be done before May.

My grandmother was getting better and worse simultaneously. Her strength was coming back. She shuffled around the apartment almost like before; she was eating normally. But with the return of her strength came the return of her depression—as if, having conquered most of her physical difficulties, she could go back to worrying about her spiritual ones. She began talking regularly about suicide. "You know," she said one day after lunch, "I've had enough."

I knew from the way she said it what she meant, but I decided it might be therapeutic for her to say it. "Enough of what?" I said.

"Of all this," she said. "Of life. I've had my share."

"Well," I said. I didn't know what to say. "You're just going to have to tolerate it a little longer."

"Yes," my grandmother said. "I guess I'll have to."

I tried my best. One day when it wasn't too cold out I took her to the department store across from the Clean Ponds metro. Despite going down to only three PMOOC classes, I had managed to save a little money by cutting down on hockey and boycotting the Coffee Grind, and I thought it might be nice to buy her a new pink sweater, since the one she had was frayed and had developed a noticeable hole in the right shoulder. The outing was not a success. As we shuffled toward the department store my grandmother started reminiscing about Soviet shopping. "It was impossible to find anything," she said, "but if you did find it, you could buy it. Everything was affordable. Of course, it didn't matter, because you couldn't find it. Most of my clothes came from America."

"What do you mean, from America?"

"Someone sent them to me from America."

"My mom?" I asked. "Your daughter?"

"My daughter?"

"You had a daughter in America."

"Yelochka?"

"Yes."

"Yes, it must have been her. She died, you know."

We walked on in silence. The store, aside from a hulking security guard at the entrance, was empty. People were still suffering the effects of the crisis. And this store was not cheap. It was not crazy, like the luxury stores closer to the Kremlin, but it was definitely overpriced. I knew this going in. But I had not anticipated—though I should have—the effect this would have on my grandmother. When I walked her over to the sweaters and found a pink one I thought she might like, she immediately reached for the price tag. It was 5,000 rubles—$160. "Oh, my God!" she cried, and dropped the price tag as if she'd been singed.

I found myself having an interesting reaction. I had myself been this person complaining about prices so many times, in so many stores, restaurants, coffee shops—everywhere. Especially in Russia, where some of the prices were very reasonable, in line with the salaries people made, and some of the prices were so outrageous, more in line with the massive theft at the top of the pyramid, that it was impossible not to complain. I mean, my grandmother was right. This was a thirty-dollar sweater. But my interesting reaction consisted in taking the side of the store. "That's how much a sweater costs!" I said. "It's a nice sweater."

"No, thank you," said my grandmother.

"Will you at least try it on?"

"What's the point?"

There must be a clearance section, I thought. I should have scouted ahead and taken my grandmother there right away. Stupid.

"Hold on," I said. "I'm going to find some cheaper sweaters. I'll be right back."

My grandmother had by now wandered over to the lingerie section and was picking up skimpy little underpants—they really did have very little fabric on them—and looking at the price tags and laughing in horror. "Three thousand rubles!" she called out after me, holding up a tiny blue thong.

I left her to this and started speedwalking through the store. There were overpriced winter coats from Sweden, overpriced winter hats from Norway, some jeans that were actually not so terribly priced, or anyway no more than jeans are normally overpriced, but all of them had some kind of sparkly spangles on them. Why was everything so overpriced? It wasn't because people along the labor chain were receiving fair wages—they were not. I knew from talking with Michael the subletter, who worked in logistics, that Russia's roads were bad, the train system was good but overcrowded, and customs duties were inordinately high. Moscow was well inland, so even under the best of circumstances it was going to be a difficult place to deliver goods to. And one of the most corrupt economic systems on Earth was far from the best of circumstances. So in the end you had a flimsy pink cotton sweater that cost five thousand rubles. I completed my tour of the store. There was no clearance section.

When I returned to the lingerie section my grandmother was no longer there. Nor was she back at the sweaters. Had something happened? I finally found her standing in front of the massive security guard.

"Tell me," she was saying, "do a lot of people come to this store? It's very expensive."

The giant shrugged. How was he to know? All he knew was that if someone tried to steal something, he would fuck them up.

"Well." My grandmother wouldn't let up. "It doesn't seem like there are a lot of people, does it?" She gestured to the empty store.

The giant's countenance changed and for a second I thought I even saw him square up slightly to my tiny grandmother. Maybe she was trying to steal something, and should get fucked up? Stranger things had happened in this country.

I took my grandmother firmly by the elbow. "Shall we go?" I said.

"All right," said my grandmother.

We walked home. For the next two weeks, whenever my grandmother called Emma Abramovna, she made sure to complain about the prices in the store. At first this hurt my feelings—I felt like she was complaining about me—but then I realized that it had given her something to talk about. She continued to wear her sweater with the hole in it. It was just a little hole. It was fine.

Emma Abramovna told us about a Tsvetaeva documentary she'd read about. Had we seen it? We hadn't. "We never go to the movies anymore," my grandmother lamented. "Andrei's too busy."

"I am not!" I said. It was true I'd been spending a lot of time with Sergei, following him around as he did his volunteer teaching, but I still had most of my evenings free, and anyway that wasn't the reason we weren't going to the movies. I said, "You don't like any of the movies we see."

"I would like this one," said my grandmother.

"Great!" I said. "Let's see it."

So on a non-hockey night a few days later, we dressed warmly and headed out into the night. Once on the boulevard, my grandmother started waving at cars. Mercedes after Audi after Mercedes sped past without paying her any mind. "That car won't pick you up," I kept saying. My poor grandmother would ignore me, wander out into the street, and come back a few seconds later disappointed.

"How did you know?" she'd say.

"Because it's a Mercedes."

Then I saw an old Zhiguli lumbering toward us. "Whereas that car," I now said, and stuck out my hand, "will pick us up." And sure enough the old wreck pulled over and the driver asked where we were going. My grandmother looked at me like I had magical powers of foresight. Then we sat in traffic for twenty minutes. The boulevard wasn't really built for cars, and yet cars had no choice but to use it. It would have been faster to walk to the theater, though this way at least we were sitting down. My grandmother, sitting up front, spent most of the ride talking about how old she was and how all of her friends had died. The driver nodded politely and occasionally made a sympathetic sound. When we finally arrived my grandmother handed him fifty rubles, which was too little. Luckily I had anticipated this possibility, and was able to hand him fifty more.

We came into the theater after the lights had gone down; my grandmother clung to me as we maneuvered ourselves to a pair of seats in the front row. This way she could stretch out her legs. And finally we were there. The movie unspooled before us: it showed Tsvetaeva's life before the Revolution, a happy life among the Moscow intelligentsia, her father the professor and founder of the art collection that became the Pushkin Museum. The Tsvetaevs lived in comfort, they had servants, but they were not aristocrats or parasites; they were the very best of the world that the Revolution would destroy. The documentary had good archival footage. A lot of it took place near where we were sitting—Tsvetaeva grew up around the corner, practically, at Three Pond Lane.

"Andryush," my grandmother said very loudly, turning to me. "Did we get tickets?"

"Yes."

"Are you sure?"

I assured her we had tickets.

"Excuse me!" someone said, meaning, please be quiet.

Tsvetaeva had her first success with her poetry at a young age and embarked on her first love affairs, with her eventual husband, Sergei Efron, and also the poetess Sophia Parnok. Then the Bolsheviks came to power. Tsvetaeva was soon cut off from Efron, who was fighting the

Bolsheviks in Crimea, while she remained in Moscow with their two young daughters.

"Andryush," my grandmother said, "I need to use the bathroom."

I took her hand and led her out of the hall. Once we were close enough I let her go. She looked awkward, in a hurry, as she went into the ladies' room. I waited for her in the cinema's empty, tastelessly furnished café. She took a while, and then emerged, my poor grandmother, looking very tired.

We had missed the Civil War, the terrible death of Tsvetaeva's daughter from hunger, and then her emigration, finally, to Prague, to join her husband, who had escaped there from the Bolsheviks.

Tsvetaeva lived happily in Prague and gave birth to a son; then she lived unhappily in Paris, wrote some of the greatest Russian poetry of the twentieth century, and tried to make ends meet. All through this her husband did nothing. Or, not nothing: He went to school. He went to school a lot. In Prague, at the age of thirty, Efron enrolled in university and started a student literary magazine. A few years later, once they'd moved to Paris, Efron *again* enrolled in university, this time to study filmmaking. I started to feel like the movie was some kind of criticism of me.

It was only in 1934, at the age of forty-two, that Sergei Efron finally got a job—and that job was for the NKVD. At first all he had to do was praise the USSR to the deeply anti-Soviet émigré community in Paris, which Efron, who'd recently been converted to Soviet Communism, could manage with a clear conscience. But eventually the job came to include political assassinations. This is what happens when you work for the NKVD. Efron helped organize the killings of the defected Soviet agent Nathan Poretsky and (possibly) Leon Trotsky's son Lev Sedov. Efron did a so-so job, and with the police on his trail, fled for Moscow. He was soon followed there by the couple's daughter, Ariadna, who worshipped him.

Here my grandmother had to go to the bathroom again. I hung out in the doorway of the theater until she came back, watching the movie and watching for her.

Tsvetaeva was now alone in Paris with her teenage son, Mur, impoverished, surrounded by a hostile émigre community that believed she had been in league with her husband and, by extension, the NKVD. She knew well enough what was happening in Stalin's Russia, though no one who wasn't there could really imagine how bad it was. She had had a fateful meeting with Pasternak in Paris in 1935. In coded language—he was too scared to speak freely—he tried to warn her. But she did not understand. All she knew was that her family had abandoned her; her friends refused to speak with her. Nazi Germany rose in the east, and France was preparing, albeit too slowly, for war. Should she return to the USSR? A few years earlier she had written one of her greatest poems. "Homesickness," it began, "what bullshit!" She wouldn't return out of some misplaced sentiment about her so-called motherland. But her husband and her daughter were there.

After a terrible period of indecision, Tsvetaeva took the train to Moscow in 1938. She found a frightened country. Her old friends avoided her; even her half sister declined to see her. (Her full sister, Anastasia Tsvetaeva, was already in the Gulag.) Efron and Ariadna were in an NKVD safe house outside Moscow, where Tsvetaeva and Mur joined them. Within six months, Efron and Ariadna were both arrested, and Tsvetaeva and her son were forced out of the house. They sought lodging with the remnants of their old family in Moscow. Meanwhile Mur, a spoiled teenager with limited Russian, had trouble adjusting to Soviet life. He made an already bad situation worse. Soon they joined the mass evacuation before the German advance, and life became even harder and more lonely. Eventually it became too much. Two years after they arrived, Tsvetaeva hanged herself. Efron, her overeducated husband, was shot by the NKVD that year. Her son, just barely out of his teens, was killed at the front a few years later, in 1944. Only their daughter, Ariadna, who spent years in the Gulag, survived.

My grandmother had come back from the bathroom now and we walked again into the theater. How much of this stuff had she been through? Some of it, for sure. She too was in Moscow when the Germans invaded, and she too was evacuated to the Soviet interior. Her father was ill and she was already pregnant with my mother, but when Stalin asked, people went, and in any case the Germans were coming. She too lost her husband during those years. But she was thirty years younger than Tsvetaeva. Her difficulties were less difficult. She survived.

The film ended and the lights came up. It had been, to my surprise, admirably understated, scrupulously documented, intelligent, humane.

My grandmother turned to me as we walked out and said, with a slightly sour expression on her face, "What did you think of it?"

"I thought it was great!" I whispered.

"I didn't. I thought it was boring and pointless."

"What?" I said, much louder than I expected to. "How can you say that?"

My grandmother pursed her lips and shook her head. I recognized the gesture because I had inherited it somehow, presumably via my mother, and used it when I was forced, almost against my will (said the gesture), to point out that some much-praised movie or TV show or book was in fact garbage. "I don't know," said my grandmother. "I just didn't get it."

She was being a snob about this movie that had described this life with such care, that had resurrected and paid homage to the sufferings of an entire generation—sufferings that she herself, my grandmother, had shared! I was inexplicably miffed. They weren't *my* sufferings. The extent of my suffering had been a mildly embarrassing car ride and having to leave the movie theater a couple of times so my grandmother could use the bathroom. (Was it something we ate?) And yet she was the one who wanted to see it!

"You know what?" I said. "If you didn't like this movie, then we won't go to movies anymore! I don't see the point."

She heard me. She stopped and turned to me. "Andryushik," she said gently, "don't get mad. I really didn't understand what it was about. What was it about?"

I had a thunderous look on my face, I could feel it, and then I felt it melt away. My poor grandmother. She couldn't hear; even in a movie theater, with the giant speakers, it must have been difficult to understand every-thing that was happening. And her memory was terrible—how could she follow the narrative if she couldn't remember anything from one minute to the next? Of course she didn't enjoy the movie.

"It was about Tsvetaeva," I said.

"Tsvetaeva?" she said. "That's a wonderful poet."

"Yes. The film was about her life."

"She hanged herself," said my grandmother. Then she added, "During the war."

My grandmother still remembered reams of Russian poetry, and she recited some now:

> No foreign sky protected me,
> no stranger's wing shielded my face.
> I stand as witness to the common lot,
> survivor of that time, that place.

"Yes . . ." my grandmother said. "Survivor of that time, that place."

I was confused. "Is that Tsvetaeva?" I asked.

"No. Akhmatova."

She let me hail the car this time. It was almost ten o'clock, the streets had emptied a little, and we encountered no traffic on our way back home.

12.

I ENLIST

THE THING ABOUT ME as a hockey player was that I wasn't very good. I wasn't bad, I was competent, but compared to my love of hockey, my skill was minuscule. In that gap lay all my disappointment. I was an OK player. But I wanted to be so much better.

Still, I did what I could. In hockey there are two types of players—skill players and grinders. I was a grinder. My shot had never been very good, even in high school, and playing with Anton's crappy stick didn't make it any better; I had no moves that would allow me to buy space and time for myself in tight spots. I was pretty good at anticipating where the play would be and getting there, though I was bad at stick-handling with my head up, which would have allowed me to see and anticipate much more. I scored some goals that year, but the plays I remember were ones where I made a nice outlet pass to Anton or Oleg; or the time I managed to knock Grisha on his back with an open-ice check at our blue line, sending our bench into a spontaneous cheer; or the time I actually caught up to Alyosha from the white team as he maneuvered the puck toward our goal.

But I was not a professional hockey player, nor would I ever be. As the rest of my life became busier, I had to cut down the hockey to a minimum. I still played against the white team on Wednesdays and Fridays, but I stopped going out to the hellscape rink next to the elevated gas line, and also the game with the locker room sheds in the parking lot.

I decided to focus my article on Sergei's departure from the university and his activities, in particular his teaching activities, since then. He had invented what he called mobile classrooms, though the mobile part of it was actually Sergei driving his old Lada. He had spent a few

223

months putting up flyers around Moscow advertising a university-trained teacher to lead literature seminars for free. It took a while, he said, but eventually he had a steady set of about six or seven groups he met with on a weekly basis.

The students in the classes were primarily, to my surprise, men, without much education, who wanted to talk about their experience of a world that was changing all around them. Sergei facilitated this, inserting the teachings of the literature they were reading where necessary, and at other times simply letting the men talk. He also taught high school students whose parents couldn't afford tutors to prepare them for university entry exams, and he taught what essentially amounted to Russian language classes to workers from Central Asia. He would typically try to teach two or three classes in a day, organizing them in such a way that he didn't have to travel too far in between. But Moscow was a big city and he did a lot of driving. I followed him for a week and by the end of those days I was so tired I could barely sleep. But Sergei seemed not to notice the exertion. He wasn't paid by any of the people, although more often than not there was food at the meetings, and during the evenings a beer, and at one of the classes I attended, in the dormitory of some workers from Tajikistan, the men gave him a traditional Tajik tambourine as a sign of their gratitude—at that point he had been teaching their class for exactly one year.

It wasn't all some kind of montage from an inspirational film about radical education. Half the classes I came to were ill attended—two or three people. At one meeting, four middle-aged men with big guts who'd decided to embark on a program of self-improvement demanded to know why Sergei had assigned them Tsvetaeva, whom the men merrily referred to as a slut even after Sergei had explained why they shouldn't. But perhaps the worst incident I saw was the mother of a boy Sergei was helping prepare for his exams—for free, alongside another boy—badgering Sergei about the theoretical nature of the small class's discussions. Couldn't he just tell them what sort of questions were going to be asked by the examiners? Sergei tried to answer that the boys needed to learn how to *think* about literature, but the mother wasn't mollified. She relented only after he suggested that learning how to think about literature in a theoretical mode would actually allow her son to answer questions about books he hadn't even read. "So he doesn't have to read all these books?" she asked.

"N-n-n-n-no, he does," said Sergei. "But there might be books on the exam that we don't have." The mother, a thin woman with big blue eyes who appeared to live alone in this neat but ancient one-room apartment with her teenage son, nodded suspiciously and retreated into the kitchen.

Still, it was incredible—not just because it was exhausting, discouraging, mentally draining, and even possibly dangerous, but because he wasn't being paid. His wife worked as an editor at Lenta.ru, a large media company, and earned a small but sufficient living, and the only money Sergei contributed was from playing goalie in the various men's leagues—he got twenty dollars every time he came out, which was about three times a week. In a sense it was not so much the actual teaching that so impressed me, though that too, but the willingness to live off his wife. Sergei admitted that it was a source of tension within the family. "It's like she married one person, and now she's living with another person," he said of his wife. "And she thinks this new person cares more about his political beliefs than about her and her daughter."

"Is that true?"

"No. Maybe. I don't know. I want my daughter to live in a fair country. But my wife wants me to get a job."

He felt bad about it, but he wasn't going to change. From each according to his ability, to each according to his need. It had the force—or should have had the force—of a biblical injunction. And that's how Sergei lived.

We were getting into March now, and I was hearing more and more from Dima. "You're definitely leaving at the end of the summer, right?" he said one day over Gchat.

"I don't know," I said. I had recently learned that my old nemesis Fishman was also applying for the Watson job—it was a mediocre college, it was isolated, the closest cultural attraction was a giant federal penitentiary, but the job market was tight and at least at Watson they

225

wouldn't make you teach German. Then my adviser told me, to my amazement and chagrin, that Watson had brought in Richard Sutherland, from Princeton, the man who had asked me to fetch him seltzer water at the airport, to head up the search committee. ("They wanted someone who didn't know anything to help mislead the other people who don't know anything" was how my adviser put it; we both knew that this meant Fishman now had an inside track for the job.) But now, talking to Dima, I tried to put on a brave face. "I'm applying for a job for the fall," I told him, "and I hope I get it. But if I don't, I think I'll stay here."

"And do what?"

"What I'm doing."

"That's ridiculous!" Dima typed. "Grandma is going to get worse and worse. At some point she's going to need help taking a shower. She's not going to want you to do that. We're going to need a nurse and it's going to cost money and it's not money that I have if we don't sell."

But there are some things that should not be done for money, I thought. I was sitting at the windowsill. It was past midnight on a Friday—I had returned from hockey and was drinking a Zhigulovskoye with some sushki. As we were arguing over Gchat my grandmother came out of her room, in her nightgown, to go to the bathroom. Her fall and subsequent stay in the hospital had disrupted her sleeping patterns, I think, and she got up now more often in the night. She saw me and waved.

Some things must not be done for money. They must be apportioned instead along communistic principles—from each according to his ability, to each according to his need. Dima could type at me all he wanted—I was staying put.

After following Sergei around for a while, I decided that I had enough material, and I sat down and wrote it up. I placed his work in the context of quixotic Russian attempts to reorganize the world. Sergei struck me as a Tolstoy figure, the sort of person who gives up everything to wander the earth and follow the dictates of his conscience. He was wandering Moscow, not the earth, and he was not doing so barefoot but in a rickety Lada.

I was not suggesting that Sergei was a saint. I was suggesting, I guess, that he was a fool—a holy fool. He was doing what all of us would have wanted to do, but were too cautious, too practical, too chickenshit to do.

I wrote the article and sent it to both Sergei and the *Slavic Review*. It was a long shot. I had sent more than a few articles to the *Slavic Review* over the years, with zero results. This one was better, but that was no reason to think it would meet with more success. The *Slavic Review* was far away. Whereas October, Sergei, my hockey team, my grandmother, and eventually, I still hoped, Yulia, were right here.

Not long after I sent off my article, Sergei asked somewhat formally if we could meet. My first thought was that he'd hated the article. My second thought was darker: that he and/or October were mad about Yulia. I had kissed her, and then I had made that comment about Shipalkin in front of the police station. Had I let my feelings about Yulia cloud my political judgment? I had continued seeing Yulia at the Marxist seminars and she seemed to have stopped being mad at me, but neither did she seem like she particularly wanted to talk. And Shipalkin, her husband, was still in Lefortovo.

Sergei and I agreed to meet at a Mu-Mu café about a mile from my place. If he was mad about the article, I could deal with that. Another alternative was that, now that I'd filed the article, I no longer had an excuse to be hanging around, and so therefore had to leave. But I didn't want to leave. I liked what I was doing. Even without Yulia, I had become very attached to the entire October group.

I played all the bad scenarios out in my mind as I made my way to Mu-Mu. Mu-Mu, as in the sound a cow makes, was in a basement and was cafeteria style and very cheap and pretty good. If it had been a little closer to our house I'd have been able to take my grandmother there whenever we needed food. I found Sergei sitting there in front of a bowl of borscht. I got my own bowl of borscht and sat down with him. Sergei got right to it.

"Listen," he said. "I don't know w-w-what your plans are or feelings are, but now that you're done with your article, I wanted to ask you about something."

I nodded.

"We—October—are going to start a website soon. We want to have a space to discuss leftist politics, educational theory, cultural events, that sort of thing. We think it's important for the left to have that kind of platform."

"That sounds good." This seemed to me a rather roundabout way of kicking me out of the group.

"And we think that a certain amount of it—not all of it, definitely, but the good stuff—would be worth translating into English, as a way of building solidarity internationally. One of the troubles with the Russian left the past few decades has been its isolation from the West. We need to end that."

I agreed again.

"So a few of us were talking, and I know you were involved largely for research purposes, but we'd really like it if you were the one who translated the texts. You understand what we're doing. And your English is good."

"Ah!" I said. I was immensely relieved. "I'd love to do that."

"We can't pay you, of course."

"No, I wouldn't want you to." This was mostly true. However little money I had, these guys had less.

"OK. Well, great." Sergei bent down and spooned some borscht into his mouth. "There's one more thing. Would you be willing to join October? It would make working together easier and I think more pleasant."

This was unexpected.

"I would consider it an honor," I said. "What do I have to do?"

"Well." Sergei seemed mildly embarrassed. "There's an oath. A few years ago when we were starting we had a long argument about it, but we decided it was the right thing: it would spell out the responsibilities of the party to you, and of you to the party."

"OK," I said. "What is it?"

It was a short oath. "I pledge to do what is best for the party in accordance with my conscience, and to try to live honestly and directly in a way that will bring credit to the party. The party in turn pledges to help me, to advise me, and to support me should I need support." Sergei stopped. "That's it."

We did it right then and there in the Mu-Mu café. I was now a member of October. In the next few weeks, I started getting the first of the texts to translate into English. And I continued attending the reading group. My entry into October meant that people confided in me more. Misha told me about his drinking problem, Boris about the fact that his mother wanted him to move out and get married. Sergei had always been honest with me, but now as his marriage moved into its death agony I felt almost like his only confidant. His wife had said that she couldn't live like this any longer; he had told her that he couldn't live any other way; they were at an impasse. Sergei felt like there was no way to fix it but he worried, as his wife did also, about their daughter. "It's normal for people to change," he said. "We got married while we were still in college. Of course we changed. But it's impossible for a child to understand. If only there were some way to tell them, from the start, that mama and papa isn't forever. That each of us will still be here but not necessarily together. There must be some way, because otherwise it's a lie." He was in a bind of his own creation, but that didn't make it less painful, it seemed to me.

Yulia continued to be guarded with me, and that was understandable: her husband was in jail and she spent a lot of time thinking about him, standing in line to visit him, talking with lawyers about his case. Yes, we had kissed, but that was long ago. I would find someone else to kiss, probably. Howard, amazingly, after months of sleeping with girls from the online hooker website, had met a nice girl who worked at Russian *Esquire* and was dating her. He had suggested to me that she might have friends who were single. And Oleg, in the locker room, had suggested the same thing. "Andrei," he asked me one day, "do you have a girl?"

"No," I said.

"My girl has a friend who might be interested," Oleg said. The word he used for his "girl" was actually *telka*, a calf—it was in this context a word for "mistress." And so it was that a few days later I found myself sitting at a gaudy, expensive café off Clean Ponds with Oleg, Oleg's calf, and Oleg's calf's friend, named Polina. Oleg's calf was a quiet, mousy girl who kept fiddling with her phone, but Polina was a tall, healthy, attractive twenty-five-year-old. They worked at a beauty salon together. A few months earlier I would have jumped at the chance, but now I couldn't find any enthusiasm inside myself. When Oleg suggested we all go to a club together to continue the evening, I said I had to get back and check on my grandmother. "All right," said Oleg, and didn't hold it against me.

One evening a few nights hence, as my grandmother was whipping me at anagrams, I got a text. It was from Yulia.

"Are you able to come out?" it said.

It was eight o'clock on a Friday. I had hockey but I could skip it. Presumably Yulia wanted to tell me what Sergei had failed to—that she wanted me out of the reading group. Maybe I could talk her out of it. I texted back that I would be happy to come out, and even, as a show of courage, added a smiley face—Russians did so by just using a bunch of parentheses, like this:))) It was an odd way to make a face, since there were no eyes, but on the other hand you could use as many parentheses as you wanted, to indicate a supersmile. I used four parentheses. But as I made my way to the Czech beer place near her house I felt like a man on his way to an execution.

She was there already when I showed up, looking pale and beautiful and nervous and already drinking a glass of wine.

"*Privet,*" I said.

"*Privet,*" she said. She seemed upset. I didn't say anything. She asked politely after my grandmother and then she said, "You were right about Petya." Petya was Shipalkin. She looked miserable as she said it.

"I was?"

"He's been released," said Yulia.

"That's good!" I said, partly meaning it.

Yulia didn't seem to have heard me. "He gave everyone up," she said.

"What?"

"He ratted them out. Told on them."

"You don't know that."

"I do. His lawyer said he was looking at five years, that there was no hope unless he cooperated with the investigation and named the other members of Mayhem."

"Don't the police know the other members of Mayhem already?"

"They seem not to have. I don't know. But Petya was released two days ago and yesterday they picked up two of the guys and another of them took a train to Kiev."

"Wow," I said. It sounded like he really had given them up. Why was Yulia telling me this?

"Well," I said, not knowing what else to say, "what's he doing now?"

"I don't know," said Yulia, "and I don't care."

She took a sip of her wine.

"Will you do me a favor, Andrei?"

I nodded.

"Will you get drunk with me?"

So we got drunk. As we did so I tried not to think too much about what I was doing. Was Yulia vulnerable right now, due to her ex-husband's shameful behavior? And was I, by sticking around while she was in this vulnerable state, taking advantage of that? And did this also mean—I couldn't help but think—that once she was no longer in this state, she would lose interest again? Yulia was wearing tight white jeans and a small black cotton sweater that hugged her torso. She was a thin girl, and very pale. Her big green eyes in such a face gave her a particularly pained look. Russian girls, even intellectual Marxist Russian girls, starved themselves. And yet in Yulia's case it didn't matter. I liked it. Not her starving, of course. But how she looked.

She was drunk after three glasses of wine, whereas I, after the same number of beers, was merely a little giddy. I walked her to her house, a twelve-story block not far from Patriarch Ponds, and on the doorstep we stopped. "Good night, Andrei," she said, and hugged me. I would have preferred that she kiss me but she also seemed so upset, so unhappy, that I mostly just wanted her to be less so. We said good-bye, and she went inside.

231

After that, we began to text each other, and go to the movies. This was innocent enough, in the sense that we weren't necessarily going to the movies romantically. I didn't want to hurry her. I did, however, want to impress her, and at first, as with my grandmother, I tried to do so by finding artsy films. Then she confessed that she actually didn't mind seeing something less high-minded, so with some relief we did that. We watched the Russian version of *Titanic*, called *Admiral*, about the White admiral Kolchak, who fought the Bolsheviks, and a kind of Russian *Flashdance*, called *Stilyagi*, "The Stylish Ones," about a group of 1950s rebels in Moscow who adopted colorful clothing and jazz music as a form of protest against the stifling sartorial conformity of Stalinism. That was the movie Yulia and I saw the night she invited me up to her apartment.

That night, Moscow changed for me forever. It went from being the terrible place where I was born to being—something else. I wanted to be at home when my grandmother woke up, so in the middle of the night I whispered a good night to Yulia and went downstairs. It was three o'clock in the morning and mid-March in Moscow, and it was still pretty cold. The subway was closed and if I didn't want to walk I would have to take a cab; but I did not feel like sharing my feelings, my joy and sense of belonging, with anyone, and so I walked. It was about a mile and a half to our place, and cold and quiet, and walking down the side streets approaching the great big, awful highway that is the Garden Ring, I felt the terrible freedom of this place. It was a fortress set down in a hostile environment. On one side the Mongols; on the other the Germans, Balts, and Vikings. So the Russians built this fortress here on a bend in the Yauza River, and hoped for the best. They built it big because they were scared. It was a gigantic country, and even now, in the twenty-first century, barely governed. You could do anything, really. And amid this freedom, this anarchy, people met and fell in love and tried to comfort one another.

On our last few dates, but also, especially, when we were lying in bed together, I'd learned about Yulia's family. She had grown up in Kiev, an only child, as most children of that generation were only children, because everyone was so poor; her parents were both engineers. When the country started falling apart, they saw the writing on the wall and decided that, since Yulia's father was Jewish, they would emigrate to Israel. Yulia was eleven when her father left to scout it out and find work while Yulia's mother sold off their things and prepared for the move. At first he was in touch often, relating the difficulty of adjusting to immigrant life, complaining about the other immigrants, worrying that he would not find work; but soon he seemed to get very busy, and was in touch less often. Yulia's mother nonetheless continued to sell off their things, because they weren't going to take, for example, their television with them to Israel, nor their sofa, and it was a few days after they sold their television that Yulia's mother heard, from a mutual acquaintance, that her husband had been seen with another woman on the streets of Haifa. Over the phone Yulia's mother confronted her husband, who confessed, but said he still wanted them to come over, that they were still married and he would take care of all the arrangements, and then, when it was settled, they could peacefully divorce. Yulia's mother screamed— Yulia was in her room, quietly reading—and hung up, and though Yulia's father continued to try to send money, through various acquaintances who were traveling back and forth, Yulia's mother refused it. As a result, little Yulia grew up very poor, albeit in a place where everyone else was poor, without a television or a sofa to help pass the time.

Her mother never recovered. She managed to get her job back but it was at a research institute and not much of a job. She put all her energy into Yulia, forming what sounded like a sometimes toxic, sometimes wonderful, always deeply intense relationship. In the dispute with her father, Yulia had taken her mother's side entirely. Eventually she had gone to college in Kiev and studied literary theory; in one of her classes she met Shipalkin, and soon, like most people they knew, they were married. Then Shipalkin got a job doing graphic design in Moscow, and Yulia applied and was accepted to grad school. They moved. Just before they left Kiev, her aunt, her mother's sister and best friend, died in a car accident. Yulia had always felt guilty about leaving, and thought frequently of moving back.

Transplanted to Moscow, the marriage began to falter. They had met when they were both awkward young people adjusting to university life; now Shipalkin was discovering that he had other possibilities. "There were so many pretty girls, and he was no longer a boy who didn't know how to button his shirt correctly," Yulia said. "It turned his head." He started coming home later from work, and eventually admitted he was sleeping with one of the other designers at his office. Yulia kicked him out; she stayed in the apartment, or rather their room in the apartment, with two roommates, though she soon found that she couldn't afford the room on her own and invited a friend of hers from Kiev to share the room with her. Her friend Katya worked the night shift at a TV production company and so, for the most part, Yulia had the room to herself at night and Katya had it during the day. It had been confusing and complicated at first but now Yulia was used to it. And she was used to Moscow, she said, or at least was beginning to get used to it.

"It was very hard for my mother when I left," Yulia said, "and I thought that after Shipalkin and I separated, I could go back. But there is no work in Kiev. The place is being robbed blind. Here at least I can make a little money and send some of it home." She tutored kids for the entrance exams and even ghostwrote PhD dissertations for government officials—exactly the sort of thing Sergei quit academia over. She went home to visit—it was a night's train ride—about once a month.

Everything here was twice as hard as in New York, I thought, as I made my way home that first night from Yulia's place in the cold. It was harder to get around, it was harder to find a sweater, it was harder to get a seat on the subway, it was harder to find somewhere to eat or somewhere to live—grad students had trouble making ends meet in New York too, but I'd never heard of two people who weren't romantically involved sharing the same bed. And this place was more unjust, it was far more unjust. Just the other day in Sad, where I'd had my date with Sonya from the internet, a man had shot a woman when she'd demanded an apology from him for spilling his drink on her. "You're a fat cow," he said. Then he shot her in the leg. He worked, like half the country, apparently, at RussOil, and would probably get away with it.

It was Shipalkin who had gotten the couple involved with Sergei and October, but it was Yulia who became committed to it. She was very taken with Sergei's critique of privatized higher education, and though she did not consider herself a very outgoing person, she did have a knack for spotting malcontents. She had met Boris at a public lecture in which he asked an aggressive question, and she had met Misha during his university protest campaign. "And you, of course."

"Me?"

"Remember I wrote you after that dinner?"

"Of course! But I've never understood why."

"Well, I got the impression that you were unhappy with the U.S. educational system, and also that you didn't like Fishman," she said. "I found this an appealing combination. You seemed a little confused, but willing to stand up for your beliefs."

I wondered if that was true. I hoped that it was. As I reached Tsvetnoi Boulevard, near our place, I saw a Kroshka Kartoshka. It was a freestanding little plastic building, the size of a Chinese takeout place, with a big white counter and a few tables and chairs; they'd plunked it down in the middle of the boulevard, a little hut on city property, no doubt because some bureaucrat had been paid a bribe. "Kroshka Kartoshka" meant "little potato," and that is what they served: baked potatoes. They'd split the top open and you could choose a filling— mushrooms, or chicken salad, or cheese, or some combination. This is what Russians had been doing with potatoes for generations. It was, maybe, a little gross, and to see it here in this hut in the middle of Tsvetnoi Boulevard—it was a little unseemly, something shameful made public. But it was our shared, national shame. "We like to bake potatoes and put gross stuff in them to make them taste better"—this is what the Kroshka Kartoshka stand said. There was a chain of them across the city, in these little huts, and I went in. I ordered a potato with bacon and onion inside, paid fifty cents for it, and then ate it contemplatively at one of the little plastic tables, without taking off my coat. Then I finally went home. It was four in the morning now. My grandmother would be getting up soon. But I was able to sleep until ten, and my grandmother didn't mind.

PART III

1.

YULIA

YULIA AND I began going out. During the day, she was usually at the university and I was reading student blog posts about *Uncle Vanya* and hanging around with my grandmother until she went to bed, but after that, Moscow was ours. It was a city that stayed up late. The subway closed early but all the bars and cafés and movie theaters remained open, and after eleven o'clock I could get to Yulia's place in about ten minutes, if I paid a hundred rubles for a car that would take me down Rozhdestvenskiy Boulevard. Afterward I could get home in the same amount of time, for the same price, though on the way back I tended to take the Garden Ring. The cabs really sped like crazy down the Garden Ring at night.

What did we do together? It was, for the most part, normal stuff. Her roommate Katya's schedule changed shortly after Yulia and I started going out, so she was around more, and this meant that spending time at Yulia's place was not entirely appealing. So we kept going to the movies; we even went to some cafés. Experiencing Moscow with Yulia was something completely new to me. I wasn't transported out of the city; in fact some of its latent violence, the way aggressive men dominated public spaces, became clearer to me when walking around with her. And in all other ways too it was the same unsmiling, expensive place. But I saw how Yulia handled it. She was exceedingly polite, even formal, with people she did not know. (I recognized in this my grandmother's politeness and formality, which she kept up even with many people she did know, because she forgot that she knew them.) She was a master of withholding her approval; outside a tight circle of friends, she kept up a defensive shield. But inside that circle, and inside the city that the circle had created within the larger city, was a whole other world. The Octo-brists had carved a little path through Moscow that allowed them to enjoy it. None of them made much money, or even any. They couldn't be full citizens of the consumer paradise that Moscow had become. But there were little cafés and bookstores and bookstore-cafés where you could sit and have tea or a beer for a couple of dollars and read Derrida for a few hours without anyone bothering you. Even critical theory, which had fallen out of fashion back in the United States, was still cool here. It was the Moscow I had once hoped existed but couldn't find. Now here it was.

For Yulia, I soon learned, the world was divided into two kinds of people: her people and other people; good and evil. Men were, for the most part, evil. Women were allies in the fight against men or they were traitors. Some were traitors out of weakness, others out of treachery. And theoretically, some men were allies also. Boris, barely masculine, sexu-ally neutered, was OK; so was weird, pathetic Nikolai, with his quixotic dacha that no one wanted to help him build. Misha and Sergei were treated with suspicion: Misha because of his drinking and not very good treatment of Yulia's roommate Masha, Sergei for more complicated rea-sons. "He's been stringing his poor wife along for almost as long as I've known him," Yulia said. "He can't stand the thought of breaking up his own family. But he's chosen his path and he needs to stay on it."

"He wants to be a good person," I said.

"He wants to keep his conscience clean. There's a difference."

Whatever bad ideas she'd already had about men, starting with her father, were confirmed, to a tee, by Shipalkin. "He was such a nice boy when we met," she said. "But he was weak." Another time: "Did you see that scarf he was wearing when he came by the reading group? He's very proud of that scarf. Fishman gave it to him, you know. He thinks it's the latest in American fashion."

She could be incredibly cutting like this, even cruel. But to be on her side of it was to be exempted. "You're not like that, are you?" she said one time, when discussing the depredations on this occasion of Misha, who was always getting drunk and cheating on Masha.

"I don't know," I said.

But Yulia insisted. "You're not," she said. "I can tell." To be chosen like this to fight on the side of good versus evil—even if you didn't totally deserve it—was intoxicating. I never wanted to leave.

In retrospect I see there was a kind of baseline pain-in-the-assness to everything we did. We didn't live that far from each other but neither of us had our own private space and in the end we spent a lot of time walking this way and that. She had an ex who was still sort of hanging around—after the arrests of his friends, Shipalkin had remained in Moscow, writing long self-justifying entries on his LiveJournal page. Yulia said she never wanted to see him again and, as far as I know, she stuck to that resolution. But even without Shipalkin her life was not simple. She had a mother in Kiev who needed help and attention; she lived in her room in shifts and had to constantly change her sheets. On top of that, when we started going out, it was still cold. I remember one night in late March, after seeing another movie, walking along Pokrovka Street, on a sidewalk that was only barely cleared of snow and not cleared of ice at all, so that it was pretty much all you could do to keep from falling down, and passing several cafés that were bright and welcoming. If we'd had more money we could have stopped, but these were places that charged twelve dollars for a pot of tea! So we kept going. I felt embarrassed and unmanned that I could not afford to get my girlfriend out of the cold, but Yulia didn't even seem to see these places. Eventually we reached a café that had reasonable prices, and for about fifteen minutes we sat there shivering, and then eventually we forgot all about our awful journey, and even split an éclair. The difficulties of being together, staying together, and getting together in the first place made me feel like, if we could just get through this one situation, or the next, that we would be all right pretty much forever.

Yulia's work situation was lousy. Her college president was corrupt, her department head was corrupt, and in large part as a result of these corruptions they needed more work from the teaching staff. They were especially distrustful of people who didn't joyfully participate in the corruption, though Yulia, with her private tutoring and ghostwriting, participated more than she would have liked. She did it because she had to but also because, like me, she couldn't bear to leave. "I have some wonderful students," she said. "I love talking with them about Avvakum"—one of the crazy old clerics she studied. "Where else would I be able to do that?" Sergei's answer—do it voluntarily, in the community, on your own time—was not an option. She needed to make money. Yulia was trapped.

We spent hours walking around Moscow—it remained cold well into April—looking for places to sit and drink a tea. I had never dated anyone like Yulia before, and I had never dated anyone in Russian before. At first I found it easy—I could sit happily and watch Yulia talk and it was not necessarily expected that I talk back. But then I started finding it difficult—when accused of something, usually something true, my vocabulary of defense was limited, and my mind short-circuited to anger.

"You have no idea how we've lived here," she said once. We had stopped to eat some dumplings in a small basement cafeteria near the university. The food was cheap and pretty good, and the only problem was that it was in the basement and kind of dark. Also on the way over we'd almost been hit by a falling icicle. In the first part of April, during the days, the temperature would sometimes rise above zero and the sun would come out, melting the winter snow, but then at night the temperature would fall again, freezing into giant icicles the water that had begun to drip from the roofs. As the weather warmed up more consistently, these sharp, massive chunks of ice started falling from the rooftops and killing people. So we had just survived these dangers and I was in a foul mood with regard to Moscow and Russia and in short I said something critical about the lighting in the basement cafeteria, and Yulia got mad. "You have no idea how we've lived. You have no idea how valuable a place like this is."

She was right. I liked the place! I should not have displaced my anger at the icicles onto it. And I think in English I'd have taken Yulia's defense of it in stride. After being a too-serious little boy I had developed an ironic disposition. Nothing affected me too deeply. Some people I'd known found this off-putting, but in this situation it would have come in handy. I'd have joked her indignation away.

In Russian I didn't know how, and I was wounded. I threw up my hands like a person who was at the end of his rope, who felt like he couldn't say anything without being attacked and so therefore had decided to say nothing. I stewed in this non-saying for a while until Yulia relented and forgave me. But I found this sort of thing happening with some regularity; Yulia was a very serious person who sometimes took things to heart, and whether I would have been able to deflect our conversations in the proper direction if they had been happening in English, I don't know. In Russian I was unable to.

But this was also OK. The same inability to joke, to parry and deflect, made me kinder. I was impatient sometimes, and angry sometimes, but I was never cutting, I was never sarcastic, I never made a quip that took a second to think up and six months, somehow or other, to take back.

For a while I was nervous about introducing Yulia to my grandmother. I worried it might upset the delicate balance we had finally achieved in our domestic arrangement. At the same time, hadn't she been urging me to get married? Not that Yulia was necessarily intent on marrying me. We had just started going out. But I was thinking about it. I had even asked, idly, if she'd be willing to move to the States. "No," she said immediately. "My mother is in Kiev and I'm all she has. It's bad enough that I'm in Moscow. If I moved to America it would kill her."

"Maybe she can move to America too?" I said.

I imagined all of us—me, Yulia, her mother, my grandmother— living in a big apartment in Brooklyn, taking long walks together in Prospect Park, saying hello to the other Russians, going to movies at the big movie theater at the corner of the park. "OK," said Yulia. "Are we going to fly there in a golden helicopter?"

Fair enough. But at the time everything seemed possible. "Just think about it," I said.

So I did very much want to introduce her to my grandmother. And

I was wrong to worry. "Yulia," said my grandmother, when I brought Yulia over one late afternoon. "That's a very pretty name." And she laughed as Yulia and I took off our coats and boots. She seemed genuinely happy. We sat down and all drank some tea.

In general, though, my grandmother was suffering. Her stay in the hospital had destroyed her mobility. Where she had previously paced the apartment like an athlete preparing for a test of endurance, she now shuffled from her bedroom to the kitchen and back again. Sometimes she brought her cane and sometimes she didn't, indicating that the cane was not absolutely necessary. But without it she was off-balance, and survived by holding on to various walls and pieces of furniture. She knew where everything was, deep in her bones, and so no matter the time of night she always managed to hang on to something. Still, it meant we weren't going on a lot of walks. For the moment, with icicles falling on people's heads, this was OK, but I wondered if, when the weather turned, she would want to be out again.

She even stopped enjoying the TV news. One evening I put it on for her in the back room and went into the kitchen to work on the windowsill. A few minutes later I heard her calling for me. "Andryush, Andryush!" she said. There was real distress in her voice and I ran to her.

My grandmother was where I had left her, on the green foldout couch, in front of the TV.

"Is everything OK?" I said.

"Oy, oy," said my grandmother, gesturing toward the television. "Who is that man?"

The man was Putin.

"Who?"

"He's the prime minister."

"Oy, what a horrible face! Make him go away," said my grandmother. I flipped through the channels a bit and landed on a Russian police procedural.

"How about this?" I said.

"OK," said my grandmother.

I went back to the kitchen. Fifteen minutes later I heard a crash in the back room. I ran there. My grandmother was standing, looking horrified, next to the TV stand. The television was on its back on the floor. It had somehow survived the fall and was showing Putin visiting a truck factory in Nizhny Novgorod. Apparently the cop show had ended and the news had come on. "Andryush, I'm sorry," said my terrified grandmother, as if I would be angry at her for knocking over her own TV. "I was trying to change the channel."

She was trying to change the channel by, apparently, pushing the TV to the floor. The TV was fine, it kept working, but as there was always the danger that Putin might appear, from now on I basically had to be in there with her so I could change the channel. Next time, after all, the TV might land on her foot.

This was not good. I could try to show her movies but she hated all the movies we saw; we couldn't go outside; and there were only so many times I could play anagrams.

It was Sergei who inadvertently came up with a solution. He was driving me home from hockey one night when he said: "We think about the Soviet Union in terms of mistakes and crimes. The camps, the lack of preparation for the war, the forced psychiatric confinement of dissidents. But for a lot of people it was an OK place. It was free medicine, free housing, free education. And above all, cultural production, above all, movies: you know, contrary to the predictions of early film theorists, movies aren't actually a highly ideologized space. They're a mass entertainment. In order to be massively entertaining they need to have some basis in reality. There weren't any Soviet films about the Gulag but there were some pretty good Soviet films. It's one of the things the workers' state needs least to be embarrassed about."

Was this true? There was a kiosk outside the Clean Ponds metro station that sold DVDs. I had bought some new Russian films there to watch with my grandmother, but most of them were unwatchable. Even the good ones were filled with violence—that was the new Russian reality, and these guys were making movies reflecting that reality. My grandmother didn't like them, and I didn't blame her.

But what about Soviet films? It hadn't for some reason occurred to me to show my grandmother old movies. I didn't know much about them. In school I'd watched the old post-revolutionary classics, and then the great works of the late Soviet underground. But aside from *Irony of Fate*—the classic 1970s movie about a very drunk doctor who accidentally boards a flight to Leningrad and then takes a taxi to the same address as his Moscow address, and finds an apartment there just like his apartment, except occupied by a woman different from his fiancée; all Russians watched this film on New Year's Eve, including my parents—Soviet popular film was not something I knew much about. I asked Yulia if she had any suggestions. "Well, you could try *Osenniy Marafon*," she said.

They had *Autumn Marathon* at the Clean Ponds kiosk, and a few days later my grandmother and I sat down in the back room to screen it. "Oh!" my grandmother said during the first sequence. "Leningrad!" We had watched numerous post-Soviet movies set in St. Petersburg, but my grandmother had never recognized it; the movies didn't present the city in a way she understood. *Autumn Marathon* did.

The movie is about a college professor and translator in Soviet Leningrad who is having an affair. His main motivation for the affair is not lust or boredom or revenge; it is a sense of guilt and obligation. Everyone takes advantage of the professor: he rewrites his colleague's poor translations; he spends hours with a visiting scholar from Denmark, helping him understand Lermontov; he is even unable to resist the importunities of his drunken neighbor, who insists that he and the Dane go mushroom hunting with him and drink a bunch of vodka. When his long-suffering wife confronts him with his affair he feels terrible and promises to break it off; but when his mistress threatens suicide if he does, he goes back to her. Through it all he has to contend with the drawbridges of Leningrad, which are raised every night at a certain hour, cutting off the old city (where he works, and where his mistress lives) from the new city, where he lives with his wife. He jogs each morning with the visiting Dane, but is also constantly running to catch a bus to take him across the bridge before it goes up, and sometimes he doesn't make it—thus, autumn marathon. Halfway through the film he resolves to change his life; by the end of the film this resolve is in shambles, and we know things will go on as before.

"That's a good movie," said my grandmother when it was over. I agreed. That night I asked Yulia for more such movies.

"Nothing is as good as *Osenniy Marafon*," she admitted, "but let me think of some others." The next day, she emailed me a list.

From then on, with the help of Yulia's list, my grandmother and I watched old and not-so-old Soviet movies. She liked all of them, even when they weren't that good (though some of them were very good). They reminded her of something. It didn't matter that she couldn't quite hear them and that she couldn't quite follow the plot; for one thing, she had seen many of them before, and for another, wherever she was in the plot, whenever her mind and eye turned to the film: There it was. The USSR. The very images, and the presentation of those images, and the things people said as they walked through those images: they spoke of values she believed in, however much, under the Soviets, they had been honored only in the breach. And I became so friendly with the guys at the DVD kiosk that if they didn't have some old film, they told me they'd put in an "order" for it. Since I was pretty sure that they were pirating the films and burning them onto DVDs, this meant they'd pirate the film and burn it just for me. This struck me as top-notch customer service.

Despite meeting my grandmother and getting along with her, Yulia did not want to sleep over; she was a Marxist revolutionary, maybe, but she was also a nice girl from Kiev, and she did not think it was proper to sleep over at the home of a man to whom she wasn't married, especially if that man lived with his grandmother, who might not approve. So I found myself spending more and more time at Yulia's place. What would have served as a living room in an American apartment had become a bedroom in theirs, so the only common area was the small kitchen and, once it got warmer, the balcony; Yulia's other roommates, Masha and Sonya as well as Katya, would sit in the kitchen for hours, drinking tea and reading and talking. All of them were used to living in close quarters and were adept at tuning out other people's conversations, so it never felt like we were bothering them if we hung out in the kitchen as well.

They were all uncommonly close. The arrangement with Katya struck me at first as borderline crazy, but Yulia seemed to think it was eminently reasonable. Why pay all that money for a room that would sit empty half the time? Why not try to have someone there? They still tried to arrange their schedules so that each had as much time as possible in the room on her own, but often they slept together in the huge bed, and if Yulia and I had been there together earlier we always made sure to change the sheets. Eventually I grew used to it. None of the girls had any money to speak of and their wardrobes were sparse, but they constantly borrowed clothes from one another to create a sense of variety. Yulia knew a woman in her mother's old apartment building who sewed clothes, and occasionally the girls would combine resources and order a sweater or a shawl. I remembered reading somewhere that Raisa Gorbachev, famed for her glamorous good looks, had been embarrassed at one of the first superpower summits because she ran out of clothes and had to wear the same cute blouse twice, while Nancy Reagan seemed to have a new designer outfit for every meal. That happened with Yulia and her roommates, but they never seemed to mind.

Misha was a frequent guest to the apartment, to see Masha and also to eat. (The other Misha, Misha impishly declared, "can't cook for shit.") To call Misha a guest doesn't quite do him justice, though. He was more like an event. He could be there for dinner, polite and gregarious, or he could show up late and very drunk and end up sleeping on some chairs in the kitchen because Masha didn't want him peeing in her bed (this had happened). I liked Misha a lot, despite the fact that he would sometimes get drunk at dinner and start hounding me to come with him to get more alcohol. He had been kicked out of grad school for organizing protests when his university had hired a deeply reactionary, pro-Putin professor. He was now writing a dissertation on the working-class opposition of the 1920s, for a German university. For a freewheeling intellectual alcoholic, he was surprisingly interested in academic politics. "There are only two countries where serious historical work is done right now," he said one time at dinner, "and that's Germany and the U.S. But in Germany people get emotional very quickly. The leftists still blame the Russians for the death of Rosa Luxemburg! It would affect my ability to get a job."

"You wouldn't want to teach in Russia?" I said.

"I would. I do. But you need to get a job somewhere else first. Russian universities don't like to make the first hire of your career. And of course they can't pay anything, so you need to be able to work the international granting system, which again is mostly German and American."

"Misha," Masha said, "maybe that's enough? People are trying to eat."

"I'm not hampering them," said Misha.

"Your talk of grant applications gives everyone indigestion," said Masha.

"OK," Misha said, backing off. "I didn't know that." He was quiet for a few minutes, and then started quizzing me, not for the first time, about the job application process in the U.S.

There was also a lot at Yulia's that I missed. I did my best to see my grandmother to bed, so I tended to get to Yulia's late, and I tried to be back at my grandmother's before she missed me, so I was rarely at Yulia's in the morning. I never saw but was told about how Sergei also ended up sleeping there a fair amount as his marriage deteriorated. And how Masha declared that if Misha didn't shape up she'd leave him. And how Yulia's relationship with Katya too was not always perfectly harmonious. So maybe I had a slightly rosy-tinted view of the situation. But I loved it. It was a kind of primitive communism—from necessity but also by choice. They took pleasure, I think, in making it work.

In addition to spending more time at Yulia's, I was increasingly caught up in the activities of October. They weren't ready to launch their website, but in the meantime they kept sending me articles to translate. They were analyses of the Russian political situation from a Marxist perspective. It was a lot of the stuff Sergei and Yulia and the rest had been saying to me for months: That the authoritarianism of the regime could best be understood in an international capitalist rather than a post-Soviet context. That the regime did not imprison its opponents because it retained a memory of Soviet methods, but because it wanted to continue making money for its clients (the oligarchs). Money, here as elsewhere, was the goal. Once you understood that, modern-day Russia came into focus; it made sense.

I translated the articles into English with pleasure. And as the weather grew warmer, there were more and more protests and other events to attend. We protested the Kazakh embassy after police fired on striking oil workers in one of Kazakhstan's Caspian boomtowns; we protested the bank that supported Norilsk Nickel after a report came out calling Norilsk the most polluted city on earth. We protested the Ministry of Education because of its new standardized college entrance exam, which was going to turn Russian kids into little test-preparation drones, just like their American counterparts, and we protested the Duma when it voted on a law to decrease government funding for education.

The protests were always peaceful and organized in such a way that we avoided arrest—either they were permitted, or we did them singly, so that they weren't considered gatherings, or we didn't present any political slogans, so they weren't considered political. "The time will come when we need to heighten the contradictions," Boris counseled, "but first we need to build a movement." There were days we spent leafleting outside factories, supporting their independent trade unions, even inviting workers to contact us about membership in October. Aside from a few run-ins with security, we were never systematically bothered or harassed for any of this. I think the fact that we were in Moscow; that we were concentrating on national-level issues rather than smaller, more contentious local ones; and that no one really knew what to make of a group of friendly young socialists showing up at their factory or outside their embassy, shielded us, for a while, from the attention of the authorities. October was simply too small and too weird to seem anything but harmless. The apparent exception was the protest the summer before against the highway through the forest, the same one my brother had been accused of somehow instigating. The authorities still seemed very angry about it, and had been trying for months to find out who was involved; as I learned from Misha, it had been a joint protest with Mayhem, the group Shipalkin had joined, and it was the Mayhem people who had come up with the idea of destroying one of the bulldozers. Despite some qualms, the October members went along with it. It would turn out to be a big mistake.

At one point Sergei invited an acquaintance of his, a grizzled old Marxist who had been imprisoned in the 1970s for calling for a return to Leninism, to give us a brief tutorial on what to do if we ever got arrested. The gist of his message was to keep our mouths shut. "The minute you get in there, consider yourself deaf, dumb, and blind, because in essence you are," he said. "You have no idea why they're asking you the questions they're asking, what they could possibly do with that information, where it might lead. Nothing you say can make anything better, but lots of things you say can make things worse. So keep quiet. Establish your identity, and that's it."

The man wore shabby clothes and was missing several teeth. He had bad breath. Nonetheless there was some romance to meeting an actual veteran of the fight against Russian tyranny. I wondered whether I might write a follow-up paper to the one on October, about this guy's life.

I never got around to it, of course. There were many things I didn't get around to.

One Sunday in late April Yulia and I finally made the long trip to Nikolai's dacha. We met up in the middle of the Novokuznetskaya subway station and took the orange line all the way to the southern end. Then we caught a bus, rode it for half an hour into emptiness, got off, and walked a mile along a patchily paved road until we reached Nikolai's dacha settlement, and then Nikolai's dacha itself.

It was at this point half built. The frame of the house—a small two-story colonial—was done, the windows and doors were in, there was even a functioning staircase installed, but the bathroom and kitchen were missing, there was no railing on the staircase, and the walls weren't painted—that was our task for the day, to start painting—and dacha season was fast approaching. The yard was a mess, with trees and bushes and tall grass all seemingly falling into one another. It wasn't clear that Nikolai was going to make it before dacha season began, or even before the fall.

The location left something to be desired. There just wasn't much in the way of nature. No woods, no lake, no river. There was a huge abandoned quarry, but it wasn't filled with water; you could climb around in it, but that was all. There was a field nearby, but it was just a big field of mud.

"So what do you guys think?" Nikolai said happily, after we'd taken a quick tour. We were, it turned out, the first ones to have come out to help.

"It's pretty close to being done?" Yulia said gently.

"Yes! You should have seen it just last year," said Nikolai enthusiastically. "It was a hole in the ground."

"And now it's an aboveground hole," Yulia whispered to me. In Russian "hole" meant a depression in the ground but also a dump. It was difficult to imagine Nikolai's dacha being anything else.

We spent the day painting the walls of one of the upstairs rooms. It was hard work and it was still cold enough outside that we didn't want to have the windows open too much, but at the same time the fumes were bad enough that we didn't want the windows closed entirely. Nikolai tried to entertain us by playing music on his phone but the sound quality was bad and Yulia kept asking him to skip songs. Finally, toward evening, we finished. Nikolai had dragged an old wooden bench and chair from somewhere and plunked them down in the jumble of weeds in the back, so after we were done we sat on these and drank vodka and ate the black bread and salami he had prepared for this occasion. He was thrilled. "That's the first room we've painted, so two more rooms upstairs, all the hallways, and the entire downstairs—probably seven more days like this," he said. "But before we do the downstairs we need to put in the kitchen and the bathroom." He was counting it up on his fingers. "Maybe we'll be done by June!"

He had been living there on weekends, sleeping on the floor, and waking up and working for as long as he could stand it. Nikolai, I had by this point learned, was a programmer at an outfit that perpetrated various online scams mostly to do with gaming advertising revenues; Nikolai said they mostly targeted major corporations and would eventually cause capitalism to collapse. He probably made more money than anyone else in October, and was now spending all of it on this dacha, but he didn't mind. "This was the inheritance my father left me," he said. "This is it. A piece of land in a shitty dacha settlement in a very hard-to-reach area. But that was all he had to give, and I've taken it. When we're done here we can all use it. We can even have retreats here for the group. Hell, if things go wrong it can be a safe house!"

"It can't be a safe house and a meeting place," Yulia said, not unkindly. "Either it's official or it's a secret. Given that your name is on it, it probably shouldn't be a secret."

"OK, OK," said Nikolai. "Anyway, who says things need to go wrong?"

By the time we left it was dark; Nikolai walked us to the bus stop and then headed back to his dacha, to keep building.

"It's impressive that he's done so much," I said, once we got on the creaky old bus and Nikolai retreated into the distance.

"We'll see if he finishes," said Yulia. "God, I'm so tired."

We got back to her place around ten, both of us so exhausted that we immediately went to sleep in our clothes. I woke up at around midnight, just before Katya was supposed to return, kissed Yulia good-bye, and headed home.

A few days later, Dima Gchatted me to say that he had lost the final hearing on his case; he had expected as much, but this put an end to the story of his gas stations.

"I'm wiped out," he said. "I need to move on the apartments."

"When?"

"In the next couple of months," he said.

"Both of them?"

"Yes." Pause. "Sorry."

"No," I typed before I could think better of it. "We're not moving Grandma. She's weak and the only reason she can get around this apartment is because she knows where everything is."

There was also something that I didn't say, which was that two months after submitting my Watson application, and six weeks after submitting my *Slavic Review* article, I hadn't heard a peep from either place.

"OK," said Dima. "How much longer is she going to be able to get up those stairs?"

"She gets up them OK now, with my help."

"You're going to stay there and help her up the stairs indefinitely?"

"Yes," I said.

"Are you fucking serious?" Dima was typing very quickly. "Have you looked out the window recently? Do you have any fucking clue what's going on in that country?"

"I've looked out the window," I said.

"You don't have a clue," Dima said. He could be very charming when he wanted something; he could also be mean. Sometimes, of course, he was right. Maybe in this case he was right. At some level I really didn't have a clue.

But also he was wrong. I liked it here. And I was not going to let him evict our grandmother.

A week after this conversation he wrote to say that a prospective buyer interested in just our grandmother's apartment was coming over and would I at least let him look at the place? If he made an offer we could decide then. But I wasn't interested. I asked the Marxist reading group to come over and stage a small protest in the courtyard. They relished the opportunity. They made little signs that said HANDS OFF OUR GRANDMOTHERS! and NOUVEAUX RICHES NOT WELCOME HERE! When the buyer showed up and saw this, he didn't even get out of his Mercedes-Benz. I watched him from my grandmother's bedroom. That evening I got a short email from Dima. "You're an idiot," it said. "Buyer is out. You're on your own."

Good, I thought. Good.

A week later he sold his apartment to a Bulgarian arms dealer named Miklos, who had been the one who wanted to buy both. "Four hundred grand," Dima wrote me. "The agent said we were lucky. If we sit on Grandma's place any longer, the market's going to collapse right out from under us."

"Sorry," I wrote him. "I'm not going."

"Whatever," said Dima.

Miklos told the soldiers they could stay until the end of the summer. I would be sad to see them go.

2.

MY GRANDMOTHER THROWS A PARTY

IT WAS FINALLY SPRING. The snow melted and for a few weeks every-thing was muddy, but the sun shone and it was warm and my grand-mother and I started going for walks again. I had rejected Dima's plan to sell the apartment on instinct; beyond that I didn't really know what to do. If I was going to stay here, Yulia and I should try to move in to-gether. I could displace Katya and move into Yulia's room, but that was the room she lived in with Shipalkin before they broke up—a bad idea. She could come live with me and my grandmother, and I could replace the bunk beds or just place them side by side—but as Yulia had thus far not even agreed to sleep over this was maybe a stretch. I walked up and down the boulevard with my grandmother, trying to figure it out.

Her ninetieth birthday was coming up. I wasn't sure how she felt about celebrating it but a few days after the blowup with Dima she turned to me and said, "You know, I'm about to turn one hundred."

"Well, almost," I said. "You're about to turn ninety."

"How's that?" she said.

"Well, what year were you born?"

"In 1919."

"And now it's 2009. So that makes you ninety."

My grandmother looked at me, unconvinced. "Maybe," she said.

Either way, it seemed like a big deal, and I decided we should throw a party. I made sure Emma Abramovna could come on that day, and I invited Yulia and her roommates, our reading group, and Sergei, as well as the soldiers. "I have invited some people to come over on your birth-day," I told my grandmother.

"You have? But how will we feed them?"

"Seraphima Mikhailovna will make a nice meal for them," I said.

My grandmother agreed, but she did not quite agree. The next day, in the late morning, she started getting dressed to go out. "I need to get some things for the birthday party," she said.

"Like what?"

"All sorts of things," said my grandmother.

I decided to go with her, and together we walked to the market. The ground was a little wet still from the melting snow but the sun was out. It was nice.

At the market my grandmother headed for the baked goods. "Do you think the guests want this pie?" she said, pointing to her favorite poppy-seed pie.

"Maybe," I said. "But the party is two weeks away. Why don't we buy it a little closer to then, so it's fresher?"

"Let's buy it now so we don't have to worry about it," said my grandmother.

I decided not to argue. And the next day I did not accompany her as she went again to get more birthday supplies; I watched her from her bedroom window as she slowly but surely made her way, sometimes leaning on her cane and other times ignoring it, out of the courtyard and toward the market. The birthday party was inspiring my grandmother to leave the house—I wasn't going to argue with that, even if some of the things she was bringing back—for example, grapes—were not going to make it. Sometimes I ended up eating the food she bought; other times she would eat it herself, forgetting why she'd bought it. I began to think of it as more of a two-week birthday feast than a waste of energy.

And why not? You only turn ninety once. Especially if you think you're turning one hundred. When the day of the party finally arrived I got up in the morning and sent out a reminder email to all the guests; I also called and talked with Emma Abramovna and her caretaker, Valya, to make sure they were still coming. (By this point Emma Abramovna had received numerous calls on the subject from my grandmother. "I'm turning one hundred," my grandmother would say. Pause. "No, I am. I did the math." Another pause. "Are you sure? Well, how old are you?"

Emma Abramovna was eighty-seven. "Really?" said my grandmother, surprised. She couldn't be thirteen years older than Emma Abramovna.)

After emailing everyone, I ate some breakfast and began doing the dishes. I noticed that the water wasn't draining. This had happened before but it had responded well to my jamming it with a plunger. I did this now and it seemed to get better, but when I went into the bathroom, the sink there wasn't draining. They were connected, these sinks, and I had merely shifted the problem from one to the other.

I now plungered the bathroom sink. The water drained but when I returned to the kitchen, it didn't drain again. At this point my grandmother came into the kitchen and saw that something was wrong.

"Andryush, what's the matter?"

"The sink is clogged. But we'll unclog it."

"Do you know how?"

"Yes," I said, and went into my room. I did not know how. It was now ten o'clock. Seraphima Mikhailovna was coming at noon, and the guests at five. We were in trouble.

I called Dima's handyman, Stepan. He picked up on the second ring. "I'm in Irkutsk," he said, "visiting family. You're an educated person, you'll figure it out. There's a snake under the sink. Use that."

"Thanks," I said.

"No problem," said Stepan, and hung up.

Stepan's confidence in me, however ironic, propelled me back into the kitchen. My grandmother had taken a seat and was now preparing to watch me defeat the clog.

I had noticed, a few times while going under the sink to fetch a rag to wipe the floor, that there was a device back there that looked like a thick, coiled wire, which I thought might be a sink implement of some kind. I took it out now. It was a coiled wire with a kind of winding mechanism. This was the snake: you stuck it in the sink and wound it until it came up against your clog. But the kitchen sink drain was covered by a metal grate that was soldered to the sink bottom—I couldn't get the snake in there. Was there another way in? I went, again, under the sink. The water drained into the wall through segmented plastic pipes. There was a pipe running straight down from the sink, which connected to a U-shaped pipe, which in turn connected to a pipe that ran into the wall. Three pipes in all. But why would they make the water travel through a U—that is, down and then up again—before going into the wall? Maybe that was the problem—the U was blocked? At least the U looked like it would come off; it was attached to the other two pipes with round coupling nuts. I tried them. Lefty loosey—they turned. I undid one nut, and the U-shaped segment detached, ever so slightly, from the pipe going into the wall. Now I unscrewed the other nut—and just like that the U-shaped pipe came off! Suddenly a cascade of water came down onto me from the sink pipe—I jumped back and out of the space and spilled water from the U-shaped pipe. The water was nasty, brackish. I took my U-shaped pipe and dumped it in the toilet. Then I came back and started rounding up rags to clean up the spill.

My grandmother was aghast. "How horrible!" she said. "How terrible. What are we going to do? We're finished. Are we finished?"

I tried not to lose my cool. After all, my grandmother wasn't wrong. I was covered in filth and I had just dismembered the sink without any clear plan of action. I was ignorant of plumbing. I was ignorant of the entire physical world! I lived in an apartment, but how had they built this apartment? What materials were in it? Why did it keep out the cold? How did heat enter it? How did water? And where did the water from the sink go after it made it through those plastic pipes?

"Andryush," said my grandmother, "should we cancel the party?"

I looked at my worried grandmother. She had stopped dressing up at home and mostly wore her worn-out pink robe. But she still wanted to have a party, I could see this. "We're OK," I lied. "I know what I'm doing. Give me an hour, OK? If I don't fix this in an hour, we can cancel the party."

My grandmother agreed and went to lie down in her room. I returned to the sink.

I had been reading Marx—a man who tried to examine every minute piece of socioeconomic detail in order to discover the laws whereby capitalist society functioned. But was there a Marx of the physical world? There was, actually: Newton. In the seventeenth century, Newton had discovered the basic laws of motion: inertia, gravity, every action has an equal and opposite reaction. Where previously people had simply seen things fall, now they could understand *why* they fell. In fact it was less that Newton was the Marx of the physical world than that Marx was trying to be the Newton of the social world. Had he succeeded? Maybe not. The laws of economics were more complicated than the laws of motion.

I considered calling Yulia to ask her if she knew anything about sinks, but it was my sense that she did not know anything about sinks. And Sergei was probably teaching a class somewhere. Not that he would know much about sinks. Of the Octobrists, Nikolai would have the best chance of knowing about sinks, but calling him now would be an implicit promise to help him again with his stupid dacha; also I had not invited him to the party. But I wiped my hands on a towel and dialed his number. He did not pick up. I went back to the sink.

The simplest thing would have been if the U was clogged. I had spilled water out of it but that didn't mean there wasn't a clog in there. I looked inside and saw darkness. I took the U into the bath and poured some water into it from the lower faucet—the water went into the U and very quickly started coming out the other side. The U was not clogged.

I returned to the kitchen only to find my grandmother going through her little phone book. "Andryush," she said, "we have to call everyone and tell them not to come."

"Why?" I said.

"Well, look!" she said, indicating the sink.

The area around the sink was terrifying—filthy rags soaked in water, a mess of cleaning products and old plastic bags, the little red doors under the sink opened to reveal that someone had torn apart the pipes. I could see why my grandmother might think we weren't ready to receive guests.

"You said you'd give me an hour. Only twenty minutes have passed. I can fix this."

I shooed her back to her room. Then I put our deepest saucepan under the sink, poured some water into a glass, and started pouring it down the drain. It appeared without delay on the other end of the pipe and splashed into my saucepan. So there was nothing wrong with the sink or its pipe, and there was nothing wrong with the U-pipe.

That left the pipe sticking into the wall. I took my glass with water and angled some into that pipe. In it went, but I could not see the other side. The other side was—I had no idea where. Outdoors? Under the apartment?

I mean, both. The answer had to be both. The pipes must have been in between the walls and the floors, eventually connecting to a larger pipe under the street. That was the only possibility. And the pipes from the street went—I did not know. That was beyond my pay grade. Into the river? It didn't matter. I just had to clear this one clog.

I stuck the snake into the wall pipe and started turning the handle. At first there was no resistance and then there was a little, but I kept turning the handle and my wire went deeper. Had I cleared the clog? Or were these bends in the pipe? I suspected bends and kept going. I was shocked at the length of the wire—there was no way to know just how quickly I was uncoiling it, and I couldn't of course measure, but it must have extended more than fifteen feet. And then it ran into something that stopped it cold, a wall of some kind, or a rock. At first I thought that this was it: the end of the pipe. If this was the end of the pipe, and I had not yet met the clog, then I was up against a mystery. Or else I had simply cleared it and not really noticed—that's how strong the snake was. I started withdrawing the snake; I'd have to put the pipes back together and test the sink again.

Except what would it mean for the pipe to end? I stopped withdrawing the snake. The pipe couldn't end. If the pipe ended, where would the water go? No, our pipe must have cleared into a larger pipe, which eventually cleared into an even larger pipe, out on the street, like I said. That's the only way this thing could have kept going.

If my snake had entered a larger pipe, why would it have stopped? No. I started turning my snake again in the old, forward direction, until it returned to the rock. This time I kept going. If there was a rock in my pipe, I needed to get it out of the way. And as I turned the snake, I felt, or thought I felt, that the rock was moving. I might also have been twisting without effect. And yet it felt like something was happening.

I kept turning and by now I was convinced, although at times it seemed immovable, that this was not a rock, but a clog. My clog. A coil of hair and vegetables and shampoo and kasha. As I pressed against it I imagined what it looked like, this coil of hair and kasha; I was amazed that any water had managed to penetrate it at all, but then again water has its ways, and also, actually, the whole point was that it had stopped penetrating it. That's why I was here.

And then suddenly it felt like my clog had fallen into space and my snake was free. I turned the handle a few more times but it was unnecessary. The clog was gone! I just knew it. Motherfucking clog! I wished I had been able to see its face as it fell into the larger pipe, to be swept into a river, and then eventually an ocean. Or whatever. Fuck you, clog! My only regret is that I didn't look upon your ugly face.

I reassembled the pipes under the sink, turned on the water, and watched it drain. I had never been so impressed; the simple draining of water in a sink had never looked to me so elegant.

"Babushka!" I said. My grandmother was in her room and when I went in there to get her, she was looking out the window into the courtyard. "Babushka, let me show you something." I led her back to the kitchen.

"Oh, my God!" she cried after seeing the mess on the floor, which I hadn't yet cleaned up.

"No, look," I said, and I turned the water on. It drained perfectly.

I was worried that she'd forgotten about the whole thing and was going to ask what I was showing her, but she hadn't. "You fixed it?" she said.

I nodded.

"I knew you would," she said, and went back to her room.

A little while later my phone rang. It was Nikolai.

"What's up?" he said.

"Oh, nothing. I wanted to consult you about a plumbing issue. But I fixed it."

"You fixed the plumbing?"

"I did."

"Good for you," said Nikolai. There was a pause. I sensed that he knew that there was a party, and that I hadn't invited him. So I invited him.

"I'd be glad to come," said Nikolai.

Soon Seraphima Mikhailovna came and cooked a monumental feast. Then the guests started arriving. Emma Abramovna came, with her caretaker; and the soldiers, plus Howard's very nice and pretty girlfriend; and the Octobrists. My linemates Anton and Oleg represented the hockey guys; I hadn't realized until they filled up my grandmother's ancient apartment just how big they were. The party was not without its ticklish moments. Misha demanded of Oleg what he did for a living, and when Oleg answered that he was in real estate, Misha asked if that meant he sucked the marrow from the life of the city. "That's right," said Oleg happily.

Misha was momentarily flustered by Oleg's amorality, and then just raised his glass to him: "You are my enemy and you know it." They got along great after that. There was plenty of alcohol at the party, and plenty of food; I hadn't realized it before but Anton and Katya were both single, and at the end of the night he asked for her number.

For dinner we set everything up in the back room and put my grandmother in a spot from which she wouldn't be able to get up and try to fetch people things. She accepted this. I worried that she would start hinting to Emma Abramovna about her dacha, and everyone would see how her oldest friend evaded her, but she never brought it up. Periodically she would ask, when there was a quiet moment, "Whose party is this?" At first it was worrisome, but then it almost seemed like she was teasing us.

"It's your party!" we said, and she said, "My party?" and we said yes. "All right," she agreed. She stayed with us until the guests left, at close to midnight, and then declared, as she watched Yulia and me finish the cleanup, that we were never having guests again, it was too exhausting. But she said it in a triumphant sort of way.

3.

I LAND AN INTERVIEW

THEN IN MID-MAY, a couple of weeks after my grandmother's party, I got an incredible bit of news. The *Slavic Review* had accepted my paper on Sergei's radical reeducation program. I sent a short note about this to the Watson College hiring committee. The cochair of the committee (alongside my old almost-employer Richard Sutherland), a German professor at Watson named Constanza Kotz, wrote back right away that this was good news and could I send the paper? I did so. Professor Kotz then wrote again to say that the committee would like to add me to the short list of candidates and could I send some dates when I would be available to come for a campus visit and interview? If I could not make it in person, Kotz suggested that we could get it done over Skype. She added, in a private note, that the committee had been impressed by my commitment to teaching and my previous contributions to Watson College but had been worried by my lack of publications. They still had this worry but a little less so, given the *Slavic Review* acceptance, and looked forward to meeting me in person, or over Skype, as the case may be.

I was at the windowsill when I received the email and I jumped up from my chair—it was easier to do than from a normal sitting position, since I was already astride the chair—and pumped my fist like I had just won a great victory. I sort of had. I owed it all to Sergei and October. We didn't have hockey that night, but we did the next night, and I couldn't wait to thank him in person.

But first I saw Yulia, and she did not feel about it quite the way that I did.

"So you used Sergei and the rest of us to get a job interview in America," she said.

"What?"

We were in her kitchen. Yulia had made us some hot dogs, and I was eating them with black bread and a beer when I told her about the interview. Their kitchen was large enough for a small aluminum-topped table, and it had a door to the balcony.

"You converted our work into cultural capital," Yulia said. "Yes or no?"

Her face had grown hard and she wasn't looking at me as she said this.

"Well, yes, I suppose, but that's what I do, it's what we do, we write about things," I said. "Is it wrong to write about things? Karl Marx wrote about things."

I was still happily eating, not quite understanding how pissed Yulia was.

"Marx wrote so he could transform the world," she said. "You wrote so you could get a job at a college with a nice lawn."

"Who says it has a nice lawn?"

"I looked it up online."

The campus did have a small old-fashioned quad, but that wasn't its most salient feature. "It's also right next to a federal penitentiary!" I said.

"Great," said Yulia, "you can make yourself feel better by tutoring prisoners."

I had not seen this side of Yulia before, though I had always known it was there. I had seen it directed at economic injustice, at her father, at Shipalkin. But not yet at me. I put my fork down.

"You know," I said, "I had thought you guys might feel this way. When I started out I thought you would. But since then I've joined October. I've translated tons of articles for a website that still doesn't exist. I've been to all the protests. At this point I think it's unfair."

Yulia didn't say anything.

"Anyway," I went on now, I couldn't stop myself, "I'm not taking the job."

"No, you should take it. You'd be crazy not to take it."

"If I get it, will you come with me?"

"I already told you no."

"Then I'm not taking it."

"You have to take it. It's a good job, you said so yourself."

We had discussed the job a couple of times, mostly in the context of my saying that I would probably never get it.

"It's not good enough."

"It's not?"

"Not if you're not coming."

"OK, you know what, don't do anything heroic, all right? Let's see if you get the job. Then we can have this conversation."

I said OK and it was in fact OK—there was no reason to have a big fight over something that might not even occur. At the same time my feelings were hurt.

"Do you really think that?" I said, later in the evening.

"Think what?"

"That I'm just using you and Sergei to advance my academic career?"

"I don't know," said Yulia. "You tell me."

This answer made me furious. I got out of bed and put on my jeans. I was leaving.

"Where are you going?" said Yulia. "Katya's not back until morning." She and Anton had taken a weekend trip to Suzdal.

"I'm going home," I said. "The metro's closing soon and I want to be there when my grandmother gets up. Or do you think I'm using her too?"

Yulia shrugged. I saw the same look on her face as I'd seen when she was telling me about Shipalkin in the wake of his release. It was a look that expressed grave disappointment and disgust at human weakness, and especially at male human weakness. Women had it much, much worse than men, and yet they bore it somehow. Why couldn't we? Were we such pussies? That is what that look said. And obviously, strictly speaking, she was right. But I thought, at that moment, that it was unfair to give that look to me.

I walked out without saying anything more, and she let me. She called me while I was on the subway and I ignored it. She called me again when I got home and this time I answered.

"Andryushik," she said when I picked up the phone. She was crying. "I'm sorry. I don't know why I reacted that way. I mean, I do know. I don't want you to leave me. I don't want you to go to America. But I wasn't being fair. If you get the job you should take it."

"I won't get the job," I said. "But if I get it, come with me?"

"I can't!" she said, crying harder. "I can't leave my mother. Don't you understand that?"

I thought of my grandmother, who also didn't have anyone.

Something about Yulia crying—I'd never seen or heard her do it before—was contagious. I started crying too.

"Yul'," I said, "I love you."

"I love you too," she said.

"We'll think of something," I said.

She sobbed. "Do you promise?"

This was a really pathetic scene. I was getting tears and snot on my cell phone. And how could I promise anything? I had no money and lived with my grandmother and the best thing I had going for me just then—a Skype interview with Watson—was also, it was turning out, the worst. Nonetheless, I thought we would think of something. I thought I would think of something. "I promise," I said.

"Do you want me to come over?" said Yulia.

"Right now?" I asked.

"I can call a cab. It'll be cheap."

"OK," I said. "Call me when you're pulling in and I'll come out."

She slept over that night, and in the morning the three of us had breakfast.

"Yulia," my grandmother kept saying, and forgetting that she was saying it. "Yulia. What a beautiful name."

I agreed.

Then, after all the hopes and arguments, I blew the interview. Maybe I shouldn't have done it over Skype, but I didn't have seven hundred dollars lying around to go flying to America. And anyway the connection on the windowsill was fine. That wasn't the problem.

The problem was me. I had spent so many years worrying that I would never get this opportunity that I was crazy with nerves. I kept interrupting the very kindly professors who asked me soft-ball questions, and then interrupting myself. The low point of the interview came when they asked me how I would try to arrest declining enrollment in Russian literature classes, and I started giving them a talk, which I didn't believe, about the pop culture relevance of certain Russian writers. I even said something along the lines of "Pushkin was a Tupac figure." There was a pause. "You know, because he got shot."

There was consternation among the search committee as they tried to determine whether I was kidding—I wished I had been kidding—and then just at that moment my grandmother walked into the kitchen in her bathrobe. I turned around—she waved. I turned back to the screen, wondering if the people in upstate New York had seen her. From the expressions on their faces I could tell that they had.

"That's my grandmother," I murmured.

"Andrew, thank you very much for taking the time to do this," Sutherland purred. "We know it's late there."

I nodded.

"We'll be in touch," he said, and I saw him approaching the screen in a weirdly menacing fashion. Watson College disappeared, and then I was staring at the big empty Skype icon.

Two weeks later, while checking the Slavic jobs website, I saw the name Alex Fishman. I saw it before I saw the rest; I was reading right to left. He had accepted an offer from Watson College.

Sometimes you know something bad is going to happen, but it doesn't help; in fact it's like you have to experience it twice. I logged on to Facebook. Even after our blowup at dinner I hadn't had the guts to unfriend Fishman—it just seemed unnecessary, he knew what I thought of him—but I made a point of ignoring his posts. Still, when I saw a big smiling photo of Fishman throwing a gang sign and the name of a college I had once hoped to teach at, I couldn't help but read his status update. It read: "I'm being shipped upstate! (To teach literature at Watson College!)"

I wondered if there was some comment I could make that would somehow puncture Fishman's incredible self-regard. Did he know how stupid he looked throwing a gang sign? Did he know that it got really cold up at Watson during the winter? I couldn't think of anything that wouldn't also reveal how pathetically jealous I felt.

At that point, really for the first time, I had to face the prospect that I would never get a job. Why for the first time? I don't know. I had always thought I'd make it through somehow, even in the face of mounting evidence that I would not. Something would turn up; my luck would change; I'd finally make it. Now it looked like I would not.

And that was OK, maybe. I could stay in Russia. Yulia and I could move in together. Or Yulia could move in with me and my grandmother. Or . . . I would likely be allowed to keep my PMOOC classes for the next year. So I would have some income. Yulia also had some income. I hadn't broached this with her yet, but I decided now that I would.

4.

I CONFRONT EMMA ABRAMOVNA

AND THEN I put it off. It wasn't that I had doubts about Yulia. I didn't. I had doubts about myself. I was still in Moscow because—why? Because I couldn't get a job in the States and because I wanted to foil Dima's evil plan to sell our grandmother's apartment. And—what? It seemed purely negative, reactive, like Russian foreign policy. It was as if I'd lost and failed my way into Yulia's life. Was this a good foundation on which to build a future?

My yearlong visa was expiring in mid-August, so one way or another I'd have to leave the country and get another one. It would probably mean going back to New York. And if I was going back to New York, it might make sense to spend a month and see if I could drum up some work. In any case, for the moment I was thinking about the summer.

It was almost June and my grandmother had still not discussed her dacha dreams with Emma Abramovna. Or, rather, she had hinted at them numerous times, and Emma Abramovna had not taken her up on the hinting. Finally I decided that I should just go over there and ask.

Emma Abramovna was an intimidating person. She had escaped from Hitler, had been exiled to Siberia as a Polish national, and had maintained her glamorous good looks that had invited a great deal of unwanted male attention, including at one point from the NKVD. Even among the generation that included my grandmother and Uncle Lev, she stood out. In short, as I sat before her, she half lying on her couch with a blanket draped over her lap, me in an armchair across from her, I was sitting before someone who was still quite formidable, no matter her age and condition.

"So what have you been up to in Moscow?" she said.

I told her about my work with October and our soon-to-be-launched website.

"They're, what, communists?" she asked.

"Socialists," I said.

"Idiots!" she said. "Socialism has been tried in this country. I lived through it. And I can tell you that the only thing worse is fascism."

"They're proposing something different," I said.

"They all propose something different, and in the end it's the same. Look at China, Cuba, Cambodia—wherever you go in the socialist world they set up camps, and sometimes worse. No, thank you."

She started telling me the story of how she'd been kicked out of the Party in 1948 for refusing to question the loyalty of Jewish citizens who supported Israel. (Stalin was convinced that with the creation of Israel, Jews would become a fifth column inside the USSR.) I had heard this story before. But I listened again.

"This group is anti-Stalinist," I said, when she was done.

"Well, thank God at least for that!" she said. Emma Abramovna was not about to get talked back into socialism by me.

Eventually I got around to what I'd come there for. "Emma Abramovna," I began, "as you know, Baba Seva lost her dacha in the nineties. Every summer she gets really sad when she has nowhere to go."

"I know," said Emma Abramovna. "She tells me all about it."

"Well, and I was thinking. Maybe she could come stay with you at Peredelkino for a little while? It would make her summer so much better."

"I don't think that's a good idea," Emma Abramovna said right away. She did not seem surprised in the least by the suggestion. She had apparently not been oblivious to my grandmother's hints. She had just chosen to ignore them.

I, however, was surprised. "Really?" I said. I knew Emma Abramovna's social life was a little more varied than my grandmother's, but it didn't seem like a round-the-clock party. She could fit in my grandmother, I thought. "Why not?" I said.

"Borya and Arkady and their families will be visiting a lot," Emma Abramovna said. "Really there's not much space."

"There won't even be a week where you'll have room?" I said, begging now. "You're her best friend!"

"Well," said Emma Abramovna, setting her mouth in a way that was unlike her, but then being brutally and entirely honest in a way that was: "she's not mine."

And that was that. I was silent, and then Emma Abramovna suggested that we change the subject, and her aide, Valya, brought out some tea and cookies, and I gulped them down as quickly as I could and then took my leave as politely as I could. But I was heartbroken. It was like a door had been shut on my grandmother's life, and she didn't even know about it.

As I walked home, I called Yulia to tell her the news.

"That's very sad," she said.

"Yes," I said. "*Starost' ne radost'*. Know anyone else with a dacha?"

"My mom goes to a sanatorium outside Kiev during the summers. Do you think your grandmother would enjoy that?"

"Maybe, but I don't think she'd enjoy the trip to Kiev. In fact I'm sure she'd refuse to take it."

"Yes. Well, maybe Kolya will be done with his dacha in time."

She said it half jokingly, but it wasn't the worst idea.

"That hadn't occurred to me," I said.

"Of course even if he does finish there won't be much to look at," said Yulia. "And nowhere to swim."

"My grandmother's not a big swimmer these days. Do you think we can ask him?"

"I don't see why not. He can say no if he wants. We did help him build the thing."

I got off the phone as I was descending into the underpass at Pushkin Square. I walked through it holding my phone in my hand. It was bright and full of people, some hurrying home, others tarrying in front of one of the many kiosks. There were fancy malls all over Moscow now but it was easier and more convenient and cheaper to buy something in an underpass. A few years earlier a Chechen terrorist had set off a bomb in this underpass, killing a dozen people. For a while people avoided it, but then they started coming again. What could they do? It was the very center of the city. I felt a surge of solidarity with all these people who did not care one way or another whether Chechnya was independent, whether it was Islamic or not, but who had to worry nonetheless when they passed through the Pushkin underpass whether someone might decide to blow them up. I passed a pie stand where I sometimes got a nice apricot pie for thirty rubles. I was sorry that I'd eaten so many cookies at Emma Abramovna's and was too stuffed to buy one now.

I emerged right next to Pushkin. In his sideburns and top hat, he towered, twelve feet tall and green, over the square. Why so big? Pushkin himself was quite short. But he was a genius. The great-grandson of an African slave brought to Russia to entertain the tsar's court, by the age of eighteen he was producing poetry that was clearly superior to any written in Russian until then. At the time, Russian literary language did not quite exist; most educated Russians wrote in French, only the very rich were educated, and what literature there was bore the marks of this double separation from actual Russian life. Pushkin managed to change this. His poetry was exquisite *and* it sounded like Russian; even now, two hundred years later, it was perfectly clear and comprehensible. His talent was eventually too much. The tsar personally censored his work. He was surrounded by intrigue; a young French officer who was flirting with his wife killed him in a duel before he turned forty.

I called Nikolai and he picked up right away. "Listen," I said, "I'm hoping to get my grandmother out of town for a week sometime this summer, and I can't really think of any place that would work, so I was wondering—do you think we could use your dacha for a week?"

"Of course!" he said. "I would be honored to provide shelter for a woman whose dacha was taken from her by unscrupulous capitalists." There was a pause. "But if the place is going to be ready for the summer, I'm going to need some help."

So for several weekends in a row I made the long trip out there and painted and sanded and helped the Uzbek construction guys unload their small trucks and set up the bathroom and the kitchen. We agreed that I could have the dacha for a week in mid-July.

In the meantime, my grandmother grew increasingly despondent. She was shrinking physically, but her personality was shrinking as well. There was less and less of her inside her. She was becoming, more and more, what she had been as a little girl: the dutiful daughter of an overbearing mother. I had intuited that she'd been this way from her stories of her childhood; now I saw this very person before me, in the guise of a ninety-year-old with a cane.

The semester was again rounding into its final stretch and this meant final papers and dozens if not hundreds of emails in which students asked for clarification about what the final paper entailed and what exactly I was looking for and could I send some samples of successful papers that they could emulate? I was able to do much of this from the windowsill, and my grandmother had become better at not interrupting. I think the fact that I was so visibly before her, at my computer, meant that she was both reassured that I was around and also convinced that I was doing something, and should be left alone.

In the evenings she still enjoyed our Soviet films. Sometimes Yulia, who remained our main source for tips on what to watch, joined us. Other times I saw her later. She slept over a fair amount now, and my grandmother seemed to find this arrangement congenial. It was as if she were sprouting a new family.

But in the late afternoon hours, after lunch, she spoke of suicide. "You know," she said one day, over tea, "I asked one of the pharmacists to give me poison. I even gave her the money. But now she won't do it."

"What? Who?"

"The pharmacist."

"Where?"

"Over there." She motioned outdoors.

"What kind of poison?" I said.

"I asked her for something that would kill me. She said she had something like that."

I couldn't tell if this had actually happened. I imagined myself showing up at the pharmacy and demanding to know, through the glass, if they had promised to poison my grandmother.

"In one of the European countries there is a place you can go," my grandmother went on, "a house, you can go to the house and if you want to die, they will help you."

She was talking about physician-assisted suicide, euthanasia. It was practiced in the Netherlands. Perhaps she had seen a segment about it on the news.

"Isn't that nice?" she went on. "If you want to go, you can go."

I no longer argued with her about these things. I agreed with her that it was nice. Sadly, I suggested, the same was not possible here.

"No," my grandmother agreed. "It's not."

My grandmother dreamed of killing herself. Her doctor had said there was no safe way for her to take anti-depressants, so I tried to give her some Saint-John's-wort tea. But she had a bad reaction: it made her hyper and paranoid. She woke up several times in the middle of the night and told me she thought she heard noises outside her window. I had to come and sit in the armchair next to her bed while she slept. I threw out the Saint-John's-wort. She remained depressed. I felt like she was asking me to kill her, and I could not do it.

A better person might have done it. A better or more courageous person. I was beginning to think that maybe I was not that better or more courageous person. I had become a slightly better person here. I had stopped looking at Facebook quite so much; I had become less bitterly jealous of all my classmates. I was being nice to Yulia, and, aside from refusing to strangle my grandmother with a pillow, I was being a decent friend to her. But compared to the vastly better person I had hoped to become, this wasn't much to speak of. And I could always go back to being the person I was before. In fact all it would take would probably be a return to the United States.

I had even begun to have my doubts about Yulia. I didn't want to have them, but I did. She too was a little depressed. And incredibly sensitive. I wasn't sure I could handle being in the constant presence of someone so morally acute. I wasn't sure I could live up to it. I was sure, in fact, that I could not.

More to the point, would I really be able to stay in Moscow indefinitely? On the one hand it was appealing. I didn't care that much about good coffee. And I liked the food. But the daily grind of life was something else. Just to do anything—to get my skates sharpened, to get a library book, to get from one part of the city to another—was an unbelievable hassle. What in New York took twenty minutes, here took an hour. What in New York took an hour, here took pretty much all day. It wore you down. The frowns on the faces of the people wore you down. The lies on the television too, after a while, wore you down.

Sometimes in the evenings as she was going to bed my grandmother asked me to sit with her while she read. She would lie in her little twin bed, her glasses on her nose, and hold up a thin sheaf of pages she'd torn from one of her books, while I sat in the armchair by her bed and read whatever I was reading then. Eventually she would fall asleep, I would gently remove her glasses, pull her blanket over her, and turn off the light. One night that spring she fell asleep and for a while I sat in my chair and wondered if I should do it. My grandmother was in pain—not physical pain, though a bit of that, but emotional pain. She was bored, she felt useless, she was sad. She lay with her mouth hanging open, her teeth out, my grandmother, the mother of my mother, lightly snoring. She had a pillow under her knees, which I could remove without waking her and then press over her face—I had already removed her glasses— and perhaps if I did it gently enough she would not even wake up. This is what she wanted above all, not to wake up! "Leva just went to sleep one night" was something she said a lot about Uncle Lev. "He just went to sleep and died." But of course she'd wake up if I tried to suffocate her with a pillow. I pictured her fighting me instinctively, even as intellectually she wanted the end to come. And then what exactly would I tell the police? That she asked me to do it? I pictured the baby-faced

276

policeman I'd talked to when my grandmother was missing—would he be understanding? Should I try to bribe him? Or would that be an implicit admission of guilt?

It didn't matter. I wasn't going to do it. I didn't have it in me. A better person would have done it, I think. I bet Sergei would have done it. He had told me the other day that he was finally leaving his wife. "It's the hardest thing I've ever done," he said. "But it's better this way." He couldn't lie, was his problem. And I felt like if an elderly person, a little grandmother, in pain, had asked him to kill her, he would have done it. Yet I could not.

I was beginning to wonder if I had promised more to the people around me than I could deliver. If I had made myself out to be a better person than I could be. I couldn't shake the occasional feeling that I was in over my head.

5.

PROMISES

AND YET, AND YET, and yet. I loved it. I loved kasha and kotlety and I loved the language and I loved the hockey guys and I even loved some of the people on the street. I loved walking down Sretenka with my hockey gear in my Soviet backpack, taking the subway one stop, emerging at Prospekt Mira and then walking to the stadium past the McDonald's, the Orthodox church, the market where we failed to buy my grandmother slippers, and then into the rink. Late at night, on my way home, I loved sometimes buying half a chicken from the Azeri guys. "Our hockey friend!" they always said, greeting me. On nights when I went to see Yulia, I loved taking a car for three dollars—a flat one hundred rubles, who could argue. One time I caught a car home from her place, up the Garden Ring, at two in the morning. The driver was in his early twenties, of indeterminate ethnicity. When I got in the car he took his mobile phone from the radio slot, in case I was a cop or something, but once I was seated he put it back in again, and as we picked up speed on the Garden Ring I saw that it was playing a film—*300*, I think, about the Spartan battle with the Persians in 480 B.C. We raced down the Garden Ring, my driver and I, occasionally looking up at the road, occasionally looking down at the Spartans in chroma-key, holding off Xerxes' army.

One night in early June, Yulia decided to have a dinner party. She invited the Marxist reading group and two of her friends from her graduate program, who were not Marxists. On the way over I walked down to the fancy grocery store next to the KGB. They had a whole huge section devoted to vodka. This was a stereotype about Russians, most of whom preferred beer most of the time, but it was also true: in addition to beer, they liked vodka. It was a matter of geography. It was too cold in Russia to grow grapes; it was too dry to age whiskey deliciously in barrels. And so Russians, like Finns and Swedes and Poles, drank a clear, wheat- or potato-based liquor. That is to say, they drank vodka. In the fancy supermarket next to the KGB the vodka section ran the gamut from insanely cheap to moderately cheap. The government kept the vodka tariffs low because they knew that if vodka became too expensive, people would start making it in their bathtubs and dying. From the cheapest to the most expensive, the vodka bottles were clear, and the light of the store refracted through them as through crystals, and I walked through the aisle, choosing my vodka, like Superman in that chamber on Krypton where the tribal elders used to meet before their planet was destroyed. Once I picked out my vodka I also got some high-quality herring. The whole thing ran me fifteen dollars. "Having a party?" the middle-aged cashier, her hair dyed red, said to me as she scanned my items.

"Just meeting up with some friends," I said.

"Bon appétit."

"Thank you."

I left the store in a state of near exaltation. I had never had such a pleasant interaction with a Russian cashier. But in recent weeks I'd had such interactions more and more. I thought, perhaps, that when I'd first arrived they'd smelled fear on me, and worry, and displacement. I had shed it now. I was an émigré. I had left. Now I'd returned. The night before, at hockey, Oleg had come off the ice looking annoyed after I flubbed a pass to him from the corner—but the fact was that I'd had to fight off two defenders from the white team and I still had Grisha draped on my back when I made the pass.

"Andrei," said Oleg, "what was up with that pass?"

"Oleg, fuck your mother!" I cried, finally losing it. "Stop making a long face all the time! Play hockey! If the puck doesn't come to you, go get it, you lazy fuck!"

I was mildly horrified by my own outburst, especially as Oleg had been having a rough time recently—the guys he was renting to, about whom the rest of the team had warned him, had stopped paying their rent and declared that they were going to take over the space as their own—but after I swore at him Oleg just laughed.

"Antosha," he said, turning to Anton. "Did you hear that? Andrei's yelling just like us now!"

I felt very proud. Now, coming out of the supermarket, I decided to hail a car—I was running late, the streets were clear, and there wasn't a good subway to catch from where I was to reach Yulia's. I got a car quickly and sat down in the front seat. My driver was from the Caucasus somewhere (most of the guys who picked you up at this point, although they drove Russian cars, were not Russian—they were from the poorer countries south of Russia), and as we reached Pushkin Square he turned to me and said, "Where you from? Argentina?"

It was a question that had freaked me out when I first arrived. Now I just said, "I'm from here." Which was true. "But I'm Jewish."

"Oh, yeah?" said the cabdriver. "I'm Jewish too. Ever hear of the mountain Jews of Georgia?"

I had not.

"We've been there thousands of years," he said. Then he asked, "You know Yiddish?"

"No."

"I do. They taught us there, up in the mountains."

"Wow," I said, and meant it.

I was in a great mood when I showed up at Yulia's. It was past ten already but that was all right. Russians keep late hours. They think nothing of starting dinner at ten o'clock. Especially now that the air was a little warmer and the sun set later in the day.

Dinner had not yet been served. People were out on the balcony, smoking and drinking beer. Yulia was wearing her pretty white cotton dress with flowers on it. She kissed me hello and directed me to the balcony. Out there Sergei was talking about a new branch of October that had started up in Saratov. "The comrades from Saratov," he called them. Apparently the comrades from Saratov came from the antifa movement, which spent some of its time engaging in street fights with neo-Nazis, and though this group had decided to go socialist they had brought some of their old ways with them to October. "If it wasn't for all the knife fighting," Sergei summed up, "the comrades from Saratov would be worth their weight in gold." After breaking up with his wife he had moved back in with his parents, and he seemed quite happy.

Yulia had gone into the kitchen after taking me to the balcony and she now called everyone in to eat.

Yulia tended to make up for a lack of quality in her cooking with volume. She and her roommates, some of whom were superior cooks, had made potatoes and kotlety and salad and even cabbage pie. We drank the vodka I brought—everyone else had brought wine or beer—and pronounced various toasts.

At some point people started talking about whether they'd leave the country.

"I would, I think," said Misha. "Academically there's only so much I can accomplish here. If I want to do serious work I need to go to Germany or Britain or the U.S. But I'd hope to come back eventually."

"Like Lenin," said Boris.

Everyone laughed. That was the consensus, it seemed—people were willing to leave temporarily, but they intended, like Lenin, to return. I waited for Yulia to say something—I wondered if she'd take a different position, in this context, than she did with me. But she remained silent.

"I'm not leaving," said Sergei. "I associate my fate with the fate of this country. No matter what."

"Even if Putin comes back?" Katya asked. She meant if he came back as president. There was a sense—not really shared by the Octobrists, but Katya was not in October—that the Medvedev regime was more liberal, and a return to Putin would put an end to that.

"No matter what," Sergei reiterated.

The table went silent. Sergei had said it very matter-of-factly, without undue drama, and still it had the effect of making everyone else feel that their attachment to Russia was inadequate.

"I feel the same," Yulia said quietly.

The table was silent again, even more awkwardly now. I felt that people were looking at me, as if at this dinner party Yulia was breaking up with me. And in a way she was doing just that. I was from America, in the end. If she wasn't going to leave Russia, then that meant we were kaput.

Unless.

"OK," I said, speaking to her (I was right next to her), but also to the table. "Then I'm not leaving either."

There was a momentary pause and then everyone laughed. We drank to me staying. Yulia kissed me on the cheek. "Don't be an idiot," she whispered to me.

"I don't want to go anywhere without you," I said.

She kissed me again.

And I meant it. These were my people. Fuck America. I would stay.

6.

SUMMERTIME

THAT SUMMER WAS MAGICAL. The weather just got warmer and warmer, to the point where it was maybe too warm, but that was OK—people simply walked around in shorts and flip-flops and took things slow. I loved walking to hockey in the heat, cooling off on the ice, and then reemerging into the summer. After hockey, Sergei would drop me off at Trubnaya and I would buy a Zhigulovskoye and then go sit with my hockey stuff on one of the benches on the boulevard and relax. The Moscow heat was a dry heat, like in Jerusalem. As I sat there I thought of how, back at the hockey rink, the Zamboni driver, in the dark Moscow night, was cutting the ice one last time so that the next day we could have a fresh new sheet. Occasionally on these evenings my phone would buzz in my pocket and it'd be Yulia asking if I wanted to see her. I always did.

Now that the weather was much better, we got to spend more time outside. It turned out there were yet more cities within the city. The city that I had always seen was a charming old European city that had been defaced and overwritten by Communism. And there was some truth to that. But over the years many of the buildings that would catch the eyes of a common tourist, the old pastel-colored cupcake buildings, had been fixed up and made to look new, whereas the buildings of the early Soviet school, which included Constructivist masterpieces, had been allowed to deteriorate. Walking around with Yulia clued me in to the great utopian experiment that had been attempted here, on the level of the buildings themselves, before it was abandoned and forgotten.

There was something else that she showed me, not having to do with Communism, exactly. The city that I knew was the city of avenues and side streets. The avenues were enormous highways; the side streets were quiet and rambling. But in between the side streets were the courtyards. You could go in, sit on a bench, drink a beer. I had seen people doing this in our own courtyard, and found it, mostly, annoying. But now that Yulia and I did it, or Yulia and I and Misha and Masha or Sergei, it was great. There were courtyards near my grandmother's place, off Pechatnikov, that were quiet and almost ancient-seeming; the buildings around them had peeling pastel paint, and there were old trees, and in a few places people had tried to plant some flowers. None of the courtyards were beautiful or particularly well kept, but I saw now they had a beauty to them; they were leftover oases inside the giant metropolis. And gradually, even in the time that I was there, they were being wiped out: as the old buildings on Pechatnikov were knocked down and replaced with near exact replicas of themselves, the new owners always made sure to install sturdy gates, so that only the wealthy residents would be allowed in. The city was closing itself off from itself. But for now at least there were still places you could go.

The warm weather was good for our political activity as well. October started running its "Street University," where various speakers would come and give a brief talk somewhere out in the open—the idea was less to attract random passersby than just to claim public space for public discussions. And also the general pace of our meetings, protests, and other activities increased, and we finally launched our website— Yulia organized a small party at Falanster to celebrate—and there were more things for me to translate, for which I was glad.

The thaw in the weather accompanied a political thaw of sorts. Medvedev was slightly more liberal than Putin, but the real change was that the spigot of oil money had finally run dry. World oil prices collapsed in the wake of the global financial crisis. In Russia, after ten years of sometimes astounding economic growth, the economy slipped into recession. You could fool all of the people some of the time, and some of the people all of the time, but as the weather grew warmer and the economy still hadn't improved, the ruble had lost value but salaries had not been adjusted for inflation—well, it was as if some kind of lid had been lifted.

In one Siberian oil town, workers whose wages hadn't been adjusted for inflation in an entire year—during a time when the ruble had lost 20 percent of its value against the dollar, meaning that they had to swallow what was in effect a 20 percent wage cut—started organizing against their employer, good old RussOil. The head of their organizing committee was arrested and thrown in jail, supposedly for having a bag of heroin on him. When the organizing didn't stop, another leader of the movement was beaten to within an inch of his life. When the workers walked out in protest, they were set upon by security, who proceeded to beat the shit out of them with baseball bats. Someone took a grainy cellphone video, and Misha sent it around to our email list: it was surreal to see these Russian guys with baseball bats attacking a group of workers. The situation was so bad that Putin himself got involved and demanded that the wages be indexed. RussOil grudgingly complied.

Sergei and the others were very excited. Labor unrest was at the heart of their concept of political action. "The liberals have never even tried to speak to these people, and in fact they have nothing but contempt for them," Sergei wrote on the October website. "They call them *sovok*. But in fact these *sovok* are the very people who have the power and the right to annihilate this regime." The protest at RussOil and a few others like it were grounds for hope. "We're not in a revolutionary situation," Sergei told me one night as we sat in his car on Trubnaya. "We're not even on the brink of a revolutionary situation. But at least we can start using the words." Throughout the summer we held pickets in support of protesting workers, handed out leaflets at Moscow factories, and published excited reports on our website, analyzing the situation and predicting more labor unrest in the future.

I was still managing a few nights a week of hockey. Our luck against the white team had hardly changed; maybe once a month we'd beat them, if that. But for a week that summer, before he went back home to Seattle to settle down and get married, Michael from next door had two college friends visiting him. He had gone to school in Vancouver and his friends were Canadian, and at my prompting he had asked them to bring their hockey gear. They had been glad to, and I brought them to hockey with me. They were regular, unassuming guys, neither tall nor short, neither fat nor thin, and I could tell when they showed up with me that the guys on my team were underimpressed by "the Canadians." But when they got on the ice the Canadians were unbelievable. The game was in their bones. We put them on a line with Oleg and they must have scored six or seven goals. The white team was so amazed they didn't even bother trying to maim them. We won both games they played in. The team was thrilled, and Sergei quietly asked some questions about the Canadian health-care system.

Something else happened at hockey that I found pretty interesting. The white team, while a cohesive unit, occasionally invited some friend or client to come and play in the game. One Wednesday night they had a new guy playing, and in the warm-ups when I saw him I immediately had a strong, deeply unpleasant reaction. I couldn't place where it was coming from and I skated by him again: he was young, blue-eyed, and had chiseled features, very familiar, and I knew I didn't like him. I'd had this reaction a few times in New York when seeing actors on the street who played bad guys on TV. Had I seen this guy in one of the movies Yulia and I watched together? I started trying to figure out which one it might have been. On the bench once the game started I asked Anton if the guy was an actor. "An actor?" said Anton. "No. He's just some asshole. His father's in the Duma."

Then I knew who it was. It was the guy who had pistol-whipped me outside of Teatr. And he was on the ice at this very moment. I couldn't believe it. It wasn't my turn to go out but I announced that I was taking the next man off and no one argued with me. When I got on the ice, the guy was still on, and I skated right at him and slashed him in the leg. He looked up, surprised.

"Remember me?" I yelled.

He looked like he didn't remember and didn't care. "Fuck off," he said.

At this I lost my mind. It was one thing for some guy to hit me with a gun for no reason. I mean, that was bad enough. But for him to show up to my hockey game, skate around like it was no big deal, and then pretend not even to care whether he knew who I was—this was too much. Without dropping my stick, I punched him hard in the back of the helmet. He fell forward onto the ice. I wanted to kick him but it wasn't possible with skates so I dropped my stick and gloves and jumped on top of him to tear his helmet off. It wouldn't come off so as he lay on the ice I started punching the back of his helmet—it was a little idiotic, but I don't think it was ineffective. "All right," I heard him say. "Enough." By this point several of the guys from both teams had skated over and were trying to pull me away. I let them do so. The guy wasn't fighting back. He wasn't a strong skater, his pads were brand-new, and apparently he felt less sure of himself on the ice than he did out on the street. Whereas I felt, just then, right at home.

"Andryush, what the fuck's going on?"

Fedya, from the white team, was in my face. He had been slipping passes by me to his linemate Alyosha for months and had never once smiled at me, or even after our first meeting acknowledged my existence, though a few weeks earlier he'd accidentally hit me in the face with his stick and apologized.

I said, "That guy hit me with a gun outside a nightclub on Clean Ponds. Without any reason. He just came up to me and hit me."

Fedya turned to the blond, who was slowly gathering the equipment he'd dropped when I attacked him. "Alexei, is that true?"

"I don't remember," said the guy. "Maybe. He was talking to my girl-friend."

"Fuck off!" I yelled. Literally, "go on a cock." I delivered the curse with total authority. "I didn't say a word to her. And you had a gun."

Fedya turned to the guy and said, "Leave."

The guy nodded and without looking at me skated off the ice, holding his gloves and stick against his chest like a little boy. I stayed. At the end of the skate, I went over to Fedya to thank him.

"It's nothing," he said. "You were right and he was wrong. He won't be invited to play again."

And that was it. The next time we played, Fedya gave no indication of being my new friend. But what happened had happened. The hockey guys were OK.

It wasn't all triumphs and victories during this period. One night on my way home from Yulia's, I saw a fire—it was the Azeri chicken and pastry stand. It was in flames. A group of people was standing around, and then a fire truck came and poured a bunch of water on the stand. No one was hurt, but, as I read online a few days later, it wasn't an accident: several Azeri-owned businesses had been torched that night in Moscow in retaliation for the stabbing of a Russian teenager by an Azeri man at one of the markets. For a couple of weeks, the burned husk of the chicken stand stood there, and then it was removed. The Azeri guys didn't come back.

Something foul was in the air. One Sunday the speakers at October's Street University were two Italian communists—"comrades of Negri," according to Boris, in the email announcement, meaning the legendary Italian communist and political prisoner Antonio Negri—and the location was right around the corner from us, at the Krupskaya statue. My grandmother was feeling pretty good that day, and I invited her along.

The Italians were sweet grad student types in their midthirties. They spoke in English and Boris translated, with some help from me. The Italians wanted to talk about "cognitive capitalism." This was a concept Negri developed to deal with the fact that actual physical capitalism had done OK by workers in Europe. They received decent wages and were able to purchase property and were no longer interested in revolution. But, Negri argued, their minds were being colonized. Not just their bodies, as Marx had said; their very minds.

I liked the Italians but I couldn't help but think that this news was, for Russia, a little premature. Here working people were still being exploited in the old-fashioned way. They did not earn decent wages; they could not afford to buy property; they had no protections. There was no need to come up with fancy new theories when the old ones were still so obviously true.

As I was thinking this a group of skinheads appeared from the far end of the boulevard and approached the Krupskaya statue. They wore combat boots and army surplus pants and jackets. There were five or six of them. I had never seen actual skinheads in the center of Moscow. Maybe, I thought, they were the good kind? Then they set up shop at the base of the statue, not fifteen feet from us, and started goofing around and taking cell phone photos of themselves with Lenin's widow in the background. "Beat the Jews, save Russia!" they yelled. Click. And then, "Heil Hitler!" Click. These were not the good kind of skinheads. They were behind the Italians, who didn't seem to notice and kept going on about cognitive capitalism. Boris kept dutifully translating, though he occasionally sneaked a look over his shoulder.

I sized up our group. There were seven of us: the two Italians, Boris, Vera, Yulia, me, and my grandmother. Of the seven of us, I was the only one who looked like he engaged in any regular exercise. We did not stand a chance against the skinheads.

"*Sieg heil!*" yelled the skinheads.

"You know," Boris said, turning to the Italians, "I think we should move a little farther into the park. It'll be quieter there."

And so we did. I thought for a moment that the skinheads would wonder what was up, or even that they had deliberately come over to our group to yell their slogans, but they didn't pay us any mind. They were busy taking photos of their Nazi salutes. Maybe they had just re-designed their website and needed some content. We found a shady spot farther along the boulevard, and the Italians finished their lecture on cognitive capitalism. By the time my grandmother and Yulia and I went back to our place, the skinheads were gone.

A few days later, my grandmother and I were walking back together from the market when I noticed, not for the first time, the group of old ladies who sat in the children's playground in the courtyard between our building and the market. These were the women my grandmother had dismissed to me as anti-Semites, but ever since the Vladlenna incident I wondered if she wasn't just imagining it. And if they were a little anti-Semitic, who cared. What an opportunity! These old ladies sitting on a bench, feeding the pigeons and keeping an eye on the neighborhood, had once been a common feature of every Soviet and post-Soviet courtyard. In the center of Moscow, the era of high oil prices had all but wiped them out. And yet here, literally one courtyard away, a little pocket of resistance remained. There was still plenty of summer left; perhaps my grandmother would enjoy coming out here and sitting with her near contemporaries and discussing the problems of the day?

Before my grandmother or my own natural shyness could stop me, I turned to address the old ladies.

"Hello!" I said. I pulled my grandmother over to them. Several pigeons the old ladies had been feeding with bread scattered loudly as we walked over. "Hello," I said again, after the pigeons had cleared out. "My name is Andrei. And this is Seva."

The old ladies nodded—there were three of them—and waited for me to continue.

"Tell me," I said, not really knowing what else to say, "what are your plans for the summer?"

The old ladies exchanged what seemed like amused looks. Then one of them, who was sitting in the middle and had a half loaf of white bread in her hand, spoke up. "We're going to be sitting right here, where else are we gonna go?" she said. "Not like some people who're probably going to Israel for the summer."

The sudden invocation of Israel wiped the polite smile from my face, which I suppose was the intended effect.

"How's that?" I said. "Why Israel?"

"Well, isn't that where Seva *Efraimovna*'s going to go?" said the woman. She put a lot of stress on my grandmother's obviously Jewish patronymic. The other two women snickered their approval.

"No," I said uselessly. "She doesn't have any relatives there."

"No?" said the woman. "Maybe she'll go to America then. There's plenty of your kind there, right?"

Now the other two women were really enjoying it. One of them clapped her hands in delight. My heart was racing. I had never met an actual, real-live anti-Semite before. I felt my grandmother beside me; I couldn't tell how much of this she could hear, but I think she sensed the hostility of these women, and knew what they were about. For my part, I couldn't believe it. And yet what could I do? Was I going to stand there and yell at them? Or fight them?

I stood for a few long moments, just kind of staring, and then without saying anything I turned with my grandmother—her hand was looped around my elbow, so we turned together—and walked away.

"Good-bye, Jews!" the women called after us, and laughed.

Still, it was a beautiful summer. One Sunday in June, Misha, Boris, Yulia, and I borrowed Sergei's car and took a trip out to a place called Petrovo, a few hours south of Moscow. Misha and Boris had found it at random on a map. They pretended that the trip was for my benefit, so that I could see "the real Russia," but they were obviously curious as well. In Petrovo we found a simple Soviet town, with the old 1950s five-story apartment buildings called Khrushchevki, a grocery store that sold local vodka, a department store where you could still buy the old Russian-made pots and pans and can openers that my grandmother's apartment was filled with. "This is real Russian vodka," Misha said when we went to the grocery store, and "These are real Russian utensils," he said at the department store; and when we went to an old-fashioned cafeteria and ate cold borscht and cucumber salad, he informed us that "this is a real Russian cafeteria and this is real Russian cuisine."

"It will give you," said Yulia, "a real Russian stomachache." Everyone laughed. I realized then how much in common I had with all of them, more than I realized; they remembered this Soviet world from their childhoods just as I remembered it from mine. They were, in a way, as nostalgic for it as I was. On our way home, we pulled off the road so that Misha, who'd had a few beers in the cafeteria, could go to the bathroom. The dirt road we found ourselves on was so narrow that we couldn't turn around and had to keep going until we reached an opening; we ended up at an old Soviet schoolhouse, obviously abandoned. SCHOOL NUMBER 3, it said over the entrance. It was dusk when we came to the school, and the broken windows and trash piled up near it gave it a kind of haunted aspect.

"You know," said Boris, "most of the rest of the country is like this." He turned the car around and we sped back toward the main road.

A few weekends later, Yulia and I took a trip to Kiev so that I could meet her mother. Sophia Nikolaevna lived alone in one of the crumbling high-rise blocks on Kiev's Right Bank; she was approaching sixty, and hadn't worked in over a decade. Yulia had warned me that in her loneliness and disappointment her mother had fallen victim to the info-war between Russia and Ukraine that would eventually, some years later, turn into a shooting war. Sophia Nikolaevna was an ethnic Russian; this didn't used to matter in Ukraine, but now it could, if you let it, and she let it by consuming Russian television, which warned her that soon the Russian language would be banned in Ukraine. There were times, Yulia told me, that she told Yulia she feared leaving the house because she thought she'd be outed as a Russian. "If she starts railing against the government, just ignore her," said Yulia as we took the subway to her childhood apartment. The Kiev subway was identical in just about every way to the Moscow subway, but older and poorer (and about five times cheaper), and the announcements were in Ukrainian (as it turned out, and contrary to Sophia Nikolaevna's fears, this was just about the only Ukrainian I heard while in Kiev). Yulia's mother was much sweeter and more together than advertised. Aside from complimenting my Russian, which, given that she was such a brave defender of the Russian language, I took as high praise, she kept her rantings about the government to herself. If anything, I found her a little distant.

"Thank you for visiting me, my friend," she said. "You didn't have to do that." I couldn't tell if this was a commentary on her sense of her own unimportance, or an expression of skepticism toward my commitment to her daughter. Or some combination.

"I'm happy to finally meet you," I said.

"Thank you, my friend," answered Sophia Nikolaevna.

Yulia's childhood room was filled with books, and the walls were covered with little drawings, in gouache, that she had done as a teenager. The apartment, on the sixth floor, was small—three rooms, low ceilings, a tiny kitchen—but it was tidy and lived-in. The building itself and the neighborhood were a different story. The elevator smelled like someone had died in it. The entrance had been graffitied over a hundred times. It was surrounded by identical buildings, some small grocery stores, and a fast-food chicken place where Yulia and I sneaked off for lunch.

"This place was OK when I was growing up here," said Yulia. "It was full of children. Every winter they would make an ice rink in front of our building and everyone would go skating."

To reach the chicken spot, we had walked through what seemed like a series of abandoned lots full of trash and broken glass (but no furniture—Ukrainians were too poor to throw out furniture). Once upon a time this was meant to be a tree-lined play area for children. That was hard to picture now.

"It was very different," Yulia said. "It wasn't just physically different, it was morally different. People had work and they weren't ashamed of themselves. They were poor, but poverty is relative. Remember the immiseration thesis? 'As capital accumulates, the situation of the worker, *be his payment high or low*, must grow worse.' The reverse is also true. People can be poor without suffering, as long as they are not abandoned, as long as they don't perceive themselves to be abandoned. My mother was poor under Communism but she had a job, she had access to medical care, she could look me in the eye and tell me things would be OK and believe it. She was a happy person. That person you see in there is not her."

The next day Yulia took me around the city; she showed me the Maidan, where people had massed together to form the Orange Revolution in 2004, and the huge old churches on the hills above it, and finally the house-museum of Mikhail Bulgakov, whom Yulia loved. "He wasn't a socialist," she said, "and he didn't like Jews. But he was a good writer and a pretty good person. That counts."

Kiev was a more naturally beautiful city than Moscow, and also a calmer one. Five million people lived there but you never felt hurried or rushed. It was much poorer too. Ukraine had few natural resources and had fumbled the post-Soviet transition. For a visitor, this meant everything was cheap. We walked around the church grounds and ate ice cream. Yulia seemed happy and relaxed here in a way she rarely did in Moscow.

I felt like she was trying to tell me something by bringing me to Kiev, introducing me to her mother, showing me around. Perhaps she was saying, "This is why I can't leave. It would be cowardly to do so." Or perhaps she was saying, "This is serious. You know everything about me now. Make a move." Sitting in the chicken place listening to her talk about her childhood, then walking among the thirteenth-century churches on the hill above the city center, then in her favorite bar, the Kupidon, where I drank a giant Ukrainian beer, I kept thinking that I should propose to her that we bind our lives together. Maybe Sophia Nikolaevna could move to Moscow. She and my grandmother could keep each other company. Or maybe we should all move to Kiev. We could live like kings in impoverished Kiev. I kept thinking in all these spots of how to phrase it, and if I should phrase it, and guessing what she'd say.

But I didn't do it. I was in part still wondering if there might not be some job opening that could happen, some stroke of luck—I wanted to prove to Yulia and my grandmother and myself that I wasn't a failure, that I could provide for all of us in some other way than by selling off my grandmother's old apartment. So I waited. And waited. And then things took on a momentum of their own.

The highlight of the summer was our trip to Nikolai's dacha. There had been some delays and cost overruns, but by mid-July it was done. Nikolai spent a week there in triumph, and then turned it over, for a week, to us.

There was no way we were going to force my grandmother to take the hell journey to the dacha on public transportation, so I borrowed Sergei's rickety old Lada. Then I had to drive. I had never driven in Moscow before, and it was terrifying. It was not just that it was a big city. It was a tremendously confusing one. The side streets were narrow; the radial avenues were enormous; on certain long stretches of the major avenues traffic lights had been eliminated, making it basically impossible to turn left. On my first drive home from hockey, where Sergei had handed me the keys to the car, I missed my left turn onto Tsvetnoi Boulevard from the Garden Ring and then could not figure out how to pull a U-turn. I tried once to take a right and another right and another so as to return to the Ring and take a left, sending me back where I came from, but I ended up in the wrong lane and had to take a right again. Finally I decided it would be easier to just remain on the Garden Ring and go all the way around. It was late and traffic was relatively light and it only took forty minutes to get back to Tsvetnoi Boulevard again and take my damn left.

The other factor I encountered, once we had packed the car with our stuff and my grandmother, was that the cars were going at different speeds. In New York most cars are as aggressive as they can be; once you get used to this, you can anticipate it. In Moscow drivers were equally aggressive, but it was hard to anticipate exactly how it would play out in practice because cars had different capabilities. There were plenty of Mercedeses and Audis—these cars were quick. On the other end of the spectrum were old Russian cars, like mine—these cars had limited acceleration. And in between were newer Russian cars, some of which looked like they'd be able to accelerate, but in fact could not. So while everyone wanted to be a daredevil/asshole, not everyone could go at the same speed, and this added a layer of complexity to an already difficult situation.

Somehow we arrived at the dacha without incident. I hadn't been there in a few weeks and Nikolai had clearly continued to improve it. The main thing was that he'd cleared out the yard. The weeds and overgrowth were gone, leaving a clearing, not yet quite covered with grass, and a few select bushes that had a bit more shape to them. My grandmother, upon seeing one, immediately said, "Raspberries!" She was right. She approached it and started pulling down raspberries and eating them.

And thus we spent the week. There was a cot on the first floor where my grandmother could sleep so she didn't have to tackle the stairs, and while the tiny grocery store was a little too far to walk, we were able to drive there every morning and pick up what we needed—they had potatoes, beets, cabbage, and bread. Every other day a local farmer set up a small fruit and vegetable stand outside the store, where we got tomatoes, cucumbers, and some greens. Finally, at Nikolai's suggestion, Yulia and I drove out about an hour one day to a village where we were able to go door-to-door and buy eggs. We had to go door-to-door because the most eggs we could buy from any one person was two. That seemed to be all they had. But we kept going until we had twenty eggs. One woman also sold us some cottage cheese. Between the two of us, and with conceptual input from my grandmother, we were able to make enough food to feed us, and everyone was satisfied.

For all of Nikolai's heroics there was no changing the fact that the house was in the middle of nowhere. We did not wake to the sound of a babbling brook or the fresh smell of dewy trees and grass taking in the morning sun. But we were also not in Moscow. One of the neighbors apparently also kept chickens, because in the early mornings we were roused by the sounds of a rooster. The first time it happened, I found Yulia already lying awake, smiling. "My dear," she said, "we're not in Moscow anymore." This was a quote from an old Soviet anecdote about an American family that comes to the Soviet Union on a trip from Chicago, and whose young daughter keeps complaining about the accommodations, to which her parents reply, "My dear, we're not in Chicago anymore." But also it was true. We were not in Moscow anymore. And that meant we were on vacation.

Nikolai had set up the house with wi-fi so in the mornings Yulia and I were able to work. (I had taken on three summer PMOOCs; the U.S. economy was still in recession but partly for that reason there was less of a PMOOC drop-off than expected.) Then in the afternoons we would go for a walk to the abandoned quarry. My grandmother wasn't up for these walks but she remained content to sit in the backyard wearing her old wide-brimmed summer hat and occasionally getting up to feed herself raspberries from the seemingly inexhaustible raspberry bush. One morning Yulia and I woke up and stumbled into the kitchen and my grandmother was already out in the yard, picking raspberries. She had in recent weeks become almost entirely reliant on her cane when she walked, but now she was stretched out to her full height, reaching for raspberries. Yulia said, "She looks like a little bear."

I had brought along a whole packet of old Soviet movies on DVD from the DVD pirate kiosk at Clean Ponds, and in the evenings we would watch them together. We watched *Office Romance*, about a mean lady boss and her nerdy but charming underling, who fall in love; and *Five Evenings*, a Nikita Mikhalkov film about a man who returns suddenly from unknown parts to spend a week (five evenings) with his old love and her teenage nephew, whose mother died during the war. Though the film was from the 1970s, the director, Mikhalkov, was still alive and active and had become a nasty nationalist, and so Yulia refused to watch it with us and went upstairs. But my grandmother and I were free of such prejudices, and we were not disappointed. The movie centers on the man's attempts to win back his old love by exerting a manly influence on her rebellious teenager. The film is set in the mid-1950s, and it's unclear why the man, Sasha, has been away—whether he was imprisoned, or he simply left, or what. His old girlfriend Tamara is wary of him but not actively hostile, whereas the boy rejects him outright. By the end of the film, Sasha has broken down the boy's resistance somewhat, and the three of them spend some time together. Still, it is a grim and unrelenting film. In the last scene, Tamara drops her hostility toward Sasha and allows him to fall asleep with his head resting on her lap. We finally learn—it's possible that to the Soviet audience of its time this would have been obvious from the start—the reason the couple was separated: the war flung them to different parts of the empire, and Sasha has only now managed to make it back. And as he falls asleep on her lap, Tamara, beginning to plan her future with him again, pronounces a kind of prayer. "Just don't let there be another war," she says. "Just don't let there be another war."

"Yes," said my grandmother, when the film ended, "just don't let there be another war."

From her mouth the phrase, which had become, during Soviet times, a kind of slogan, contained so much. Her husband, my grandfather, dying at the front; her parents, forced to evacuate Moscow despite her father's poor health; in the midst of all this, her pregnancy and the birth of my mother. Just don't let there be another war: a mixture of terror and hope.

We were sitting next to each other on the couch that became, with the removal of some pillows, her cot. If her husband, my grandfather, had survived the war, she could have had other children. Or if she'd agreed to remarry sooner than she did. If she'd had other children, one of them could be here now, and she would have had more grandchildren, probably, than just me and Dima. "But you don't get to say how your life is going to be," my grandmother said suddenly. And that was also true. On a whim I took her hand in mine. For such a tiny little grandmother she had surprisingly big hands.

7.

END OF A BEAUTIFUL ERA

THAT WAS REALLY the end of it, for me, the last good thing that happened. After we got back from the dacha, things started falling apart.

One day in late July, Howard rang our buzzer. He looked upset.

"Tea?" I said.

"Russians and Brits can have tea in any weather," he said. "But it's too hot for me."

I had some half-liter Zhigulovskoye beer bottles in the fridge; my grandmother was in her room napping, so we sat in the kitchen and drank those.

"I need your counsel," Howard began. "I met a girl online and we set up a date. She was hot. And—"

"Wait," I said. "What about the girl from *Esquire*?"

"Vera? She was away. But that's part of it. So, I, uh, this girl was hot. And she had her own place, which is pretty rare." Howard paused to see if I was still indignant about Vera, or listening. I was listening. "OK, so in retrospect her place seems a little weird, like there wasn't much in the way of personal stuff. It was kind of anonymous, you know?"

I nodded.

"So, um, you know, we hung out and I paid and went home and that was that. Vera came back. I tried to put it out of my mind.

"And then this guy just fucking cold-calls me. He says, 'Howard, my name is Vitaly, we need to meet, I have some information about Natasha'—that was her name—'that I need to share with you.'

"So I'm a little freaked-out, naturally, but I go to meet this chap for lunch, he's very nice, he's well dressed, quiet, says he works for an 'information consulting agency,' and he hands me a thumb drive and says, you know, 'This was sent to us the other day, with your contact information, and we wanted to make you aware of it, in case it wasn't something you wanted getting out.'

"And it was a fucking tape of me and Natasha in her room, screwing around!"

"Ho ho ho!" I cried. "*Kompromat*! Amazing."

"Yes, right? I mean, there are two issues. Or three."

"Vera," I said.

"Yes, but, actually, she's quite understanding about that. She knows I'm not the world's most abstemious person."

"OK, but still."

"Yes, true."

"And the *Moscow Times*?" I said. I was trying to earn my role as his adviser.

"Yes, but, actually, I don't care. I've been there three years, and I'm ready to move on. And in terms of being a freelancer, I mean, I'm not saying I'm some kind of sex hero, but if this ever came out, I'd be like a hero, right?"

It was an actual question. "A sex hero?" I said.

"Yes, you know, I'm in a sex tape."

"OK," I said. "Let's suppose."

Howard nodded and looked at me expectantly.

"So Vera forgives you," I said, "and you're a sex hero. What's the problem?"

"Well, that's what I wanted to ask you about. I don't think my friend Vitaly is really from a private information security company, do you?"

"I guess not," I said. Howard was implying, not without justification, that he was from the FSB.

"So I guess I'm wondering, if they'd go to the trouble of doing this, what else might they do?"

"That's a good point," I said.

Howard had been working on a piece about the tenth anniversary of the Moscow apartment bombings. The bombings had taken place shortly after Putin became prime minister (the first time) and had been blamed, immediately, on Chechen terrorists; in response, Putin launched the Second Chechen War, promising, in a famous early moment of his leadership, to wipe out the Chechen enemy wherever he might hide, even if it were the shitter. The war immediately made him the most popular political figure in Russia and guaranteed his election to the presidency in early 2000. He had not looked back since.

But over the years questions had been raised about the bombings. The terrorist suspects had never been produced; several of them supposedly died while being apprehended. The Duma tried to convene an independent investigation; two of its members ended up dead. Two former FSB agents who voiced suspicions publicly about possible state involvement in the bombings were arrested; one eventually emigrated, doubled down on his claims, and was poisoned in London by polonium. As time went on, and no further light was shed on the supposed terrorist masterminds of the bombings, more and more people came to suspect, rightly or wrongly, that the government itself had done it.

"Am I in danger?" Howard asked.

"How should I know?" I said.

"I don't know," Howard said. "You seem to know Russian history."

I did know Russian history, I thought. And it wasn't good. "I'll tell you what my grandmother would say," I said. "She'd say it's a terrible country and you ought to leave."

Howard seemed relieved. "You know," he said, "I was thinking the exact same thing."

A few days later, he came by to bid farewell. He was especially attentive to my grandmother, who seemed quite moved by this and then immediately asked, when he left, "Who was that?" Not long after, someone with very good aim came by and threw a rock through Howard's bedroom window.

Then Oleg got shot. I found out about it from Anton, who found out from Oleg's wife. Oleg was at a meeting in central Moscow and was getting into his car to go to hockey when a guy in a mask came up to the driver's side window and started firing. He shot Oleg three times in the torso and then raised the gun to his head. When Oleg saw this he instinctively started falling sideways, onto the passenger-side seat. This saved his life. The bullet entered his head at an angle, only partly entering his brain, and doctors were able to remove it. He survived.

He was relatively certain that his troublesome tenants were responsible. After they'd declared that they weren't paying rent, he had tried to negotiate with them, and when that didn't work out he'd gone to the police. That, apparently, was a mistake.

The Sklifosovsky emergency clinic where he'd been taken was close to my house, and Anton and I went by there a couple of times before he was finally able to see us, about a week after he was shot. His head was bandaged from the surgery, and his speech was slurred—something he said the doctors thought would get better with time—but otherwise he seemed OK and in surprisingly good spirits. He must have figured he was going to die and was pleased not to be dead. He had decided, after the shooting, to go ahead and sign away the property to his bandit tenants. He still had the other property to lease, and plenty of money squirreled away, and he didn't need this sort of craziness in his life. He thought he might go to Spain for a bit when he was ready to travel. Anton and I agreed this was a good idea. "You guys are going to have to get a new left wing," Oleg slurred. Anton and I told him not to worry about that, that we would keep his spot for him as long as it took.

When we walked out together, Anton said, "He's not going to play hockey again."

He was right. Oleg got better and went to Spain, but his hip had taken a bullet and hockey was out.

After Oleg got shot I received an email from Dima. The other soldiers had followed Howard out of the country, for their own reasons, and Miklos the arms dealer was going to start working on renovations to his place right away. If we wanted him to buy Grandma's apartment as well, now would be the time, before he plowed too much money into repairs. I thought about it—Oleg's getting shot seemed like a bad omen—but I said no again. We weren't moving Grandma.

Then we ended up moving her anyway, and it was all my fault.

I'll start from the beginning.

In early August, Sergei wrote to the October email list to say that the union organizer jailed at RussOil's behest had not yet been released and was now staging a hunger strike. There was nothing or nearly nothing about it in the papers—the pro-Putin papers suppressed it, and the liberal papers weren't interested in worker struggles. "RussOil workers don't use iPhones, so they don't care," Sergei wrote. Was there anything we could do, any action we could plan, that would bring attention to the plight of the RussOil workers and shame RussOil? Would anyone, he continued, be up for something in front of the RussOil headquarters near Clean Ponds? For example, what if we dressed up like injured oil workers and held signs that said something like RUSSOIL IS SUCKING THE BLOOD FROM THE RUSSIAN EARTH? Did people think that would be effective?

There was some debate about the slogan on the email list: Was it anti-Semitic, given the number of oil executives who were Jewish? Was it unnecessarily nationalistic, turning Russia into a physical body whose blood could be sucked, rather than a social compact between free people, with no particular physical manifestation, or anyway not in the sense of some sacred "Russian" land? But there were also more serious, strategic objections. RussOil was one of the nastiest players on the Russian political scene—they came out of the criminal 1990s and then adapted brilliantly to the kleptocratic aughts. They were well connected to both the mob and the Kremlin and the general prosecutor. On top of that, they were still very angry about their bulldozer and it was rumored that they'd been the driving force behind the prosecution of Mayhem. "We might be walking into a shitstorm," wrote Boris.

People were not insensitive to this argument—maybe we should put it off, or do something less confrontational?

But the more I thought about it, the more I wanted us to do it. I had been living for a year—and, more to the point, my grandmother had been living for years—in the shadow of that giant RussOil building. Every time she saw it she was reminded of what they'd done to her beloved husband. Fuck those guys, I thought, and for the first time ever, I wrote to the list. I told the story of my grandmother and Uncle Lev and RussOil. I said it was one of the reasons I'd joined October. I thought we should get in their faces and tell them what we think.

I sent the email. In truth, I thought that people would express admiration for my passion and say that nonetheless I did not understand the domestic situation and that really we should proceed with caution. But that's not what happened. My email carried the day, and we proceeded to plan the protest.

On the day of the protest, August 7, I taped a couple of pieces of paper together and made my sign (RUSSOIL SUCKS, it said, a pun). Then I went to the pharmacy where I usually bought my grandmother's medicines and bought some bandages. My grandmother had hurt her shoulder a few years earlier and we still had the sling in the apartment. I spent some time in the bathroom dressing myself up to look like an injured worker. My grandmother came in at one point and asked what I was doing.

"I'm going to a protest," I said.

"Oh," said my grandmother. "OK. Be careful. The police don't like protesters."

And she left. A minute later she was back again.

"Andryush, are you sure you need to go to this?" she asked. "I think it's dangerous."

"It's OK," I said. "I will be careful. And Yulia is coming."

"She is?" said my grandmother. If Yulia was coming, in her book it couldn't be too bad.

A few minutes later, the doorbell rang and it was Yulia. She had bandaged her head and added ketchup to it. She shared some ketchup with me. We made a nice pair.

My grandmother laughed. I kissed her on the forehead and we headed out the door. It was a hot day, dry and dusty, and the sun was out. Making our way to the RussOil building in our costumes—it was a four-minute walk, and one we'd done many times—was interesting. People stared at us, trying to determine whether we were actors or performers (there were several theaters in the neighborhood) or if we'd been in a bad accident. We smiled at everyone and kept walking.

We all met up on the pedestrian strip across from RussOil—there were ten of us, in various costumes depicting various severities of injury. Sergei had a white T-shirt that was covered in something red that looked much more like blood than ketchup did. Misha asked him if it was blood and he said that it was beet juice. "Looks like blood," Misha said admiringly.

The RussOil colossus was built back from the street so that there was a plaza in front of the building, which was elevated above the sidewalk and enclosed by a transparent and probably bulletproof fence. The entrance to the plaza was tightly guarded. Employees in suits showed their badges to get in. Because the plaza was elevated, all you saw from the sidewalk were their shoes.

"Ready?" Sergei said when we had all gathered. We were ready. We walked across the street and took up positions in a bracket shape outside the fence, thirty feet from one another, as agreed, so that technically we were not having an unpermitted public meeting, and facing outward, toward the street. Yulia and Sergei were at the hinge of the bracket, directly in front of the entrance to the plaza, with the rest of us, four in each direction, fanned out down the two intersecting streets. Our spacing meant that the last person in line was already beyond the fence, but so it goes; I decided that, as I was new to these things, I should be on the end, and so I stood 120 feet from Sergei, on Rozhdestvenskiy Boulevard.

Around the corner was Sakharov Avenue, formerly Labor Union Avenue, renamed in 1995 for the physicist and Nobel Peace Prize winner who'd tried to de-escalate the nuclear standoff between the Soviet Union and the West. On this street there stood the former Ministry of Trade, designed in the late 1920s by Le Corbusier himself, and one of the great monuments to the period of post-revolutionary modernism. In front of me was the 1890s shopping center that was now occupied by luxury apartments and that terrible store where my grandmother and I had failed to buy a sweater. A few hundred feet farther along was the

Krupskaya statue and the spot where we'd had to flee the skinheads. Around the corner was the pharmacy where I suspected my grandmother had arranged with the pharmacist to give her poison.

It was all so familiar to me now.

I held my sign and looked into the faces of the people who walked past me. Most of them looked the other way, but some of them looked at us and read our signs. In general, the better dressed someone was, the more likely they were to hurry past, and the less well dressed someone was, the more likely to linger for a moment and take it in.

We weren't there more than ten minutes before things went south. A police car arrived quickly. Two officers approached Sergei; I couldn't hear the conversation, but presumably he explained to them that this was a legal picket. The two policemen walked away from him and got on their phones, presumably to ask for instructions. Then more policemen arrived, and they sort of fanned out around our perimeter, keeping an eye on us.

At this point I saw Grisha, the bald, violent defenseman from the white team, walking past me with another guy, both of them in suits. I knew Grisha worked in oil, but I didn't know which company. He saw that I was looking at him and he looked back, and then his face took on a look of surprise. "Andryush?" he said. He was smiling. He came up to me and shook my hand. "What are you doing?" he said.

"I'm protesting."

"You're protesting us?"

"Yes. RussOil framed a union leader out in Tyumen' and we're trying to bring attention to the matter."

"Yeah, I heard about that." He shook his head and chuckled. "Did someone pay you to do this?"

"No. We've been following this story for a while. Sergei's down there." I pointed to him.

"Holy shit!" He laughed. "What are you, a communist?"

"Not quite. But close."

"All right then. I never knew. Are you coming to hockey tonight?"

"I wouldn't miss it."

"Ha!" he said, and shook my hand again. "I'll see you there, international agent."

And with that he rejoined his friend and kept walking toward the RussOil building.

To the left of me, Misha was looking over, as if to say, "What was that?"

"I know him from hockey!" I said, and almost as soon as the words were out of my mouth, two policemen had grabbed me by the elbows.

"Come with us," they said.

"OK," I said. I did not try to fight them. "What happened?"

"You talked to your friend over there. That makes this a public meeting."

"You're kidding."

"Do we look like we're kidding?" They walked me toward a small police jeep and pushed me up into the tiny back compartment, where there was a wooden bench. They slammed the door behind me and aside from a few breathing holes in the roof through which sunlight entered, I was completely in the dark.

I leaned back on the bench and considered my situation. Just a few minutes ago I was on the street, free to do whatever I pleased, and suddenly I was trapped in this jeep. It was four o'clock. Unless they let me go right away I was going to miss dinner, but hockey wasn't until nine, so I might still make that. If they held me very long I'd need to call my grandmother and lie to her about why I was going to be late. Those were the sorts of things I was thinking about.

Outside I heard Sergei arguing with the police. "He's an American citizen," he said. "You want to pick up an American citizen for protesting against RussOil? It's going to be in all the papers."

"I don't care if he's a citizen of Portugal!" said one of the policemen. "We have the law and we follow the law."

"Whatever you want," said Sergei. "For now it's still your country."

"What's that supposed to mean?"

"We'll see," said Sergei.

He came up to the jeep and knocked on my door with the palm of his hand. "Andrei, it's Sergei. How are you doing in there?"

"OK!" I said.

"Listen," said Sergei. "They'll take you to the station and have you sit for a while and try to scare you. But you'll be out fast and then we can all get a drink, OK?"

"Yes," I said.

Now I heard Yulia. "Andryushik," she said. Her voice was coming from next to Sergei's. "Are you OK?"

"Yes," I said.

"Don't let them scare you," she said. "We're going to raise a fuss and they'll let you out soon."

"OK," I said. "Will you call my grandmother and tell her we'll be late for dinner?"

"Of course."

"Let's go!" I heard someone say, and then two doors opened and shut up front, and the jeep's engine started, and we began to move. They drove fast and I bounced around in back a little, but before I even figured out how best to sit so as not to get jostled against the back door, we had stopped and I heard the officers opening their doors. Then they opened mine. The first thing I saw was the Hugo Boss. I thought I must be hallucinating, and then realized they had simply taken me to the station on Sretenka. I was two minutes away from my house.

I've gone over in my mind what happened next a fair amount, though maybe not as much as I should. It's hard to tell whether what I said to the police had any bearing on what happened later to Sergei and the others, but I can't help but feel like it did. And does.

For a moment I thought they were just going to let me go, having put a little scare in me, but instead the two officers who'd arrested me, one a blue-eyed Slav, the other with a more Asiatic look, both of them in their midtwenties, flanked me and walked me up the stairs into the station house. I had been here that one time I lost my grandmother, and I half hoped I'd recognize the duty officer behind the desk, but it was a different guy and in any case it's unlikely he would have remembered me. The new guy buzzed us through the turnstile into the station, and then there was a waiting room with some benches. We stopped there and at this point the Slavic officer asked me for my phone and my "documents."

I had brought my passport with me, in case this very thing happened, and I now took it out and handed it over. Months earlier I had purchased a little leather passport case for it, so that it wouldn't get totally destroyed from sitting in my pocket as much as it did, and therefore the first thing the cop saw was the ordinary black passport cover with the word "Russia" on it. He hadn't been there, apparently, when Sergei urged one of the officers to let me go because I was American, and it was only when he opened the passport that he realized I wasn't Russian. He kept his poker face momentarily and then broke down. "American?" he said incredulously and with, I thought, some anger.

"Yes."

"Well, fuck your mother." He turned to his partner, who had ducked into a nearby door and was returning with some paper forms in his hand. "Marat, this guy's a fucking spy."

"We caught a spy?" Marat said curiously.

"I think we did, Marat." The cop gave me a hard stare and, tucking my passport and phone into his front shirt pocket, led me by the elbow to another waiting room adjacent to this one. This one had a guy in it, definitely the worse for wear, sitting on a bench with his elbows tucked into his knees, like he had a stomachache.

"Stay here," said the cop, and pushed me toward a bench across from the guy.

I soon saw that the guy was just very drunk. He wore filthy jeans and a button-down shirt and his face was red from being outdoors all the time. He started looking me up and down, and I wondered if this was the moment when I found out if I had the mettle to last in prison. But my cellmate did not make an aggressive move. Instead he said, "So they got you too, huh?"

I nodded.

"Fuckers," he said loudly. "Bloodsuckers!" he yelled.

Holy shit, I thought, it's the dumpster guy. But no one responded, and he went back into his cocoon. We sat there awhile longer, though the door to the room—it was just an ordinary wooden door, like in any other Russian institution—opened a few times. First, two beefy, short, middle-aged men in black jeans and button-down shirts opened it and stood in the doorway. They looked at me for a while and then one of them said, with unconcealed aggression, "International agent, huh?"

I was taken aback. "No," I said, smiling, thinking he might have been kidding.

He wasn't kidding, and he soon slammed the door. These two were followed by slightly younger, taller, thinner men, in street clothes that were more expensive and better shoes. They opened the door, gave me a quick look, and then nodded politely. They looked oddly familiar. After they left I spent a few minutes trying to figure out where I knew them from—TV? Hockey? The neighborhood?—until I figured it out. The Coffee Grind! I'd seen them in the Coffee Grind. They were FSB officers. It made sense. The older guys were police detectives; the second pair were from the FSB.

I was still unsure of what was happening—I thought I'd be cited for disturbing the peace or participating in an unsanctioned public meeting and maybe fined, but certainly let go pretty quickly. It was obvious to me what I had done, and surely it was just as obvious to them. If I was a spy it was unlikely I would have been out with a protest sign in front of RussOil. I'd have been trying to infiltrate RussOil instead. I figured it was now about five. I was going to miss dinner, but if we got this taken care of in time I'd at least make it to hockey.

Soon my arresting officers came to get me. I left my drunk dumpster friend where I'd found him and followed them to an office where, I felt confident, we were about to clear things up.

It was an ordinary rectangular office, with two small desks in the back and a large meeting table in the middle. The two police detectives, my FSB officers from the Coffee Grind, and one older, uniformed officer were inside. They dismissed my arresting officers and asked me to sit down.

Later on, I would think about all the books written about the interrogations of the 1930s, as well as of the '40s, '50s, '60s, and '70s. All the '60s and '70s dissidents and semi-dissidents, like Brodsky, had a story of how they'd sat down with the KGB and told them off. I have no reason to doubt those stories. But that's not how this worked out with me.

Solzhenitsyn begins *The Gulag Archipelago* by listing all the tortures to which people were subjected in NKVD custody. It's a long, impressive, inventive list. If those tortures were not enough, for whatever reason, the NKVD could and sometimes did offer to bring in family members and torture them. Under such pressure, who could resist? And yet Solzhenitsyn had some advice for the person who is suddenly seized on the street or from his home in the middle of the night and wants to survive his interrogation. Solzhenitsyn's advice was simply this: You are now dead. You have no family, no home, no attachments. YOU ARE DEAD. If you can convince yourself of this, there will be nothing the interrogators can do or say to you that will cause you to break. "Before such a person," writes Solzhenitsyn, "the interrogation will *tremble*."

And there I was, wondering if I might make it out in time for hockey.

"Is it Androo," the uniformed officer said, looking at my passport, "or Androov?"

"Andrei," I said.

"Ah," said the officer politely. "Andrei. Excellent. Why does it say Androo here?"

"It's the English equivalent. My parents changed it when we moved to the States."

"Understood," said the officer. "Well, Andrei, these men are going to ask you some questions about what happened today, and what you're doing in Russia, and what your plans are, and then we can all go home. The more help you can give them, the faster this will all go.

"They're good men. They're not going to torture you or beat you or any of the stuff you see in Hollywood movies. They're just going to ask some questions. Is that OK?"

"Sure," I said.

"Great," said the officer, and stood up to leave, handing my passport to one of the FSB guys.

I felt like some kind of performance was being put on for me, but I couldn't understand what it consisted of. What did dawn on me, with some force, as the officer moved out of the room, was that he could leave and I could not. I was not allowed to leave. Just down the hall was the door that led back out to Sretenka, to my grandmother's house, and the road where I could hail a hundred-ruble car to Yulia's place at pretty much any time of the day or night. But on this side of the door was me. And these men—four men, the detectives older than me, the FSB guys about my age—could keep me here. It wasn't *terrifying* or anything; it was just strange. I was sitting in an office like any other office, "taking a meeting" by the looks of it, and though it was not, I think, a friendly conversation, it was a conversation nonetheless. We were all people here. And yet these people could walk out the door and I could not.

It occurred to me that I would do just about anything to get back on the other side of that door—back on Sretenka, out of this station, away from these people—and never have to think about them again.

"So, Andrei," began one of the young FSB officers, "please tell us about yourself."

This seemed like an innocent enough question, and I wondered if I should answer. I remembered the informal arrestee training we'd done with the old Marxist—don't say anything. But he'd also said we should confirm our identity. So I answered. I told them about our emigration, that I grew up outside of Boston, that I had studied Russian literature. One of the police detectives claimed not to believe me, at which point one of the FSB guys whipped out an iPhone and offered to look up my profile on the university's website. I hadn't visited the site in months and wondered momentarily if I was still on there. But then there I was; there was even a little photo of me, and the FSB guy held up the iPhone in front of him, as if checking the photo against my face. "I think it's him," he said, showing the phone to the skeptical detective. The detective agreed that it was me.

Now the other FSB officer, the one holding my passport, said, "Andrei, so, you're an educated person. How did you get involved with this extremist group?"

I laughed. "Extremist?" I said. "No. They're not extremists. I met them through hockey." This was not entirely accurate, but even at this point I felt I shouldn't drag Yulia into it. I said, "Sergei Ivanov, who's in October, is our goalie. He's a good goalie." I said this in a way that made it clear, I hoped, that no one who played hockey could be an extremist.

"Oh?" said the FSB officer.

"Yes!" I said. "They're students, for the most part. They're very sweet."

"Oh?" said the FSB officer again. He was taking notes and didn't look up when he spoke.

"Yes!" I looked around the room to see what attitude the others had taken. As I did so I remembered again the grizzled Marxist who told us to keep our mouths shut. But that was then, back in the Soviet era. These guys I was talking to were different; they had iPhones, and even if they weren't different, still I could clear this up. If they only knew how harmless October was, this whole charade could quickly end. So I kept talking. "They have a reading group," I said. "Usually it's at Misha's house. They discuss the news over email; occasionally they hold a public protest to bring attention to some event. They're not extremists!"

"Is that Misha Vorobiev?" said the FSB guy. I stopped and looked at him. They knew Misha's name. So they knew about October. So they knew they weren't "extremists."

I hesitated before answering.

"Vorobiev, right?" the FSB guy said again.

"Yes," I said.

"If they're not extremists," said the skeptical detective right away, "what are they, in your opinion?"

"They're run-of-the-mill European social democrats."

313

"What does that mean for Russia? We're not exactly Europe, after all."

"What does it mean?" I didn't quite understand.

"Enlighten us," said the police detective.

"Well," I began. They seemed to be all ears. And why not? Sergei had taught me that just about anyone could be convinced of the October cause if you just put yourself in their position and explained things in a sensible manner. These were still young men, living in a corrupt and dying country. They probably wanted things to get better.

"Well," I said again, "I think we can all agree that Russia is in a difficult situation. It makes a lot of oil and gas, but its economy is not diversified. The entire country is hostage to oil price shocks. For the past twenty years it's essentially been living off the infrastructure built during the Soviet era, which is now deteriorating. Faith in public institutions is very low."

I looked around the room. The FSB officer was still taking notes. I took this as a cue to continue.

"The government's answer to this seems to be twofold. On the one hand, more liberalization of the economy, and at the same time more repression of political dissent. No offense."

They all nodded: no offense taken.

"So what October says is, Look, the answer to the crisis is not to defund schools, hospitals, and infrastructure projects and put them in the private sector, where the money can be stolen by capitalists, but to make it the government's responsibility to protect the people. All the people. And until the government is willing to do that, Russia will continue to suffer, and its people will suffer, and there will be unhappiness and unrest."

I looked around the room.

"Maybe you're right," the FSB officer with the iPhone said.

I smiled. I was very pleased. "Maybe," I said humbly.

"There's one thing, though," the other FSB officer said thoughtfully, looking up from his notes. "We used to have a communist government here. But we don't anymore. And calls for the country to have a communist government again could be interpreted by some passionate people as calls for the overthrow of the current regime."

"I've never heard anyone at October call for the overthrow of the current regime," I said quickly. This was not, it occurred to me, technically true. October defined itself as a "revolutionary party." So in that sense they did advocate the overthrow of the current regime. And it turned out my new friends already knew that.

"It says here," said the FSB guy with the iPhone, showing me the October website, "that they're a revolutionary party. So they do want a revolution?"

"That's just a figure of speech!" I said. "Everything's revolutionary now. People say the iPhone is a revolutionary technology. Does that make you a revolutionary?"

"OK," the note-taking FSB guy now said, "let's not get worked up. I think we can wrap this up now, right?" He was addressing Mr. iPhone.

That guy nodded.

"Great," said the other.

They both thanked me and gave me their hands to shake. Not knowing what else to do, I shook them. "Oh, one more question," the FSB guy with the iPhone said, as if suddenly remembering it. "Which of your friends was there when you destroyed the bulldozer out in the forest?"

"I don't know," I said. "I wasn't there."

"They never talked about it?"

"Not in front of me," I said. This was a lie, as they could probably tell, but they let it go. They had enough, apparently. They thanked me again and left the room.

Then it was over. The police detectives handed me my passport and my phone; they even said I should come by and see them if I was ever in the neighborhood; and I walked out, back onto Sretenka, a free man. It wasn't even seven o'clock; I had spent less than three hours in custody.

A bunch of people were standing across the street from the police station: Yulia and Sergei and everyone from October, Elena and some other well-dressed youngish people, a guy from the *Moscow Times* whom Howard had once introduced me to, and another guy from one of the wire services. The October people were talking to one another while all the journalists were having intense conversations on their cell phones. They didn't see me at first when I came out, and as I stood at the top of the stairs I had a strong impulse to walk quietly around the corner before they saw me and try never to talk to any of them again.

I had thought, back in that room, that once I got out I would have such a newfound appreciation for everything, for the shitty bookstore with the strip club on the second floor and the Hugo Boss and the cars parked on the sidewalk, and of course my grandmother and everything else. Now here I was, and that's not how I felt. Instead I felt like something had happened back in that room that I didn't yet understand. But I had a bad feeling about it.

Someone from the group saw me and called my name, and they came over to me in a bunch all talking at once and looking like they were happy and indeed lucky to see me. Yulia gave me a hug whose intensity I found embarrassing, given the mildness of what I'd just been through, and all the Octobrists gave me correspondingly solemn handshakes.

Sergei was the first one to speak. "Everything OK?" he asked.

"I think so," I said.

Something about the way I said this must have given Sergei pause, because he now said, "Yeah?" As in, was I sure everything was OK? Obviously I was not sure.

"They asked me what October was," I said. "And I told them it was a discussion group."

"OK," said Sergei.

"They were saying it was extremist but I told them that was ridiculous, that the group had no plans to overthrow the government."

"O-K," said Sergei, more slowly than the first time.

"I told them that I met you through hockey and that we met to discuss Marx at Misha's place. That was about it."

"OK," Sergei said again. He looked thoughtful. "I thought we'd all agreed that we don't talk to the police."

"Yeah," I said. "They just seemed pretty normal to me. I felt like I was recruiting them, to be honest."

Sergei took this in.

"We can recruit the army, not the police," he said quietly, like you'd say a quick catechism. Then he spoke normally again. "I'm sure it's fine," he said. "Should we all go out and get a drink?"

I really did not feel like a drink. I felt like going home and taking a shower. I still had ketchup in my hair. I told Sergei as much, and he nodded.

"Maybe tomorrow," he said. I agreed.

Yulia had been listening to all this. "I'll come with you," she said to me. I agreed to that as well.

Now Elena and the guy from the *Moscow Times* politely approached and asked if they could talk to me. I said yes but kept walking in the direction of my grandmother's, to indicate that I didn't want to talk long. Elena put a microphone in my face and Howard's friend took out his notebook and I told them that the whole thing was pretty innocuous and that I did not feel like I'd been ground under the heel of the regime and in fact I'd been happy to tell them about the activities of October— I thought it'd be nice to make a plug for October on Echo—and that was about it.

Yulia and I walked the rest of the way alone. "Katya called me," she said. "She says there are a bunch of articles already online about the American academic arrested in front of RussOil."

There was something bitter about the way she said it. I didn't answer.

"Did they beat you?" she asked.

"No. Not at all."

"Then why'd you tell them about October?"

"They knew all about it already!" I said. I said it in a pleading sort of

317

way. The October website literally said that it was a "revolutionary" organization. What had I told those guys that they didn't already know?

"Oy, Andryush," said Yulia. "Let's go check on Seva Efraimovna."

"OK," I said.

We walked the rest of the way in silence.

My grandmother was sitting at the table eating alone when we came in. "Andryush!" she said. "Yulia! Where have you been?"

"Sorry, Grandma," I said. "We got delayed. Everything's fine."

"You must be hungry," she said. "Let me cook you something."

She still referred to cooking things even though mostly what this meant now was reheating the food that Seraphima Mikhailovna had left in the fridge.

Yulia and I agreed to eat but insisted that my grandmother sit while we heated up the portions.

My computer was sitting on the windowsill. "Here, I'll do this," Yulia said about the food. "Have a look."

I did as I was told. There really were a bunch of articles about the American academic arrested by the despotic regime. On Facebook everyone was asking after my well-being, even Fishman. It made me sound like a brave martyr, which I found embarrassing. Maybe this was what Yulia was mad about. If I was such a brave martyr, why had the police let me go so easily, and with such pleasant smiles?

Then my phone rang. It was my adviser.

"Are you out?" he asked.

"Yes," I said. "I just got home."

"OK, great. Jesus, you gave us a scare. Listen. I got the strangest call from Phil Nelson just now. He saw the news coverage and was asking about you. He even suggested there might be a line for you in the reconstituted GSLLD." That's what my adviser had taken to calling the Germanic and Slavic Languages and Literatures Department. A "line" was a job.

"Wow," I said. "Why—why would he do that?"

"Who knows. I mean, Columbia just made some splashy hires. And you know Phil. He loves hugging babies and releasing prisoners. And our finances haven't taken quite as much of a hit as they should have, I think. We might even get some of that Obama stimulus money. Anyway, when he called asking about you I told him you had a big article coming out in the *Slavic Review* and that you should have gotten the Watson job. So, heads up. If he calls with an offer, make sure he's talking about a genuine line, not a visiting appointment. And ask him about housing."

"Seriously?"

Housing was a subsidized apartment. They weren't luxury apartments but they were spacious and they were in Manhattan; in fact it was about as close to socialism as you got in New York.

"Yeah, why the hell not," said my adviser. "If he wants to hire you to get some publicity, make him really hire you. OK?"

"OK," I said. "Thank you."

I had walked out of the kitchen as I talked with my adviser and now I came back in. Yulia was sitting with my grandmother and holding her hand. "You see," my grandmother was saying, "all my friends have died. All my relatives have died. Everyone is dead except me. What's the point?"

"I know, Seva Efraimovna," Yulia said. "I know."

When I came in she looked up at me with a question on her face, as if to say, "Who was that on the phone?"

I shrugged, as if to say, "It wasn't anyone important. It was a wrong number. It was nothing."

I really did feel like it wasn't worth getting into, given that it could well end up being nothing, like the Watson job. My adviser had a pretty good sense of these things, but President Nelson was a guy who frequently changed his mind.

"Who was that on the phone, Andryush?" my grandmother asked.

"No one," I said. "A friend from America."

"Ah, America," my grandmother said. "I went there once. I didn't like it."

"And you were right, Seva Efraimovna, you were right," Yulia said.

Then she stood up and, to my surprise, brought her lips to my grandmother's forehead. "Thank you for everything, Seva Efraimovna," she said. "Thank you for taking me into your home. I am very grateful to you. Stay strong."

My grandmother didn't understand where this was coming from but she loved to be touched, and she laughed happily. "Thank you," she said to Yulia, who was now heading for the front hall. But it sounded to me like Yulia was saying good-bye to my grandmother.

I followed her into the front hall.

"What's going on?" I said.

"Nothing's going on," she said coldly.

"Why did you just say good-bye to my grandmother?"

"I don't know that I'll see her again."

"Why not?" I said, and then repeated: "What's going on?"

Still without betraying any emotion, she answered my question with a question. "What did you tell the police?"

"Nothing! I didn't tell them anything they didn't already know!"

"You know it doesn't work like that."

"Like what?"

"They were nice to you and pretended to think what you said was interesting, right? And you talked and talked. Yes?"

That was approximately what had happened. My silence now confirmed it.

"Oh, Andryush. You haven't learned anything about this place, have you? You're still such an American. You still believe in words."

"What's wrong with that?" I said. "What else am I supposed to believe in?"

"Who was that on the phone just now?" Yulia said.

"My adviser." In Russian the word is longer—*nauchny rukovoditel'*, academic supervisor, or *nauchruk*. "*Nauchruk*," I said.

"And did he tell you they have a job for you now?" Yulia asked.

"He said maybe, yes," I said.

"I knew it," said Yulia, half to herself.

"I'm not going to take it," I said. "If it even exists."

"No, Andryush. You will take it."

"Yul'," I said. "What's going on?"

"I don't know," she said. "We'll see. I could be wrong. I hope I'm wrong. But I'm probably not wrong.

"Good-bye, Andrei."

She kissed me on the cheek, not on the mouth, sort of like she'd kissed me on the cheek when I came into Sergei's party, but in reverse. It seemed like years had passed since then.

She opened the door and left. I let her. I was angry and confused. But I was also worried that she was right.

It was eight o'clock now, I still had time to go to hockey, but I didn't feel like it. I cleared our plates and played a couple of games of anagrams with my grandmother. Then I answered as many of the emails and messages I'd received as I could. All of it left me feeling uneasy; something had happened back there, and I still didn't know what it was.

The next morning, a Saturday, they arrested Sergei and Misha and charged them with "extremism." I heard about it from Boris, who called to ask if I knew anything.

"*Blyad'*," I said. "Could it have been because of me? Because of something I said?"

"I don't know," Boris said coldly. "I have no idea what you said or didn't say. So the answer is: I don't know."

I tried Yulia. She didn't answer. I kept trying her and she still didn't answer. Finally I got dressed and went outside and took a car to her place. I called up to their apartment and Katya answered.

"Yulia doesn't want to see you," she said.

"But she's there?"

"Yes, she's here."

I asked her if she knew about the arrests, and she said she did.

And that was it. I tried Nikolai, whose phone seemed to be off. I called Boris again and asked if he had any news about Nikolai or anyone else; he said he didn't and also that he didn't think we should be talking on the phone. I told him I was near Mayakovskaya and asked if he wanted to meet up, and he said no, he didn't, as if I were some kind of spy.

I walked down to Patriarch Ponds and sat on one of the benches. This was one of the beautiful spots of Moscow; a small pond inside a small park, with benches and a walkway shaded with old trees, and then all around some old, mostly non-ugly buildings from early in the twentieth century. Yulia and I had come here a few times once the weather was nice enough. There were seldom any really drunk people causing a ruckus here.

Now it felt useless and sterile and sour. Because of me, two good friends were in jail, and Yulia wouldn't see me, and even ice-cold, robotic Boris was mad. I felt both wrong and wronged.

I called Anton, from hockey, and asked if he could meet me. Anton may have been a tax attorney, but that was the closest thing to an attorney I knew. He was at his office, nearby, and half an hour later he met me at the Starlite Diner. I told him what had happened. He didn't blame me, but he was upset. "We need to tell the guys," he said. "That's our goddamn goalie."

He got on the phone and soon we had six guys from the hockey game, including Fedya and Grisha from the white team, sitting in the diner with us. Anton and I saw each of them pull up in their Mercedeses and BMWs and park quasi-legally within a convenient distance of the diner. Watching their sleek black cars slowly maneuver into place—"That's Tolya," Anton said. "That's Fedya"—and then watching them enter the diner, in their weekend sweat suits, and all of them bigger than I remembered them, I took a momentary pride in how far I'd come in the past year. That I could convene such a meeting was amazing to me; at the same time, it was also being convened because I had managed to land our goalie in jail. Each of the guys came in, shook hands with everyone around the table, ordered food, and only then heard out Anton and me. Then each of them got on the phone to people they knew. Grisha called his friends in management at RussOil. Fedya and Vanya both had connections in law enforcement. Tolya called some of his banker friends, just in case. Mostly people came up with nothing, but Grisha and Fedya talked to people who were in the know.

"This is coming from pretty high up," Grisha reported. "They're still pissed about the bulldozer in the forest. It's over my head. I told them we needed a goalie. They said we should visit one of the sports schools."

"What'd you say?"

"I hung up."

"Fuck," said Anton.

The guys sat for a while longer, trying to think of people to contact, but it was clear that this was their best shot at it, and that once they left the diner, that was it.

"There's no one we know who knows someone who could take care of this?" I said.

"Andrei, I talked to the assistant to the chairman of the company," Grisha said. "He said the boss has taken a personal interest and wants these guys in jail. That's the very highest level—it's way beyond us."

He took a bite of his burger.

"He also said they're looking to make more arrests. He said there was some girl involved."

Oh shit, I thought. Oh no. "Grish," I said, "listen, that's Yulia. Remember, she came to one of the games?" Yulia had come to one of the skates and watched from the bleachers; the guys had all been very polite to her. "Can you call your friend back? If Yulia gets arrested, tell him I'm going to the embassy."

I didn't know what I would do if I went to the embassy, but it sounded like the thing to say. Grisha looked thoughtful for a moment and then picked up his phone again—most of the guys still had regular old mobile phones, and Grisha's looked tiny in his massive hand.

"Sash, listen," he said. "That girl you mentioned—that's the American's girl. They're planning on getting married. I think if they pick her up the American's going to raise hell. It's going to be a huge pain in the ass . . . Yeah . . . I understand. Just keep it in mind."

Grisha hung up and gave me a look that said, "I did what I could. We'll see what happens."

After that, in a subdued and somewhat defeated manner, everyone finished their burgers and, shaking hands all around, took off. Anton and I remained with a heap of uneaten French fries.

I went outside—I had not developed the Russian habit of holding phone conversations right in front of other people—and called Boris again to tell him that more arrests might be in the offing. "OK," he said and hung up. I later learned that he took the next train to Kiev. I was unable to reach Nikolai, but he later told me that after hearing about the arrests he'd gone to his dacha for a day, just as he'd once imagined, and then taken a train to Estonia. After trying and failing again to call Yulia I sent her a text warning that more arrests might be coming.

She wrote back this time. "I'm not going anywhere," she said.

I was elated to hear from her, but it was nothing she hadn't said to me a dozen times. And when I tried calling her again she did not pick up. I went back inside the diner to join Anton.

"Andrei," he said, "don't take it into your head. It's not your fault. Sergei knew what he was doing."

"Thank you," I said. And I was thankful. But it didn't change the fact that this was all my fault.

That evening, I got a call from Phil Nelson. We'd spoken very briefly once or twice during my time at the university, but he greeted me like an old friend. He said he'd always been very impressed with my work and that he loved my *Slavic Review* article (which he could not possibly have seen), and then just as my adviser had predicted he offered me a job. He had been thinking for a while, he said, that the university needed to start thinking systematically about the historical experience of the Gulag, both in Soviet Russia and other places, and given my research interests, as well as my recent brush with Russian totalitarianism, how would I like to be the inaugural chair of Gulag Studies at our great university?

I had expected the call, though not in all its crazy details, and I had hoped my instinct would be to say no. But it wasn't. My instinct was to say yes. I tried to put it off. "I've got a lot of stuff," I said meekly, "a lot of projects, under way here right now."

"Sure, of course!" said Nelson. "I think we could do a fifteen-thousand-dollar research budget to help you get back and forth a bit. Would that work?"

Jesus, would it work. I could fly back every other week, practically.

I was trying to formulate some response to this, but Nelson must have mistaken my silence for toughness, because he said, "And look, now that we're talking numbers, how would one hundred be to start? That's not including health insurance and other benefits."

I was speechless. Most people I knew made sixty-five or seventy. But he wasn't done.

"And look, I know it's tough to find a place in New York when you're in Moscow, so let me see if we can come up with some housing for you. It might be in the new construction, but you'll still be able to walk to campus." The university had recently completed some new buildings in the East Village. He was offering me housing and I didn't even have to ask for it. I gave a small laugh of disbelief, which I think Nelson understood correctly to be a surrender.

He decided not to press his advantage. "So how about this," he said. "Take a day, walk around the block a couple of times and noodle it over, and we'll talk again tomorrow, all right? I think we can come to terms."

And he hung up. The next day he called again, confirming his offer of a one-bedroom apartment in the new building near Astor Place. After everything I'd said and thought about the inequities of the academic job market; after all the progress I'd made here on starting a new life; after all my promises of how I'd never leave my grandmother behind; after all that, and much more, when it finally came time for me to act on my supposed convictions, I did not. I took the job and the research funding and the apartment.

Having done so, I did not have to sell my grandmother's apartment. I now had a salary and could contribute to paying for a caretaker, as I'd said I would. For all his bluster, Dima wouldn't actually have sold it without me. But I no longer had a moral leg to stand on. Dima had to leave our grandmother because they were readying a case against him. Whereas I left of my own free will. Who was I to tell Dima he couldn't sell if he needed the money? Here, as in other things, I took the easy way out. I wrote my brother from the windowsill: "I'm ready to sell."

It took all of twenty seconds for him to write me back. "Finally!!!!" he said.

And that was that. Miklos came by the next day and offered two eighty. We accepted. I asked Seraphima Mikhailovna if, once we found a new place, she'd be willing to come live with our grandmother. She said yes.

Miklos said he'd be working on Dima's place for at least another month, so if we wanted to take that long to move our grandmother, we could. But I didn't want to. I wanted to get it done and over with. I had ten days before my visa expired, and I spent the first days looking for an apartment in our neighborhood with a real estate agent recommended by Anton. But nothing worked. Most of the buildings near us were old, and though the apartments I was looking at had been remodeled, there were no elevators, and all sorts of stairs for my grandmother to fall down. Finally Dima heard of a place through a friend; it was in a quiet neighborhood across the river, it had a balcony for my grandmother to sit on, and most of all it had an elevator. The rent was just fifteen hundred dollars a month. Dima needed a hundred thousand out of the apartment sale for his legal fees, which meant that we had one eighty left over; if we paid Seraphima Mikhailovna one thousand, and budgeted another thousand for everything else, we didn't have to worry about any Grandma expenses for the next four years. We took the apartment, and three days later Dima flew in to help with my grandmother's move.

Once again he stayed in our room, and in virtual silence we packed up my grandmother's books, her clothes, all the photos and little knick-knacks, her medicine, her letters. We told our grandmother that she would be moving temporarily while this apartment underwent renovations, and she accepted this, then forgot, then accepted it, then forgot, then accepted it again. It took three long, miserable, hot days to pack the apartment into boxes, and at the end of it two guys came with a small but adequate flatbed truck, and while the driver sat in the truck and smoked, his partner helped us load my grandmother's stuff, including all the furniture from her room, so we could basically re-create it verbatim in her new bedroom. Then we went. We thought it would take us two or three trips, but all our grandmother's stuff fit onto the flatbed, and we managed in just one. Seraphima Mikhailovna was already at the apartment, and after unloading the truck I left her and Dima to unpack and went back to our place to keep our grandmother company in the now almost empty apartment. She was sitting on the lone remaining chair in the kitchen when I got back, looking through her phone books. Instead of waiting in that ravaged apartment, we went outside for a walk and sat in one of the neighboring courtyards and took in the sun. It was still the middle of the afternoon. Eventually my phone rang; it was Dima, who had returned in the small Nissan he'd rented at the airport, and it was time to go.

I sat in the back, my grandmother in front, and Dima drove. It was a ten-minute drive, but it was far too long. Coming out of our courtyard onto the boulevard, Dima had to turn right, and as we went down the hill toward Trubnaya, for a second a vista of Moscow opened up before us—the golden steeples sparkling in the sun, a few glass towers, and the blue sky over the city. "Ah," said my grandmother, "how beautiful! Look!" she said to both of us. "Look how beautiful it is."

We got to Trubnaya, and Dima pulled a U-turn. "Why are you turning around?" asked my grandmother. "Where are we going?"

The right we took must have made her think we were going to Emma Abramovna's—that was usually where we went when we went in a car in that direction.

"We're going to the new apartment," said Dima.

"The new apartment," said my grandmother. It was half a question, but we did not answer.

Everything was quiet for a while, but then we passed Clean Ponds and my grandmother suspected something was up.

"You know," she said, turning to Dima, as if just thinking of something, "let's go back. I think it's time to go back."

"It's OK," said Dima. "We're almost there."

My grandmother saw that we were not turning back, and she tried to take an interest in the sights. We were traveling along Clean Ponds, one of the most beautiful areas of Moscow, and it was a warm summer day, and there wasn't much traffic, so we sped along.

I thought I was going to cry. What were we doing? Already so much of her memory had been erased. And much of the city she knew had been erased. Now we were erasing her physical connection to the place she'd lived for fifty years.

We crossed the bridge over the Yauza River, in the shadow of one of the huge Stalin-era stone skyscrapers, and here my grandmother tried again.

"You know what," she said, as if very casually. "Let's go back. Don't you think it's time to go back?"

"Grandma," said Dima. I looked up when I heard the tone of his voice. He was crying. In the back I also started crying. Dima said, "We're almost there."

And in just a few minutes we were. By the time we got out of the car our eyes were dry again.

Dima and Seraphima Mikhailovna had done a good job with the apartment: the bedroom was set up to look almost exactly like her old bedroom, with her same cot, her old desk, and all her photos of us and Uncle Lev arranged on a little shelf above it, and next to her bed the green armchair on which I'd started sitting while she read. Into the living room we had imported the green foldout couch and, heroically, the standing closet. Nonetheless my grandmother was confused. She was tired from the ride and we brought her into her new bedroom so she could lie down. She recognized her bed and her bedding. "This is my bed," she said experimentally.

"Yes," we said.

She lay down and we left her, but a few minutes later she came out and asked, very politely, like a guest, where the bathroom was. I walked her there. Then she came into the living room, where we were still unpacking the boxes, and said, "How terrible!" about the mess. "Andryushik," she said, "tell me, where do I live?" I walked her the few steps to her bedroom, and once again she recognized it, and turned to me and asked, "This is my room, right?"

I said yes.

In the late afternoon, as we continued to unpack, she took a long nap in her room. When she woke up she was even more disoriented. When I came into her room to check on her, she was happy and surprised to see me. "Andryushik," she said, "my Andryushik." Then she asked me when we were going back to Moscow.

"We are in Moscow," I said.

"Oh," she said. She looked confused. If we were in Moscow, why weren't we in her apartment? "Well," she said, "just let me know what time the train is."

"What train, Grandma?"

"Back to Moscow. Just tell me the time and I'll be there."

"OK," I said. The move had somehow triggered a deep confusion in my grandmother. I started heading out of the room but she called me back.

"What time is the train?" she said.

"Grandma," I said again, "to where?"

"Pereyaslavl'." It was where she'd been born.

I knew if I tried to say anything I would burst into tears, and that this would worry her. So I didn't say anything.

"Just tell me what time the train is," she said again.

"In the morning."

"What time in the morning?" She was very businesslike now. "How are we going to arrange it? Will I call you?" She pointed to me. "Or will you call me?" She pointed to herself.

I waited a second before answering.

"Let's do this," I said. "I'll come over in the morning, and we'll have tea." This was a lie—my flight out was early the next morning—but I couldn't think of what else to say. I said, "OK?"

"Tea?" said my grandmother. "Yes, that sounds good. I'll see you in the morning." And she closed her eyes.

It was almost nine by the time we finished unpacking. The books were all out of the boxes and on the shelves, all the framed photographs and the few works of art my grandmother had collected over the years were on the walls, the plates and silverware were in their cupboards, and Seraphima Mikhailovna set up the green foldout couch and was ready to sleep on it. Dima and I were going to sleep on our bunk beds back at the old apartment.

I peeked into my grandmother's room one last time. There was still a bare penumbra of light coming through the window, and she was sleeping on her back, as she always did, with her hands folded gently across her stomach.

We left.

We drove home and showered. Dima pounded angrily at his computer for a while as I packed up my big red suitcase, and then asked if I wanted to go to Gentlemen of Fortune. I didn't. "Well, I'm going to go, if you don't mind," he said. I didn't mind.

I finished packing and it was still only ten o'clock. It was my last night in Moscow. I had already said good-bye to the hockey guys, and I hadn't tried calling Yulia in over a week. I had tried to visit Sergei and Misha in Lefortovo, but was turned away. The October email list was totally silent. The only one who still talked to me was Nikolai, from his friend's place in Tallinn. He told me over an encrypted chat program— Gchat's off the record was bullshit, he said; Dima had been right about that one—that he really liked Tallinn, there was a thriving tech sector, and he thought he might stay awhile.

"What about your dacha?" I said.

"I'll return there in triumph after the Revolution," Nikolai said. "We'll throw an enormous party."

"))))," I said.

On that final night in Moscow, I texted Yulia one last time. "I'm leaving tomorrow," I said.

She texted back this time. She said, "Have a good trip."

I considered asking to see her, but I was pretty sure she'd say no. Instead I said, "Thank you," and went to bed.

My flight was at eight in the morning, which meant I had to be out of the house at five thirty. I decided to take a cab. It would mean an extra half hour of sleep, and I could afford it now: I was about to start getting a regular grown-up salary for the first time in my life.

Dima wasn't yet home when I got a call from the driver that he was downstairs. I took one last look around the Stalin apartment and then left my keys under the doormat in the stairwell. If someone broke in and stole Dima's computer, that was his fault for staying out so late. And anyway no one broke in.

The cab took a right on the boulevard and then kept going once we reached Trubnaya. It was so early in the morning, and a weekend, that the streets for once were almost empty. The driver took a right at the Pushkin monument, onto Tverskaya, and past Emma Abramovna's, and Yulia's, and Misha's old place, from which he had been taken just the other day. We drove in silence. I remembered the feeling I'd had, exactly a year before, on the way into town on the train, that feeling of fear and excitement and worry that I'd be spotted as a foreigner. I probably no longer looked or sounded like a foreigner, and even if I did, I no longer cared. I sat in the front passenger seat and watched the city of my birth race by, decrepit building by decrepit building, and here and there some poor carless bastard walking along, scrambling through the broken glass and heaps of piled-up shit.

EPILOGUE

I HAD THOUGHT my research budget would mean I'd be flying back and forth almost all the time, but I soon got sucked up by the semester—the teaching and committee meetings and office hours. I enjoyed it all, I wore corduroys and a sweater to class and discussed the Gulag, but it didn't leave much time for other things. I managed to make a short visit over Thanksgiving. My grandmother did not remember me.

"It's Andryusha," Seraphima Mikhailovna said to her. "You're always asking after him."

"No," my grandmother said, shaking her head. "I don't remember."

Nonetheless we sat for a while, drank tea, and played a few games of anagrams. My grandmother was still unstoppable. There was no place for me to stay in the apartment. I stayed instead in a pretty filthy hotel a few stops north of Olympic Stadium, and though I had left Anton's stick at my grandmother's place, I had not brought my skates. Anyway I hadn't had any time to play back in New York, and I didn't want to get embarrassed.

Sergei and Misha's trial took place in early December, during the last crunch of the semester, and I couldn't get away; I thought it would last awhile, into break, but the prosecutors made short work of it and they both received three years in labor colonies for extremism. After that happened I did my best to bring attention to their cause, and even wrote a *New York Times* op-ed. President Nelson sent me a note to say how much he loved it, as did the woman who ran alumni development, but it didn't seem to do much for Sergei and Misha. I continued trying, but I couldn't get out of a peculiar loop, wherein I received praise, and speaking invitations, for bravely championing their cause, and they remained in prison. I did hear one time from Yulia, who had been to see Sergei—he had asked her to tell me that neither he nor Misha blamed me for what happened. "We knew what we were getting into," Sergei said.

Misha was released after his three years were up. He had had a bad time in the colony—he started drinking the moonshine some of the prisoners made from potato peels and it eventually made him sick. After getting out he moved to Germany, where he was living off fellowships. I saw him at the last meeting of the Association for Slavic, Eastern European, and Eurasian Studies in D.C. He did not look well. His prison experiences had not done as much for his career as they had for mine.

I saw Fishman at that conference too. Things had not worked out for him at Watson—there was some kind of scandal with one of the faculty wives—and he had taken a job as a Russia expert with one of the D.C. think tanks. Occasionally he wrote columns in the *Post* about how the U.S. should finally "get tough" with Russia. Every time I saw Fishman the hawk in print, I wondered what our old classmate Jake, who'd once thrown Fishman halfway across a room, thought of that.

As of this writing, Sergei is still in a labor camp. He got in trouble with the colony administration for organizing the prisoners to protest against unfair working conditions, and when he had his release hearing, he was unapologetic. "I will go back to that prison colony, or whatever colony you want to send me to," he said. "But someday I will go back to the colony out of curiosity, to see what people have built on its ruins. And the ruins of this court, and this rotten system, also."

The hearing was public, and I watched it on YouTube. Sergei got another five years added to his sentence.

Boris had remained in Kiev after the arrests. When the protests at Maidan broke out in 2013, he criticized them for a neoliberal tendency, and eventually, to the shock and dismay of at least some of his old friends, moved to Donetsk and started writing in praise of the Russian-backed Donetsk People's Republic. I worried for his safety—according to his

Facebook page he had briefly been arrested during one of the governing crises in Donetsk—even as I was still kind of mad at him: after Misha and Sergei's trial, he had taken it upon himself to kick me out of October.

Not that it mattered. After the arrests they had to shut down the website, and soon people started arguing with one another. When the anti-Putin protests that they'd been predicting for years finally arrived, Sergei and Misha were still away and October for all intents and purposes had ceased to exist. What was worse, the protests were fundamentally liberal rather than socialist in character, appealing to free speech and voting rights rather than to economic justice. They were not the protests October had hoped for, and they were, eventually, crushed.

Oleg mostly recovered from his injuries and then moved to Spain. Anton and Katya dated for a while and then broke up, and he also moved to Spain, to be closer to his ex-wife and son.

And Yulia—after writing to me that Sergei didn't blame me for what happened, she had not written again. But I heard from Nikolai that she kept visiting Sergei, even after he was transferred to a camp in the Far East, and that in fact they had gotten married. In a way, I'm happy for her. She finally has someone who will not let her down. And I'm happy for Sergei too, if that is the word. He is doing what he always wanted. I just hope it doesn't kill him.

My grandmother lived less than a year in her new apartment. She had been declining already; the move accelerated it. The last time I saw her, over my spring break, two months before she died, she could no longer have a conversation. She formed sentences but they were unrelated to anything that was happening. Emma Abramovna died six months before she did, and this closed her last connection to the world she had known.

On the day she died I was able to reach Seraphima Mikhailovna over Google Talk. She didn't have video but she had sound and she brought her laptop into my grandmother's room.

"Grandma!" I said.

She was moaning in pain. She had been for an entire day, according to Seraphima Mikhailovna.

"Grandma!" I yelled into Google Talk. I was in my office at the university. "It's Andrei. Do you remember me? It's Andryusha."

She moaned back. I don't think she understood me. She appeared to be in terrible pain.

"Grandma," I said meaninglessly into the computer and wept. On the other end I heard Seraphima Mikhailovna weeping also.

My grandmother died later that day. In her final moments, Seraphima Mikhailovna told me, she kept calling for Dima.

We went to Moscow again and buried our grandmother.

I have not been back since.

ACKNOWLEDGMENTS

I am deeply grateful to a small group of people who read parts of this book over and over and over again and were always encouraging and kind: Rebecca Curtis, Mary Hart Johnson, Eric Rosenblum, and Adelaide Docx. Chad Harbach read an early draft and wisely urged me to make it shorter. My father, Alexander Gessen, and his wife, Tatyana Veselova-Gessen, and my younger brothers, Daniel and Philip Gessen, allowed me to stay with them for weeks while I rewrote this book time and again. One could not imagine a more hospitable writing retreat, and my father caught a mistranslation of *telka*. My sister, Masha Gessen, made some timely corrections and was, as always, wise and generous with her counsel; her wonderful book, *Ester and Ruzya*, was a great help and in many ways an inspiration for this one. The final edits for this book were completed at the home of my very kind aunt, Svetlana Solodovnik, in Moscow.

I am immensely grateful to the Dorothy and Lewis B. Cullman Center for Scholars and Writers at the New York Public Library for the opportunity to spend a year reading books about hockey, oil, and Russian history. The support I received there from the amazing Jean Strouse, Paul Delaverdac, Lauren Goldenberg, Marie d'Origny, and Julia Pagmagenta was invaluable. I am grateful to Carlos Dada, Ayana Mathis, and Michael Vasquez for staying late, to Megan Marshall for her conversations about life and literature, to Hal Foster for his humor, to Steven Pincus for explaining neoliberalism to me.

During two crucial moments in the writing of this book, Brian Morton gave me a source of income. I owe much to him practically, but even more to his example. I am honored to consider two of the greatest magazine editors of our time, Henry Finder and Cullen Murphy, my friends as well as my editors. The incredible group that has coalesced around *n+1*, led by Mark Krotov, Rachel Ossip, Cosme Del Rosario-Bell, Nikil Saval, and Dayna Tortorici, continues to inspire me with its brilliance and commitment. Carla Blumenkranz is a genius. Mark Greif is present in everything I write. Ben Kunkel and Marco Roth are my ideal readers. Nell Zink sent me a note while I was writing this book that actually allowed me to finish it. Elif Batuman assured me that this was a novel. Eddie Joyce, himself a novelist, promised me that at least one person would read it. Christian Lorentzen's commitment to literature, and to his friends, is unmatched by anyone I know.

In Moscow I could not have survived without my friends Igor Alexandrov, Scott Burns, Anatoly Karavaev, Lenka Kabrhelova, Leonid Kuragin, Kirill Medvedev, Grant Slater, Courtney Weaver, and Marina Zarubin.

I'm grateful to my bosses and colleagues at the J-School for letting me start a semester late so I could finish this. I'm grateful to my old teachers from Syracuse, Mary Karr and George Saunders, for three incredibly valuable years, and much support and encouragement.

The brilliant Allison Lorentzen is the editor of this book. Everything good about it is her idea, but the bad parts were written by me. I am grateful to Diego Núñez for altering his diet so that he could more authentically shepherd this text to publication. At the Wylie Agency, Sarah Chalfant and Rebecca Nagel have been incredible supporters and counselors.

I am grateful to my mother- and father-in-law, Kate Deshler Gould and Rob Gould, for helping so much with Raffi when he was little and I was trying to finish a first draft. Ruth Curry's bracing monologues on tenant law and literature, as well as her unfailing generosity, were a comfort and an inspiration.

Without Emily Gould, who took a job she didn't much like so that I could keep writing, nothing would be possible and nothing would matter. Without little Raphael Konstaninovich Gessen-Gould, all we would do is sleep.

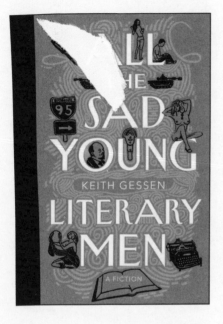